THE

PRIEST

THE

PRIEST

ELLEN GUNDERSON TRAYLOR

WORD PUBLISHING

NASHVILLE

A Thomas Nelson Company

This is a work of fiction. Apart from obvious historical references to public figures and events, all characters and incidents in this novel are the products of the author's imagination. Any similarities to people living or dead are purely coincidental.

Library of Congress Cataloging-in-Publication Data

Traylor, Ellen Gunderson.
   The priest : a novel / by Ellen Gunderson Traylor.
      p. cm.
   ISBN 0-8499-4099-0
   I. Title.
PS3570.R357P75 1998
813'.54—dc21
                                                      98-8854
                                                         CIP

Printed in the United States of America
8 9 0 1 2 3 4 9 QPK 9 8 7 6 5 4 3 2 1

To my mother,

Carol Gunderson,

who took this book to heart

The Lord said:

"My temple shall be called a house of prayer for all people!"

Isaiah 56:7 TLB

CHAPTER I

October/*Tishri*

David Rothmeyer stretched his long legs and twisted stiffly in the molded chair of the airport terminal. Airplanes and waiting-room chairs were not made for people over six feet tall, he thought, and he exceeded that height by five inches. He had not been comfortable even in the first-class seat on the flight that had brought him to New York.

"You are related to the Philistines!" his Grandma Rothmeyer used to say. "On your mama's side!" That was the only way she could account for his quick growth and lanky stature as a child.

Rothmeyer smiled a little at the memory. For years he had barely thought of his Jewish grandmother; the past few days he had thought of her a lot.

Through the haze of the terminal's smogged-up windows, Rothmeyer saw that the fall sun was setting. Red-orange, it smudged through the huge chrome-and-glass room, seeming to sink into the dingy scarlet carpet. The flat-napped floor had been worn by thousands upon thousands of feet into definite paths, the widest and best traveled leading straight through the terminal to yet other terminals that would take travelers across the map; other paths, narrower but faded, led toward men's and women's rest rooms, a clutch of obscenely priced tourist shops, and an indoor "sidewalk" café complete with umbrellas that were never touched by sun or rain.

From this café the aroma of tobacco smoke and reheated popcorn wafted over the gigantic room, and David's keen, hazel eyes flitted from the endlessly scrolling TV monitors suspended over his seating area to the bumping walk of the miniskirted barmaid who seemed to be the little eatery's only employee. Daring to leave his chair, his single suitcase, and his briefcase for a second, he adjusted the brown leather cap on his unruly shock of sandy-colored hair and approached the young woman. "I'll have some popcorn," he said, reaching for his wallet.

Casting her chewing gum from one side of her mouth to the other, like a cud-chewing cow, the thin-limbed barmaid thrust one hip forward, then rested her tray upon it. "We're out," she said.

David wondered how two words could reveal so much about character. Yet, they were so heavy with Bronx twang, so enveloped in snarl, that they instantly evoked the stereotype of the obnoxious New Yorker so repulsive to foreigners.

David was not a foreigner, but he may as well have come from a distant planet, so little had he in common with this female. Pushing his wallet back into his pocket, he returned to his seat without a word and wished he could hop the next plane back to Columbus, Ohio.

The sterile black and white chairs arranged in locked rows about the red floor reminded him of the checkerboard his grandfather used to put on the dining table each holiday evening. Every Purim and every Hanukkah when he was a boy, he and his family would wile away the sacred nights playing board games. This activity, of course, was indulged in only after his grandfather had recited the history and moral lessons of the feastday for the children. But David remembered the holidays of his youth more for the games and family closeness than for the pedagogy.

Still, it was not like David to give his childhood so much

thought. His recent ruminations on his Jewish heritage were sparked by this trip and the invitation that had brought him to JFK airport.

Leaning back in his seat, he absently thrummed his fingertips on the chair's plastic arm. Since his flight had arrived early, he still had fifteen minutes to kill in this unfriendly place. Then he would take the escalator down to the lower level where his hosts were supposed to meet him.

He had mixed feelings about this imminent encounter.

Pursing his lips, he reached inside his tweed sport coat and pulled out a rumpled letter. How many times he had folded and unfolded, read and reread this document since receiving it a week before, he could never count, but it had become the focus of almost all of his thoughts.

He knew the contents by heart now, but he scanned it once again, trying to imagine the full import:

Dear Dr. Rothmeyer:

You have been referred to us by Rabbi Yitzak Schiller of Temple Beth Shalom, Columbus, Ohio, who speaks highly of your work as an archaeologist and your commitment to the Jewish community.

We are a committee of rabbinical and historical researchers, involved in a project of highest importance to the future of Israel and the welfare of our people. We have been seeking a practiced Jewish archaeologist and linguist to assist us in this project.

After investigating your credentials and your reputation, we are convinced that you would be a great asset to our endeavors, and we would like to meet with you in New York City on the afternoon of October 9.

Knowing that this date might be inconvenient to your duties at the university, we have already taken the liberty of contacting your department chairman, Dr. Kenneth Aronstam. He indicated that you have accumulated leave time during your tenure at the school, which could be used for research, if you choose.

To that end, we have also taken the liberty of enclosing an airline ticket to bring you to New York. We will pick you up at the appropriate terminal when you arrive.

Due to the sensitive nature of our project, we cannot divulge more than this. But trusting that a man of your scholarship and heritage could not reject an opportunity to be involved in research of monumental historical significance, and an opportunity to be of invaluable assistance to his people, we look forward to our meeting.

Sincerely,
Rabbi Horace Benjamin, Th.D.
Rabbi Menachem Levine, Sc.D.
Dr. Carl Jacobs, M.D.
Rabbi Uriel Katz, Th.D.

As always, David was impressed by the heavy, cream-colored stationery with its gilded letterhead. The quality of the paper alone, which revealed a fine watermark when held to the light, lent an air of authority to the contents. The credentials that followed the signatures were enough to raise the hair on the young professor's academic hide. However, he had never heard of any of these men, nor had he heard of the Temple Consortium, the agency they represented. In fine gold letters the group's name was embossed at the top of the page, and next to it, in the left corner, was an embossed menorah, the seven-branched candlestand that symbolized Judaism. Precise in detail, the little menorah, although only one inch tall, was so radiant its miniature candles may as well have been lit with real flames.

Naturally, when the letter had first been delivered to David's cluttered college office, he had scratched his head in bewilderment. Rabbi Schiller and Temple Beth Shalom were figures out of David's childhood. The old rabbi had officiated at his bar mitzvah over twenty years ago, but rarely since then had David set foot in the synagogue. As for his "commitment to the Jewish community," it had rarely been tested, except for the occasional playground skirmish, wherein he had retaliated against some childish ethnic slur.

And what did the consortium mean by calling him a "practiced Jewish archaeologist"? True, he was an archaeologist, and he was Jewish. But that was where the connection stopped. His expertise as a scientist was in cultural anthropology, but his studies, his fieldwork, and his digs had been primarily in the Mayan and Aztec regions of Central America. Never had he been to Israel. Never had he studied biblical or Hebraic archaeology, nor had he any interest in doing so.

Furthermore, it was quite disconcerting to think that there were strangers out there who had been "investigating" his credentials and reputation—that people he knew nothing of, knew a great deal about him!

Not the least bewildering aspect of the letter was its imposing nature. Not only did the committee, whoever they were, conclude that David would be interested in their mysterious project, but they had presumed to make airline reservations for him without so much as a by-your-leave.

Chagrined, David refolded the letter and put it back in the inside pocket of his jacket. Of course, he *was* sitting in the New York airport. He *had* left his cloistered classrooms and his tiny office to fly halfway across the country on an unknown errand. The letter *had* spellbound him, and he had thus far complied quite nicely with the demands of the document's drafters.

With a shiver, David pulled his jacket across his chest and crossed his arms. Maybe these people, whatever they were about, knew him better than he cared to think. Maybe he knew less about himself than he cared to admit. At any rate, he was on their journey, at their expense.

Ken Aronstam, who, in his mid-thirties, was the youngest chairman ever to head the anthropology department of Midwest University, had been of no help when David barged into his office waving the freshly opened letter. Looking up from a pile of grade sheets, Ken had slipped his wire-rimmed glasses down his large nose and shrugged. "I don't know who these guys are," he said glibly. "So they really wrote to you, huh? I thought their call was odd, but I forgot about it. You know, we get calls now and then from agencies, looking for cheap research help. Usually they want some starving grad student to do summer work, that sort of thing. I've never run into anybody who requested a Ph.D., and certainly not a Jew in particular. But I guess I just didn't think much of it."

"Have you ever run into people who would send a first-class airline ticket to someone they've never met?" David asked. "Doesn't sound like a lean outfit to me."

Scooting forward in his castered chair, Ken lifted his spectacles again to his eyes and reached for the ticket. "Let me see that," he said. Intrigued, he read the fare. "Five hundred and thirty-six dollars!" Handing it back to David, he blew on his fingertips, as if they were red-hot.

"Look at the letter," David replied. "Weird, right?"

As Ken perused the letterhead, his dark eyes grew wide. "Pretty classy, Dave!" he replied. Then as he scanned the contents, he frowned slightly. "Temple Consortium," he muttered, rubbing his neatly clipped beard. "I remember thinking it was a funny name when the guy called. But," he added, handing it back, "like I say, I didn't think much of it."

"Well," David said, "if it were just a letter, I wouldn't think much of it either. I'd probably throw it in the circular file and see if they called again. But this ticket . . . "

Turning it over and over, he stood before the desk in silent wonder. "Do you remember who called you?" he asked, glancing at the signatures on the bottom of the letter. "Was it one of these guys?"

Ken ran over the list and settled on the top name. "Benjamin," he said. "I'm pretty sure that's the one. It wasn't a secretary, but one of the rabbis themselves. And I remember thinking the name was as strange as the call. 'Horace Benjamin.' Quite the classic moniker!" He laughed.

"And ethnic," David added. Then, looking at the floor, he shrugged. "But I guess that's not so bad."

"I suppose it wouldn't hurt either of us to trek to synagogue now and then," Ken said. He placed his pen on the pile of grade sheets, then looked sideways at David. "How easily we forget who we are."

Rarely had David and Ken spoken of their mutual heritage. Each knew the other was a Jew, but when, in their far-removed world of freshman seminars and Central American file cards did they have cause to talk about it? Oh sure, they told each other Jewish jokes and wished obligatory Happy Hanukkahs. But if any colleague had joked about their ethnicity like they themselves did, David and Ken would have labeled that person anti-Semitic.

David was about to leave, to ponder the mystery in his office cubicle, when Ken reached for the ticket once more.

"Just a minute," he said. "Let me see that again."

Reading down the figures, his eyes grew wider than ever. "Check this out!" he marveled. "Did you notice that this ticket is one-way?"

Quickly David grabbed it back, gawking at the fine print. "You're kidding!" he exclaimed. "I'll be. . . . It is!'

With a vacant stare, David slumped down onto the folding chair across from the administrator's desk.

"Looks like you have a deeper riddle than we thought," Ken teased.

When he saw that David did not appreciate his humor, he

leaned back in his tilting chair and studied the young professor soberly. "What are you going to do?" he asked.

For a moment, David squinted at the ticket and the letter. At last, he jumped to his feet. "The whole thing's crazy!" he fumed. "I'm a teacher, not an international sleuth." He headed out the door. "They need a detective, not an archaeologist!"

It was just such words that turned Ken's crank. "What's the difference?" he called after him.

Stopping, David growled, "What did you say?"

"What's the difference?" he repeated. "Aren't a detective and an archaeologist pretty much alike?"

Exasperated, David returned to the office and poked his head in. "Are you suggesting I go on this snipe hunt?" he muttered, glaring down at him.

Ken shrugged, then picked up his pencil and doodled on his grade sheets. "Did you have something better to do this winter?" he inquired. "Look, you've got tenure and earned leave. You're due to present the committee with your plans for a sabbatical. Your grad assistants can cover your classes for you. Maybe this project could be a start—"

"I can't believe what I'm hearing!" David interrupted. "You know that whatever these jokers are up to, it's about as related to my field of interest as fish to bicycles!"

"Or the modern world to Mayan architecture?" Ken goaded.

With a scowl, David reentered the office, threw the documents on the desk and leaned across them, staring the chairman in the eye. "What is that supposed to mean, Ken? Are you saying I use my studies as an escape?"

Ken gave a fake gasp. "Would I suggest such a thing?" Then, more compassionately, he added, "No. Not always, Dave. But . . . ever since Susan . . . went away . . . "

That was a mean blow. It was true that for the past three summers David had buried himself in the ruins of an ancient village high in the Guatemalan mountains, as much to flee a broken heart as to outline a pottery history. The death of his precious wife and coworker, Susan, had nearly killed him, though it had also meant an end to her torment as a cancer victim. The childless couple had thrived on going on digs together and on studying the dust of the past. That dust had been David's healer after her passing, and he thought it was cruel of Ken to criticize him for it.

Wounded, David said not a word but turned again for the door. Sweeping up the letter and the ticket, Ken left his desk and pursued him down the hall.

"Look, Dave," he pleaded. grabbing him by the arm, "I didn't mean . . . I mean—maybe this is an opportunity to turn your thoughts elsewhere." Quickly he pushed the papers into David's hand. "Look. Don't make a decision today. Sleep on it and talk with me tomorrow."

With a sigh, David nodded. "Okay. But what about this crazy one-way ticket? How do I get home?"

"Take your Visa card." Ken grinned and hurried back to his grade sheets.

Hard to believe that conversation had taken place just a week ago, David thought. It seemed years since the inscrutable letter had arrived.

As "Muzak" floated through the mammoth terminal, blending with the sounds of travelers coming and going and planes whooshing on and off the ground, David hunched down in his seat and tried to relax.

The busy place hardly invoked serenity, however. The droning voice on the intercom, announcing arrivals and departures, and the ceaseless churn of escalators full of tired families and harried businessmen were hard to shut out.

David was about to pull his leather cap over his eyes for a forced rest, when a peculiar gathering of people drew his attention to one corner of the waiting area.

A group of Orthodox Jews were standing together in a cluster. They were dressed in plain black suits that buttoned to the neck, and wore various sorts of hats: broad, fur-rimmed platters, or little embroidered *yarmulkes*, like the one David donned on his rare visits to synagogue. Wearing striped prayer shawls, they faced the darkening windows that provided a ribbon of view toward the eastern sky, over rows of airport buildings, and they nodded and bobbed their heads in prayer, their lips moving in a low, murmured chant. Some held small prayer books, while others gripped their hands close to their chests.

Although they were gathered together, no one led them. Each was alone in his own world of meditation, eyes closed or lifted toward the east.

Toward Jerusalem, David thought, remembering the evening prayers that older men in his family had said.

Fascinated, the professor observed them. He could make out a few of the words they softly recited, the movements of their lips recalling certain phrases:

If I forget thee, O Jerusalem, let my right hand forget her cunning.
If I do not remember thee, let my tongue cleave to the roof of my mouth;
If I prefer not Jerusalem above my highest joys.

David had not thought of these words for years. He wistfully smiled, and a surprising sense of nostalgia settled over him.

But it was all too fleeting. A shuffle near the praying men broke in on his reveries.

A small boy, probably no more than four years old, had wandered close to the group and stood looking up at them in curiosity. This little fellow was also dressed in ethnic garb, but not of a Jewish variety. He was wearing an embroidered, striped tunic and a small boxy hat of like material. Noting the outfit, as well as the boy's dark hair, large, dark eyes, and olive skin, David deduced he was of Middle-Eastern heritage.

The little boy watched the praying Jews with wide, round eyes. Then tentatively, he raised a hand and reached for the tasseled fringe of one man's striped prayer-shawl. Giving a little tug, he got the man's attention, jolting him out of his meditation.

"Hi, mister," he said, his wee voice cheery and inquisitive.

The startled Jew stared down at the upturned face and smiled slightly. Gesturing toward the waiting area, he asked, "Where is your mother?"

Barely were the words out, however, before an olive-skinned man, with black eyes and blacker beard, swept across the room, grasped the lad's arm, and jerked him away. He barked at the boy and thrust him toward a woman who sat in one of the waiting-room chairs. Apparently the lad's mother, she was dressed in a long kaftan, her head and face concealed by a broad scarf.

The man gave her a spearing look and growled at both of them. Then, gesturing toward the Jewish group, he spat out a stream of epithets in Lebanese.

David's linguistic training picked up on the gist of the nasty phrases, as the angry man drove home to his son that these were "untouchables, the enemy, the Jews!"

The man's invectives were startling enough. But his voice, itself, was more so. Unusually rasping and coarse, it caused people to stop in their busy rush through the terminal to turn and stare at him.

The little boy now sobbed in his mother's arms. Glancing at the onlookers, the man said no more, just snapped his fingers and motioned for his wife and child to follow him. Together they joined the flow of foot traffic down the concourse.

Although the incident did not involve David, it took on special significance, both because of his trip and because of an incident he had just learned about that morning. As he had prepared to depart Columbus, David had caught a snippet on CNN about a bus being blown up in Tel Aviv. Arab terrorists were blamed. Of course, such news was all too commonplace anymore, and in the past it would not have overly concerned him. Lately, however,—ever since the Temple Consortium letter—he had been much more in touch with his own Jewishness, much more aware of the hallmark of his ethnicity, his thin, hooked nose.

As the Lebanese Arab and his little family passed by David's seat, the professor felt, for the first time in his life, the deep and terrible chill of racial fear.

Turning his head, he avoided eye contact. Once they were gone, he nervously cleared his throat.

A clock on the terminal wall said it was time to go downstairs. He felt strangely relieved as he descended the escalator, suitcase in hand.

He watched for a group of rabbis, who, like the men upstairs, should not be hard to spot. No such greeting committee was to be seen, but just as he reached the main floor a flash of evening sun reflecting off gleaming metal drew his attention to the street. Just pulling up to the loading area was a sleek limousine, the longest he had ever seen. Like a shining gray whale, it glistened beside the curb, its black windows inspiring mystery.

As David watched, the chauffeur jumped out, ran to the passenger door, and opened it. From the depths emerged a most unusual character, a man in a long black coat, wearing a wide black hat, beneath which dangled fluffy white curls. As this fellow straightened, facing the terminal, David was amazed by another tumble of curls that descended to his chest, a veritable snowfall of a beard.

From behind this figure emerged three other men, all dressed in black and conservative gray, all with distinctive hats: two broad-rims edged in ebony-colored ermine, and one the more common, skull-fitting *yarmulke*. All the men were bearded, their beards carved so that the corners were left long. Their hair was of varying lengths, but they all wore the traditional *poyis*, long ringlets on either side of the face.

The young professor from Ohio felt his pulse race again, but this time out of awe more than anxiety. As the men stood on the curb, they searched the terminal windows, then moved forward as a body to enter the building.

David clutched his suitcase nervously, and shoved the letter deeper into his pocket.

No one needed to tell him that the drafters of that invitation had just arrived.

CHAPTER 2

Father Ian McCurdy knelt in the soft brown dirt of his Oxfordshire garden, mulching his rose bed for winter. Although it had been ten years since he had worked in the Israeli desert, the moist soil of his English garden often reminded him, by contrast, of the long, hot days he had spent there. It seemed he could never get enough of the solace he found in his dark-earthed haven.

Leaning back, he rubbed his hands on his khaki work slacks, leaving streaks of soil on his thighs, and loosened the neck of his plaid shirt. It had also been a long time since he had worn his clerical collar, the mark of the priesthood that he was seldom called upon, these days, to practice. He wondered if he should put it on today.

Though he lived only a few miles from Pembroke College, one of the few Catholic institutions among the thirty-five campuses of Oxford University, he was emeritus and rarely lectured there anymore. He had not received a professional visitor in a long time. He avoided the thought that he should dress the part of a priest or a faculty member.

Ian McCurdy had never enjoyed standing on ceremony. It had been the bane of his existence as an Irish

Catholic priest. That was why he preferred the realm of scholarship to the role of the pastorate, and he had buried himself in archaeology because it was the field of study most removed from the formal classroom.

Digging in his English garden had nothing to do with archaeology, however. He had cloistered himself in this quaint corner of Britain because it was as unlike the Judean desert as possible, its fertile dirt yielding no great finds, only the glory of roses and greenery.

No, he would not wear his collar. He would not even have granted the upcoming interview if the young journalist who made the appointment had not been the daughter of an acquaintance—his sister Emily's acquaintance, not his own.

His lips tightened in a line of resentment as he realized the power Emily had over him. She was his only living relative, and it was to indulge her that he had decided to break his vow of public silence and meet with a reporter.

Having lived as a virtual recluse for months, he knew it would be tempting to say too much. He must guard himself against that vulnerability. He had seen the media's warped coverage of his character and his life's work. It would be a longed-for relief to unveil himself, to stand before the world and cry out in his own defense. But this he must not do. He must phrase all responses carefully, to protect the dreadful secret that was his to bear, even if it meant he must go to his death unvindicated.

Father McCurdy brushed his gray-white hair from his round face and reached for the ash-tipped cigar he had set on a rock. Besides Emily, his cigars were another weakness he indulged. He took a long drag, then blew circles in the air and tried to clear his mind. The interview would not last long; he would see to that. When the young reporter left, she would wonder why she had bothered to come. Emily would be satisfied, and he would be none the worse for it.

A rattle of the gate behind told the priest his afternoon of solitude was ended. John Cromwell, his tall, thin-boned houseman, had entered the garden, looking for him.

"Your visitor is here, Ian," he announced.

Standing up, Ian removed his gardening gloves, dusted the dirt from his pants and put a hand on Cromwell's shoulder. "The dog returns to its vomit," he quipped in his Irish brogue.

Cromwell sighed. "How can you make light of this, Father? Did you see the morning's headlines?"

"I saw CNN," he replied. "Something about Allaman and the Deadly Duo."

Cromwell didn't like the priest's satiric reference to the very people who were disparaging him *and* the church before the world. "Allaman has come out with a full endorsement of Bailey and Lee's Deception Theory. How much more of this will you allow to go unchallenged?"

"Allaman has always been an atheistic maverick, looking for any opportunity to promote his heresies! Remember," Ian chuckled, "this is the same clown who insisted the followers of Jesus were a mushroom cult! He did the team the greatest of favors when he left Israel. Now," he said, rubbing his ample stomach, "fetch us a snack."

B ritta Hayworth sat on the edge of a wing chair, notepad and pencil in hand, and breathlessly watched the parlor door. Any moment the elusive Father McCurdy would be entering the room, granting her a reporter's dream, the chance to interview an international enigma.

For weeks she had waded through stacks of journals and newspapers, reading anything she could get her hands on regarding the Cave Scrolls and the controversy surrounding them. Of course, most literate people had heard of the famous scrolls, discovered in the forties in the Dead Sea wilderness, at the ruins of the ancient settlement of Qumran. Most knew that they contained records of a mysterious sect called the Essenes, though that designation was now disputed.

When the public first heard of the scrolls, they were touted by the media as the archaeological find of the century. Along with their unique chronicle of Jewish culture before the sacking of Jerusalem by Rome in 70 C.E., they also appeared to contain proof that Old Testament scriptures that seemed to point to Jesus as the Jewish Messiah, had not been "revised" after his death.

For four decades they had caused no end of embarrassment to scholars of the "modernist" camp, who had discredited the notion that Jesus was foreseen by Isaiah and other pre-Christian writers.

Now, however, the scrolls were back in the news, this time at the center of an unparalleled debate challenging the very foundations of the Christian world.

Father Ian McCurdy was at the center of that debate, though he did not openly participate in it and had made no public statement about the scrolls for nearly a decade. In fact, it was his very silence that had turned public scrutiny increasingly in his direction, for he was the senior member of the original team of scholars that first translated the scrolls.

Britta smoothed her tailored pantsuit, the "professional woman" attire she had adopted since she graduated from the casual college scene three years ago and entered "the real world." She knew she had a more credible image as a reporter when she dressed this way, and Britta, with her cherubic face and unruly blond curls, needed all the credibility she could muster.

Actually, twenty-four-year-old Britta came from a long line of newspeople, her great-uncle being a legendary photojournalist who had worked for the *London Times* during World War II. He had made an indelible mark on the profession by his risk-taking feats in the line of duty, even receiving the coveted George Cross for wounds received on assignment at Normandy.

Britta had always admired her uncle, visiting him twice during college breaks at his home in Nazareth, Israel.

Having been assigned to photograph the immigration of Holocaust Jews to the emerging nation of Israel in the postwar years, he had fallen in love with that land, and with a young Jewess, whom he eventually married there. From that time on he had divided his work between Israel and England, taking up full-time residence in the Holy Land upon retirement.

It had been Britta's lifelong dream to be as proficient with her writing as that heroic reporter had been with his camera. Presently, she worked as a stringer, a freelancer employed by the same legendary newspaper for which her great-uncle had worked. The *Times* already paid her more for her stories than most stringers received. If only she could impress them with one really big scoop, she felt she might have a chance at a regular position. This interview with Father McCurdy might be the break she had been looking for.

In preparing for this meeting, the reporter had read everything she could find on the enigmatic priest and had pumped his sister for details. Britta learned that he had earned a reputation for genius as a lecturer at Trinity College in his native Dublin, Ireland, teaching courses in archaeology. He had been courted by Oxford, hiring on at Pembroke, which specialized in Middle-Eastern studies, when he was only twenty-eight.

His scholarly interests leaned toward ancient languages, and his courses in Hebraic archaeology were always full of enrollees.

After the Cave Scrolls were discovered, Oxford sent him to Israel to work at the field site under the direction of the head of the archaeology team. Eventually, he spent more time in Israel than England, until his sudden and unexplained return to Oxford ten years ago.

He was now in his late seventies, and his mystique had only grown with his inaccessibility.

When McCurdy finally entered through the french doors leading from his garden and approached Britta across the parlor, she was surprised at his appearance. If she had gone out of her way to look professional, he looked anything but the part of a priest.

Father McCurdy drew a handkerchief from his back pocket, wiped his soiled hands once more, then reached out to greet her.

Britta managed to conceal her jitters and, poking her notepad under one arm, stood up, giving him a hearty handshake. "Father McCurdy," she said, "I'm Britta Hayworth, with the *Times*. Glad to meet you." She liked linking herself with the prestigious newspaper, regardless of her fledgling status.

McCurdy surveyed her quickly and deduced that this would be a quick and uneventful encounter. He need not have worried about an inquisitor who looked like Shirley Temple.

"A pleasure, Ms. Hayworth," he replied, using the generic title for sake of political correctness. Likely she considered herself a feminist of sorts, in her male-dominated world of ink and newsprint.

"I'm a bit of a mess," he acknowledged. "Would you like to talk in the garden?"

"I would," she said, admiring the sunlit grotto.

Cromwell brought them tea and cookies on the flagstone veranda, as they chatted about Ian's sister Emily and then his flowers.

Britta, eager to get to her subject, asked, "Did you do much gardening in Israel?"

McCurdy puffed on a fresh cigar and looked at her knowingly. *Clever*, he thought. *She's not new to this game.*

Before he could answer, she laughed and added, "But of course you were digging for other things than weeds when you were there!"

McCurdy blew smoke from the side of his mouth. "I'm sure you're aware of all the digging we did," he muttered.

"I have tried to educate myself," she said, pushing back a lock of her wayward hair. "The questions I would like to ask may be rather repetitious to you," she proceeded. "I hope you will indulge me."

He knew what Emily liked about this young woman. They were two of a kind.

"If they've been asked before, they've been answered before," he said, "and you've doubtless read anything I've had to say."

He had her there. He knew she'd never read any such thing, for none had ever been written.

She blushed a little. "Very well," she conceded. "Then, I do appreciate this opportunity. I will get right to the point."

Good, he thought. *Then you can get right back to London.*

"What do you think of the Deception Theory?" she began.

McCurdy's eyes narrowed. "You know what I must think! It fits in the same category as Allaman's poppycock book that claimed the early Christians ate 'magic' mushrooms! It's balderdash! Pure foolishness. And if I weren't a priest, I'd use stronger language!"

"How so?" she went on, jotting on a notepad.

"If you've read the Deception Theory, you know it essentially says that the Christianity of the Bible is a perversion of Jesus' teachings. It equates 'The Teacher of Righteousness,' referred to in the scrolls, with Jesus, and 'The Wicked Priest,' who was out to destroy the Teacher, with St. Paul."

McCurdy frowned at her as she wrote down key phrases. "The theorists," he went on, "say that the scrolls present the Teacher as an adherent of the Jewish law and that Paul, because he taught that the law was not the source of salvation, was a heretic. Hence, the Christian committee that was in charge of the scrolls hid this dreadful revelation from the world, for fear it would undermine the very roots of the Church, showing the Christianity of the New Testament to be a fraudulent distortion of Jesus' original doctrine!"

Britta scribbled quickly, wishing she had taken a shorthand course along with her writing classes, and trying to follow the priest's explanation.

"So," she mused, looking up from her notes, "the drafters of the Deception Theory claim that the Qumran writings are truer to the teachings of Jesus than those of the New Testament and that what the Gospel writers came up with was heresy?"

Ian nodded curtly. "They say that Jesus was essentially a Jewish teacher, with no intention to deviate from traditional Judaism. They say that Paul was the culprit who planted the idea that people no longer had to abide by the Judaic law and could be saved by faith alone."

He took a breath. "As for me," he reiterated, "if the Teacher and the Priest do represent Jesus and Paul, which I sincerely doubt, the Qumran doctrine is the heresy, not the New Testament!"

Britta, who had an Anglican and Jewish background, had not gone to church or synagague much and knew very little about the Bible. Looking up at the priest, she commented, "But isn't Christianity full of rules and regulations? What's the difference?"

McCurdy had not anticipated the interview to go in this direction. Sighing impatiently, he blew out more smoke. "Christianity as it is misconstrued, yes! One of the things I've always loathed about the priesthood is its rules and rituals. I think I would have liked Paul."

Then, leaning forward, he peered directly into the young woman's open face. "But this is not why you are here. You want to know if we were, indeed, covering up this . . . 'revelation.'"

Britta nodded. "Isn't that what everyone wants to know?"

Ian gave a chuckle. "Dear girl! If we wanted to cover up every pseudo-Christian line of thought, we'd have to burn every *Book of Mormon*, every *Watchtower* magazine, and every book of Ellen G. White! They all teach salvation through works!"

"So," Britta marveled, "you're equating the monks of Qumran with certain sects of today?"

"They were Jewish traditionalists, that's all. No more sectarian than any Jew then or now. *If* their writings refer to Jesus and Paul, instead of outright rejecting Jesus as Messiah, they merely redefined him, like any good Mormon or SDA. That set them apart from the Jews who wanted nothing to do with him, just as they were already set apart from the temple in Jerusalem, which had become 'ceremonially' unclean. No, my dear, the Deception Theory is a bunch of wishful thinking, a contrivance to shame the Church!"

For a moment, Britta was at a loss as to how to proceed. To buy some time, she studied her notes. Finally, however, the source of her bewilderment took on focus: All of this had been much too easy.

Shaking her head, she found only one question to ask. "Father," she said, "when you come right down to it, there is nothing earth-shaking in your answer. Why then have you avoided the press?"

Ian was caught off guard. He took the cigar from his lips and twirled it aimlessly. "Well," he grunted, "perhaps I didn't expect reporters to be so easily satisfied."

Ian's heart pumped uncomfortably. In being very forthright with her, confident in doling out doctrine, he had made it appear he had no real reason to hide from the press. He could have anticipated her next words.

Britta closed her notepad and looked squarely at him. "I sense, Father, that we have been dealing with a smoke screen. You say you have no secret. Yet, for almost half a century, the scroll team sat on their cache of parchments. It is believed that even today there are scrolls you have not released to the scrutiny of the scholarly community. What then *have* you been concealing?"

Ian squirmed in his patio chair. "Can't you just accept that I am an old man?" he offered. "I would like to live out my years in peace. I granted this interview to appease my sister, and I have nothing more to say. My original colleagues have nearly all died off. The scrolls are in the hands of our apprentices and the world at large. Some of our students have turned out to be renegades, making personal fortunes off absurd conspiracy claims. You have the scrolls. Go and read them. You'll see that there is nothing to hide!"

With this, he stood up, straightened his stiff knees, and bowed curtly to her. "Cromwell will see you out." He waved her off and turned to his rosebeds. "My garden is calling."

Britta rose and stuffed her notepad under her arm. "What about the rumors of other scrolls?" she called after him. "Scrolls not yet released to the public?"

By now, Cromwell was ushering her back through the house.

"Thank you for coming," he said, as he opened the front door. "It has been a long time since Father had such charming company."

CHAPTER 3

David Rothmeyer sat in the side seat of the glistening gray limousine as it sped from the airport into Manhattan. He had never ridden in such a vehicle before, and he appreciated its spaciousness, stretching his long legs into the center of the passenger compartment.

His hosts studied him quietly, obviously sizing him up.

One of them, the one whose name headed the signatures at the bottom of the mysterious letter, sat in the seat against the window separating the back of the limousine from the chauffeur. He made amiable conversation, discussing the weather and asking chatty questions, the answers to which David was certain he already knew: Have you family? Oh, you are a widower—so sorry. When did your wife pass away? You have been at Midwest for seven years? How do you like it? What classes do you teach? How many digs have you been on? etc. etc.

David replied to each question simply, directly. He knew that old Rabbi Horace Benjamin was trying to break the ice, but until the young professor knew what this visit was about, there would be a virtual iceberg between them.

It was the tail end of rush hour, which meant that this trip would be excruciatingly slow. Somehow, the chauffeur managed to maneuver the huge car through the traffic with a minimum of delays. The tedious pace, however, allowed too much time for silences between stabs at conversation.

David felt it was not the time to be asking his own questions. He thought that was best reserved for when they arrived at whatever their destination was.

The other three men in the car interjected pleasantries, but David found Rabbi Benjamin to be the friendliest. He was the awesome-looking gent with the cascading beard David had seen emerging from the limousine at JFK.

The rabbi struck David as almost holy. At the very least, the man evoked wonder and respect, not only by his appearance, but by his gentle voice and kind mannerisms.

David's linguistic background clicked in, once again, the instant the rabbi spoke. He noted that the gentleman had a thick Jewish accent, often ending his sentences on the downswing, rather than in the typical upbeat ending of American English: "You are a widow-*er*. We are so sor-*ry*." His speech did not have the nasal characteristic common to the Yiddish dialect, however. Instead, his distinctive talk pinpointed him as highly educated and refined, while a hint of the Queens/Brooklyn "r-dropping" was evident.

Actually, all the men but one spoke this way. They also used their hands more than the ordinary American. David's trained eye and ear allowed him to assess these things easily. In fact, it was second nature to him to make such analyses.

Of the four hosts, Rabbi Uriel Katz was the most reserved. He sat in the backseat between Menachem Levine and Carl Jacobs, whose broad, ermine-trimmed hats cast him in shadow. Rabbi Katz, more than the others, seemed engrossed in studying David, saying little and occasionally closing his eyes, as though to imprint something in his mind.

Perhaps because he was a slighter fellow than the others, or perhaps because he sank back into the seat, keeping his head against the headrest in a contemplative posture, Rabbi Katz seemed to blend with the background, and his silence lent him mystique. He wore an elaborate yarmulke embroidered in many colors, which was secured to his thinning hair with gold clips. He, too, had a beard, close-cropped and streaked with gray, though he did not appear to be older than forty-five.

His first name, Uriel, seemed rather ethereal, and David recognized it as the name of one of the archangels of folklore.

When he spoke, which was not often, his accent was distinctly foreign, that of an Israeli-born Jew. David figured he must be one of the first generation of Jews born in the newly established state of Israel after the exodus from the European Holocaust.

All of these facts made the man intriguing, though each of the hosts was part of the enigma that had haunted David since he received the letter.

The limousine had passed through the Queens-Midtown Tunnel, and as it sped up First Avenue, which was relatively free of congestion, it passed the United Nations Building.

David gazed out the car window at the sprawling structure, with its flags of many nations illuminated in the evening sky. Although he did not know where he was headed, he appreciated this chance to sightsee. As the car sped west down Forty-ninth Street, David's eyes were drawn up, up the sides of skyscrapers, and he wondered if they were near the building that was bombed in 1993.

"Are we close to the World Trade Center?" he asked, scanning the slit of horizon above the street.

Dr. Jacobs shook his head. "The financial district is on the southwest side of Manhattan," he said. "But we are not far from Rockefeller Center and Grand Central Station."

David perceived the pride in the man's voice. He evidently enjoyed showing off his city to an out-of-towner.

Passing block after block of New York's multistoried monoliths, the professor remembered well the day of the dreadful bombing of the World Trade Center. He had been home, making lunch in his small apartment kitchen between class sessions. The little TV on the kitchen counter was tuned to CNN when the regular news was interrupted by the special report of the explosion in one of the world's most famous skyscrapers. Shots of men and women being hauled out of the building on stretchers, blood-spattered victims hobbling between less wounded coworkers, and the cries of onlookers would remain forever a part of American memory.

He also recalled his gut reaction. Almost without thinking, he had called Ken Aronstam at the university and announced, "Ken, wait 'til you see what the Arabs just did in New York!"

It had taken the media much longer to draw that same conclusion. At first they had posited that either a gas line or a container of some other volatile substance in the mammoth skyscraper's subterranean chambers had malfunctioned, leading to the deadly blast. When that had not proven itself out, they had surmised that a disgruntled janitor or other manual laborer at the building had driven a bomb-laden van into the basement.

Only after clues began to trickle in as to the possibility of a terrorist attack had they begun to zero in on a violent Egyptian cult led by a blind Islamic holy man. The ensuing investigation revealed that the terrorists had been on the verge of fulfilling other plots, including the bombing of the Holland Tunnel during rush hour. Fortunately, that scheme had been intercepted.

Since then, any disaster that smacked of subterfuge opened immediate speculation that Muslim terrorists were the instigators, from the bombing of the Oklahoma City Federal Courthouse, to the TWA disaster over Long Island.

As for David, he was no genius of international politics, but quick reasoning had led him to suspect Arab terrorists the moment he saw the World Trade Center coverage.

"What makes you think it's Arabs?" Ken had asked him.

"Come on." David had laughed. "Think about it! If you wanted to get at the wealthiest and most influential Jews in the world, where would you go?"

Ken's silence spurred David to fill in. "You're thinking Israel, right? No way, Ken. The thickest concentration of Jewish power resides at the World Trade Center! Any anti-Semitic message delivered there will be heard loud and clear!"

So it had followed. The Muslim perpetrators had eventually been caught and tried, and their leader had been imprisoned. Interestingly, however, although the Egyptian cult was the same one that had been accused of assassinating a Zionist leader in this same city in 1990, no media commentary had ever given the explanation David gave. No one, he figured, had dared touch the obvious.

As David lowered his eyes from the tall buildings, he noticed how people on the street tried to peer through the darkened windows of the car in which he traveled. On the rare occasion that he had seen a limousine pass through Columbus, he had done just as these onlookers were doing: He had peered quizzically into the obsidian-like glass, wondering who the passengers could be. Celebrities? Tycoons? Now, David was the limousine passenger, and people were giving him the same unfocused stares he had leveled at luxury cruisers.

He felt foolish. The further he went into this conundrum, the more ridiculous it seemed.

David should have figured his hosts would not be quick to reveal much about themselves. As much as they knew about him, he was proportionately ignorant of them. It appeared that they intended to keep it that way, at least for a while. The first suggestion of this was the fact that they would only meet with him in a neutral place, not in a home or office.

Smoothly, the limousine veered toward the curb in front of the Waldorf-Astoria Hotel. As it pulled to a stop at the Park Avenue entrance, the hotel's crisply uniformed doorman rushed out and saluted the unseen occupants.

The chauffeur beat him to the passenger door, and as he let the rabbis out, he told the doorman to fetch a bellboy. In a moment, a sharply-groomed adolescent was unloading David's luggage from the trunk and taking it to the elevator of the elaborate, muraled lobby. All tips were paid by the chauffeur, and soon David and his hosts were escorted to a posh tenth-story suite.

David's modest salary had never allowed him to stay in such a place. Even if he had been blessed with a windfall, he would not have spent it on the luxury of a New York hotel. He would have used the money to fund a trip to some primitive Central American dig. Still, he could not help being impressed with the three-room suite. Crystal chandeliers and gilt wall sconces graced the ceilings and walls; bouquets of fresh flowers lent life and aroma to the room, and a marble-walled bathroom, which David could see through the arch beyond the vast bed, added a final touch of opulence.

David's wide eyes said the "wow" he was too dignified to say.

Then he spotted something that made his academic spine tingle. One low table beneath the parlor window was covered with books, some of them so ancient they could have been from the cloisters of a medieval monastery. Speechless David walked toward the table, then stopped and turned to the rabbis gathered in the middle of the room.

"Go ahead, Dr. Rothmeyer. Look at them. They are here for you to study," Rabbi Benjamin said.

"Study?" David repeated. "Now?"

He walked to the table and gazed on the musty old volumes. Most of them were in German, some in other esoteric languages he vaguely recognized, like post-Roman Latin, Syriac, and ancient Aramaic.

Many of the books were half- or full-bound leather, with raised compartments on the spines and gold-tooled titles. Daring to touch them, he opened to pages of parchment and vellum, many of them illuminated, the designs intricate and elaborate. As David ran his hands over the priceless works, his fingers quivering, Rabbi Benjamin and the others drew near.

"We know you must be tired from your journey and all this strangeness," Benjamin said. "We want you to rest this evening and get a good sleep."

The kindly rabbi placed a hand on David's shoulder. "You must have a thousand questions. All in good time, my boy. Meanwhile, there is plenty here to amuse you."

Then, pointing to a stack of newer books and leaflets, he said, "Some of your questions will be answered by these." He picked up one pamphlet and suggested David start with it.

"This will tell you enough for now," he said. "We will meet you for breakfast in the hotel dining room at seven A.M."

As David glanced at the pamphlet, the rabbis left the room.

The professor did not think to say good-bye as he turned the little booklet over in his hands. At the top of the front flap was the same shining menorah that had graced the letterhead he received a week before. The pamphlet's title promised to explain some things: "Temple Consortium, Paving the Way for Messiah."

CHAPTER 4

Father McCurdy woke suddenly and sat up in bed, his heart racing. He had not had one of his recurring dreams of Qumran for months. It was clear why he had this one tonight, however. The interview with the young journalist had provoked old fears, old anxieties.

He reached out and pulled back the filmy curtain that gave him a view of his garden. Usually, the pleasant bower, especially when seen in the moonlight, salved any restlessness of his spirit, but tonight it only added to his agitation, making him feel quite alone in the world.

He swung his legs out from under the covers and shuffled to the kitchen. A mug of warm milk might relax him, he thought. The house was quiet. Only the ticking of the old wooden wall clock above the sink filled the silence.

Fumbling through the cupboard, he found a saucepan, poured in some milk, and warmed it to a steamy froth.

He had just sat down to the comforting cup when his dear friend and houseman, John Cromwell, entered the room.

"Father," he greeted him, "I heard you rustling about. Having trouble sleeping?"

"Sleep is not the problem," Ian answered. "It's what comes with the sleep."

"How Shakespearean!" Cromwell chuckled. "'To sleep. Perchance to dream . . .'"

"'Ay, there's the rub!'" Ian joined him. "Yes, yes," the old priest said with a shrug. "I guess Hamlet and I do have something in common."

Cromwell rubbed his bleary eyes, placed his spectacles on his nose, and went to the cupboard for his own mug. He was hesitant to say what he thought, but when he sat down, he couldn't help letting out a heavy sigh. He took a sip from his steaming cup and stared intently at the tabletop.

"Come, old friend," Ian nudged him. "You can say it."

"Well, it almost seems irreverent," John replied. "You know, Shakespeare and all. But I think you have Hamlet beat by a long shot."

"How so?" Ian asked.

"The Prince of Denmark bore only the secret of one royal murder and an incestuous conspiracy. You bear the burden of the world's future—the security of the entire planet!"

To a chance listener, such a declaration would have seemed melodramatic, even ludicrous. But to the two men sitting in the Oxfordshire kitchen in the dark of night, the statement was anything but absurd. It was altogether factual, an unearthly load to bear.

The two of them had borne it together for ten years!

Cromwell had never been to Israel. He had been caretaker for Ian's residence since the professor's early days at Pembroke College. In the 1950s, when Ian began to spend months at a time at Qumran, John had been his mainstay, keeping his home in his absence. Though one was Anglican and the other Catholic, the two had become fast friends, and the houseman had followed with interest letters sent from the Holy Land while Ian was working there.

When the letters became less frequent, the tenor less personal, Cromwell had chalked it up to distance and infrequent visits between the two men. Even the best of friendships must suffer under such strains, he figured.

But then Ian had returned, suddenly, unannounced, keeping close to the house and avoiding society. That was when the facts of Ian's trials in Israel became their mutual secret.

"Let's go to the parlor," the priest said. "I've never been good at talking in a kitchen."

The last embers of the October hearth glowed amiably on the grate. Two wing-backed chairs faced the warmth, and the flannel-robed gentlemen settled into them like monks in quiet cells.

Here, it always seemed, the world was not so much with them, though in this quaint corner of Britain, on this country road, well back from the flow of English life, there was little likelihood of eyes or ears within miles.

Beside the priest's chair were baskets piled with current issues of *Biblical Archaeology*, the *Jerusalem Post*, *Mid-East Scholar*, and newsletters from a dozen Israel-based agencies, all more or less related to the fields of Middle-Eastern history and the Bible. Next to these were other baskets and boxes, stacked with issues of international newspapers and magazines, ready for the fire. Upon inspection, these publications would have revealed gaping holes, where articles had been neatly cut out and placed in scrapbooks that lined the shelves of Ian's study.

In that study, which was adjacent to the parlor beyond a set of glass doors, were older BAs and bound volumes of the *Jerusalem Post*. Ian never permitted those publications to be cut or altered in any way.

How many evenings the two men had sat before this fire, reading, clipping, and cataloging, was impossible to say. Once they had finished, even on summer nights, Cromwell burned the international papers in a barrel stove in the garden. And morning duties in the house included arranging clippings in the scrapbooks.

Ian figured that the young London journalist who had visited earlier that day had noted the horde of publications near the wing chairs. Undoubtedly her notebook contained an entry to the effect that he was still obsessed with the Middle East, and with developments in the arena he had supposedly forsaken.

Since the release of a good number of the scrolls for public consumption, and until the recent blast from Allaman and the Deadly Duo, the media had calmed down to a tepid simmer over the whole issue of the Cave Scrolls. Except for *Biblical Archaeology*'s ongoing pleas for the release of more information to the scholarly community, there had been only the occasional offbeat conspiracy theory to keep the matter in the public eye.

Every print medium, from the *New York Times* to the *National Investigator*, had made a stab at the mystery of the scrolls' contents. The latter posited everything from the secrets of alien spaceships and interplanetary flight, to the genealogy of Bigfoot as the great riddle that was being withheld.

The clamor on the part of Allaman and his cohorts was only one more in a string of suppositions trying to guess at what kept the committee from releasing its hold on the scrolls for nearly half a century. To Allaman's credit it must be conceded that this latest attack was the best thought out and most cleverly "supported" of the theories.

John leaned forward and prodded the embers with the poker. As he did, Ian reached under his ottoman for a back issue of BA. It, like all the publications received at this house, was addressed to J. Cromwell; the less Ian's name was associated with such matters, the better. He chuckled as he opened the magazine to a review of *The Cave Scroll Deception*.

"You know," he said, "I rather think it is a good thing the blockheads have gained such a spotlight. In time, their silliness will blow over. Meanwhile, the shakeup has taken the newsmongers off the scent of the trail."

Cromwell was astonished. "But, Father, what of the church? What of the integrity of—"

"Come, come, John," Ian interrupted. "In two thousand years nothing has prevailed against the Word of God. This sham of intellectualism is nothing new. Nothing new at all!"

Though Ian had many fine qualities, John liked this part of his priestly friend best of all. The two were of different creeds, but when it came to Scripture, Ian knew it inside out, and he knew the God of Christianity with a faith that never bowed in the face of challenge.

"You are right, of course," John said. Grabbing a hunk of the *New York Times*, he crumpled it for the fire, and Ian glanced at it thoughtfully.

"I must say, though," Ian observed, "those New Yorkers tend to give me a scare sometimes."

He took a cigar from his side table, bit off the tip, and held it close enough to an ember to light it, then put it to his lips and blew out a long breath of smoke. His mind drifting through the flames of the fresh fire, he relived one of his worst experiences as though it played on a screen before him.

"You are thinking of Father Ducharme," Cromwell surmised.

"The New York paper did not know how close it came that time," Ian replied. "Had the old fellow lived . . . well, perhaps things turned out for the best . . . . May his soul rest in peace."

John sat back and studied Ian's sad face. He knew what a harrowing few years Ian had spent with his mentor, the original master of the scroll committee, as that French scholar had destroyed himself with drink and madness.

"Never has a student loved a teacher more than you loved Ducharme," Cromwell said. "You did all you could—no one could have done more."

"But the paper was right," Ian recalled. "They guessed he went mad with some horrible burden, something he hid from the world." The priest's eyes glistened in the light of the fire, and he blinked back a tear.

Then he gave an ironic chuckle. "Such a legacy he left me! Shall I, too, go mad, John? Shall we go mad together?"

"Don't say such things!" Cromwell demanded. "Ducharme had too many weaknesses. You are stronger."

"True." Ian snorted. "I have no great need for wine or liquor, like my mentor. I have no penchant for female parishioners or for choirboys, like others I have known."

Cromwell gave a sad grin.

"No, John," Ian conceded, "I do not have those weaknesses. But to live with the revelation of the infernal scroll is enough. I think it was enough to produce Ducharme's madness!"

At this, John jerked violently. "Enough, Ian!" he exclaimed. "You are my employer, but you are also my friend. I will not have you tormenting yourself with things that will never come to pass, secrets whose finding out is as likely as . . . "

A long, deathly silence passed between them. The fire crackled, rising up in images of unspeakable misery and annihilation.

"As likely as the Holocaust?" Ian offered.

Cromwell shuddered. Sinking back into his chair, he put his hand to his lips and spoke no more.

"I must tell you," the priest muttered. "I am not afraid of the journalists *or* the conspiracy theorists. There are others, others more resourceful, more motivated than any hack writer. They are on a quest to fulfill their God-given destiny, and their quest requires my secret."

At this, he opened to the back of the old BA he had retrieved from beneath the ottoman. Pointing to a small classified ad buried on the last page, he handed it to his friend.

"If you doubt me, see here," he said.

"Committee of Orthodox rabbis seeking Jewish archaeologist with background in linguistics for sensitive study. High pay and world travel guaranteed to qualified applicant. All references considered. Contact Temple Consortium, 36 Rebi Josef Street, Jerusalem."

The little ad was highlighted with the figure of a tiny menorah.

Cromwell's eyes went wide, the pupils large and dark. Peering over the rims of his spectacles, he asked, "You know these people?"

"I know of their work," the priest replied. "It would surprise me if they have not already found their linguist. They move very quickly when they set their minds to something."

CHAPTER 5

David's eyes felt dry as sand as he stepped from the elevator and entered the hotel's sumptuous Peacock Alley Restaurant. He had barely slept all night, poring over the maze of reading matter that his hosts had left for him.

For much of the early evening, he had been alternately fascinated by the esoteric materials and angered by what appeared to be a huge academic joke. Could it be that this entire episode was nothing more than an expensive and elaborate farce conceived by his coworkers at the university, some kind of scholarly prank to send him off on sabbatical with a gleeful "gotcha!"?

He knew better, of course. None of his coworkers had the kind of money it would take to pull off such a charade. No, the rabbis were for real. It was up to David to make some sense of the material they bestowed upon him, at least enough to ask intelligent questions in the morning.

Around midnight, he had decided to arrange the books and pamphlets in chronological order. Since the oldest volumes had no copyright dates, he had had to go by inference. This took time, since not all the writers were historians and dates seemed quite unimportant to them. He was able to deduce that many of the ancient books went back to about 1500 C.E. Some of these were written in Ladino, a blend of Spanish and Hebrew spoken by the "Sephardic" Jews living in Spain in the Middle Ages and later. Others were written in Yiddish, a blend of German and Hebrew spoken by the Jews of Eastern Europe.

Next he was able to pinpoint writings that dated close to these, encompassing nearly five centuries thereafter. To his bewilderment, the non-Hebrew texts were not Spanish, German, nor even European. These were Syrian, and full of lengthy discourses on Jewish law. The only thing they had in common with the first were long lists of genealogies.

Then there were pieces from a scholarly group in the Balkans, dating back as far as the early Renaissance, and first-century manuscripts from the famed rabbinical schools of Alexandria, Egypt.

Later writings were from the 1800s, during the rise of Zionism as a philosophy. Even more modern writers from Brooklyn, New York, and New Jersey added their two cents.

Sometime toward dawn, a theme began to emerge from the plethora of seemingly mismatched and haphazard material. While the writings spanned the gamut of history, law, and philosophy, all of them dealt directly or indirectly with the quest for one enigmatic figure. Some called him the Messiah; others distinguished him from the Messiah, referring to him as the heir to a great priesthood and calling him "high priest" of Israel.

Some volumes seemed to be repositories of that priestly ancestry, line-by-line tomes keeping account of his family tree. Others debated just what he would mean, whether he was real or symbolic, and whether he would ever exist at all.

Just before the front desk rang David's room with his wake-up call, he had lain down and fallen into a fitful sleep, replete with the smell of old paper, dried leather, images of shepherds and archaeologists and mitred priests. Like the tigers of Little Black Sambo, the cartoonish characters chased each other round and round the hotel room, until they dissolved into a buttery blur of pancakes and syrup that splattered into dawn's light when the phone rang.

Upon waking, David had a craving for flapjacks.

In a private, glassed-in dining room of the Peacock Alley Restaurant, the rabbis waited for David. Tall green plants along the crystal wall provided a screen against the bustle of customers who took seats in the main dining hall.

Rabbi Benjamin, seeing the professor had arrived, hailed him congenially, waving him into the quiet sanctum and pulling out a chair. "Good morning, Dr. Rothmeyer," he greeted, handing him the menu of strictly kosher dishes the rabbis had requested. "We trust you had a good rest."

All the hosts nodded and smiled warmly. Even Uriel Katz seemed a little less shadowy in the morning light that filtered through the room's tall windows.

David took a seat and sighed audibly. "Good morning, gentlemen," he said. "But I doubt you trust any such thing. You knew that anyone with my background would be awake all night with the stash you left me to sort through."

"Ah!" Rabbi Benjamin brightened. "You found the material interesting!"

David scowled at him and his colleagues. Leaning back, he gestured to the sumptuous surroundings. "It is obvious you are doing your best to impress me," he said, "courting me with the finest your city has to offer."

When Dr. Jacobs and Rabbi Levine only nodded proudly, David shook his head. "No, gentlemen!" he snapped. "Enough parlor games! You have had me on puppet strings for a week. Now it is my turn to ask questions."

Rabbi Benjamin grew grave. "Very well, Dr. Rothmeyer. I told you we would give you answers in time. Begin."

"Well," David said, "I know that through the night you had me on a scavenger hunt. One piece of information, if analyzed properly, could fit in with another and lead forward. But this hunt was more puzzling than most, because you never told me just what I was to look for."

The men glanced at one another, avoiding David's angry eyes.

"We gave you a clue," Dr. Jacobs said, the portly gent seeming genuinely concerned about easing David's mind. "Rabbi Ben told you to start with the pamphlet first."

David thought back. That gesture had seemed days ago.

"All right," he replied. "I'll grant that much. So you wanted me to deduce from that little bit of information that all of the material I would be reading related to this so-called 'paving the way for Messiah.'" His face flushed, he felt more the brunt of some ungodly joke than ever.

When the men only smiled quietly, he grew more agitated.

"You're not serious!" He gave a derisive laugh. "You people really think there's some great New Age about to dawn, and you want me to help you usher it in?"

Rabbi Levine jerked his hands up from the table, his long, thin face stern and corrective. "We don't use the term 'New Age.' That has the wrong implications!"

David rolled his eyes. "New Age, Golden Age, Aquarian Age . . . what's the difference? You don't really expect a scientist to take any of this seriously, do you?"

The men turned to one another and muttered quietly.

At last, Rabbi Benjamin reached out and touched David's arm. "Professor, true science does not avoid inscrutable matters. It does in fact embrace them. We hired you exactly because you *are* a scientist."

"Yes," Dr. Jacobs enthused, his round face red with ardor. "And a linguist."

"And an archaeologist!" Rabbi Levine added.

"And Jewish," Uriel Katz said somberly, his brooding eyes boring through David like those of an owl at night.

For a long moment, David was fixated upon this one man, at once fascinating and frightening.

Then Rabbi Benjamin's kind voice broke in. "Consider it all a great dig!" he said. "You may find nothing, but then again, you may come up with trowels full of treasure!"

David ripped his gaze away from Uriel Katz and shook himself. "But why?" he asked. "What is this all about? What is in it for all of you, if we learn something about this ancestry stuff and law stuff and Jewish stuff?"

Dr. Jacobs leaned forward eagerly, his ample paunch doubling over the table edge. "We will be able to build our temple!" he declared. "We will be able to build the temple that Ezekiel prophesied!"

Rabbi Benjamin hushed him and looked anxiously through the glass partition, into the main room.

"Temple?" David snorted. "Where? Jerusalem? Like . . . in the Bible? Come on! You can't be serious!"

Suddenly Uriel Katz filled David's sight. Like a cloud, the little man loomed larger, rising from his seat, pressing in close, his face directly in front of David's.

"There is nothing more serious in all the world than what we speak of, Dr. Rothmeyer! Nothing more serious for us, or for you, or"—he gestured toward the roomful of diners beyond the private chamber—"for all of humanity!"

David was stunned. Sitting back, he swallowed hard and watched mutely as Rabbi Katz sank again into his seat.

"And just what is it you want from me?" David finally managed to ask. "How do my 'talents' fit in with your quest?"

Horace Benjamin scooted close and spoke softly. "First of all, David, you must understand that we do not presume to search for the Messiah. He will come of his own accord, in his own time. What we want you to do is help us find our high priest. Without him, we have no use for a temple. Without a temple, Jerusalem is a crown without a star, the Messiah has no place from which to reign, and Israel is a dream unfulfilled!"

David stared at the rabbi mutely. From what Benjamin was saying, it seemed that if David accepted this assignment, he would be responsible for the world's future! It was more than his mind could absorb.

Flashes from his crazy nightmare darted to mind. His head fuzzy, he scanned the kosher menu. "Do they serve pancakes here?" he muttered.

CHAPTER 6

April / Nisan

Mel Wester settled back in the seat of his modest rental car and sped up Highway 95 out of Coeur d'Alene, Idaho. Drinking in the April green of the forested hills, he lowered the driver's window and let a sun-warmed breeze spill across him.

Just an hour ago, he had disembarked at the Spokane airport from a flight out of Los Angeles. Already he could feel the tension of twelve years on the Los Angeles police force, and the stress of five years of a high-profile legal case, easing out of his broad shoulders.

This would be the best move he ever made, he told himself. Leaving California to join his older brother, Pete, in the hills of Montana would forever change his life—might even save it.

"Should have done this long ago," he muttered, glancing at his early-forties reflection in the rearview mirror.

He passed through names on the map that had long peppered his brother's conversations.

Sandwiched between humps of rolling hills and verdant valleys, along clean rivers and lakes at the foot of tall, forested mountains, such towns as Hayden, Chilco, Athol, and off the beaten track,

Rathdrum and Spirit Lake, were more than just bucolic villages. According to Mel's brother, they represented a mind-set and way of life that challenged the "sheeplike indifference of the apathetic masses."

If Pete was right, rusty junkyards and tacky R.V. parks belied the fact that deep thinkers lived here, "men and women who have clearly seen the truth of America's wretchedness and have removed themselves from it."

Oh, sure, yuppies had invaded the region, clearing forests for multimillion-dollar golf courses, erecting posh resorts with "wilderness" themes, "restoring" failed sections of the little cities into "old towns" for the marketing of "primitive art" and espresso.

"In the name of nature, they rape nature!" Mel snorted as he passed through one such restoration.

This statement was not original. He was quoting his brother. After all, who was Mel to criticize what he had accepted all his adult life? The L.A. scene was as far from "nature' as any scene could be.

But Pete had always been ahead of Mel when it came to truth seeking.

As he passed beneath the shadow of black bluffs to the west of Lake Pend Oreille and wound through dark evergreen bowers, Crosby, Stills, and Nash crooned on the radio, reminding him of his youth in Seattle, when he and Pete had decided to become hippies.

"Become yourself," the songsters implored, because the past was just a "good-bye."

Mel and Pete's parents had died a thousand deaths when the boys grew their white-blond crewcuts into braids and exchanged their button-down collars for beads.

With the encouragement of such mentors as CSN and the Grateful Dead, they had set out to abandon the establishment, donning the regalia of the counterculture, trying a little pot and marching against the war.

Then Mel had been drafted and went off to Viet Nam, serving in the final conflicts. He returned "without a conscience," Pete said, joining the L.A. police to fight all over again in the ghettos.

Pete, who had dodged the draft with a bad back incurred on the Queen Ann High School football field, had retained his integrity and carried his dropout spirit into the hills, first the Okanogan region of Northeastern Washington, and then, five years ago, the Bull River Valley of Western Montana.

Somewhere in those transitions, Pete had left off his childhood nickname and insisted on being known as "Peter," in the style of his hippie cohorts. After a while, Mel had adjusted to the new name. For years, his brother had been "Peter" to him.

Mel had noticed, however, that in the past few letters his brother had sent, he had reverted to "Pete." At first, Mel thought this was just evidence of middle-age mellowing, of a maturing comfort with his past that did not need counterculture posturing. But other things had changed in Pete's letters, and in his infrequent phone calls. Whereas Pete's antipathy toward "the establishment" in his younger years had always been pacifistic, his language was now more activist. He wrote and spoke about the government as the enemy in a way he had never done before.

No longer was there a Viet Nam to protest. Yet Pete's antipathy toward "the central bureaucracy" was more venomous than it had been even at the height of the war. And he mentioned gatherings that Mel wondered about, meetings with people who had never been pacifists and who seemed anything but hip.

Sometimes Mel wondered if Pete had become too chummy with some of the "rednecks" in the region, although he could not believe Pete would go far enough to actually befriend gun-toters.

Mel was looking forward to a life free of the violence he had known in L.A.—the race wars, the bloodshed, and the legal traps that could pin a racist rap on a good cop like himself. He would be happy, now, to live without a gun. He might learn to hunt for deer or elk, but he would never again point a gun at a fellow human being.

A prick of envy stabbed Mel's heart as he made his way farther into the outback of the Northwest. Even the names of the dirt roads that took off from the highway, disappearing into the mysteries of piney shadows and leading to overgrown, Emersonian hideaways, made him jealous: Homestead Road, Timberland Route, Remington Way, Granite Loop, Blacktail Road, Log House Way conjured up images of calming cottages and long-haired women in macramaed dresses setting up preserves from naturally grown gardens.

Mel knew it couldn't be that perfect, that utopian. Whatever the folks had here, though, it was better than what he had known, and he wondered why he had waited so long to seek it out.

Now and then, incongruous tourist traps with names like Ponderosa Condos or Big Valley B & B jolted him. An amusement park featured the Big Bear roller coaster and fake holdups by cowboy bandits on the miniature railroad that carried dazzled families through pristine groves. Eventually, though, such commercialism was less conspicuous than logging roads and real railroads. Taverns, posted as the spots "where good friends meet," replaced yuppie bistros. Horse trails through the brush were more frequent than jet trails overhead.

What seemed to Mel a peculiar blending of cultures led from billboards advertising "See the Wolf People—Gifts and Souvenirs," to a marquee announcing a Celtic harp concert; from a classy little sign pointing out an elite ski resort, to an Adopt-a-Highway marker, sponsored by a gospel mission.

Mel remembered the gospel missions in the L.A. area. Pockets of reprieve on hopeless streets, they served an admirable purpose, and although the cops trusted the managers to help them make a dent in the crime scene, the missions were also sad reminders of the depths to which men could sink, and the long way up they had to climb.

Mel wanted to be away from all that, never to return.

Somewhere near the Montana border, as the sun was begin-ning to sink and the heavens began to spread out in that phenom-enon known as "the Big Sky," all vestiges of blatant commercialism seemed to fall away. Southeast, along Highway 200, which fol-lowed the Clark Fork River down the west side of the state, teepee burners—the smokestacks of shingle mills—spiked the sky, the only human counterpart to the tall tamaracks that graced the sky-line. Wildhorse Saloon, Hoot Owl Saloon, and a dozen other such establishments sat alongside little chapels and Jehovah's Witness Kingdom Halls in the small burgs that dotted the road. Solar-paneled houses and earth berm holdovers from the back-to-the-earth movement of the seventies sat alongside roads like Deer Hoof, Moose Jaw, and Hope Route.

Montana was the only state in the union where, instead of "60" or even "65 Miles Per Hour," speed limit signs said "Reasonable and Prudent."

The wild west is alive and well, Mel thought, grinning to himself.

Yet, in this land of the independent cowboy, folks were savvy enough to use the government to their advantage. On the edge of one town, a ranch-style house sported a cage door on its garage. "This Pet Cougar Protected by Federal Law," a sign warned.

That sign was one of the markers Pete had told Mel to watch for. About a mile after that, the highway would bridge the Bull River, where it met the Clark Fork. Just before the town of Noxon, an unmarked road would take off from the highway east into the hills of the Kootenai National Forest. "I'll tie a red bandanna to a tree where you're supposed to turn," Pete had said. "It's a dirt road. Hit it before sundown, or you'll get lost before you reach the house."

Once, when Pete had lived in the Okanogan, he had given Mel similar instructions. He had been living in a wigwam at the time, as he built a stone house without benefit of power tools, deep in the sagebrush hills. On his one and only visit from L.A., Mel had indeed gotten lost. Had it not been for a kindhearted hippie who had come rumbling by in a VW bus, Mel might have spent the night with the rattlesnakes.

This time, he was running ahead of the sun. He would make it up the rugged road just in time for dinner. At the thought of the meal his brother would set out, his mouth salivated.

Pete's "significant other," Honey, who had been with him ever since his Okanogan days, had split a few months ago. Pete had not gone into the reasons why. But the couple, while not strict vegetarians, had learned together the marvels of homegrown gardens, herbs, and real nutrition. Even Mel, who had to have meat with every meal, came to admit that wonders could be worked with yogurt and tofu.

The red bandanna was tied to a white birch on a road between the Naughty Pine Tavern and a cute, cabin-style Baptist church. The narrow, bumpy road that cut a swath between dark woods became barely more than a trail as it ascended Cricket Creek. At last, a couple of crook-necked turns brought the rental car out of the woods onto a slope of ground that lay like an open palm before the house of Peter Wester.

"Good grief!" Mel sighed, as he saw the place for the first time. It was beautiful! And his brother, who earned a decent living as a freelance carpenter, had built it with his own hands.

A spacious log house, graced by a broad front porch, it was a true work of art. The big roof, which came down over the porch in a sweep of hand-hewn shingles, sported dormers for the loft Pete had told him about.

"You'll sleep there," he had promised, "like you've never slept before."

"It's quiet, huh?" Mel had asked.

"It's so quiet you can hear the quiet," Pete had bragged.

The porch posts were as elaborate as any machine-turned

columns. They were each made from a single, twisted log, with gnarls and burls that looked like totem faces. Mel remembered Pete's letter, telling how he and Honey had hiked into the woods day after day, looking for just the right tree trunks for those pillars. When they had found six, they had called friends together to help them haul them to the house site, and with a big party, they had celebrated their placement.

Mel had not heard mention of those particular friends for some time. He wondered if they had moved away or if Pete just didn't see them anymore.

Stopping his car on the grassy slope, he turned off the motor and breathed in the quiet.

Soon, the quiet was outdone by an even better sound. Pete was on the porch, calling his baby brother's name. "Hey, Mel, ol' buddy! Welcome to the Promised Land!"

CHAPTER 7

Spring in the Montana hills brought cool evenings. Pete Wester grabbed a padded flannel shirt off a hook by his front door and bounded off the porch to greet his brother.

Though they were two years apart, the men were twinlike, with their husky builds and white-blond hair. Tall and muscular, they were distinguishable primarily by dress and hairstyles: Mel in citified slacks and sweater, his hair cropped close, while Pete, in jeans and plaid, still wore his hair long and tied back with red string.

The main mark of Pete's transition from pure hippiedom to the Montana outback was his new footwear. Whereas he used to wear sandals, he now wore cowboy boots, much more practical in the hills.

"How's the refugee from the asphalt jungle?" he asked with a smile, tiny crow's-feet about his eyes the only sign of aging in his youthful face. The two men enjoyed a brisk hug, and Pete took Mel's suitcase from the backseat.

"Good to be here!" Mel admitted.

"Come on!" Pete said, as Mel hung back, studying the trees and the sunset sky. Like a stained-glass dome, the red-pink glow hung over dark green spires.

"Gorgeous!" Mel said.

"Sure! But there'll be plenty of nights just like it. Supper's waiting."

The log house was as warm and inviting as Mel had imagined. His brother's craftsmanship gleamed in every cabinet, every rafter. With a sweep of his eyes, Mel tried to absorb it. A grand rock fireplace filled the entire south wall. Though it was April, the crisp mountain air called for a fire, and a small blaze glowed on the grate. The wood hues of the room were complemented by colorful Indian blankets draped over the loft rail and braided rugs on the floor, lending further warmth.

"Braided rugs!" Mel exclaimed. "In L.A., we don't see those even in antique shops."

Pete spoke softly. "They're not antiques. Honey made them."

Mel detected the sadness in his brother's tone and knew it was not the time to ask about her. "Something smells good," he said instead.

The kitchen was open to view, taking up the north end of the big room. A hallway led toward a pantry and another smaller porch in the back.

Between the kitchen and the fireplace, a steep set of half-log stairs led to the loft, which, Pete had told him, was divided into two bedrooms, with a bathroom in between. Filtering through the log posts of the banister, the glow of sunset descended through the front dormers.

The only other illumination was from oil lamps. Electricity, which was supplied only by a generator, was used sparingly, and none was in evidence that night.

Mel was glad he had sold off his few sticks of furniture and his Spartan kitchen supplies before coming here. Pete's home was fully equipped, and nothing Mel could have contributed would have been worthy of the place.

The ex-cop had arrived with literally all his worldly goods in his rental car: a few books, photo albums, and mementos in boxes, and a suitcase full of clothes. His old beat-up car had died, just before he left L.A.—a symbol, he had thought, that it was time to leave everything behind.

Pete bounded up the stairs with Mel's only suitcase. "I'll just set this on your bed. Make yourself at home. We can unload the boxes after supper."

Mel wandered past the dining area where a huge pine table was set for two. An old matte-black cookstove, the kind with shiny nickel decorations, warmed the north end of the house, radiating enough heat to take the edge off the chilly spring night.

Atop the stove, one huge kettle bubbled, and Mel, potholder in hand, lifted the lid. A savory steam escaped, and Mel made out hunks of colorful vegetables and potatoes simmering in a ruddy broth, with only a few pieces of meat for flavoring.

"Elk," Pete said, joining him. "I try to get one a year, and it makes enough for . . . well, more than enough for just me."

That was a comfortable cue to Mel that he could ask about Honey. Pete ladled up two big bowls of stew, and the men took seats on the table's split-log benches.

"Must be kind of lonely here without your lady," he said.

Pete dunked a piece of homemade wheat bread in his bowl and held it between his fingers a moment before taking a bite. "Sure, it can get that way. I keep busy."

"What happened?" Mel asked directly. "I thought you two would be together forever."

Pete shrugged, avoiding Mel's gaze. "I guess she got spooked."

"What?" Mel asked, wondering if he had heard right.

Pete chewed on the bread and swallowed hard. Aimlessly stirring his stew with his soup spoon, he appeared to try to look casual. "There's plenty of time to talk about these things," he hedged. Then rolling his eyes toward his brother, "What about you? Any more trouble from that case in L.A.?"

Mel took a bite of stew. "I think I kept you updated," he said.

"I was vindicated. But five years of legal hassle and death threats took it out of me."

Flashes of the scene in the streets that had nearly cost Mel his life, let alone his job and reputation, swept over him even now. Never would he forget the call that came that evening, the last night he worked the force on a regular beat. A small all-night market in a Watts neighborhood, one of the most notorious black ghettos in L.A., had been held up. A routine incident, he and his partner figured.

They had not expected that one of them would die in an ensuing scuffle outside the market.

Surrounded by a group of foul-mouthed ruffians, the officers drew their weapons. Most of the boys backed off, but one of them, high on crack, made a lunge, knifing Mel's partner in the kidney. Jorey Evans, the finest cop in the racially torn city, had not lived to see morning, dying in the E.R. of the Angel of Mercy Hospital.

Mel had not been able to be at his side when he died, as he had stayed behind when the ambulance left, interviewing witnesses and writing up the necessary reports. That fact alone had been enough to ruin Mel's sleep for months. But it was his own eyewitness account that nearly cost him his own life.

It was customary for one white and one black cop to work the Watts beats. Jorey Evans had been a great officer and had built good relations, as far as they could be built, with the people of the streets. Mel had believed that everyone involved in the event that night, including his partner, was African-American, and he had written in his report that a young black man had wielded the death instrument.

When the case went to trial, however, the issue was not over whether or not the suspect in question had actually wielded the knife, but whether or not the report was trustworthy. After all, the defense lawyers argued, Billy Olivera, the defendant, was predominantly Chicano, not black. If Mel Wester could not report an ethnic identity correctly, how could he report a murder correctly?

By the time the trial came to court, all other witnesses had retracted their statements, undoubtedly frightened by threats from the neighborhood ganglords. Mel knew how that felt. He had received more than his share of the same threats from the same hoods. What the ganglords had not counted on was Mel's depth of devotion to his fallen comrade. If he had to die in the process, he would not give up his fight against the killer of his best friend.

Shaking away the awful images of that night, Mel focused again on his brother. "I guess I'm just lucky I never went through something like the Rodney King case, or"— he snickered—"the O.J. trial."

Then, remembering his brother's efforts in behalf of civil rights in their hippie days, he quickly added, "Don't get me wrong. I think those bozos were way out of line. Kicking the life out of a guy—they were no better than the street gangs! And that investigator on the Simpson case—wow! A smart cop doesn't use racial slurs. He deserved getting kicked off the LAPD."

Pete, who had seemed less than intrigued by Mel's comments, suddenly sat up straight. "You mean the detective who got shafted by Judge Ito?" he asked. "Did you know he moved to Idaho?"

"Yeah," Mel replied, wondering if Pete took pride in the fact. "I also heard the people of Sandpoint didn't want him.'

Pete sank back, and Mel couldn't read him.

For a long while, silence passed between the two brothers. Mel could taste the awkwardness as easily as he could taste the stew. *What is going on?* he wondered. Had Pete changed so much that they couldn't even talk?

"Hey, bro," Mel said. "For years you gave me no end of grief for being a cop. Do I detect some kind of admiration toward that racist fuzz?"

Pete removed his napkin from his lap and set it on the table, then rose and began clearing the dishes.

His silence was disconcerting, but Mel did not press the issue. Instead, returning to a previous subject, he asked, "So, what about Honey? What did you mean, she got 'spooked'?"

Pete stood at the sink, his back to Mel. At last, he turned around and faced him squarely. But once again he ignored the direct inquiry.

"You've come to the right place, baby brother," he said. "This is the 'last best place,' you know. And not just because we escape things here."

Mel listened respectfully. He knew this part of his brother, this serious side, this pedantic side. He had been on the receiving end of many a lecture through the years, about social ills, war, poverty, racial injustice, and the right way to live. He was ready now to hear it again. Whatever Pete had to say, he felt it would be worth hearing.

He did not know that this time it would scare him. Always before, Pete's lectures had pricked his conscience or made him rethink his life, even make drastic moves, like this one to Montana.

Never before had Pete's opinions made him recoil.

"We don't just escape things here," Pete was saying. "Not me, not my friends, not anymore. We have not just removed ourselves from the wicked world. We are now prepared to do something about the wickedness!"

"Prepared?" Mel said. "How so?"

Pete came closer and leaned on the table, his fists pressing down like axeheads. "By first being aware of the enemy," he said, peering deep into Mel's blue eyes. "By not being so naive as we have been. By not believing that there are no such things as classes or good wars or races."

A shiver went through Mel. He was not sure what all this meant, but he did not like the sound or the feel of it.

At last, he swallowed and managed to ask once more, "What spooked Honey? Why did she leave?"

Pete stood up straight and looked out the window, in the direction of the road which could not be seen and the highway that led to the outer world.

"Have you ever heard of Ruby Ridge?" he asked.

CHAPTER 8

Peter Wester stood on the cedar deck of his log home, a steaming cup of coffee in hand, and breathed deeply of the cool morning air. The sky over the Bull River Valley was vivid blue and cloudless where it stretched between the cathedral-like grove that covered his acreage. He watched the sky for a moment, hoping that the old bald eagle would appear again, the one he'd seen a hundred times since moving there five years ago.

In the house, his brother enjoyed a deep sleep, and would probably not set foot out of the loft for at least another hour. Pete had not had the heart to tell Mel that their solitude and the quiet of the retreatlike grounds would be broken in a couple of days.

Before Mel had left Los Angeles, Pete had been notified that the committee might need his house for a "gathering." Pete had attended such events in Idaho. He knew they usually came together quickly, people involved in the network being notified sometimes only hours beforehand. He had not known for sure that the "gathering" at his house was a go until Mel was on his way to Montana.

Maybe it was providential that his brother had arrived at this time, Pete thought. Meeting his new connections might be the best way for Mel's education to begin. After all, Big Brother Pete carried only so much weight with Mel. There were things the ex-cop would need to learn from other sources.

The tall, Nordic-looking Westers were stubborn fellows. They had come to blows more than once as youths. In their late teens, they had seen eye to eye on most things, but Mel had always been less comfortable with the revolutionary scene than Pete had.

When Mel went to Viet Nam and then became a cop, Pete had nearly given up on him. Still, the two were fast friends, and Pete knew it would take more than politics to truly separate them. Now that Mel had moved to Montana, Pete hoped he would hear him out on his newest beliefs, accept his latest comrades and give them a chance.

Actually, the tenets of Pete's current faith were not so new. They had been growing in him for a long time, and when he analyzed them, it seemed that, although they involved tolerance of a more militaristic mind-set than he would have once embraced, they were the ultimate outgrowth of his hippie days.

He grinned sardonically. When he thought about it in light of Mel's arrival, he realized that his new views actually embraced many of the things he used to criticize his brother for espousing.

Pete walked out on the grass, and after placing his coffee cup on a low rock wall bordering a flower bed, he stretched in the sunlight. His azure eyes mirroring the heavens, he watched for the eagle but kept his ears pricked for the sound of a radio on the front porch, the ham radio that was, apart from a small transistor Walkman, the only technological connection he allowed himself with the outside world.

When he had first met the folks who would be coming to his house, their leader, Jim Fogarty, had been pleased to learn he was a ham operator. Fogarty had used him many times as a relayer for messages to and from members of the brotherhood in distant places.

Usually, the voices on the ham radio were American, but some had foreign accents. The messages were often a jumble of code words. Pete had tried to decipher the code, for his own curiosity, but had never been able to figure out more than a few phrases. He had never asked questions, though. He respected Fogarty and felt rather privileged that, when the leader was in the area, he used the house as headquarters.

A few days ago, an Irish-sounding voice had told him to expect a message today. It was supposed to come before ten A.M. He hoped it would come before Mel got up. He preferred to take the message in private.

Sitting down on the rock wall, he sipped his cup of coffee and studied Honey's outdoor handiwork. She had landscaped the yard. He wished she were here to give it the feminine touch. He tried to keep up the flowers, but they didn't do so well without her.

As the coffee-cup's steam drifted into the cool air, so, too, did Pete's thoughts drift to Honey. Nothing did so well without her, he admitted.

Suddenly the radio emitted a garbled bunch of static. Pete lurched, spilling his coffee. He darted across the lawn, fumbled with the headset, placed it quickly over his ears, then picked up the microphone.

"Cricket, here," he said, giving the code name that referred to his location on the nearby creek. "Over."

The static was thick. That could indicate either bad weather somewhere in transit or radio interference from anywhere on the globe.

Even when the voice became clear enough for Pete to make out, it was an odd one. Not only was it obviously foreign, the accent recognizably Middle Eastern, but it had a raspy, grating quality, not accountable to bad transmission.

Between bouts of interference, Pete could make out several of the code words that had become familiar. "Eagle-eye" was one, and "happening" was another.

Pete had heard these terms often enough to figure that, in con-text, they meant, "This message is for Fogarty." Eagle-eye was Fogarty's code name.

The next terms, however, were a mystery: "Relay to Swastika. Bailey's Bug is a go."

Strange, Pete thought. *What in the world could that mean?*

As he listened to the coarsely spoken phrases, he scribbled them quickly on a piece of note paper. The riddle in combination with the unforgettable voice gave him the heebie-jeebies.

The last line of the message added to the mystery: "Cedars ready to drop on Shekinah."

Pete hastily wrote it down, then heard, "Over—out," followed by loud static.

As he sat pondering the scribbled notes, the bald eagle he had awaited came swooping out of the mountains and circled on soft currents over the property.

"Eagle-eye happening," Pete muttered, a chill working down his spine at the thought of the voice.

Suddenly a sound from the house caught him off guard. Mel had come downstairs and was standing in the front doorway.

Pete shook himself and quickly put the message in the pocket of his flannel plaid shirt. Standing up, he feigned sunny cheerful-ness. "Heckuva morning, huh, bro?" he greeted. "How 'bout some scrambled eggs?"

CHAPTER 9

Spring brought a different sort of beauty to the Holy City, Jerusalem, than it did to the hills of western Montana.

David Rothmeyer had never anticipated that he would spend a spring in Israel. Of course, when he had committed to working with the Temple Consortium six months earlier, his university colleagues having accepted his application for earned leave, he had not anticipated any of the strange twists and turns his life had taken since.

But here he was, in the capital of Judaism—the capital, in fact, of three world faiths—and the international hub of contentious politics.

The fact that, three days ago, Arab suicide bombers had set off explosions at the busiest intersection in the city, killing themselves and several civilians including tourists, was testimony to the perpetual strife that flared over every inch of Israel's soil, and over Jerusalem in particular.

The Holy Land had been contended for by the children of Abraham, today's Arabs and Jews, since the days of the patriarch, each claiming the right of inheritance. Jerusalem, its spiritual and geographical capstone, was the most highly prized gem and was the central focus of Muslim and Jewish jealousy.

Then, since the time of Jesus, it had been the faith-heritage of Christians the world over, and no end of bloodshed, in the name of the cross, had occurred on its soil.

David strode down one of the narrow streets of the Jewish Quarter this bright April morning. A bag of hot bagels dangled from one hand, and he gripped a stack of file folders with the other.

He was learning, after half a year here, that life in this strife-torn city had a way of going on with amazing normalcy, despite confrontations. He might have been walking across the campus in Columbus, Ohio, carrying a pile of lecture notes and grade sheets, and balancing a cinnamon roll picked up at the Student Union Building. But he had developed a taste for bagels since coming to Israel, and he was not presently teaching classes at Midwest.

He was mentally preparing, however, for an academic presentation.

He hurried to the cloisterlike apartment that the rabbis had reserved for him in a wonderful old house that had become his home away from home. His employers were to meet him there in a few minutes, having flown in from New York to look in on him and see how he was progressing with his assignment.

He had been up since dawn, getting ready for the meeting, thinking through just how he would explain the steps he had taken in his research and what the results had been. An hour in an open-air coffee shop had been a welcome reprieve, but even there he had pored over notes and outlines. There was no more time for preparation.

The yellow-white rock of the Old City pavement was already warm with morning sun. Palm trees threw stripe-like shadows across the awnings of little shops as he rushed by. Jerusalem was all abloom with flowers that did not grow in Ohio, succulents and poppies that would have been more at home in the California hills.

David's work had not allowed him much time to admire the city. The reading material that the rabbis had provided in the Waldorf-Astoria hotel room had been shipped to Jerusalem along with the professor. It had taken him months to go through the material and to make enough sense of it to produce an outline of the contents.

The rabbis had sufficiently explained their goals so that he knew what to look for and what questions they were trying to resolve. What he had not realized, however, was just how involved his research would be, until he saw that the building in which he lived was the repository of an enormous library of such books.

If he had been asked to provide a description of his job, he would have had to say that he was like a scribal monk, secluded in a stone building, writing and researching night and day. He was no prisoner, but he was not permitted to call his colleagues back home or to share what he was learning with anyone outside the select circle from New York.

Sometimes he resented his isolation. But Israel, as far as he had observed it, was a fascinating place, and no one was holding him against his will. Besides, he had been hooked the night he was left alone with the old books in the New York hotel.

His suite of rooms was part of an ancient house located along the southern wall of the Old City, the central portion of Jerusalem that bore the most history. The wall against which the house was built was a conglomeration of stones from several periods—Crusader, Byzantine, and along the lowest layers, rubble from the days of Herod and the Romans. Often, when David approached the place, he was transported back in time, as he wondered what stories the stones could tell if they could speak.

The house, which was also the residence for the Temple Consortium, bore no sign over the entry. The path that led to it veered off one of the narrower streets. Several stone steps led to a barred gate. Vegetation concealed most of the building from the view of passersby. In fact, it would be easy to miss its presence altogether, if one were not looking for it.

The first time David had come here it was with Rabbi Benjamin, who had accompanied him to Israel to help him get settled.

"This house dates to the time of the Crusades," the rabbi had told him. "Of course, the invaders simply built upon the rubble of the city they overran, so the foundations probably go back much further, as is true of most places in the Old City. You will be living with the ghosts of millennia past," he said, with a wink.

Now holding the bag of bagels in his teeth, David took out the key he kept in his pocket, opened the gate, and let it swing back with an antiquarian creak. He had learned the hard way always to lock it behind him. One evening a bunch of street kids had entered the yard, tearing up the flowers so lovingly tended by Anya, the immigrant housekeeper.

Anya, a plump and pleasant old woman, had recently arrived in Israel from Russia. For a time, she had made her way by playing a violin on Ben Yehuda Street, where the terrorists had set off the recent bombs. She spoke only a smattering of English and a rough version of Hebrew. The rabbis considered her no threat to their business and, because she knew how to cook kosher, hired her to keep the place.

David rarely conversed with her, other than to praise her for the sweet Russian breads she was fond of presenting him after a day of baking in the antique kitchen.

He opened the front door, a tall thick slab composed of half a dozen cedar boards and fitted with heavy iron straps. Like the gate, it moved with a groan of age, and David stepped into the cool sanctum of the lobby.

David had grown quite fond of the strange old house, which was more like a series of ascending caves than a man-made building.

As were all the rooms of the house, the entryway was furnished with massive antiques—a coat rack, a side table with a beveled mirror, and heavy straight-backed chairs that looked as if they could have been brought overseas by the Crusaders.

David tossed his keys on the sideboard and took the next steps three at a time, rushing to his apartment up a winding corridor that was a series of stairs and landings leading past the parlor, the kitchen, and several private rooms. Passing a large vaulted chamber lined with books on shelves that reached to the ten-foot ceiling, he stopped short.

To his dismay, he could hear voices coming from his suite, the last one in the house. Making the final turn up the stone hallway, he jockeyed his bagels and files under one arm while he smoothed his breeze-blown hair and straightened his rumpled shirt, recalling with chagrin that he had not changed it since yesterday.

If you aren't the epitome of the absent-minded professor! his wife used to tease him.

Placing his hand on the door's handle, he took a deep breath, then entered the apartment.

His friends—for indeed, some degree of trust had grown between them—sat around a table in the front room of the suite. Spread out on the tabletop was a roll of paper, composed of several smaller sheets taped end to end. The roll was so long that it ran onto the floor in overlapping waves.

The men, intent on studying the paper and talking excitedly among themselves, did not hear David come in.

Clearing his throat, he greeted them. "Rabbis! I guess I'm tardy for class!"

Looking up, they returned his greeting, and Horace Benjamin rose to meet him. Of the four men, Horace was David's favorite, and the two shook hands warmly.

"Professor!" Benjamin said. "Welcome. My colleagues and I have been looking at your work. We are amazed at your accomplishments!"

"Yes, I see you have been reading the chart," David noted,

placing the files and the bag of bagels on the sofa. "Can you interpret my scrawls? My wife always said I should have been a medical doctor, my handwriting is so bad."

Dr. Jacobs chuckled at this. "Well, I for one am used to interpreting such scrawls, as you say. It is the science of your work that is truly gratifying."

David stepped up to the table and surveyed his handiwork with a flush of unconcealed pride. "I guess I have been busy, haven't I?" he said.

Upon the wide ribbon of paper David had drawn a chart. One long line ran across the top, composed of dates going back into antiquity on the left, and up nearly to the present toward the right. Below this, a complex series of lines looking like trees spread across the pages, a veritable forest of branches. Upon each branch was a name, and each branch connected to other branches, down to the trunks where yet other names were recorded. Probably one hundred of these trees made up the chart. The trunks, branches, and most of the names had been filled in with black pencil, although each tree also contained names written in red. Some of these red names were connected horizontally through time by another line, which was also red.

David had made such charts before, though never anything this detailed, when he had traced pottery styles or other artifact types on time lines. Such tools were used in archaeology to unravel the history of a culture or to see its inter-relatedness to other groups, as represented in its handicrafts.

But this chart did not deal in pottery styles. This chart dealt in human names. Family names.

The effect of the dark red line across the expansive charcoal forest was that of a bloody ribbon, a stream of blood on a background of history.

And in truth, it *was* a bloodline.

As David traced his finger across the crimson strand, the men pressed in close about him, Rabbi Benjamin and Dr. Jacobs almost blocking his view, while Dr. Levine and Rabbi Katz leaned from the far side for a better look.

Their bushy beards and side-curls dangled on the paper, and they adjusted their spectacles, taking it all in with wonder.

Nearly breathless, they asked the silent question.

"Yes," David said, "this is the Cohen line. To the best of my knowledge thus far, all the records you have given me play out this way."

As they all knew, the name "Cohen," and its many cognates, were derivatives of the name "Kohath," the patriarch from whom Moses and his brother, Aaron, were descended. From the time that Aaron was installed as high priest of Israel, his male descendants, through his firstborn son, were set apart for priestly duties. They came to be called the "Kohathites," or "Kohanim."

Any quest for a legitimate heir to the high priesthood must follow that line, which in modern times was called the "Cohens."

The rabbis let out a collective sigh, like men who had gazed on the contents of a royal tomb or who had just lifted the lid on a treasure chest.

"So," Rabbi Benjamin said, "the records are incredibly intricate. To think, our people have kept their genealogies this perfectly!"

"The *Cohen* people," Rabbi Katz interjected. "Not every Jewish family can claim as much."

"Of course, of course," Dr. Levine muttered. "But what race of people has survived the centuries and the vagaries of history like the Jews?"

"Yes—*all* the Jews!" Dr. Jacobs asserted. "It may be true that the Cohens—including the esteemed Katzes," he said with a bite, "have been more particular. But the mere fact that the Jewish people still exist at all is a wonder!"

Rabbi Katz only crossed his arms and rolled his eyes.

"Gentlemen," Benjamin said, "this is no time for the eternal quarrel. Let's keep peace for now."

But Rabbi Katz was only more piqued. "Let us hope the quarrel is not eternal," he spat. "Did we not hire Professor Rothmeyer just so the contest would be resolved, once and for all?"

Horace Benjamin drew back and blew softly through pursed lips. "Must you see all this as a contest, Uriel? Is it not God's will we are seeking, and not the glory of some human bloodline?"

At this, Katz looked aside, avoiding Benjamin's eyes. But his pride was still evident by his clenched fist.

David took all this in silently. Always it was like this, when the rabbis came to visit: little squabbles and power struggles that led nowhere. After witnessing several such interludes he surmised that Katz was greatly invested in the outcome of his studies.

David realized, not only from his recent research, but from his Jewish upbringing, that there were many names related to the line of the Kohanim, or the Cohens. "Katz" was one of them, being a contraction for two words: Kohen, meaning priest, and Zadok, meaning righteous, rather like "Kodak," of camera fame.

Uriel Katz apparently had reason to believe he had a greater stake in the findings of this study than that of other people with his rather common surname.

Actually, it was not impossible that Dr. Levine, being in the line of the Levites, the priestly tribe from which Aaron and his brother Moses were descended, could potentially be in the line of the high priest. Even Dr. Jacobs, being lumped with the patriarchy of Jacob, who was the original "Israel" and who was the father of *all* the Jewish tribes, could potentially be of the same lineage.

However, since their names were part of broader branches, and were not specifically Cohen, they apparently had less at stake in the outcome.

As for kindly old Rabbi Benjamin, there was no possibility that he was in the priestly line. The tribe of Benjamin was distinct from that of Levi and had never had a priestly function. Perhaps this helped him to maintain his objectivity and to fulfill the role of moderator, with which he seemed to be invested.

Actually, as far as David could see at this time, the possibility that Katz, let alone the others, might be in the true high priestly line was no greater than it would be for any one of the millions of Cohens throughout the world. But David had been hired to narrow down the search, and he had spent the past six months working toward that goal.

Despite their ongoing sparring matches, the men seemed to be pleased with his work.

Benjamin, in an effort to redirect their attention, perused the chart again. The long red line, which connected the various historical segments, was not a continuous strand. Here and there, large gaps showed up, before the line resumed again and went on in relative wholeness for years at a time.

"As we would expect, there may be places where the chart can never be complete," Benjamin observed. "The gaps come exactly where they must be."

"Yes," David said, pointing to a vague area dated around the sixth century B.C.E. "The period of the Babylonian Captivity, for instance, is a hazy one, although copies of scribal records brought back by the returning exiles have helped somewhat."

Passing his hand to the right, David pulled the paper and smoothed out a section from the eleventh century C.E., and following. "There is also quite a set of discrepancies that arises in the period of the Middle Ages. I am sure most Jewish scholars, yourselves included, are aware of the ethnic split."

Katz stiffened, and the others looked at one another knowingly.

"You speak of the social division between the Sephardic and Ashkenazic families," Benjamin surmised.

Again, Katz tensed. "Far more than *social* division!" he

exclaimed. "We Jews divided along every imaginable line: political, religious, scholarly . . . "

David sensed another debate coming. Intervening, he stopped it before it flared. "Gentlemen," he said, "I do not know what issues divide you, but my job would go easier if you brought cooperation to our meetings, rather than constant quarrels."

The men quieted, and David tried to bring them together. "Regardless of your individual roots, you are all scholars," he said. "Now . . . shall we proceed?"

Directing them again to the paper, he pointed to the area near-est the end. "Of course, we all know that the Holocaust of this cen-tury caused monumental losses to the recordkeeping of our people. I do not know how you wish for me to address that issue. I have really done nothing with it, to this point."

Rabbi Benjamin nodded. "We have much to tell you about work in that arena," he said. "For now, are there other periods you wish to point out to us?"

David moved the paper again so that the generations nearest the Roman period were on the table.

"Here is one of the most difficult sections," he said, pointing to the first century. "As would be expected, following the destruction of Jerusalem in 70 C.E., during the great Dispersion, there is a lot of information missing."

Then, gesturing to the back wall of his parlor, he reminded them of the books they had provided. "I was able to find some help from the records of the Jabnians, of the first century."

A look of grave concern clouded the professor's face. "Despite those clues," he said, "it will take keys of information, which I am not sure we will ever find, to legitimize the rest of the line."

The rabbis hung on his words.

"What I am saying, gentlemen," David explained, "is that, up until 70 C.E., when the temple was destroyed, we can pretty much accept that the Jews had done their homework. We will probably never find records any better than what they had, to fill gaps existing at that time—such as the Babylonian period. When they installed a high priest, unless they were capitulating to some outside pressure, they went by the best records known, records that we will not be able to top."

Rabbi Benjamin nodded. "There were, of course, spurious installations during the time of the Hasmoneans."

"And later, during the Roman occupation," Rabbi Levine said. "Anything to please Caesar."

"That's right," David said. "We can see this in the broken lines around the time that Annas and Caiaphas were the temple chieftains. Always, there were those who maintained the true records, and sometimes impostors were deposed."

"Very well," Rabbi Katz said, anxious to move on. "We are aware of this. So, what you are saying is that the gap we must be most concerned with comes around the time of the temple's destruction. Up until then, we must rely on the wisdom of the genealogists of the day."

"I think we can do no better," David said.

Dr. Jacobs jumped in. "And, after that time, without a good record of the first century, anything we deduce must be held in question."

David crossed his arms and studied the men carefully. "I guess you answered that when you first contacted me. If you felt you could trust tradition from the time of the Dispersion, you never would have hired me."

At this, he began to roll up the scroll, again toward the time of the temple's destruction. "In fact," he said, "you probably could have saved me a lot of time and energy by having me trace the line from 70 C.E. on, and leaving the first half to history. You surely knew that the only real controversy arises after that point."

Rabbi Benjamin smiled sheepishly. With a shrug, he turned his palms upward. "You have us there, David."

"So," the professor said with a half-smile. "This has been a test? I suspected as much. Well, it's your money, gentlemen. Pay me for wasted effort, if you will."

"Wasted?" Rabbi Levine marveled. "Surely not, David! No study of our past is wasted! Besides, how did we know but what you would turn up something new?"

David shrugged. "Okay. Let's get back to the record." He placed a finger at a point on the scroll. "There was a lot of controversy going on for two hundred years or more before the fall of Jerusalem," he said. "The split in the records is phenomenal!"

Again, the men bent close, gathering around the paper. David observed them closely. The factious splits that preceded the Roman invasion were familiar to the scholars.

Rabbi Benjamin looked at David inquiringly, his bright eyes studying him with keen interest. "This is the time of the great division in the temple administration. Have you read much about the Essenes, Dr. Rothmeyer?"

"Those were the fellows at Qumran," David replied. "I suppose everyone has heard of the Cave Scrolls. Of course, I came across many references to them in my study here."

Katz jumped in. "Then you may know that the temple priesthood came under sharp criticism at that time. In fact, the people of Qumran may have been disgruntled priests themselves, who left the sanctuary because of the corruptions they witnessed."

David nodded. "That is one of the theories. It might explain their apocalyptic views, the insistence that the world was divided between the Sons of Light and the Sons of Darkness, and that a great war would soon be waged between the sides."

"Well, for our purposes," Dr. Jacobs offered, "there was undoubtedly a huge dispute over which priests were legitimate and which were impostors."

David rubbed his chin. With a shrug, he said, "There certainly are confusions in the genealogical records of that time. As to direct references to the heir to the priesthood, however, I found nothing in any of the quotations from the Qumran scrolls."

At this comment, the men glanced at one another furtively. David perceived, in the thick, awkward silence, that they wished they could say something but dared not.

"What is it?" he asked. "Have I hit on something?"

Benjamin hedged. "There may, or there may not, be such references."

A chill worked across David's shoulders. He realized, now, that they knew much more than he did, and he felt like a mouse between the paws of four cats.

Drawing back from the table, he scrutinized them with sparking eyes. "Now, hold on!" he said angrily. "What kind of game are you playing? You obviously know something that I do not—something essential to my work. If I thought you had nothing better to do, I could believe that you took me away from the university as part of some perverse need to toy with a stranger! Before I go another step, I want you to come clean with me!"

Dr. Jacobs and Rabbi Levine glanced covertly at one another, and Katz cleared his throat. Gesturing to the sitting area of David's parlor, Benjamin directed everyone to find a chair.

When they were seated the old fellow took a long breath, blew it out softly, then began speaking. "Of course, as you surmise, there are things we know from years of dealing with these matters that you could never have known. You have quite accurately deduced that what is essential to our goals is information from the Temple period. Yes—the time of the Essenes and other radical groups who asserted that the priesthood was corrupt."

David sensed a pronouncement coming, but when the rabbi was only silent, he knew he must prompt him. "Let me guess," he said, half in jest, "we are on the prowl for some mysterious lost scroll. Ah! A story for the tabloids! 'Secret Jewish Group Discovers Genealogy of Christ in Desert Cave.'"

But the rabbis did not laugh.

Dr. Jacobs, his usually good-natured face tensing with soberness, stared at David from across the sitting room. "You do not know how close you come to the truth," he said. "We do not seek the Messiah's bloodline, but we seek the next best thing. And, yes, there is the distinct possibility that there is a scroll—probably from Qumran—that will give us what we need."

David's eyes grew round with wonder. "You're serious," he marveled. "But weren't all the scrolls finally released to the public just recently? They're available to be read by anyone who is interested."

Rabbi Levine lifted one eyebrow. "So it would seem. So certain people mean for it to seem."

David ran the damp palms of his hands down his thighs. "Now, let me get this straight. You believe that all the hubbub about the scroll committee and its sequestering of the scrolls is not really resolved? You believe there is still some material hidden away?"

Katz would have the last word. "We not only believe it; we know it to be the case. And we want you, Dr. Rothmeyer, to help us track it down!"

CHAPTER 10

The Daisy Pub in the old square of Oxfordshire was relatively quiet. Most students who had not gone home for Easter break were outside, enjoying the serene beauty of the university town—the wide greens between the campuses or the sloping banks along the River Cherwell, where rowboats dotted the water.

Britta Hayworth, the young reporter from the *London Times*, and Emily McCurdy, sister to Father Ian McCurdy, were having lunch in the pub. This was one of Emily's favorite places at Oxford, and since she did not visit England often, she always had her choice of rendezvous.

The last time Britta had been in Oxford was over six months earlier to meet and interview Emily's brother, a feat achievable only because the elderly Irishwoman had arranged it.

Emily was a longtime friend of the girl's family, and Britta held her in great esteem. She had been a Red Cross nurse when Britta's great-uncle Reginald had been wounded at Normandy during assignment as a photojournalist there. Emily had tended to him during his recuperation at an army hospital in France, and then she had been transferred to Germany, ultimately helping in the evacuation of the Holocaust death camps when the survivors were freed.

Britta, having grown up with stories about Emily's and uncle Reginald's experiences in World War II, had decided as a child that she would be a heroine, if she could. Though no great opportunity had presented itself, she was determined to serve humanity grandly, if the chance arose. So it was that a twenty-four-year-old, moppet-curled blond and a tall, dignified woman in her seventies sat together that day in a pub, chatting over tuna on rye and drinking Guinness.

Dark, polished oak beams and wainscoting, accented by gleaming brass bar rails, sconces, and hardware, and soft, multicolored light from Tiffany lamps lent a warm and endearing mood to the place. Conversation was easy, backed by the strains of folk music, laughter, and the hypnotizing plunk-plunk of cue balls and pinballs. They were in England, but it was easy to forget this when a sign on the wall, advertising Bailey's Cream, asked, in letters four inches high, "Is There Any Irish in You?"

After half an hour of girl talk, catching up on Emily's Dublin garden and Britta's latest fashion spree in London, the conversation inevitably turned to their common interest, Reginald. It was no secret that Emily and Reg, as he was usually called, had once been "a thing." Their romance, which blossomed during Reg's stay at the army hospital, had been brief and was interrupted by their duties. After Reg had recuperated, he had been whisked away on another assignment, and Emily had been transferred to Germany.

Correspondence had kept the fire of their feelings alive for years. But like so much in the wake of war, their relationship had been a casualty of long separations and stress, and was now a fond memory. Reg's meeting of a young Jewish Holocaust survivor, his eventual marriage to her elder sister, and relocation to Israel had eliminated any hope of Emily reuniting with him. But the Irishwoman still cared about Reg and always asked after him.

"He is doing well," Britta said. "I got an e-mail from him last week. His grandson, my second cousin, recently celebrated his bar mitzvah. Reg scanned me some photos of the event. Quite the party!"

Emily shook her head. "I still cannot imagine your uncle marrying outside his faith. Why, my Catholicism versus his Anglicanism was one of our stumbling blocks. And then he went and married a Jew!"

Britta smiled wanly. She did not understand why religion of any kind should be an impediment to love.

"Apparently Aunt Deborah was not a devout Jew when they met," she said. "She converted to Uncle Reg's faith before they married."

Emily sighed. "I guess you told me that before. Then, why . . . "

"Why did my cousin celebrate his bar mitzvah?"

"Yes, especially as an adult. Don't they usually go through that rite at twelve or thirteen?"

"Cousin Zachary embraced some new form of Judaism," Britta said with a shrug. "I really don't understand it, but Uncle Reg seems quite proud of him."

Emily leaned back from the table and chuckled. "How do you keep it all straight?" she asked. "I thought it was difficult in Ireland. All we have to worry about are the Catholics and the Protestants!"

The two laughed together, and Britta was relieved at Emily's good humor.

Then, Emily grew more sober. "Speaking of the Jews, as I've said before, I came to admire them greatly when I worked with them in Germany. I don't know much about their religion, but many of those who survived the camps were inspiring." She took a sip of Guinness, then continued, "Did you know that one of the ways in which the Jews kept their traditions and the memory of their Scriptures through all they endured was by writing them in secret places?"

"Secret places?" Britta repeated. "What could be kept secret in the camps? Besides, they had no paper, no way to store anything."

"Ah, but they were resourceful! They did have the clothes on their backs, clothes given them by the SS. Using bits of charcoal from fires the guards had them build, they wrote on the insides of their prison garbs, inside their shoes, or on the thin blankets of their bunks. If the guards came across these scrawls, they ignored them, having no respect for Hebrew and considering it nothing but childish scribbling. I remember how some of the survivors clung to the rags that held these precious documents—the remnants of religious and ethnic history they had risked everything to record."

Thinking back, she recounted a particularly memorable scene.

"I recall coming upon a little group of huddled prisoners, intent on unearthing a pile of the very rags I have described, near the foot of one of the guard towers. Apparently, they had been in charge of burning the clothes of the prisoners when they became louse-infested or if they had been removed, for any reason, from the bodies about to be burned in the ovens. In their unique position, they had been able to rescue many of the clothes that bore these documents I speak of, and had stashed them in a small pit dug when the guards were not looking—a pit right under the noses of the SS!" She smiled wanly. "I think they got some pathetic sense of enjoyment out of that trickery."

Britta was intrigued by this account, and covertly reached for her notepad. "What else do you remember?" she asked.

Emily looked at her suspiciously. "Why? You aren't thinking there's a story here, are you? Child, there are millions of such tales from the Holocaust. This one is nothing."

Britta shrugged, placed her notepad on the table, and scribbled a few words. "You never know," she said. "I just like to keep notes on any possibilities. I doubt I'd ever do anything with it, but it might get me thinking about other story ideas."

Emily looked at the girl with almost as much admiration as Britta bestowed on her. "If grit has anything to do with it," she said, "you're sure to win the Pulitzer someday!"

The reporter smiled. "I don't know. The really great stories seem to elude me."

Emily knew she was referring to the interview with Ian.

"I remember your saying that my brother was not much help," she said. "Well, at least you got in to talk with him. You're the only reporter he's even opened the door to."

"And I have you to thank for that much," Britta said. "He, of course, denied that there was any story to be had at all. I went away with nothing."

Emily looked down at her plate. "I wish I could have done more—"

But Britta interrupted her. "No, I take that back," she said. "I did come away with something—a feeling that your brother is still hiding something. He was so adroit at handling the Deception Theory that I was left wondering what all the mystery is about. I was left with the sense that there *is* a mystery, though not the one everyone has been pursuing."

Britta had spoken little with anyone about her experience with Father McCurdy. She had told her editor she had reached a dead end with the story. Still, a persistent hunch nagged at her.

Emily was clearly in the dark. She gave no hint that she knew anything of her brother's doings. "What about another interview? I could try—"

"No," Britta said. "Thanks, anyway. I wouldn't know what to ask him if I did see him again."

Then, purely from politeness, she inquired, "I hope he is well. Are you enjoying your visit with him?"

"I am," Emily replied, brightening. "But he is going to London this afternoon. He'll be gone when I get back to the house today and won't return until tomorrow."

Britta looked at her friend quizzically. "Why would he leave home when you are here for a visit?"

"Once a year, he has an appointment at the British Museum to look in on his cubicle."

"Cubicle?" Britta said. "What cubicle?"

Emily explained. "Oxford professors, particularly those who deal in history or languages or, as in Ian's case, archaeology, may use study closets at the museum. They are usually assigned them for the length of their tenure here. They may work there privately or with students, with access to the materials in the Hall of Manuscripts."

Britta was intrigued. "And Ian has one of those cubicles?"

"Yes," Emily said. "He is still emeritus, and may keep the cubicle so long as he checks in annually, though I doubt he ever works with students at the museum anymore."

"So," Britta said, "these cubicles . . . are they exclusively for the use of the ones who are assigned them?"

"Oh yes," Emily said. "It is quite an honor to have one. And it is almost like a vault, accessible only by the assignee or his assistants."

Britta leaned back and cocked her head. The wheels of journalism were whirring in her brain. "Does Ian have assistants?" she asked.

Emily laughed. "Oh no. Not any longer. What would he need graduate assistants for when he no longer has classes? But Ian is a proud member of Oxford. And I never knew an Oxfordian to give up his privileges lightly. In fact, he never misses going to that cubicle punctually this time of year. If he overlooks using it by this deadline, he must relinquish it to a more active member."

Britta tried not to ask more questions, though her instincts were humming.

"So, you will be keeping house with dear Cromwell?" she guessed, remembering the dignified fellow.

Again, Emily shrugged. "No—Ian is taking John with him. They always make this annual trek to the museum together."

CHAPTER 11

The next morning, Britta was back in London. She had spent a leisurely afternoon with Emily, visiting the shops in Oxford, then had caught one of the late-night buses back to the city.

Leaving her apartment early, she took one of the underground trains heading for the British Museum. Sunlight stabbed her eyes as she emerged from the tube station at Tottenham Court and hastened down Great Russell Street. The spring day was cool and crisp, almost fallish, though the trees were brilliant green.

The reporter figured that Father McCurdy and John Cromwell would have arrived at Victoria Station too late to go to the museum before closing time. They would probably waste no time this morning, however, making their way to the great complex and its fabulous library. She intended to be there when they arrived, even if she did nothing more than observe their level of tension.

The British Library, housed on the ground floor of the immense museum, was best known for its manuscript hall. Called the "Manuscript Saloon," the main room covered a good city block, its ceiling soaring to the height of three stories. Each wall of this and adjacent rooms was lined floor to rafters with leather-bound volumes, each one handwritten. Those manuscripts on the higher shelves were reachable by long ladders and catwalklike galleries.

Astonishing as this collection was, the contents of glass cases, arrayed along the floor, were the most breathtaking. Many of the greatest documents in the history of humanity could be viewed here, from the Magna Carta to the original score of Handel's *Messiah*; from the Codex Sinaitica, the oldest manuscript of the Holy Scriptures, to the poems of Coleridge and Shelley.

Pausing at the museum's main desk, Britta reserved the use of one of the library's reading rooms. Since the museum had only just opened for the day, there was no waiting list.

As she made her way through the Manuscript Saloon, she skirted Handel's score on the way to the Medieval hall. She had been there more than once in her life as a Londoner, but she stopped on a double-take, amazed at what scraps of paper filled the case next to Handel's great oratorio.

Scrawls and doodles from jam sessions of the Beatles were on temporary exhibition, accorded equal honor with Beethoven and Bach. "I Wanna Hold Your Hand" was on display across the aisle from "The Unfinished Symphony."

Chuckling to herself, Britta shook her head and entered the huge chamber of illuminated Medieval manuscripts. A door led from this hall, down narrow corridors through which no one was permitted to go without a pass, to the offices and staff lounge, and then to the reading rooms, or students' rooms, of the library. She assumed that cubicles such as Emily had described, assigned to scholars like McCurdy and his Oxford cohorts, were probably nearby.

After showing her admission slip to the guard at the door, she went down one hall until she came to the main reading room of the manuscript collection.

Here she was obliged to check her purse, while she told the

attendant what she wanted to see. She had given much thought to a plausible alibi for being there.

"I'd like to see William Blake's *Europe*," she said.

The man looked at her from his perch behind a high desk. He was old, balding, and smelled of ancient leather, like the volumes on shelves behind him. Britta wondered if he had known Blake personally.

Peering down his long nose, he said, with a sniff, "Of course, the original is housed in the archives. The best we can do is let you see a rare imprint."

Britta glanced down the gleaming oak table that stretched from the desk to the far side of the room behind a low oak partition. There were no other students or readers here. "That will do," she said, imitating a version of scholarly haughtiness.

The attendant reached under his desk and pressed an unseen button, releasing the lock on the partition's gate. Britta pushed against the gate and entered the room. She took a seat facing the entry, in the hopes that, should McCurdy arrive, she might see him. She had a hunch that the scholars' cubicles were down yet another hall visible behind the warden's desk.

After she had taken her seat, the attendant picked up a phone and spoke softly into it, ordering the book she wanted brought in from the stacks.

Since there were no other patrons present, Britta felt free to speak to the man.

"Sir," she called out to him, "is it possible to reserve a study carrel? I have heard that there are such rooms available to researchers."

The attendant looked down the table toward her, obviously unused to conversing freely in the quiet sanctum. Pursing his lips, he sniffed again. "Are you on the faculty of one of the Queen's colleges?" he asked, his doubtful tone thick as London fog.

"Uh, no," Britta replied. "But I *am* with the *London Times*."

The man lowered his wire spectacles and eyed her skeptically. Nonetheless, he seemed to mellow a little. "I see. And what use would a reporter have for a cubicle?"

At that moment, a delivery boy entered the room, bringing Britta's copy of Blake's *Europe*. The attendant waved Britta over, and she took the book, returned to her chair, and placed the volume on the felt-covered stand that sat on the table before her. Carefully opening it, she pretended to survey the art-nouveau etchings and Blake's fine, swirling penmanship.

"Well," Britta continued, "say there was a hunt for a missing Blake plate and we needed to research the history of the piece and its various owners. We might need more than a day or two in a reading room to do the work."

There. She had not lied. She had only presented a possibility.

The attendant seemed to be impressed, his interest piqued. Still, he maintained his stiff demeanor. "In such a case," he said, "you could apply for an extended reservation. But assignments are quite limited."

Britta looked up at the old fellow with a melting smile. "I see," she said, repeating his earlier phrase. "Now, say that our research was of a highly sensitive nature. Say that we wished to be assured that our research materials were available only to us for that certain period of time."

The man took her persistence as evidence of her sincerity. "You want to know about security measures here?" he said. "My dear girl, the museum prides itself on its impeccable guardianship. Whatever a scholar needs is reserved in his—or her—name, until the research is done."

Now Britta was getting somewhere. "Very well," she said. "And what of materials the researcher might wish to bring into the library? Are there ways of storing such items?"

"Oh, indeed," the man answered, beaming with pride. "Each carrel has its own strongbox. The researcher may rest in perfect confidence that all materials are safe day and night."

Britta's cheeks warmed. She could hardly believe her own clev-
erness. If her hunch was right, she hardly even needed to see
McCurdy's arrival. She certainly did not need to test him with questions—not at this point, anyway.

What purpose could the emeritus professor have with a permanent cubicle, and with a strongbox, if he was not hiding something
there?

Britta stood up from her seat and gently closed the Blake book.
Taking it to the attendant, she smiled again and told him she would
speak with her editor about the library's superior service.

"Come again," the man said with a nod.

As Britta slipped down the hall from the reading room, she kept
her eyes open for McCurdy and Cromwell.

The timing was perfect. She had just reached the door at the
head of the hall, when the Irish priest shuffled in, his houseman
close behind him.

Feeling quite confident now, she hailed him. "Why, Father
McCurdy!" she exclaimed. "Fancy seeing you here!"

Father McCurdy stopped abruptly, wavering on his feet. John
Cromwell nearly collided with him from behind and then held on
to him to lend support.

"M-Ms. Hayworth," the priest stammered. "What are you doing
here?"

Britta laughed lightly. "So much for 'howd'ya'do,'" she teased.
"Perhaps I should ask the same of you. After all, I am a Londoner
visiting a London museum, and you come from seventy miles away."

McCurdy blushed, and John intervened. "How pleasant to see
you, Miss," he said. "I hear that you were visiting our fair village
only yesterday."

He had her there. "Yes," she said. "I spent the day with Emily."

A long span of awkward silence passed between the three, the
two men studying Britta for any hint of suspicion and she surveying
them for the same. Each side awaited questions that did not come.

"Well," McCurdy finally said, stepping sideways past her, "charmed, as always."

"Charmed," John echoed.

"Greetings to your sister," Britta returned. And with that, she exited.

McCurdy looked up at his friend, his face white as paper.

"Now, Father," John said, "do not be concerned. What can the girl know?"

The priest glared down the hall angrily. "I am going to find out," he said.

Making his way to the reading room, he approached the high desk.

The attendant greeted the professor warmly.

"Professor McCurdy!" he said. "I was only just yesterday looking at your file! You've just crept in under your deadline again!"

"So I have," McCurdy grumbled. "Say, old fellow. Was there a blond woman in here just moments ago?"

The attendant glanced down the table to where Britta had sat. "Nice girl," he said. "Do you know her?"

"I know her slightly," the priest replied. "Did she have business here?"

"So it seems. She wouldn't say much, but it seems she's on the trail of a lost work."

McCurdy froze, his heart thundering. "Lost work?" he repeated, his throat dry. He reached up and gripped the edge of the tall desk, as flashes of his beloved scroll, the despicable, damning scroll, careened through his head.

"Yes," the man said. "Watch for it in the *Times*."

CHAPTER 12

Pete Wester paced the broad porch of his Bull River home, checking his watch and keeping his ears pricked for the sound of approaching vehicles.

Pete had broken the news to Mel, over breakfast two days ago, that they would not be enjoying their solitude for long. They would be receiving company this afternoon, a large group of people, who would probably be staying for a while.

Mel had asked a lot of questions. Pete had fielded them pretty well, explaining as much about the upcoming gathering as he could without frightening his brother away.

"You used to enjoy hanging out with my hippie friends when you came to the Okanogan years ago," he said. "These fellows will seem a little strange, but give them a chance. You may learn something."

Mel, who remembered the spontaneous parties Pete had taken him to, had actually responded with relief. "Hippies?" he replied. "I'm glad to hear you still know a few. I can handle hippies!"

Apparently Pete had not made himself clear. "No—I don't mean these guys are hippies. I mean, you learned to appreciate the weird friends I had once. These guys are weird in a different way. Some are ex-hippies, but most of them wouldn't claim that identity any more."

Mel was thoroughly confused, but he quit asking questions, content to wait it out and make up his own mind about the visitors.

The fact was, Pete didn't know what to expect completely, himself. He had entertained Jim Fogarty and a few of his upper-echelon cohorts whenever they had used his premises as their headquarters. He had taken the mysterious messages that crackled off the ham radio. He had long ago bought into the anti-government rhetoric of Fogarty and his Freemen when he attended meetings at a camp in Idaho. But he had never hosted a large gathering of such people. So, apart from preaching the doctrines of the revolutionists, there was not much he could say to prepare Mel for what was coming.

And he chose not to preach. He figured Mel would get his eyes opened quickly enough.

When Mel had called from Los Angeles, saying that he wanted to come to Montana, Pete's first urge had been to short-circuit his plans, to make up some excuse why his baby brother shouldn't come. But, on second thought, he had decided it might be an opportune time for Mel to learn the truth—not only about Pete's new life, but about the realities of the world.

Mel was in the house, washing up the lunch dishes, when Pete stopped his pacing and cocked his ears toward the road. "I think they're here," he called through the screen door.

Mel wiped his hands on a towel and stepped outside. Up from the woods through which he had driven the other night, Mel heard the sound of rumbling engines. "Gosh, sounds like an army!" he said. "What are they driving, anyway?"

Pete grinned nervously. "I think it's the hogs," he said.

As the distant rumble became a roar, and then an earthshaking thunder, Mel's eyes grew wider and wider. Suddenly, like black knights on metallic warhorses—rather stubby, and very hairy

knights who rode with their knees to the saddle horns, their hel-
meted heads at an obtuse angle—a dozen leather-clad bikers burst
out from the forest. Several of them had riders behind them, skinny
women with windblown hair held down with bandannas and glistening chrome studs stamped all over their skintight pants.

"Hogs," Mel sighed. "I get it. Harleys."

Pete shrugged, trying not to show his embarrassment.

Mel leaned close. "You've got to be kidding, Pete," he said
through gritted teeth. "These are your new friends?"

"Don't let the extremes throw you," Pete said. "They always
take the lead, but they're not the leaders."

As the bikers rumbled into the yard, they tipped their
machines and circled in front of Pete's cabin, kicking up the dust
of his driveway.

Mel noticed Pete wince, and he shook his head, wondering
what he had gotten himself into. The last time he had seen Harley
hogsters had been in the ghettos of L.A., a part of the culture he
had hoped to leave behind.

As the hogs quieted to a thumping chug, seeming to function
on one cylinder apiece, other vehicles came into view. One after
another, they entered the yard and parked along the edges of the
open area.

Most of the rigs were pickup trucks, the majority at least seven
years old, Mel guessed, many older, showing the scrapes, dents, and
bent fenders of rough wear. Almost all of the trucks had rifles on
back-window racks, and some carried loads of firewood or hay bales.
There were absolutely no foreign makes among them.

Mel gawked at the incongruity of the gathering on the lawn.
What in the world, he wondered, could a bunch of gangsters have
in common with farmers and ranchers?

His capacity for amazement was about to be further stretched.

As men in baseball caps labeled Cenex, John Deere, and
Budweiser piled out of the trucks, their middle-aged, overweight

wives, and passels of kids clambering out with them, a little caravan of VW Bugs and buses arrived.

From these vehicles—apparently the only sanctioned foreign make—a peculiar group of folks emerged. Coming close to Mel's image of the perfect back-to-the-earth female, thirty-something women in long dresses appeared, their straight hair woven into braids and their smocked bodices jangling with beads. Their menfolk, many wearing tie-dyed T-shirts, ambled up to the farmers, shaking hands as though they spoke the same language, while the women joined the farm wives, bearing linen-covered platters and picnic baskets.

Food, food, food was carried from the vehicles—canned goods, pickled goods, breads, pies, and meat ready for barbecue.

Pete certainly did not have the means to feed this crew, Mel thought, so it was a good thing the visitors had come prepared. The women had brought tablecloths to spread on the ground, and a few tables made of boards and Pete's sawhorses were set up on the grass, but the tailgates of all the trucks would be needed to accommodate the fare.

The arrival of the gathering was not really a processional, but the various contingents did tend to come in clusters. The next bunch were of a different stripe altogether than the first three. These arrived in battered four-wheel-drive rigs and were dressed military style, in camouflage or army surplus olive drabs. They were skinheads, their pates, as well as their faces, clean-shaven and their bare forearms boasting Nazi tattoos.

Among all these sorts, there were those who were less noticeable. They were small-town folks, for sure, Mel thought: loggers, mechanics, shop owners. There were no yuppies here, no rich people, and no white collars.

Still, Mel could make no sense of the diversity. What neo-Nazis could have in common with ranchers, or bikers with New Agers, he could not imagine.

Although Mel did not know it, this diverse processional was only the prelude to the arrival of the grand master of them all.

As the people greeted one another, the women laying out the food and the men talking bikes, guns, planting, or taxes, the mood was one of quiet eagerness. Mel noticed that they all watched the woods, listening, just as Pete had done, for the sound of another rig.

At last, as though the timing was deliberate, a shiny vehicle flashed into the open: a dark blue, four-wheel-drive Suburban, glistening with a recent wax job, whitewalls slick and chrome sparse but gleaming. This rig, with its dark windows, looked as if it might be armored.

Everyone stopped talking as the car pulled into the center of the green. But the moment the front passenger emerged, the crowd burst into cheers.

Mel watched over Pete's shoulder as Jim Fogarty stepped into the sunlight. Taller by a head than most of the men present, he was attired to match his car, in dark, uniform blue. Crisp pants and shirt with epaulets gave him an official look. His collar-length white hair and neat beard were accented by a blue beret.

The crowd clapped and hoorayed.

When he motioned to the backseat of the car, calling forth a newcomer, the onlookers grew hushed.

This man was also tall and bearded, with shoulder-length hair pulled back in a black ribbon. He wore camouflage shirt and pants and thick combat boots, and Mel thought he saw the bulge of a shoulder harness beneath his padded vest.

As he was introduced, he stood straight, chin raised, not disdainfully, but with supreme self-confidence.

"Ladies and gentlemen," Jim Forgarty announced, leading the stranger into their midst, "this is our friend from Germany, Monte Altmeyer. I know you will show him your warm, all-American hospitality."

The people were utterly thrilled. Mel sensed that they had

heard much about this fellow and had come from great distances just to meet him.

In respectful groups, they came forward, reaching out to shake Altmeyer's hand and expressing gratitude for his coming.

Mel nudged Pete. "Who is this guy?" he asked.

"Altmeyer?" Pete said. "Just one of the great social geniuses of our time! You've never heard of him because keeping a low profile is a key to his success."

CHAPTER 13

Eating and conversation took up the afternoon. The aroma of barbecued hamburgers lured Mel into the throng, which by midday had grown to about two hundred. Pete took him from group to group, introducing him as his ex-cop brother from Los Angeles, who had given up the ghetto and the concrete to find some peace in Montana.

Mel did a lot of listening throughout the afternoon. He did not need to ask many questions. Once people knew who he was, they seemed eager to fill him in on their viewpoints and reasons for being there. As they did so, he picked up on recurring themes—beliefs and experiences held in common. After hours of taking in their expressions of personal anger, political frustration, and social hatred, he began to see that it was indeed plausible that such diverse types could come together.

Window stickers and bumper decals on pickups, buses, and even on the fenders of the Harleys expressed the sentiments on which the people elaborated: "I Love My Country, but I Fear My Government," was popular among the pickup trucksters, along with "Return Prayer to the Schools So the Kids Can Pray for the Government—It Needs It!" Then, there was a new slant on an old classic: "America—Love It, but Don't Pay Its Taxes!"

The bumper stickers on the buses were still as counterculture as during the sixties, only more militant: "Nuke the Nukes—Over the White House"; "Ban the Bomb but Bomb the IRS"; or "One More Long-hair Who Don't Care to Share—Keep America for Americans!"

Mel could not help but grin at the one that said, "Beam me up, Scotty! The taxman's after me!"

The most radical of all, however, were the hogsters. "Revenge Ruby Ridge" and "Wacko about Waco" were tame compared to "OK City—Only the Beginning" and "You Ain't Seen Nothin Yet," emblazoned over a silhouette of the Murrah Building in flames.

Mel wandered through the crowd, paper plate in hand, munching on his second hamburger, unaware that he had drawn his shoulders into an avoiding hunch, subconsciously trying to appear inconspicuous.

Passing one more cluster of VW buses, he glimpsed an intriguing sticker: "Zap Zog." He stood looking at it, wondering if it was something from a Star Trek convention. Zog must be some alien planet, he thought, and the owner of the bus was probably a comic-book collector.

He did not realize how alien he, himself, felt in this environment until someone tapped him on the shoulder. As though he had been shocked, he lurched, sending his plateful of food flying to the grass.

"Sorry, ol' buddy," one of the ranchers said as he turned around. "Didn't mean t'spook you."

Mel's face burned. "That's all right," he muttered, amazed at his own jitters. A couple of pet dogs raced over from a family rig and made quick work of the spilled food.

Mel drew back as the flannel-shirted rancher helped him brush crumbs off his clothes.

"So yer Pete's brother," the man said. "Hank, here, Hank Dwyer."

He stuck his hand out, and Mel, first wiping mustard off his fingers, returned the gesture. "Nice to meet you, Hank. My name's Mel."

"Hear yer from L.A. Wow, is that a sty, huh?"

For some reason, although Mel agreed completely, the description of his former hometown seemed a bit insulting. "It has its problems," he said.

"Phew-eee, yeah!" the man laughed. "I guess! All them spooks and spicks! And they call 'em minor-tees. Why, the white race is the minor-tee in them places!"

Mel shrugged and made an innocuous grunt.

Hank motioned toward a dull brown crew cab around which five young children played, and called a woman over to join them. Mel noticed that she seemed to have forgotten to take a couple of rollers out of her salt-and-pepper hair.

She came obediently, straightening her cotton dress as she walked. She had a neat, work-hardened body, but her veined legs would have looked better in pantyhose, Mel thought. He didn't know they even made bobbysocks anymore, but she wore white ones, unselfconsciously rolled above the ankles of her black loafers.

Mel noticed that Hank's truck proudly bore the emblem of the Montana Militia, with the initials A.C.E. stamped in gold foil. Mel had already met several ACEs and knew the letters stood for All Citizens Equal.

Hank introduced his wife, Lucy. "Mel here's from L.A.," Hank told her. "I was just tellin' him he made the right decision, comin' to Montana. Keep the races sep'ert, we always say." He drawled on, "L.A. ain't fer the white man anymore. Heck—prob'ly never was. We took it from the spicks, and the spicks always wanted it back. Good riddance, I say!"

Lucy laughed softly, the gap of one missing tooth marring what might have been a pretty face. "Not that we got anythin' against anybody," Lucy chimed in.

"Heck no!" Hank said. "It's just best to keep the races to theirselves, don't you agree?"

Mel gave no reply, only a twitch of a smile.

"At least we ain't farmers," Lucy said. "Geez—they gotta work with the wetbacks every harvest!"

Hank grunted. "Yeah. Let the wetbacks work, I always say, just don't let 'em shake theirselves off in my backyard!"

At this, the man whooped hilariously. Soon, others were gathering around, wondering what the gag was.

"Thorny here's from Spokane," Hank said, drawing a man to the front of the group. "I bet he has a few things to say about wetbacks!"

"John Thornton," the new fellow said, thrusting out his hand. Then, he threw in, "I think Hank's confusing Spokane with Yakima. We don't have wetbacks in Spokane—just niggers!"

Again, the air was filled with raucous laughter.

Mel cringed. He had worked the beat for years in "nigger" territory. His best friend, Jorey, killed in the line of duty, had been a black man.

Thornton went on. "Yeah. Spokane used to be a nice little town. Could leave your car on the street, your screen door unlocked. If there was any niggers, they knew their place."

Hank nudged Thornton in the side. "The good ol' days, eh, Thorny?"

"You bet."

"Gone fer'ever," someone else chimed in.

Mel was growing agitated. He knew if he didn't break away soon, he would lose his temper and say something not in his own best interests.

Glancing over the heads of the group, he pretended that his

brother was calling to him from the porch. "Hey, guys," he said, "I'll get back to you. Pete needs some help in the kitchen."

Hank and Thorny nodded, then went back to their conversation, as Mel made a quick exit.

Of course, Pete had not really called him. In fact, he did not see Pete anywhere. What he did see was a group of skinheads watching him from a corner of the yard. He nodded to them, but moved toward the house quickly, not needing to hear what they had to say. Their message could only be more offensive than that of the farmers and ranchers, which, to Mel's way of thinking, was inflammatory enough.

"Hey, friend," someone called as he started up the steps to the porch.

Wheeling about, Mel froze. A man the size of a mountain was approaching from the driveway, having left the huddle of bikers who were never more than a few feet away from their machines.

Mel gulped. "What's that?" he said.

"I said, 'Hey, friend,'" the giant repeated.

Mel had never seen anything like this fellow, not in all his years working with toughs on the L.A. streets, not in an entire career in the worst parts of hell.

This man was seven feet tall, if he was an inch, and his grizzled hair hung down his back almost to his waist. It was nearly as long as his bushy beard, which came to his belt buckle. He was dressed all in black leather, which is to say that what clothes he wore were of that material. Apart from skin-tight pants, he wore little. Only a short vest covered any part of his upper body, and the vest did not meet in the middle, but flew back with each step, revealing a torso that could have been a sampler for a tattoo shop. His bulging, rock-hard arms were covered with hair, but tattoos were visible even there. Mel noticed one in particular as the biker stuck his thumbs in his belt loops and eyed Mel up and down. "Born to be Wild," it said.

Mel had no doubt about it.

"Bored with the clodhoppers?" he asked, spitting a stream of tobacco on the bottom step.

Mel dodged the saliva and cringed. "Clodhoppers?"

"The farmers—the cow-pokers," the big fellow replied, nodding his head in their direction.

"Oh—yeah," Mel said. "Nice folks . . . "

The biker only looked him up and down again, like a butcher sizing up a piece of meat.

"So," Mel said weakly, "what brings you people here?"

As soon as he'd asked this, he regretted it. He was curious, indeed, as to what a bunch of hogsters would find important about such a meeting, but he didn't really want to engage this guy in conversation.

"I hear yer from L.A.," the biker said. "I guess you think all Harley riders are Hell's Angels, huh? Well, let me tell you, we ain't got no part with them jokers. They're nothin' but junkies and junk dealers, y'know. A real syndicate, that's what they are, into pimpin' and the whole nine yards!"

Again he spat on the ground, this time having courtesy enough to aim away from the steps.

He removed his thumbs from his belt loops, wiped saliva from his lips, and stuck out his hand. Mel shook it, having no other choice, and tried not to be obvious as he wiped his own hand on his pants leg.

"Willard's the name," the big guy said.

Mel grunted his own name. "So, you fellows aren't anarchists?" he quipped, trying to be facetious.

To his grave concern, the big guy's face clouded. Mel couldn't tell if he was angry at the question or just didn't understand it.

Mel would have explained, but Willard huffed, "Libertarians, that's what we are! Not right wing, not left wing—just the ultimate freedom fighters!"

Mel tried not to stare at the man's tattoos, but saw one that indicated he had served in the U.S. Army. "I suppose some of you are vets," he surmised.

"Some?" Willard spat again. "All of us, man. Ain't hardly a one that ain't, 'cept our ol' ladies!"

This last reference caught the attention of the bikers and their girlfriends. The women began to amble over, and the men followed.

"You gettin' mouthy again, Willard?" one of the women teased. "Leave this poor bugger alone. He mighta been headin' for the john."

"I was just tellin' him we ain't no antichrists," Willard said.

A number of the bikers looked quizzically at one another.

"I . . . I said 'anarchists,' not 'antichrists,'" Mel corrected, unable to keep from smiling.

Willard drew closer than Mel liked and looked down at him threateningly. "You laughin' at me?" he growled.

"Back off, Willard!" one of the male bikers warned. "Sorry, mister," he said, nodding at Mel. "Willard here wouldn't know anarchy from an anchovy if it bit him on the behind!"

By now Mel had overcome his desire to flee. He was intrigued by this strange lot and wondered what made them tick.

The second biker, who was much smaller than Willard but impressively built, black bearded, and notably tattooed, stuck out his hand. "Crossley," he introduced himself. "Hear you were a cop."

Mel's hackles rose. He wondered if the fact of his background made him their target. Reticently, he shook the biker's hand. "Willard says you guys are freedom fighters."

The men straightened proudly, and the women raised their chins or draped their arms through the bikers', apparently proud to be in the men's shadows.

"Heck, yeah!" Crossley replied. "I guess that about sums it up."

Mel glanced over at their gleaming hogs. "So tell me," he said. "Those stickers on your bikes—do you really mean that?"

The men turned to see what he was referring to.

"You know," Mel went on, "'OK City—Only the Beginning,' or 'You Ain't Seen Nothin Yet . . . ' You mean that?"

Crossley sneered. "Would we advertise it if we didn't mean it? Look, Melvin," he said with a snarl. "That is your name, huh? It's one thing to talk politics, like the farmers, or wear tattoos, like the skinheads, it's another to be willin' to lay down your life for what you believe."

"Yeah," one of the women joined in, her hands on her hips, "we got sick a long time ago of hearin' how this farmer lost his farm to the international agriculture monopolies or how sweet Suzy-Q got aced out of a job by affirmative action. Our boys are willing to take affirmative action of a different kind. That's why we're here today, 'cause Fogarty brought in this Altmeyer, a die-hard activist!"

The woman raised a clenched fist, and her friends cheered.

"We ain't like the New-Ager quasi-White Supremacist survivalists who don't know whether to wait for the Hale-Bopp comet or lie down on the Nuke Train track," another added. She snickered over her shoulder at the hippies. "We ain't waitin' for no one to save us, man. We're takin' action now!"

Mel darted another look at the VW vans. "Say," he said, "is Zog related to Hale-Bopp?"

Again, the bikers looked quizzical. Then, the light dawned. "Zog?" someone said. "Oh—Zog! You saw the Zap Zog sticker! Zog is the Zionist Occupied Government! The U.S. government, man! The world government!"

"Yeah, and the bankers—the Jew bankers!"

Mel was bewildered, and looked it.

Crossley, who seemed to be the leader, shook his head. "You gotta be kiddin', man. Are you really that out to lunch? Surely you know that the Jews run the world! Man—come to think about it, I guess that's what brings all of us together—farmers, ranchers, New

Age freaks, skinheads. The one thing we all agree on—the one thing we all know for sure—is the nature of the enemy."

Mel bristled. "You mean, the main thing that unites everyone here is that you're anti-Semites?"

Willard drew close to Mel again, breathing on him from his towering height. "Who you talkin' about? We ain't against no semis. My dad was a trucker!"

Crossley grabbed Willard by the arm and pulled him aside. "Keep a clamp on it, Bozo!" he snarled. "We ain't talkin' about semis or truckers. We're talkin' about Jews!"

Willard was dazed, then comprehending. "Oh—yeah! The Jews—we all hate 'em. Need to start with the Jews. We all see that real clear!"

CHAPTER 14

Dusk brought a chill to the Bull River Valley. After the long afternoon of barbecue and "fellowship," the men began to gather up wood for a bonfire, apparently to be built on Pete's driveway.

Mel found his brother, who had spent the day in a round of fetch and carry, serving Jim Fogarty and his henchmen their umpteenth cups of coffee on the broad porch. "Hey, Pete, look at this," he said, drawing him aside and pointing to the wood gatherers. "Do you want a fire on your property?"

Pete observed the activity with apprehension. "Gee, I guess it's okay," he faltered.

Mel heard the hesitation in his brother's voice. "You have the last say, don't you?" Mel challenged him. "This *is* your property!"

Pete shuffled. With a glance back toward Fogarty, who sat sprawled like Saddam Hussein on one of the handmade deck chairs, he muttered, "Let it go. Jim's managed plenty of bonfires."

With this, Pete hurried off on yet another errand, and Mel watched him helplessly. He hardly recognized his elder brother anymore. He used to be so strong, so opinionated and "in charge." What had these people done to him?

As stars appeared in the purple canopy above the treetops, someone set a torch to the tall stack of brush and pine logs. Hank, Lucy, Thorny, and their friends gathered just beyond the brightest part of the firelit circle, their kids scrambling for blankets strewn on the grass and sitting cross-legged in anticipation of something.

Gradually, the rest of the crowd congregated as well, always leaving room before the fire. Resting on the porch rail, Mel leaned against one of the posts, expecting that some show was about to be staged.

Whatever was coming up, however, his attention was grabbed by the sight of the skinheads along the crowd's shadowed boundary. He saw yellow armbands on their camouflage sleeves, something they had not worn earlier. He did not need to stare to recognize the emblem stamped boldly upon the saffron ribbons: The Nazi swastika was impossible to misconstrue.

Mel's stomach tightened, the hair on his arms rising in goose flesh. He knew now, more than ever, that he wanted nothing to do with these people. Pulling on the plaid jacket Pete had loaned him, he peered over the crowd toward his car, which was parked by a small outbuilding at the far side of the yard. Slipping silently from the porch—unnoticed, he hoped—he headed for the darkness that ringed the group, intending to skirt the edge.

Suddenly, however, he was stopped in mid-escape by the sound of a whoop and a cheer, accompanied by the wild strumming of guitars, the jangle of tambourines, and the piping of flutes.

Hidden in darkness, he stood spellbound by the sight of twirling women and wild-haired men bounding into the firelight. It was the bus contingency, the New Agers, leading the crowd in song.

On cue, the people began to clap and sway, to tunes Mel had heard before. The assortment of music, however, was as odd as the assortment of people. How they managed to find common meaning between "If I Had a Hammer" and "Onward Christian Soldiers," or "The Battle Hymn of the Republic" and "The Times They Are

A'Changin'" was a wonder to Mel. But they sang them all with equal gusto, their mood swinging from brotherly love to religious zeal to social defiance, without missing a beat.

Mel wondered, in fact, if they were paying any attention to the lyrics. When Peter, Paul, and Mary had hammered out "love between my brothers and my sisters all over this land," they had surely never worn Nazi armbands. And when the old North had sung the Civil War "Battle Hymn," they had never dreamed that leather-clad bikers would someday declare, "In the beauty of the lilies Christ was born across the sea, with a glory in his bosom that transfigures you and me!"

Incongruous as all this was, however, Mel was further appalled by other armbands, other emblems. The bikers, he noticed, now sported their own ribbons, black with white silhouettes of raised fists.

He had been a preteen when the Black Panthers had been on the move in the sixties. He remembered that their symbol had been the black fist. The meaning of the new White Power emblem was unmistakable.

Mel could have stayed. It might be his only chance to see such a gathering firsthand. Until now, he had seen such things only in movies and on news footage. Probably these events took place far more often than the average Joe had any knowledge of, but he doubted he'd ever be so close to one again. And he could stay for his brother's sake. For the first time in his life, he felt like Pete needed him—like his big brother could be in big trouble.

But Mel wanted nothing more than to be out of there and down the road, back to the pit of L.A. or the lethargy of Spokane, or any-where but here, before anyone missed him.

He was almost to his car. Only one hurdle of Harleys, moved aside to make room for the meeting, stood between him and free-dom. He was fumbling in his jeans for his car keys, when a shadow suddenly loomed through the moonlight across his path.

Frozen, Mel looked up, and up, to the leering face of Willard, the brain-dead biker.

"What's yer hurry?" the giant growled. He had planted his feet wide, straddling the path. From behind him came Crossley.

"Hey, ol' buddy," the pack leader spat, "you wanna miss a good show?"

"I—I forgot my glasses," Mel lied. "In—the glove box," he said, pointing toward his car.

"Don't think so," Crossley said. "Top Cops don't wear glasses."

What had made Mel think he could fool guys who knew the law well enough to stay outside it?

Willard planted an arm across Mel's shoulders. "Now, we wouldn't want you to miss anything," he snarled. "You just come back with us."

Mel stumbled along beside Willard, or rather, Willard dragged him, back toward the throng.

By now the dancers were really wild, the women in their ankle-length calico skirts, colorful scarves, and long beads, the men in striped vests and silky pants bounding around them. One of the women carried a large American flag on a long pole. As the crowd sang "Hooray for the Red, White, and Blue," she waved it over their heads, while the men, some of whom were old enough to have burned similar flags in the seventies, strummed and banged away on their guitars.

As Mel cringed under the pain of Willard's grip, another woman flashed into the light, twirling round and round as she tied a scarf around her forehead. To Mel's horror, it was yellow, like the skinheads' armbands, and also bore a swastika. As she danced, the crowd cheered wildly, until what seemed the ultimate irony took place.

One of the skinheads, representative of the rightest of the rightwingers, jumped into the circle with her, symbolically joining his ideology to her leftist agenda, and the two spun together until the people were nearly frantic with joy.

Crossley leaned close to Mel. "Amazin', ain't it?"

Mel's throat was dry, and he pulled against Willard's hand. "You bet," he said with a grimace.

Willard finally let loose of him, and Mel rubbed his shoulder.

"I—I guess I have to admit," the cop said, "I don't get it."

Crossley exchanged a knowing look with his sidekick. "Surprisin', huh?" he said. "Well, think back. You remember Rajneesh?"

Rajneesh . . . Rajneesh . . . the word was familiar. "Oh, yeah," Mel recalled. "The commune in Oregon."

"In Antelope, Oregon," Crossley said. "They renamed it for their New Age swami, remember?"

It was coming back to Mel now. He remembered how in the eighties, a far-out group of New Agers had followed an East Indian guru to the tiny town of Antelope and had completely taken it over, driving out the locals. They had then brought in busloads of homeless people from big cities—mostly runaways, drug addicts, and the like—and had proceeded, under the guise of giving them shelter and food, to turn them into a bunch of programmed zombies.

The last he had heard, the Rajneeshis had disappeared when their leader was sent packing back to India and his thugs were incarcerated for a plot to poison the water system of a nearby city.

Crossley reminded him, as if it were something to be proud of, that the Rajneeshis had renamed Antelope's town dump "Adolf Hitler Landfill."

Mel's skin bristled. Now that he thought about it, he remembered seeing photographs of the Rajneeshis wearing Nazi armbands for the benefit of the media. Finally, it was dawning on him: The frailty of philosophy was that, in the extreme, extremes were compatible.

Around and around the hippie woman and the skinhead

danced, while the mesmerized crowd absorbed their harmony of hate and glutted themselves on it.

Mel had enough presence of mind to see that Jim Fogarty was now standing. Doubtless, old Eagle-Eye would use the fervor of the hour to give a mind-numbing speech. The L.A. cop braced himself, knowing there was nowhere to run.

Fogarty came down off the porch and stood in the firelit circle. As the dancers fell at his feet, the crowd received him with wild applause.

Throwing his arms wide, he shouted, "Welcome to the Promised Land!"

Mel cringed again. His brother had greeted him that way only two nights ago.

At the time, it seemed he had entered a perfect world. Now that world was the Twilight Zone.

CHAPTER 15

Jim Fogarty was a credit to his race, so his father had always said. Fogarty came from a long line of Aryans. His great-great-grandfather's racial ethic, instilled at birth, had been passed on through the Fogarty line at great price, beginning with the losing of the Civil War. And one of the Fogarty ancestors had been a founding father of the KKK in Georgia.

Jim was carrying on a torch handed to him with firm expectations. He must work valiantly, as had his forefathers, to bring about the purifying of the Great Race and the founding of a New Jerusalem in a new Promised Land, sanctified for the rebuilding of the Aryan Nation.

Tonight, as he stood before the bonfire on this piece of the New Heaven, he was a striking figure. Tall and white—even his once blond hair had turned a gleaming silver—strong, defiant, and intelligent, he was the perfect example of his ideologically perfect man.

He had earned his nickname, Eagle-Eye, by virtue of his cold, steely gray eyes, which seemed to penetrate the people in any crowd as if sifting it for impostors. More than once, when giving a speech at just such a rally as this, he had been known to single out those who were there under false pretense. He had an uncanny ability to ferret out hypocrites, reporters, undercover agents, or just plain party-crashers and humiliate them to the point of leaving.

If humiliation did not force them out, there were always men in the crowd, like Willard and Crossley, who were willing to make any gate-crashers wish they had never shown up.

Tonight, Eagle-Eye was in fine form. As the flames leapt and crackled behind him, he stood like a crucifix, arms spread, his shadow stretching and contracting hypnotically against the ground.

The dancers, who had brought the spectators to a fever pitch of anticipation, slowly rose from the places where they had collapsed and eased back into the crowd, leaving Fogarty the sole focus of attention.

The audience was already under his spell, ready to believe anything he said.

Mel was not very familiar with White Supremacist dogma. He knew that Hitler had taught the doctrine in his speeches to enormous rallies of Brownshirts at Nuremberg, and throughout the "Fatherland." He knew that the Ku Klux Klan, with its cross burnings and lynchings, had spouted a variation on the theme.

He also knew that in the years since the Civil Rights Movement, new groups had arisen, groups who harped on a spectrum of political grievances, all of which, they believed, could be blamed on what they called "subhuman" races, of whom, they asserted, Jews were the archetype.

Not until that day had Mel realized the extremes bound together by the racist teachings. Still, he did not know much about the particular beliefs that had spawned the likes of Fogarty.

Fogarty's leadership style, which had won for him the esteem of these diverse groups, capitalized on the themes that drew them together and minimized the points on which they differed. One of his favorite teaching techniques was to give a mini-history lesson at each rally, complete with maps and charts, slanted in a way that would never have been accepted in any university or anthropology department.

A hodgepodge of evolutionary theory, religion, and mysticism, it amounted to nothing more than wishful thinking, convincingly presented. But as Mel was about to learn, it was eagerly embraced and supported with all sorts of personal "evidence" by those who wished to blame their disappointments on convenient scapegoats and those who wished to believe they were part of a superior race.

Before Fogarty began speaking, he led the crowd in one last song. Building on the euphoria already generated by the previous songs and floor show, it was set to the tune of "The War Song of the Army of the Rhine" and was called "One Race Über Alle."

Mel tensed as the song commenced. Perhaps Willard sensed his reaction, for, pretending to place a brotherly arm about Mel's shoulders, the big fellow squeezed until the ex-cop thought his shoulder blades would crack. An unspoken reassertion of power, the gesture reminded Mel that he had no choice but to stay put and listen.

"Fogarty wrote this, hisself!" the giant said, bending close to Mel's ear. "Ain't it glorious!"

As the song ended, Mel saw tears in many eyes.

Suddenly Fogarty boomed out, "Brothers and sisters, is it not a blessing to be part of the Great White Race?"

Choruses of amens and yeah-mans echoed his sentiment.

"Have you ever asked yourself," he cried out, "'Why me? To what do I owe the privilege of my birth?' Have you ever asked yourself why you were favored not only to be born in this country, but to be born with white skin and superior intelligence? How is it that we were blessed to be born part of the Super Race, when others are born in poverty, cursed from birth with the inability to better themselves because of their genetic makeup?"

The people nodded, and Mel wondered if they ever looked at themselves in mirrors. If Lucy and Hank and Willard were part of the Super Race, the world was in hopeless shape indeed. But Mel dared not reveal his thoughts, not even with a roll of the eyes or the tiniest of smirks. Super Willard would as soon crush him as hear logic, though Mel doubted he would recognize logic if it slapped him in the face.

Fogarty's question had sounded rhetorical, but he actually intended to answer it. "Well, dear brothers and sisters," he went on, "let me tell you why you, and not others, were so blessed."

This was a cue, for from the shadows near the porch, two of Fogarty's henchmen appeared, carrying a large easel between them. They set it on the driveway, in plain sight of the crowd, then threw back the cover of a large tablet.

The first page was a colorful map of Europe and the Mediterranean. Across the top half was a band of reddish pink, with bold arrows flowing southward through continental Europe and fading as far as Persia and even India. "Expansion of the Pre-Germanic Nordics—1800–100 B.C.," it was labeled.

The audience shuffled for a view, some coming closer to the fire and sitting on the ground, as Fogarty's assistants shone large flashlights on the map.

'Here, my friends, you have a quick layout of the origins of the Aryan race. Strong, robust, 'barb-aryan,' the Norsemen were bred to endure extremes of climate. By the law of evolution, only the fittest survived the harsh world of the North," he said, running his hand across the regions of Scandinavia and upper Russia. "And by the laws of nature, they maximized human potential!"

The crowd hung on his words, many of them nodding, even clapping one another on the backs, apparently considering themselves to be examples of the lesson.

Spreading his fingers wide, Fogarty next drew his hand down the European continent toward Italy and then did the same toward Mesopotamia and India. "You see here that your forefathers brought their blood into the Roman and Eastern worlds, through conquest and subjugation of inferior races. From those lands, civilization arose, along with all the arts and sciences we have today. This was all due to the influence of the Super Race!"

Mel let out a sigh. By now, Willard and Crossley were caught up in the teaching and did not notice his agitation. *Where had Fogarty learned his history?* Mel wondered. Even grade-school children knew that civilization had arisen in the Fertile Cresent of Mesopotamia and Egypt, had been perfected in Greece and Rome, and had then spread to "barbarian" Europe. Fogarty had it backward.

The silver-haired orator was relentless. "Let me tell you," he continued, "our forefathers did not accomplish all of this by inter-breeding with subhumans!"

At this, a loud cheer went up from the crowd. Men stomped and women clapped.

Next, Fogarty flipped to a chart of various types of monkeys, trailed by humans representing supposed levels of evolution. "Let's change gears," he announced, "from history to biology. All you ranchers out there, you breed cattle, right?"

Men like Hank waved their hands and whistled.

"Tell me," Fogarty said. "What happens when you breed a thoroughbred with a donkey?"

"A mule!" the men shouted.

"Why not a thoroughbred?" Fogarty asked.

The men looked at one another and shrugged, until one of them shouted, "Because water seeks its own level!"

"Exactly!" Fogarty said. "In the rules of breeding, refined traits always bow to primitive ones!"

The crowd oohed and aahed, their faces lighting as though full of insight.

"And now," Fogarty drew them on, "what happens when you cross a white man and a Negro?"

"A mulatto!" someone answered.

"A white man and an Indian?"

"A half-breed!"

"A white man and a Jap?"

No ready name came to anyone's mind. At last, Willard hooted, "Somethin' nobody wants to see!"

The crowd loved this, and Fogarty gave Willard a thumbs-up.

The litany could have gone on, but someone cried out from the middle of the crowd, "What about the Jews? Are they white or what?"

The crowd mumbled, some shaking their heads and others shrugging, until Fogarty flipped the chart again.

Here he displayed a drawing of a tree with a snake wrapped around it and a woman holding an apple.

"Neither!" Fogarty declared. "The least of the low, the spawn of Satan—the Jews cannot be accounted for except as the offspring of Eve and Lucifer!"

Obviously awestruck, the crowd clapped again, not asking for the proof of such a statement.

Fogarty drew closer to the people, now, looking at them with such sincerity, they hushed with reverence. "My dear friends," he went on, "the reason you have been blessed with your heritage is because your forefathers had the foresight to keep themselves pure! You are the result of the pure Aryan will. And you are the foundation of the New Aryan Nation!"

Exultation swept over the crowd, and there were more congratulatory handshakes and back-claps.

"The future of our beloved race has been entrusted to your care," the leader challenged. "Upon the hills of the great northwest, we will establish a pure land, free of inferior beings, the New Israel!"

Mel could hardly believe his ears. What was this about Israel? A New Israel in the Northwest?

"Rejoice, Lost Tribes!" Fogarty cheered them. "Your wanderings are over! You have come to the Promised Land, and your time is at hand!"

Mel had not a clue as to what this was all about. It sounded about as ludicrous as belief in the Hale-Bopp snatch, by which disembodied souls would have been transferred to a higher planetary existence.

He had no opportunity to question Fogarty's statements, however, for suddenly Mel felt the eyes of the crowd upon him. Then he saw that Jim Fogarty, himself, was giving him the eagle-eye.

Mel's heart thrummed with fear. Did Fogarty sense his hypocrisy, did he know he was not a true believer? The Aryan leader studied him for a while, and the crowd was breathless.

Strangely though, Mel had the feeling that Fogarty was not suspicious. He sensed that Fogarty was actually admiring him.

"Ladies and gentlemen," the leader proceeded, "in a few moments, our guest, Monte Altmeyer, a prime example of German manhood, will be speaking to you. Before he comes, however, I want to say that we are honored tonight to be hosted by two of the finest specimens of Aryan blood I have ever laid eyes upon."

Mel glanced around, wondering who Fogarty was referring to. He noticed that everyone was still looking at him, and Fogarty's eyes had not shifted.

Without taking his gaze from Mel, Fogarty lifted his hand and waved someone up from the shadows. "Pete Wester!" he called. "Come out here! And you, the other Mr. Wester—yes, you . . . "

He was pointing at Mel.

"Come up and join your brother!"

Willard and Crossley, standing on either side of Mel, snapped amazed looks toward him. Mel swallowed hard, barely registering what was happening.

When he saw Pete come out from the porch, joining Jim Fogarty in the firelight, he knew he had not misunderstood. The Aryan leader was calling him forward as a representative of Nordic manhood.

Both brothers were red-faced as they came to the front, Mel from sheer embarrassment and Pete, most likely, from awe.

"Ah, see there!" Fogarty declared. "Only the white man can blush! Only the white man, Adam, was made in God's image—Adam, which in Hebrew means 'red face.' No other race can claim such a trait! Therefore, no other race is divine!"

Mel did not hear all of this. His head was buzzing with fear and humiliation.

Fogarty now had one brother on each side, an arm about each man's shoulders. "Have you ever seen truer specimens, ladies and gentlemen?" he shouted. "Hair blond as sunlight, eyes fair as the sea, skin white as birchwood! And tall! Aren't they tall! And strong!"

Mel wanted to run. He felt like a slave up for sale.

"All the qualities of perfect manhood, if ever I saw it!" Fogarty repeated. Then, turning to Pete, he gave him a special endorsement. "And brave!" he said, displaying the host proudly. "You all know what Pete did to keep himself pure!"

At this, many people in the crowd clapped and whistled, but Pete shook his head and whispered in Fogarty's ear.

Mel wondered what special heroics his brother was being praised for.

"Like a true Aryan!" Fogarty went on. "He is not only brave, but humble! He doesn't want me to praise him publicly!"

Now the people clapped and stamped more loudly. "Go, Pete! Go, Pete!" they hollered.

Mel noticed that Pete was avoiding his gaze. Whatever Fogarty was about to announce was something Pete did not want his brother to hear.

But there was no stopping Eagle-Eye. Proud as a cigar-passing papa, he sang his disciple's praises. "Your host, Peter Wester has given one of the ultimate sacrifices in his devotion to the Super Race. This man used to cohabit with a Jewess. When he learned the truth about her despicable race, he chose to endure the heartbreak of sending her away, rather than continue to soil his own body with hers. Yes, my friends, he cut the filth of that relationship from his heart and stands before you today, a clean Aryan man!"

The dazzled crowd applauded, whistling and cheering the shamefaced Pete.

Mel was dumbstruck. Visions of the sweet and beautiful Honey ripped at his heart. Honey—sent packing. Honey—the best thing that had ever happened to Pete Wester—kicked out of the Promised Land.

CHAPTER 16

Mel paced in the dark behind Pete's house. The party out front was breaking up, and he waited for his brother to be done with his guests for the night.

As soon as Fogarty had released the brothers from center stage, Mel had disappeared into the house. Being one of the heroes of the evening, no one questioned him. Even Willard and Crossley left him alone.

For an hour, he seethed with anger. It was probably a good thing he had a few minutes to cool down before confronting Pete. He would have decked him if he had gotten to him sooner. As it was, he was still fuming when Pete sheepishly came looking for him.

The last song of the evening had been sung, and the last cheer for the Great White Race had been whooped. Mel had missed Monte Altmeyer's talk, but he figured he could live without it.

The crowd was dispersing to campsites about the yard when the screen door on Pete's back porch creaked open, sending a shaft of yellow light across the garden patch behind the house. "Little Bro," Pete called, "you out here?"

Mel clenched his fists and growled through gritted teeth, "I'm here, Pete. Just long enough to hear where Honey is, and then I'm gone!"

Pete stepped off the porch and joined Mel in the dim light. When he spoke, his voice was dry, as though he were talking through cotton. "Look, Mel," he began, "I know you think I'm scum."

"You got that right!" Mel muttered, turning on him with a vengeance. "How could you? How could you send Honey away? That garbage about her leaving because of Ruby Ridge—that was just a smoke screen, wasn't it?" Flashing angry eyes toward the tree-tops, he snarled, "Pete, how could you buy all this trash about races and bloodlines? Where's your brain?"

Pete sighed. "I can't expect you to understand," he said. "You haven't learned all the stuff I have. You haven't seen what I've seen—my friends losing their homes, their ranches. You haven't read the stuff I've read. Give it time, Mel. You'll see. . . . "

Mel stared at Pete in disbelief. "You've actually bought the idea that Jews control the world?" he fumed. "Everything's a big conspiracy? Tell me," he challenged, "how did Honey conspire against you? You lived with her for nine years! Did she grow horns or a tail in that time?"

Rolling his eyes, he spat, "Besides, when did you figure out she was a Jew? I don't remember anything like that ever coming up before. Her last name—Aronstam—is that Jewish? I never would have known it was Jewish. So what does it matter, anyway?"

Pete stuck his hands in his pockets and looked at the ground. "It didn't matter, not years ago. I wouldn't have cared if Honey was a black African. I loved her, Mel—you know I did!"

Mel's eyes burned with exasperation. Blinking, he fought tears. He knew it was no use asking Pete to explain. Whatever had driven him to his desperate act, it must have been based on rhetoric such as Fogarty spewed. There was no reasoning with the irrational.

Gritting his teeth, he tried to listen. "So, what happened, Pete? What finally convinced you to send her packing?"

Pete grew very quiet, and Mel wondered if he would speak at

all. For a long while, he gazed deep into the woods. Finally, his voice soft, he said, "Lots of my friends, the ones I used to run with, turned to farming and ranching after their partying days. You remember Cy and Michael, and the others?"

Mel remembered. They were the ones who had helped Pete build his house. Still hippies in their hearts, they had been forced to grow up when families came along, little by little giving up their marijuana and their footloose lives to earn a living from the soil. A lot of them had worked as part-timers or itinerants in the orchards and fields until they could afford to buy land and go into business for themselves.

"Sure, they were good guys," Mel said.

"Well, most of them are gone now, forced out by the agricultural conglomerates—forced out by the banks in hard times. Their farms are now owned by international monopolies, Mel. There is hardly such a thing as the family farm anymore."

Mel shook his head. "All in the last ten years?" he asked. "How did all that happen?"

Pete tensed his jaw. "Well, brother, that's where I'd have to start preaching my heresies. I don't think you really want to hear any of that."

Mel tried to be patient. "I see," he said. "That's where the theories about the Jewish bankers come in. Well, let me tell you, coming from the ghettos in L.A., I've known a lot of bankers and a lot of slumlords. They sure aren't all Jews, and no matter what they are, some of them even have hearts. Besides, as I recall my history, the very word 'ghetto' comes from the hellholes where the Jews had to live for centuries. They sure haven't all been wealthy or powerful."

Pete shrugged. "You're not going to listen, I know that. This thing's a lot bigger than either of us can understand. It's international, Mel."

The ex-cop glared at Pete. "So much for that, Big Brother. I want to know about Honey. What pushed you over the edge?"

Pete took a deep breath. "I had been going to a lot of these meetings. Honey never came. One night, when I got home, she was already in bed. We had had words before I left. I couldn't understand why she wouldn't ever go with me, why she couldn't see the truth behind what my friends were saying. Well, I was just putting a log on the fire, and I reached up to the mantel to get the matches."

At the memory, his face twitched. "You remember Honey's music box? The one she always kept above the fireplace?"

Mel nodded. "Sure. It was really special to her."

"Well, I accidentally knocked it off the mantel. It fell to the hearth and broke apart." Pete's hands shook. "I can still hear the tune playing over and over while I tried to pick up the pieces."

Mel felt his sadness. "'The Blue Danube,'" he said. "Sure, Pete, I remember."

"I took the parts to the kitchen table," Pete went on. "I was hoping I could get them back together and that Honey hadn't heard the crash or the music. As I fumbled with the sides of the broken box, the bottom came off in my hands, the part that the little crank sticks out of."

"Yeah, go on," Mel said.

"Well, there in the bottom was a piece of cloth. At first I thought it was just some padding, insulation or something, for the sound box. But when I took it out, meaning to rearrange it, I noticed it was something odd." Pete stopped, his eyes moist and red.

"So . . . what was it?" Mel prodded him.

"It was a little rag, a funny little thing. It was kind of a grayish yellow and shaped like a star—not just any star, Brother. It was a Star of David. You know, a Jewish star."

Mel didn't make much of this. "So? Probably some holiday ornament she made when she was a kid. You know, some little-girl memento?"

Pete sighed. "I wish," he said. "No, it was more than that. I looked at it real close, and it had funny writing on one side. I can't read Hebrew, of course, but that's what it was. All crimped and jagged, like whoever wrote on it had a shaky hand. And the writing was old, you know, like it had been there for years. Besides, the rag was dirty, not a nice little decoration the way you're thinking."

Mel shrugged. "Are you telling me that finding a Jewish star in your lady's music box was enough to turn you against her?"

Pete glared at his brother. "You'd like to think I'm that stupid, wouldn't you? No, Mel, I didn't want to think anything bad about Honey. It's what she told me that finally left me no choice."

Mel listened as Pete recounted that strange night.

"The crash woke Honey up, and she came out to the kitchen to see what had happened. When she saw what I had—the little rag—she suddenly got real weird."

"Weird?" Mel repeated. "How so?"

"She came over to the table and grabbed the star out of my hand. She started to cry, and I thought she was mad about the music box. But it wasn't the box she was upset about. It was the rag. Man, you'd think I'd broken into her diary or something! She said it was something very private and that no one was supposed to touch it! She said it was a secret and not to tell anyone about it."

Mel looked quizzical. "That doesn't sound like Honey. She was always real level-headed."

Pete nodded. "Exactly. Now, you're beginning to see how weird this was. Anyway, after that, things changed between Honey and me. We'd never had secrets from each other—at least, not that I'd known about. Suddenly it seemed like Honey was real fidgety. Whenever I'd talk to her about the Militia or what I was learning, she'd get real antsy—paranoid-like. Finally, one day, I put two and two together. I started to think about her name. I remembered how Moses, in the Bible, had a brother named Aaron. And then, I realized: Aronstam had to be a Jewish name!"

Mel tensed. Pete knew what he was thinking.

"Now listen, brother," he said defensively, "I swear to you that's not what broke us up. No matter what I've come to believe, I never would have sent away the woman I loved because of her last name—not if Fogarty himself held a gun to my head. But, it was Honey; it was the way she started acting, like she had this big secret and she wasn't safe with me anymore. She stopped entertaining our friends, the ones I was bringing home from the meetings. And she kept a close eye on them whenever they were in the house. I swear, that funny little rag had come between us!"

Mel frowned. "So, is that what pushed you to send her away?"

Pete took awhile to answer. It seemed to be hard for him to find the words. "I don't know if you can believe me," he finally said. "But I didn't send her away because we had problems or because she had changed. I sent her away to protect her."

Mel was doubtful. "Sure!" He sneered.

Pete glanced toward the house, as if fearing eavesdroppers. "Listen, bro," he said, "did you know it's possible to believe certain things and yet fear the ones who preach them? Well, I've come to believe a lot of what the Freemen preach, but sometimes I think they take it too far. I don't know where to draw the line. I think they're onto something with the racism stuff. But I happen to be in love with a Jew. In fact, sometimes I don't know who the enemy is. I'm one mixed-up guy, Baby Brother. I'll tell you this—when push came to shove, I sent Honey away because Fogarty is a dangerous man. As much time as he spends here, with his scary thugs, I knew it wouldn't be long before he'd learn about Honey, maybe even find that crazy rag. So I sent away the one I love, and I'm harboring her enemy."

Mel was incredulous. It occurred to him, not for the first time, that Pete had lost himself, that he was behaving like a programmed freak from some kind of cult. "Man, you're in one strange position!" he said, taking him by the arm. "Did it ever occur to you that it was a lie that sent you down this slippery slope? Why don't you just follow your heart, man? We have to get out of here and go find Honey!"

Pete looked confused, as though two voices were speaking in his head simultaneously. At last, he nodded, like he was about to take Mel up on the idea. But, before he could say anything, the screen door creaked again on the back porch.

In the light from the house's warm interior, Jim Fogarty stood, tall and gleaming with his frosty hair. "Hey, fellas," he called. "My men and I are having a private meeting with Monte Altmeyer. Come on in and join us. He wants a few choice folks to hear what the future holds."

Pete and Mel stood hesitantly in the yard.

Again, Fogarty motioned to them enthusiastically. "Come on," he called. "How often do you get to glimpse the inner workings of the world?"

The two brothers tried to look impressed as they walked toward the house. When they reached the door, Fogarty clapped them on the backs. "Welcome to the inner circle, boys!" he exclaimed. "You've done yourselves proud!"

CHAPTER 17

Honey Aronstam walked down the hall of the anthropology department at Midwest University, reading the various names on the office doors. The receptionist had offered to call her cousin's office to announce her arrival, but Honey told her it was to be a surprise.

"I haven't seen Ken in years," she said. "I just happen to be in town, and I'd like to say hi."

Actually, Honey didn't want her name being spoken over any telephone. She had come to think that the less her whereabouts was revealed by any electronic device, the safer she would be.

Honey had never gone out of her way to look attractive, but she was a natural beauty. Wherever she went, heads turned. Her dark hair fell in natural waves, and she wore it that way, without pins or barrettes. Only a touch of lipstick brought extra color to her light olive complexion and big, brown eyes. With Honey's looks, even in her mid-thirties, less was best.

Now, more than ever, she wanted to be understated. She preferred the backwoods look that worked best in the Montana hills to anything flashy or trendy. Because she was in a big city, she had worn her one really nice dress. Even it was nothing fashionable, an old Gunne Sax that she'd had since the eighties. The last time she had worn it had been to the wedding of friends in Thompson Falls. She had often thought she would wear it if she and Pete ever formally took vows. That had never happened, and now she figured, it never would.

Honey clutched her small travel bag, the only one except her large shoulder purse that she had brought with her from Bull River. Passing door after door labeled "Graduate Assistant" and "Graduate Fellow," she finally came to the last two in the hall.

The door to the right was shut tight, the frosted glass panel on the top showing no sign of interior light except what came from some outside window. "Dr. David Rothmeyer, Professor of Ancient Cultures and Linguistics," the door was labeled. Below the name was taped a note written with black marker pen: "On Sabbatical."

Straight ahead was the office Honey was looking for: "Dr. Kenneth Aronstam, Department Chairman."

That door, too, was shut, but warm yellow light shone through its frosted glass, and the receptionist had assured her that the chairman was in.

Honey smoothed her flowered dress, then knocked on the door.

"Come in," her cousin called.

He sounded so professional, she thought, not like the kid she'd grown up with.

Slowly she opened the door, stuck her head inside, and waited for Ken to look up.

Busy as always with a pile of papers, he did not immediately respond, until she stepped in and placed her travel bag on the floor. "Come in, come in," he finally said, motioning to a chair, but still not raising his head.

When he did at last glance Honey's way, he gasped in surprise. "Honey!" Jumping up from his swivel chair, he took one giant step and reached for her, lifting her slim body off the floor and hugging her tight. Then, as if remembering his professorial image, he put her down, shot a look toward the door, and shut it.

"Honey, girl!" He laughed and hugged her again. "What on earth brings you here? Did some grizzly chase you out of the mountains?"

Honey laughed with him. "No such luck, Ken," she said. "I wish it were just a bear that drove me out."

She had intended to keep her first moments with her cousin lighthearted. But, suddenly, feeling the comfort of his presence, she let down her guard, and tears welled in her dark eyes.

Holding her at arms' length, Ken studied her sad face. "What is it, cousin?" he asked. "Here, have a seat."

He led her to the folding chair upon which so many people had sat through the years. A department chairman filled many roles beyond that of administrator, he had learned, from tutor to diplomat to psychological counselor. He had a hunch Honey's needs surpassed any he had dealt with thus far.

Honey was Ken's favorite relative. The two had grown up together, children of two brothers. They had gone to school and synagogue school together, had enjoyed the post–Viet Nam era together, with all that the holdover hippie culture afforded the young. They had even gone to this very university together, before Honey, whose real name was Clarissa, adopted her "back-to-the-earth" name and took off for Seattle.

Ken had met Pete a time or two when he visited Honey on the coast. He had liked the offbeat fellow well enough, but he had worried that he was unstable, fickle in his devotion to various causes, and he wondered if Pete was good for Honey. When Ken had heard from her, during the holidays or on his birthday, she had always seemed happy, and so he had hoped for the best.

"So, what's going on?" he asked, handing her a tissue from the ever-ready box that chairmen learned to keep near their desks. "If Pete's turned mean, I'll—"

Honey sniffed and wiped her eyes. She felt foolish, showing her emotions this way. "No, no," she said. "Pete's not mean. A little crazy," she said, with a half-smile, "but not mean."

Ken said nothing, knowing she would tell him what she wanted to.

She took a deep breath, wondering just where to start. Of course, she had thought about this long and hard ever since deciding to come to Columbus.

"I'm going to ask a strange question," she said.

Ken nodded. "Okay."

Honey looked around the little office, got up, and glanced out the window, then turned to him.

"Is it safe to talk?"

"Safe?" Ken shrugged. "Anything you say is safe with me."

"No, I mean really safe. Like . . . " She nodded toward the walls.

"What?" Ken laughed. "You mean bugged? You wonder if my office is *bugged*?"

Honey blushed. "I told you it was crazy," she said, taking up her bag and making as though she would leave. "Maybe I shouldn't have come here."

Ken lurched forward. "Now, *that* is crazy!" he huffed. "What is this all about, Honey? Are you in some kind of trouble?"

With this, Honey broke down. In a gush, all of her pent-up fears came tumbling forth.

"Oh, Ken, you have no idea! Pete . . . he fell in with some bad people! I don't know if I'm in trouble or not. I only know that I can't be too careful, and I must seem like—really flipped out!"

"What kind of people?" Ken asked, frowning.

Honey sighed. "You know how Pete was always hopping on some bandwagon, always into some cause or other? Years ago, I loved him for that, for the caring and daring it represented. He seemed like a leader, but after years of being with him, I learned that he could be taken in . . . you know—duped."

"So," Ken tried to interpret, "he's in with some bad folks, and you're in danger?"

Honey fidgeted. "I—I don't know. That's part of the problem. If I knew for sure, maybe I'd know what to do. But Pete thought I might be in danger, so—" Her chest heaved with a sob. "He sent me away!"

Ken tried to envision it. He knew that Honey had been happy with Pete, happy in those beloved hills he had never been privileged to see. In the cards and letters she had sent over the years, she had expressed her excitement about what she was learning, as well as her hopes for the future. He knew she wanted children and suspected that the lack of them created a hollow spot.

But for her to leave Pete and Montana must have taken something traumatic indeed.

"What kind of people, exactly, is he involved with?" Ken asked.

Anxiously, she spoke of the Militia, of Fogarty, and of the rallies. She spoke of what they had done to Pete's head and how he talked, now that he had been swayed by Fogarty's awful lies. "Fogarty wooed Pete by giving him a special job," she said. "Lots of evenings he sits by his ham radio on the porch, and he waits for messages."

"Messages?" Ken repeated. "What sort of messages?"

"I never heard them very clearly. I'd usually be in the house, doing dishes or something, when the crackling and the popping would start. Pete would tense up, grab a pad, and get ready to write. I swear, the words were some sort of code! They didn't mean much to me at all. But the voices, that's what weirded me out! They were usually foreign, although some were Southern. But the foreign ones, they sounded like they were Arab—or some type of Middle Eastern. Then, there was this German voice, and once or twice a voice that sounded Irish."

Ken's eyes grew wide. "You've got to be kidding!" he muttered. "You poor kid. No wonder you're scared to death!"

Honey lowered her head, and Ken handed her another tissue. "You understand, then? You don't think I'm nuts?"

Ken leaned back in his chair and cupped his hands behind his neck. He blew out softly and shook his head. "From what you describe, you'd be crazy not to be scared!" Leaning forward again, he gazed at her intently. "I know you don't have a TV at your house, but you've surely been in touch enough to think those sorts of connections might insinuate trouble."

Honey swallowed hard. "Of course, Ken. We get the paper when we go into town, and we have a transistor radio. We're not hermits!"

Ken sensed her defensiveness. "All right. You've suspected anything I could suggest. Pete's got himself hooked up with some group much bigger than any stateside militia. Sounds like this Fogarty's using Pete's naiveté and his enthusiasm to rope him into being a go-between."

Honey's hands were cold. She tucked them against her lap.

Ken observed her pale look. "Now," he asked, "how are *you* in danger? What happened to make you think they would come after you?"

The woman shook her head. "It all seems too far-fetched. It seems like something out of a movie. Maybe I'm imagining all of it."

"Nonsense," Ken said. "What you've told me so far is only too believable."

"Okay," Honey sighed. She set down her purse, and reached for her little travel bag, setting it on her lap. She opened it gently, and drew out an envelope. She placed the envelope on the professor's desk as tenderly as though it were a Fabergé egg, then smoothed it with a caress.

"Here," she said. "This is what it's all about."

Ken looked at it quizzically and gave her a questioning glance.

"Go ahead. Open it," she said. "Just be careful."

As he picked up the envelope and peeked inside, he frowned.

"I have never shown this to anyone before," she said. "My dad gave it to me when I enrolled at the university. I think he knew he would not be here much longer. He said I was grown up and ready to take care of it."

Ken pulled out a little piece of yellow, ragged cloth, about three-and-a-half inches long and cut in the shape of a Star of David. He studied it in bewilderment.

Honey's father, his uncle, had died of lung cancer shortly after Honey entered college. Having lost her mother not many years before, she suffered a long bout with grief, but she had never told Ken about the strange gift.

"Is this what I think it is?" he marveled.

Honey nodded. "It's a Jew badge, worn by our great-grandfather Aronstam in the camp at Dachau."

Ken was stunned. It had been a long time since he had heard reference to his great-grandfather, who, as a very old man, had been liberated by American GIs when they freed Holocaust survivors.

"Great-grandpa Aronstam?"

"That's right," she said. Then, reaching out, she gestured to him to turn the star over. "Look at the back side."

Ken did so, and his eyes grew even wider.

"What the . . . " He pulled it close to his face. "This looks like Hebrew!" Glancing up at his cousin, he saw that she agreed. "Do you know what it says?"

Honey shook her head. "Great-grandpa sent this to the family by means of the Red Cross the day he was set free. It went to his eldest son, our grandfather, then to my dad, because he was the oldest."

She continued, "The instructions were that it was to be a family secret until"—she stopped and looked at Ken quite sincerely—"until we could show it to a wise man in Jerusalem."

Ken blinked. "Wow! That sounds pretty strange. Are you sure you have that right?"

"I heard it more than once. My dad told me several times. It was real important to him, so it's always been very special to me. That's why I hid it. I kept it in the base of a music box all these years, and never told a soul—not even Pete."

Honey gazed out the window, her thoughts in the Bull River Valley. "You know," she said, "I don't think Pete ever really realized until just recently that I'm Jewish. For all the years we spent together, and as close as we seemed to be, we never talked about much of anything deeper than politics, gardening, and natural foods."

Ken smiled at her sadly, then scratched his forehead. "So let me guess," he said. "Pete found your star, and with his connections, he got scared."

"Exactly!" Honey exclaimed. "How did you know?"

"Pete's no dummy," Ken asserted. "He recognized a Jewish secret when he saw it. No one would have to read Hebrew to know that this is old, and probably a message of some kind. In the circle Pete runs in, a secret, especially a Jewish one, can have international significance."

As Honey pondered this, Ken surveyed the cloth like a hungry man at a bakery window. "What I wouldn't give to study this out!" he declared. Then, looking disappointed, he added, "But I guess I don't meet Great-grandpa Aronstam's specifications."

Honey did not reply, her mind still on her predicament.

Observing her, Ken scooted his chair close and patted her knee. "Pete was wise to send you away," he said. "Not only do you have a Jewish name, but you were hiding something Jewish. His new friends were always going to be snooping around your house. He knew you'd never destroy that cloth, and short of that, there was no other answer."

Honey looked amazed. "I-I don't know," she stammered. "I never thought of all that."

"No?" Ken replied. "You may not have it all figured out, but you've sensed the danger of your position." Then, with a wink, he asked teasingly, "Why else do you look for bugs in people's offices?"

Honey grinned, the tension easing a little, despite the realities that seemed to be settling in.

"So, what should I do?" she asked. "I don't have much family left. I've been on the run for months—Seattle, Wyoming, staying with friends. Can you help me?"

Ken Aronstam was a secularist and a rational scientist; he claimed no particular religion. But ever since David Rothmeyer's invitation to Israel, he had been thinking more and more about his Jewish heritage.

This visit from Honey pricked him in more ways than one.

Clearing his throat, he tried not to sound too grave. "You know me, Honey," he said, "old 'science brain.' I've never believed in God or fate. But I have to admit, this little cubbyhole of an office is attracting strange vibes these days."

Honey listened respectfully. After what she'd gone through, nothing much surprised her.

"Believe it or not, you're not the first person to come through here lately with a Jewish secret. One of my top professors was contacted a few months ago by some Jewish agency looking for help with a mysterious project. In fact, right now he's in Jerusalem working for them on something so sensitive that he can't even tell me about it! To avoid questions, we put a note on his door saying he's on sabbatical, but actually, he's only on earned leave, not even under our auspices at this point."

Honey raised her eyebrows. "That is peculiar," she said. "I wonder what the mystery project is."

"Who knows?" Ken shrugged. "Well, so much for the cloak-and-dagger stuff," he said with a laugh. Grabbing for an address book and a notepad, he began to jot something down.

"This does give me a thought, however," he said. "Do you have a passport?"

Honey was baffled. "It's with the personal papers I brought from home. Why?"

"Is it still active?" he asked, busily writing away.

Honey shrugged. "Yeah, sure," she replied. "Pete and I went with his brother to Costa Rica a few years ago. Why?" she asked again.

"What would you think of going to Israel?" Ken inquired, looking at her over the rims of his glasses.

Honey was astonished. "Israel? Me?" she gasped.

Ken sat up from his desk. Trying not to frighten her, he said firmly, "Cousin, I do believe you are in danger. You need to leave the country, and Israel is a natural. It's where Great-grandpa Aronstam said the star should go, and you could find safe harbor there."

Honey's brain was whirring. "S-safe harbor?" she stammered.

Ken tried to ease her fears. "Sure," he said with a smile. "After all, according to Great-grandpa, Jerusalem is where the wise men are."

Shoving his notepad across the desk, he pointed to a name and address in the Old City. "Now that I've heard your story, I understand your fears of being followed. I don't think we should notify anyone," he continued, "but I want you to hook up with my friend when you get there. If there ever was a wise guy, it's David Rothmeyer!"

CHAPTER 18

Rabbi Horace Benjamin never felt more in his element than when he was walking down a street in Jerusalem's Old City. Although he was not a proud man, he always held his head a little higher and wore an expression of sincere satisfaction.

People passing him could not help but take a second look. He was used to tourists, in Jerusalem or in New York, taking pictures of him as he strode along in his long black suit and wide, flat hat. Had he been dressed in red, he would have resembled a Santa Claus, save that he had no round belly. His friend, Dr. Jacobs, filled that requirement better than he. But Benjamin's bushy white hair with its long tendrils, and his glorious fatherly beard, which hung nearly to his waist, were eye-catching indeed.

Unlike many of his colleagues, Benjamin did not avoid the eyes of the public. He did not keep his face downcast or don the aspect of a preoccupied mystic, which in too many cases was not indicative of holiness, but a ruse to shun interaction with humanity.

Nor had he ever been known to take offerings from naive seekers of blessings, as was the habit of some of his fellow rabbis.

Benjamin was an Orthodox Jew, of the Hasidic

type, his roots going back to the followers of Israel Ben Eliezer in southeastern Europe during the eighteenth century. Known as Baal Shem Tov, the "Kind Master of God's Name," Eliezer taught the suffering Jews of the southern provinces to seek joy in everyday things, that God loved them, and that the Mosaic Law was made for them, not them for it. Certain aspects of the Cabala, an ancient mystical and magical interpretation of the Scriptures, wove their way into Eliezer's teachings, so that, between the mixture of joyfulness and mystery he brought to religion, his followers gained a new understanding of the word "Hasidic," Hebrew for "pious."

Dancing and singing, which were frowned upon among the scholarly Talmudists of northern Europe, enlivened Hasidic celebrations, making them gay and bright. Hasidism spread like wildfire across the spiritual desert that was legalistic Judaism. After a while, the Hasidic approach to religion was the Judaism that the world recognized, and it came to be considered the main form of orthodoxy.

It was true that in the centuries that had passed since Baal Shem Tov, Hasidism had lost some of its gaiety. It had fallen back into a form of legalism that sometimes made it indistinguishable from the rigid teachings of northern Europe. The all-embracing love for mankind exhibited by Eliezer was often nearly extinguished among some sects of Hasidism.

Yet, there was still a fascination for the Hasidics that drew people to observe and even to envy them—to lift cameras in the streets of New York and Israel and snap photos of them, to marvel at their animated debates in the restaurants and marketplaces, and to honor their devotion to God.

Horace Benjamin was among the most sincere of Hasidics. David Rothmeyer did not know much of the history of his sect, but if he had been asked to name the warmest and kindliest man he had ever met, he would not have hesitated to name the rabbi.

David walked proudly beside Horace today, his long stride

matching the rabbi's enthusiastic pace as the old fellow led him down a cobbled street toward Temple Mount.

Rabbi Benjamin had taught David a few things about that sacred mountain. Jews called the area of the Wailing Wall, or Western Wall, "Temple Mount," because that was the site upon which the ancient temple of Judaism had once stood. Presently controlled by Arabs, the platform now occupied by the Muslim Dome of the Rock was once the foundation of Solomon's and Herod's fantastic edifices. The building that stood there now, housing the rock on which Jewish sacrifices were once offered up, was one of the most sacred mosques in the Islamic world. And the Muslims did not even acknowledge that the sacred ground was related to Jewish history.

While living in Jerusalem, David had taken many a trek to the Western Wall. He had witnessed Jewish festivals at the high stone structure, which, since the destruction of Jerusalem in 70 C.E., was the only remnant of Herod's vanquished temple, and which was, itself, merely a part of an ancient retaining wall.

"Wailing Wall" was a fitting nickname, for Orthodox Jews were known to spend long hours literally wailing there for the lost pride of Israel. Also, they prayed there for the day when their temple would be rebuilt, a "house of prayer for all nations" as the Bible promised. Along with this, their prayer was for the coming of the Messiah, who must one day reign from the Holy Mount.

The mount was known by various names, especially Mount Moriah, meaning "Wisdom Teacher," and Mount Zion. It was from this second name that the term "Zionism" arose, the political movement that had given birth to the new state of Israel, making it possible for men like the rabbi to even go there.

Benjamin's colleagues had returned to New York City, and he had stayed in Jerusalem to help instruct young rabbinical students at the Consortium's seminary or "yeshiva." He spent some of his nights at the school, and had met David at his apartment door this morning, promising to show him things he never dreamed of.

David hastily showered and dressed, while the rabbi visited with Anya in the kitchen, feasting on her cinnamon rolls for breakfast.

Now, as they walked together, the rabbi was radiant. "Prepare to be 'blown away,'" he said, chuckling at the use of slang.

"Where are we going?" David asked.

"To a gallery," Horace replied.

David was disappointed, and his face showed it. The rabbi laughed again. "Not just any gallery, David. This is the gallery of the world's future!"

The professor had no idea what this meant, but realizing Horace was enjoying the intrigue, he asked no more questions.

The street down which they walked, like most of the streets in the Old City, did not accommodate cars. It was ancient and narrow, and was solely for foot traffic. But it was one of the grandest of the Jerusalem avenues, its buildings full of intriguing history.

Much of the architecture was from the Crusader period and then the Ottoman, that time in which the Turks nearly wiped out all Christian advances in the culture, along with Judaism. Evidences of the British Mandate period lay farther out, along the newer streets and broader avenues beyond the Old City walls.

Ahead, wide, banistered stairs led to the courtyard of the Wailing Wall. From the vantage point of a large veranda at the head of the stairs, one could take in a fabulous view of Temple Mount, the Kidron Valley at its foot, and the Mount of Olives beyond.

Rabbi Benjamin stopped, as was his custom, long enough to breathe a prayer upon viewing the holy site. David waited respectfully, removing his leather cap and bowing his head.

The rabbi then took him by the arm and, with the excitement of a young boy, he said, "We go this way." He pointed down a narrow lane that ran left off the veranda, paralleling the distant Western Wall.

A few doorways down the street, a little sign hung over the entry to a tiny set of descending stairs. "This is it!" the rabbi announced.

David would never have noticed the sign or the stairs had he not been directed to them. "Temple Jewels Exhibition," it said, and then in smaller letters beneath: "Temple Consortium, 36 Rebi Yosef St., Jewish Quarter."

David fumbled with his cap, not knowing whether to put it on or leave it off. Although Horace continued to wear his rabbinical one, David decided, in the split second before he was ushered into the place, that it was probably not fitting that he wear a hat in a building that housed "Temple Jewels," whatever that meant.

A small reception desk at the front lent the air of a typical tourist trap, complete with pamphlets and books for sale on the history of the exhibit, commentaries on the Scriptures regarding a prophetic rebuilding of the temple, little packets of slides, and knickknacks such as miniature menorahs.

Rabbi Benjamin introduced David to the young women who handled the reception desk and sold the trinkets. Then he said, "This way, my friend," and led David toward the central hall.

Above the doorway that opened onto the exhibit itself was a huge oil painting, an artist's conception of a glorious building. Awesome in detail, the dreamscape lifted the soul and the imagination. From a gleaming, alabaster court, a fabulous edifice arose, its aquamarine facade reflecting the light of heaven and the gleam of many candlestands. In proportion to the small figures who peopled the court, the building appeared to be several stories high. These people were garbed in elaborate robes and turbans, like actors in a Mideastern pageant.

"What is this?" David asked, pausing long enough to gaze on the work.

Rabbi Ben beamed. "That is what our temple will look like when we build it," he replied.

David studied the painting in amazement. Positioned about the temple court were ornate furnishings and various implements that the professor assumed to be ritualistic. A gilt-framed plaque beside the painting announced that these items were on display in this very exhibit.

"So," David marveled, "this gallery is about plans for the temple."

The rabbi nodded. "Not just the plans! The exhibit shows much of the actual work we have done to this point."

Looking at his watch, Benjamin said, "Why don't you wait here, while I go and fetch our guide?" Then gesturing down the hallway, he suggested, "There are several items on the wall that will introduce what you are about to see."

As the rabbi hurried off, David scanned a short history of the Jewish yearning for a temple, which was displayed in easy-to-read posters and articles, illustrated with scenes from the Bible, from the wanderings of the Jews, and from the reestablishment of the nation in 1948.

Under a poster of a Jewish family gathered about a Passover table, David read: "The hope of the rebuilding of the temple was conceived on the very day of its destruction, nearly two thousand years ago. Throughout those centuries, the Jewish people have never forgotten the temple. On our holidays we pray: 'Build your house as at the first, set your temple on its foundations, allow us to see it built, and make us joyous in its establishment . . . '"

The words reminded David of his childhood and of the many such feasts he had celebrated with his family. Indeed, he remembered reciting that very prayer and wondered, now, why it had never much impressed him.

He was gazing at the poster and at the prayer, lost in thought, when the rabbi returned with another gentleman. "Dr. Rothmeyer," Horace announced, "I want you to meet Rabbi Shalom Diamant, curator of this gallery. He is going to take us on a little tour."

The guide was dressed in more modern clothes than Horace's but wore a yarmulke like that of Uriel Katz and was bearded, as were all the Orthodox Jewish men David had met.

"Glad to meet you," said David, shaking the rabbi's hand.

"I am happy to show you around, Dr. Rothmeyer," Diamant began. "I have been following your work with keen interest for months."

This should not have surprised David. He knew that his whereabouts and his activities were monitored by numerous people he had never met, just as his credentials and background had been scrupulously investigated by the Consortium. Nevertheless, the reminder of that fact gave him the same sense of uneasiness he had experienced countless times since committing to this assignment.

He should have also anticipated that the "gallery" to which Horace had brought him would present him with yet more surprises, but he never could have been completely prepared for what he was about to see.

As the three men stepped through the arch that led to the first display area, Shalom Diamant launched into a monologue that he had apparently given often. His affection and enthusiasm for his topic were not blunted, however, by repetition.

Directing his guests toward a reproduction of the bas-relief from the Arch of Titus in Rome, he said, "We all know that the temple of Israel was destroyed in 70 C.E. at the sacking of Jerusalem by Rome's General Titus. We see here a depiction of Jewish slaves being forced to carry away items from the temple as booty for the conquerors. The great menorah that lit the court, the silver trumpets used by the Levites . . . these things and many other treasures disappeared during the destruction of Jerusalem."

David nodded. Many memories were pushing through the cobwebbed years that had separated him from his upbringing. He remembered reciting the mournful refrains of the Jewish prayer that stated, "It would be a delight unto my soul to walk barefoot upon the desolate ruins that were your holy courts."

As he followed the curator through the exhibit, he was surprised by a strange sensation of otherworldliness.

"The dream of rebuilding the temple spans fifty Jewish generations," Diamant was saying, gesturing emphatically. "It has been cried out upon every continent, sea, and ocean. The prayer for its rebuilding has been spoken in all human languages, and in all places, from synagogues to yeshivas, from prisons to ghettos, from homes to fields, each day for two millennia of exile!"

He had now led David and Horace into a room lined with tall, glass-fronted cabinets. Before directing them to the contents, he went on, "After seemingly endless centuries of peril and persecution, the dream of the actual reestablishment of the temple has taken on new hope with the return of the people to the Land of Israel and with the rebirth of the Jewish state.

"Twenty-seven hundred years ago, the prophet Isaiah declared that one day there would stand on Mount Zion a 'house of prayer for all people.' On that day, 'God will be king over all the earth!'" Diamant's eyes glistened behind his horn-rimmed glasses, and he clenched his hands together in front of him.

"Dr. Rothmeyer," he said, "the Temple Consortium was founded to fulfill God's command to build him a temple. For years, we have been researching the materials, measurements, and design of that temple as described by the Torah, the prophets, and our traditions. We have also been researching the sacred vessels, implements, musical instruments, and priestly garments necessary to the temple rituals. What I will show you now is the result of that research."

Inside the tall cabinets that lined the room were cups, platters, and censers of various types, all made of brass and fine metals. Gleaming beneath indirect lighting, they showed the finest of craftsmanship.

As the professor listened to Diamant's description of their purposes and uses, he was incredulous at the scholarship that had gone into the work.

Cups for the measuring of wine, water, oil, and grain, according to the specifications of Moses; vessels for the preparation of flour and other ingredients for the making of grain offerings; tongs for the carrying of coals to the altar; a huge copper wash basin and stand constructed after the biblical ordinance for the washing of hands; decanters, spices, incense trays . . . on and on the display went.

One showcase held little jars of spices, the result of intensive research into the components of temple incense. Another held little vials of substances for the making of the dyes that would be used for the fabrics and vestments of the court. Although he was taken aback by the fact that some of the implements were related to animal sacrifices, he had seen enough of such things in the world of archaeology that he did not, just now, question it.

In an adjacent room, the most magnificent of artifacts resided: a seven-branched menorah, as tall as a man, made of beaten brass. "This is only a model," Diamant said. "The one that will stand in the Holy Place, before the entrance to the Holy of Holies, will be made of pure gold, just as in the days of Solomon!"

David was no jeweler, no dealer in precious metals, but he knew that such an artifact would be utterly priceless.

Reminded of the letter he had received that had sent him on this adventure, its logo being a small, golden candlestand, he was astonished, trying to imagine the expense and dedication that must be going into the making of all these items. "This is incredible!" he exclaimed. "Why hasn't the world heard about your work?"

The two rabbis looked at each other and smiled feebly.

"Our work is not 'politically correct,'" Diamant replied. "The media barely acknowledges the right of Israel to exist, let alone what we are doing here."

Horace shrugged and lifted his palms to heaven. "The fact that this little agency resides here at all is a miracle," he said. "We are well aware that we have many enemies who would squash us, if they got the chance. In fact, there is no reason why they have not wiped us out of Jerusalem, except for the protection of God."

David had to agree. The consortium was brazenly situated mere meters away from the Dome of the Rock, the Arab sanctuary. Only the Western Wall courtyard separated it from the footstool of Israel's enemies, and there were no guards stationed anywhere nearby.

As he considered the exhibit's location, however, and as he stood surrounded by evidence of the temple's preparation, facts began to coalesce in his mind. Suddenly a fearsome understanding flooded David's consciousness, and with it a fledgling appreciation for the tremendously sensitive nature of the rabbis' work. Dumbfounded, he felt like a child on his first day at school.

Diamant, noting his awestruck expression, asked, "What is it, Dr. Rothmeyer? Are you all right?"

The professor shook himself and stared at his guides. "Let me get this straight," he said. "The Temple Consortium wants to rebuild Israel's lost temple where it once stood, right?"

The rabbis nodded, glancing at each other as though they knew what David's mind must be processing.

"That is right," Horace said. "Mount Zion."

David waved his hand and shook his head again. "Okay, okay!" he exclaimed. "But that is the present site of the Dome of the Rock. Correct?"

Rabbi Diamant followed his train of thought. "Also correct, Dr. Rothmeyer. Mount Moriah or Mount Zion. The two are one and the same."

David closed his eyes, actually feeling the blood drain from his face.

Rabbi Benjamin stepped closer to him. "Surely you knew this!" he exclaimed.

The professor opened his eyes again, feeling quite foolish. "I-I did . . . and I didn't!" he stammered. "I mean, somehow, despite my upbringing, despite years of watching CNN and thinking I'm informed, the sensitive nature of this situation has gone right over my head!"

The rabbis smiled sympathetically.

"You are not alone, David," Diamant observed. "Many intelligent, educated people have missed what goes on here. The fact is that the Arabs, and their Dome of the Rock, now occupy the sacred mountain where the most holy place in Judaism once stood, and where, the prophets tell us, it must stand again!"

Rabbi Benjamin showed untypical surliness when he said, "We can hold the news services liable for such lack of understanding! They do not tell the rest of the world why there is such jealousy between the Arabs and Jews over that tiny piece of real estate. But it is, indeed, the piece of property over which all Middle-Eastern conflict arises!"

David shrugged. "I am certainly vague on it all!" he confessed. "I thought most of the squabbles were over the Palestinians being edged out of their ancient territory."

The rabbis were not surprised at this admission, but Diamant's blood began to boil. "Of course!" he exclaimed. "That is all you have been told. But tell me, where will the Jews live, if there is no Israel? The Palestinians now own Bethlehem and Hebron, and will not be satisfied until they own all of Jerusalem, to make it *their* capital, not ours! The Arab world stretches from India to Libya, and from Bosnia to the Sudan! Do they really need more of the speck of dust that the world conceded to the victims of the Holocaust? Why doesn't CNN show a map sometime?"

Rabbi Benjamin placed a calming hand on Diamant's shoulder, then turned to David. "Dr. Rothmeyer," Horace said, "we did not expect to speak of such things today. But perhaps it is good we are doing so. After all, everything we are about relates to the bigger picture."

David nodded gravely. "I would say 'relates' is an understatement. I would say that the minute you and your agency set foot on Mount Moriah to build anything, it could spark—"

He shuddered, and Rabbi Benjamin filled in, "World War Three? Yes, David, we hear this objection every day!"

The professor was speechless, his body tingling with fear. At last, finding his voice, he observed, "I do not recall discussing any of this with the committee. It must seem strange to you that this has not hit home with me before. But do you really think I want to be part of something with such horrific international ramifications?"

Hearing this, Rabbi Diamant glared at David and then at Rabbi Benjamin. "You told me he was a secular Jew, Horace. But you didn't tell me he was against us!" he spat. In a huff, he turned on his heel, as though to leave.

"Shalom!" Horace pleaded, grabbing the curator by the arm. "Be patient! Put yourself in Dr. Rothmeyer's place. He has not been as close as we are to all of this. Now that his eyes are opening, we must expect this reaction!"

Not for the first time, David was observing Rabbi Ben's peacemaking abilities. This time, however, the professor himself was on the receiving end of the rabbi's diplomacy.

Diamant calmed enough to turn around and faced David with doubtful eyes, while Horace focused on the professor's concerns. "Please don't be hasty in your conclusions, Dr. Rothmeyer," he said. "Although you are not part of our 'orthodox' camp, I trust you do have a heart for Israel, or you would never have come with us this far."

The tightness in David's chest eased a little, and his hands, which had been balled up in fists, loosened.

He took a deep breath. "I suppose that is true," he admitted. "But this whole aspect of things does give me pause. . . . "

Benjamin nodded. "And so it should," he said. "We would not want you to be part of our efforts, if you took them lightly. It is good that you see the larger implications so that, if you proceed, it is with full understanding."

David might have asked why that "full understanding" had not been shared with him earlier. He knew, though, as they probably did, that if it had been, he never would have signed on.

Rabbi Benjamin was not one to preach, but his next words did prick David's conscience. "Dr. Rothmeyer, we looked long and hard for a man of your stature. We do feel God led us to you. Won't you at least see the rest of the exhibit, meet a few more people? And try to do so with the eyes of faith. Then, if you still feel you made a mistake . . . we will understand."

David looked around the display area. "I can do that," he replied, his voice smaller than he intended.

Rabbi Diamant reacted stiffly, obviously not certain that he wanted to spend more time with this heretic. But Benjamin, grasping the curator by the elbow, gave him a look that convinced him to go on.

"This way," Diamant said, his tone clipped.

Directing David to a display of musical instruments, he stood beside a dark wooden stand on which several silver trumpets were arrayed. Returning to his role as guide, the curator said, "You will note that these items are patterned on instruments shown in the Arch of Titus, which we saw earlier. The arch shows the slaves hauling off instruments just like these." Beside the trumpets were gleaming, handcrafted harps of fine Israeli hardwoods, small enough to be carried but large enough to produce an impressive sound, as Diamant demonstrated, running his hands across a set of strings.

Gesturing to the trumpets and harps, he said, "Hundreds of these instruments are being constructed for the use of the musicians in the new temple courts. Four thousand of these wonderful harps are being made, even as we speak, for the use of the temple choristers, the Levites."

Despite his perplexity, David could not help but be impressed, once again, by the craftsmanship and scholarship of the consortium.

He followed Diamant into another room, where they stood before a display of garments to be worn by the priests in the court. Diamant explained that hundreds of such garments were being made. In one corner of the room stood a huge computerized loom and a spinning wheel for the making of thread. The difficult pattern called for in the robe, headdress, belt, and pants of the priestly garb was based on ancient writings, and Diamant explained that the only weavers who seemed capable of reproducing it were from a Native American tribe.

"Research is still underway," he said, "for the identification of the precious stones of the high priest's breastplate, the twelve of which are meant to represent the twelve tribes of Israel."

It was as David stood in this room, where a faceless mannequin wore the first attempt at the reproduction of the high priest's garments, that he suddenly experienced something for which he had no name.

Only moments ago, he had been ready to run from this entire assignment. Fear, confusion, and anger had gripped him. Now, something beyond emotion filled his heart. Perhaps it was that brush with the divine, which mystics call "revelation," or perhaps only the jolt of facts coming together, so that, in one bullet of time, the meaning of his life was condensed, readable, foreseeable.

Whatever it was, it made his hair stand on end, for it relayed to him, in terms nothing short of supernatural, an interpretation of all the strange events that had befallen him since receiving the letter in Columbus.

Above the display of the priestly garments was a sign quoting the words of a traditional Jewish prayer: "Return priests to their service and Levites to their songs and music, and return the people of Israel to pleasant places, and there we will ascend and be seen and bow down before you."

David was mesmerized. Long and hard he studied the words, letting them sink into his bewildered heart, as they had already blazed through his spirit.

"Return priests to their service and Levites to their songs . . . "

Right there, in black and white, was the purpose for which he had been hired by the consortium. He, David Rothmeyer, bored professor of Central American antiquities, lonely widower, sorely empty of faith of any kind . . . *he* had been singled out of humanity to find the Keeper of the Temple's flame, the one who would govern all that went on in the only-dreamed-of Holy Place.

Why? he wondered. *Why me?* Surely he did not merit such a calling! Surely, he had never even believed in such things!

"Dr. Rothmeyer," a voice jolted him. "Dr. Rothmeyer, we have more to show you."

David looked into Rabbi Benjamin's smiling face, sensing his empathy.

"Are you ready for another glimpse of eternity?" Horace asked.

David's knees were shaky. "Stay beside me, Rabbi," he said softly. "I am not used to walking on streets of gold!"

CHAPTER 19

Shalom Diamant and Horace Benjamin led David briskly through a narrow back corridor of the consortium exhibit. According to a sign over the hall's entrance, they had left the public area and were now entering into the institute's private offices. Little cubbyholes, marked "Consortium Administrator" and "Secretary," were empty of people. David figured the administrator's office belonged to Rabbi Diamant. They passed a small room labeled Staff Lounge, where a pot of coffee sent off a stale aroma.

At last, they descended another small flight of stairs, which took them briefly outside to a lovely flowered patio whose high wall blocked a view of the Western Wall courtyard. Leading back into the basement of the institute was an open doorway, from which could be heard low voices.

"Step this way," Diamant directed the professor.

David, taller than anyone else here, ducked into the entrance and found himself in a long room full of workers seated at tables lined with computers. Flickering screens jumbled with words and images, nimble fingers flying over keyboards, contrasted strangely with piles of ancient books and the musty smell of deteriorating scrolls.

"What is this?" he asked, more amazed than ever.

"This is our research room," Diamant said.

Leading him toward one work station, he introduced David to a young colleague who was probably still of yeshiva age, his face not yet bearded, though he probably coaxed his peach fuzz each morning. Bushy tendrils of hair groomed into side-curls laced the edge of his face, and a small, crocheted yarmulke covered ample hair where in older fellows a bald spot might be hidden.

"This is Samuel Goldstein," Diamant said. "Samuel, meet Dr. Rothmeyer."

The young scholar pushed his chair back and thrust out a hand never hardened by outdoor work. "Glad to meet you, Dr. Rothmeyer," he said with a smile. "We have been waiting for you to come."

At this, about a dozen young men, ranging in age from mid-teens to thirties, stopped working and smiled at him. Several of them wore thick glasses, possibly the result of years before back-lit screens.

David nodded to them, and Diamant said, "Samuel is our chief computer guru, but all these fellows are indispensable."

Samuel smiled again, a blush bringing color to his pale cheeks.

"Sam," Diamant directed, "can you bring up a page of the floor plan?"

"Sure," Samuel replied, and with lightning speed, his deft fingers tickled the keyboard, scrolling through several screens and menus until he came to one boldly headed "Master Plan/Temple Layout."

David had seen such programs on computer screens in deluxe hardware and home-supply stores in Columbus. He had never owned a home but found the displays, usually in the kitchen-cabinet section, fascinating to watch.

Samuel ran the cursor around the courts of the computerized blueprint, clicking here and there to enlarge various chambers.

"Here we are," he said with a chuckle, "standing in the Holy of Holies!"

David grinned broadly, and Rabbi Horace nudged him. "Enjoy it this way, David. No one except the high priest will ever enter the real thing."

David remembered his synagogue school teacher showing the class a layout of the temple on a flannel-graph when he was about seven years old. He remembered how the teacher had emphasized that in the times of the temple, the inner chamber beyond the Holy Place, the Holiest of the Holies, was visited only once a year, on the Day of Atonement. On that day, the high priest entered by himself, after going through intricate ritual cleansings, and there he offered up prayers for the sins of the people.

If that priest had even so much as a sinful thought when occupying the sacred room, he could die in an instant. No one would be able to go in after him, for the Ark of the Covenant and the Glory of God resided there. For that reason, he wore bells on the fringes of his robe so that the people outside could hear his movements. If the bells were silent, they would know that he had collapsed. For that eventuality, he also wore long cords on his garment, which trailed behind him beneath the curtain that separated the sanctuary from the adjacent court. Lesser priests could pull his dead body out from the chamber by means of those cords.

"But," the synagogue school teacher had said, "we have no record of this ever being necessary. The high priests must have been quite holy indeed."

All of this flashed through David's head in a second of remembrance, just as much of his childhood had returned to him during his work with the consortium.

"I don't see the Ark of the Covenant," he observed, leaning close over Samuel's shoulder. "Shouldn't it be in the center?"

Samuel glanced up at him. "We are looking at a rendering of

Herod's temple," he said. "So far as we have been able to determine, there was no Ark present at that time."

David stood up and shrugged. "Of course," he said. "I saw *Indiana Jones!* The Ark was taken to Africa, right?"

The rabbis grinned, and the young scholars laughed. "You believe the movies?" Diamant said, his tone once more challenging. "Surely you are too much a scholar for that!"

David's face grew red. "Well, where *is* the Ark? Does anyone know? Will you have it in your new temple?"

Horace sensed David's embarrassment and stepped in again to cover for his handpicked professor. "Of course, the Ark of the Covenant is not Dr. Rothmeyer's specialty, Shalom. Let's not be hard on him. From what we've seen of David's work, if we were to assign him to the quest for the Ark, he would find it in short order!"

Again the roomful of computer jockeys chuckled. But this time, they were more respectful.

David's face was still red, not because he was ignorant regarding the Ark, but because he doubted he deserved Rabbi Benjamin's glowing endorsement.

Shalom continued. "Speaking of your work, Professor—assuming you will be staying on—you will be collaborating closely with our staff here."

No one could miss Diamant's sarcastic tone. The young men did not know what was behind it, but Horace glared at Diamant, and the curator backed down.

Leading the professor about the room, from work station to work station, Diamant continued. "The consortium utilizes cutting-edge technology in all of its research for the coming temple. Architects and engineers feed data from the Talmud and other ancient writings into our data banks, to prepare these blueprints, the clothing designs you saw upstairs, the formulas for the dyes, the identity of the metals and precious stones for such things as the priestly vestments, and so on.

"We have been fortunate," Diamant explained, "to have the help of experts from all over the world in setting up our data bases and keeping current with the best programs for our work."

He had brought David to the last work station, this one larger than all the others, and staffed by three men, each with his own computer. "Gentlemen," he said, "meet Dr. Rothmeyer. David, you will be working especially closely with these young men, for they are sorting Jewish genealogies from all over the world."

One by one, the staffers shook David's hand, introducing themselves as Clement, James, and Shofar.

David was not one to categorize people, but if he had seen these fellows on any street corner in the world, in any café or on any bus, he would have pegged them instantly as computer nerds. Complete with horn-rimmed glasses, pocket protectors, and rumpled shirts, they fit the image of the classic lost-in-cyberspace soul, though distinguished by their side-curls and yarmulkes.

Their work station was cluttered and old paper coffee cups and bagel wrappers were strewn about. But David had been around enough of such fellows at the university to know that those trappings could be the sign of sheer genius.

"Glad to meet you, Dr. Rothmeyer," they said, almost in unison.

"These fellows have been following your work with more than cursory interest," Diamant said. "What we want to do now is begin to feed the findings you have compiled into the work they have been doing on current family lines."

Clement, who headed the team, joined in. "Dr. Rothmeyer—"

"Call me David," the professor offered. Then, glancing sideways at Diamant, he added, "Since we *are* going to work so closely, let's not be formal."

Clement nodded appreciatively. "David," he said, "do you read the *Jerusalem Post?*"

"I guess I have been a lax patriot," David confessed. "Until I came to Israel, I rarely saw a copy."

"Well then," Clement replied, "you might not be aware that, for years, the agency has run ads in the international edition asking Jews to send the names and family information of any Cohens they might know of. We have been compiling this information into our data banks, and now literally have millions of names, both living and dead of the Cohen line, in our computer library. As we follow up on the leads, we are also able to create family trees, going quite far back."

Now Shofar jumped in. "You might be surprised at how many amateur genealogists there are out there. Among Jews, genealogy is quite popular, because we are so anxious to reconstruct our lost history and create a feeling of roots for ourselves."

"Yes," James added, his small dark eyes even smaller behind his thick lenses, "did you know there's even a site on the Internet specifically for Jewish genealogy? We have found all of this to be of enormous help."

Rabbi Benjamin joined in. "Of course, not all of the genealogy information we receive is applicable to the high priest. But we also need hundreds of qualified personnel to fill the lesser priestly stations in the temple courts. Any information we receive on the Cohen families is useful to that end."

David shook his head. "I was not aware of any of this work," he replied. "It sounds fantastic! So, how does my research add to yours?"

Clement explained, "What we have lacked was a scholar who had the breadth of your linguistic background. All of us here are knowledgeable in Hebrew, and some of us know a smattering of Greek and Aramaic, though those studies are confined mainly to the Septuagint and related writings. When it comes to the plethora of languages with which you are knowledgeable, we are in the dark."

Clement rubbed his chin hairs. "In fact, Dr. Rothmeyer, there are not even computer programs to aid us when it comes to some of the ancient, lost languages of the Diaspora. Judaized Syriac, for instance, or barbarized Roman Latin—where would we ever come up with such things?"

Horace beamed behind David, taking in this praise as though it were his own. "So," he said, leaning around the professor, "you see why you were chosen? Your education and experience have singled you out."

As Rabbi Benjamin gave this endorsement, Rabbi Diamant was steely jawed. When Horace saw this, he nudged him in the ribs.

"Uh, your ethnicity also qualifies you," the curator muttered.

David, heedless of this interaction, was caught up in his own thoughts. He felt as if he were standing on the edge of a high precipice. "So, now you are ready to begin meshing the information I have researched, in the hopes of finding links that may lead us forward to—" The professor stopped, awed by the concept.

"To lead us to the right one," Horace filled in. "To the one who should be priest!"

David felt another tingle cross his shoulders, just as he had felt upstairs when he stood before the display of priestly vestments. It seemed inevitable that he should have come to Jerusalem. Despite all misgivings, he found himself irrevocably drawn to this project.

"I guess I never realized that my background was so unique," he marveled. "I've been engrossed in Mayan and Aztec studies so long, I never thought of applying such knowledge to my own heritage."

He paused and fought that thrill again. "Or to the future of my people."

CHAPTER 20

Two evenings later, David sat on the veranda of his thousand-year-old house, looking over the Hinnom Valley, which paralleled the Old City's southern wall.

Except for Anya, the housekeeper, who was in her own apartment, David was alone in the medieval building. Rabbi Benjamin was spending the night, as he often did, at the consortium's yeshiva, a seminary where young Cohens were trained for priestly duties.

The sun was just setting, casting a coral glow across the modern high-rise hotels and clustered apartment houses of the opposite ridge. Beautiful as the contemporary buildings were, they lacked the character of the Old City, but they were nonetheless a part of the history of Jerusalem, exemplifying the growth and the youthful spirit that typified the modern state of Israel.

One of David's favorite parts of Jerusalem was the section that lay between the high-rises and the Old City wall, leading up from the Valley Hinnom to the new section. It was an artists' colony, full of studios and shops, its quaint buildings of yellow brick and stone terracing the hillside between ribbons of flowered gardens.

Over a century old, it had a noble history, for it represented the first Zionist attempt to develop a residential area beyond the city walls. The brave little village had been named Yemen Moshe, after Moshe Montefiore, a wealthy European Jew who poured much finance and personal risk into the dream of an Israeli homeland. Despite its hopeful beginning, however, it quickly met with failure, as wandering bands of Bedouin marauders made life for its inhabitants impossible. Creeping back inside the Old City walls, the dreamers gave up Yemen Moshe but never abandoned the dream of Israel.

A testament to the courage of those pioneers, Yemen Moshe had left its mark on the landscape. One of its most prominent buildings stood in sharp contrast to the fortresslike architecture of the many conquerors and cultures that had defined the look of Jerusalem. A windmill, used for the grinding of grain in that early colony, stood witness to the influence of those nineteenth-century Europeans, its charm lending permanent testimony to the melting pot of domesticity that was the Israel of the returning Jews.

David feasted on the beauty of the hillside village as sunset pulled a crimson brush across its canvas. But when he looked over the Hinnom Valley, he also thought about less romantic periods of Jewish history.

Valley Hinnom, meaning "Valley of the Children," was so named for the atrocities that had scarred it. In the times of ancient Canaan, worship of Molech, god of the pagan natives, had been observed there. This worship involved the sacrifice of children upon huge bonfires on the valley terraces. With the snuffing out of those young lives, generations of potential Jewish families had been sacrificed in that valley, just as surely as they had been extinguished by the German Holocaust.

It was a sad part of Israel's story that she often took up the practices of her neighbors and forgot the laws of Moses and the warnings of her prophets.

Sometimes, when David sat there of an evening, looking over this haunting view, he could almost imagine he heard the cries of those little souls as they entered the fire.

And then, there were other stories that fit exactly with the view he loved.

One of those was a story of another David, the great king for whom so many Jewish men, himself included, were named. The tale went that King David used to walk upon the rooftop of his palace when the nights were warm. Situated farther to the east and just below Temple Mount, on a parallel with David's residence, the king's palace commanded a view quite similar to that which the professor enjoyed.

One evening, as the king walked there, his eyes fell upon a beautiful woman bathing, as was the custom, in a bathing tent, upon a distant rooftop. Just how much of her loveliness he was privy to, no one could say, but it was sufficient to set his soul on fire with desire.

The legend of David and Bathsheba was one of the most well known in Jewish and biblical lore—how he had sent for the woman, lying with her despite the fact that she was a married woman, wife of one of his best soldiers; how she had become pregnant with his child; how David had summoned her husband, Uriah, home from the warfront in the hopes he would lie with his wife and claim the child as his own; how the valiant Uriah would have none of such luxury when his comrades were in danger; and how, at last, fearing exposure, David had sent the man to the front lines of the battle, fully expecting him to die.

King David, having added murder to adultery, spent much of his remaining life paying for his sins. But ultimately, Bathsheba, whom he took as wife, gave birth to Solomon, the king who would build the temple and bring Israel to the position of a world power.

From pondering the mystery that was Israel, the professor's thoughts turned to his work. He had just spent a full day entering his long paper of family trees on several computer disks, with a genealogy program provided by the Consortium. The next day he would take the disks to the institute, where Clement and the others would begin weaving it into their own findings. Although he was exhausted from his work, he was excited to begin the intermeshing of the separate researches. As much as he loved the history of Israel, he was also fascinated with its future.

Would they actually be able to pinpoint a single individual after all their work was done? Such a dream seemed very unrealistic. Yet, David knew that in this age of global communication, computerized language, and the ability to trace the most minute movement of people and events, it was just possible that they could succeed.

Still, there were great gaps that they might never be able to fill. One of the major obstacles was the Holocaust period. Even if they could say with some certainty that the line of the high priest could be defined through the eons previous, that period alone had produced a chasm in recorded knowledge that might never be bridged.

David closed his eyes and found his heart whispering something like a prayer. For the professor, this was a new experience. He had not truly prayed for years.

Even when his wife had died, he had not been able to pray. His heart had been too broken, his spirit too dark, to believe in anything. Now, however, he found himself thinking of the future in a new way.

And he thought of himself differently. He had a purpose and a work that was important, though he did not fully understand it. He had a growing sense of wonder in everything he did, in every new encounter.

"God, guide us," he whispered. "If you are really out there, if you really have a stake in all this Israel stuff . . . well, just help us out."

For such an educated man, for such a man of the world as David considered himself to be, he felt quite inept as he prayed. Though he could sort through tomes of ancient languages and deduce reams of genealogy—though he was a *linguist*, of all things!—he had a difficult time finding the right words when it came to prayer.

Opening his eyes, he shot a glance heavenward, like a little boy, wondering if anyone had heard him. He believed that, somehow, he *had* been heard. And he felt good.

Well, back to work, he thought, as he turned to the laptop computer on the patio table. Being single, he kept late hours and did some of his best work at night.

As he clicked a key, engaging the screen's backlight, something caught his eye on the roadway that hemmed the Old City wall, the highway that ran through the Hinnom Valley.

A taxi was just pulling up to let a passenger out at the foot of the wide stone walkway that led from the road to the Jaffa Gate. David watched as the occupant emerged from the cab.

Long-haired and lovely, a woman of about his own age stood beside the taxi, fumbling through her shoulder bag for change to pay the driver. The cabbie was opening the trunk and pulling out a single travel bag.

David noted that she almost grabbed the bag from the driver, as though she did not want him handling it. Mostly, though, he noticed her loveliness.

Smiling, he considered the fact that this was no bathing beauty on a housetop, but he had a fresh appreciation for just what that ancient monarch might have felt that long ago night. This woman was beautiful, as Bathsheba surely must have been. Though David had no power to summon her, he would have if he could.

Through the soft night air, it was actually possible to make out the words spoken below. At first, the professor figured his fantasies were playing tricks on him when he heard the woman speak his name. Leaning over the balcony, he listened closely to the quick conversation that passed between the driver and his fare.

"Dr. Rothmeyer?" he heard the man say after the woman had paid him. "I have no idea, lady. As for any temple agency, that is located in the heart of town."

The woman held out a scrap of paper and looked up the walkway toward Jaffa Gate.

"But I was given this address. You say this is the closest entrance to reach that street?"

"That's right, lady," the cabbie said. "But you won't find any consortium there. Not that I know of."

The woman looked very tired. She thanked the driver and began walking up the ramp.

"Sorry, lady," he called after her. "I would drive you there"—he gestured toward his old Mercedes—"but the streets are just too narrow."

The woman waved back to him. "That's all right," she called. "I'll find it."

"The streets are quite safe," the driver added, "but don't linger."

David knew he had heard his name. Who in the world was this woman, and why was she coming to see him?

"Just one more of your many mysteries," he muttered, speaking to the spirit of Jerusalem, from whom he had come to expect surprises.

Suddenly it occurred to him that he had not put on a fresh shirt that day. He rushed to the bathroom, smoothed his hair, and splashed cold water on his face, then hurried to his closet for a nice pullover.

If Bathsheba was coming to visit, David would be ready.

CHAPTER 21

David listened from the doorway of his apartment as Anya answered a buzz from the front gate. After dusk, the gate to the residence was always locked, and so the woman who had come from the cab could not approach the main door.

The cavernlike corridor that led down several flights of steps, past private rooms, the kitchen, and the parlor, to the main entrance, acted like a megaphone, sending Anya's voice through the multistoried house.

"Who is it?" she inquired over an intercom.

"Hello," the woman replied. "I am a visitor from the United States. I have come to see Professor David Rothmeyer."

Anya, obviously protective of her house and its occupants, hesitated. "It's quite late, Miss," she said, in her broken English. "You come back tomorrow?"

There was a long pause before the woman answered, "I was told I could find help here. I was sent by Dr. Kenneth Aronstam, of Midwest University. He is a friend of Dr. Rothmeyer. Is it possible to at least speak with the professor?"

At the mention of Ken Aronstam, David jolted.

Who this could be and what she wanted, he had no idea. But if she knew Ken, David could not turn her away.

Rushing down the stairs, he called, "Anya, it's all right. I'll speak with her. Let her in."

The housekeeper shrugged and turned aside, letting David press the button that deactivated the gate lock.

"Hello," David called over the intercom. "This is Professor Rothmeyer. Come in. Meet me in the lobby."

Within seconds, the beautiful creature whom he had admired from the veranda was standing in his house. Obviously tired and looking a bit overwhelmed, the woman put out her hand and said with a sigh, "Dr. Rothmeyer, I'm so glad to find you. I just arrived in Israel today from Columbus. I took a bus and then a cab from Tel Aviv. I hope I am not imposing."

David shook her hand, looking her over carefully. "You were sent by Ken Aronstam?" he repeated.

"Yes," she said. Then, flustered, she added, "I'm sorry. I didn't introduce myself. My name is Clarissa Aronstam. I am Ken's cousin. Most people call me Honey."

"And what brings you to Israel?" he asked. In a fleeting deduction, he knew it had to be more than tourism that would send a woman straight to his door on the day she entered the country.

Honey set her travel bag on the floor, and David could see the weariness in her face, more weariness than would be produced even by a long plane flight and jet lag.

"Now it's my turn to apologize," he said. "Here, let me take your bag." He bent over to pick it up, but Honey grabbed it as if it were gold—just as she had earlier, David thought.

He straightened and gestured to her to follow him. "Anya," he directed, "please fetch Ms. Aronstam some tea."

The plump housekeeper looked the visitor over suspiciously, then hastened toward the kitchen.

"Honey, is it?" David said. "Why don't you come sit in the parlor? You must be very tired from your trip."

"Thank you," Honey said and followed him back up the hall.

The parlor of the great old house was always cool. The massive stone walls kept all heat at bay, so there was always a fire burning in the hearth.

"Have a seat," David offered.

Honey chose a large armchair but did not really relax. She perched on the edge of the cushion, tightly holding on to the handle of her travel bag.

As Anya came bustling in, setting a tray of tea and cookies on the footstool, David poked the embers of the fire, then sat across from the woman, trying not to stare. She was, indeed, quite beautiful, even more so in the glow of the firelight.

It had been years since David had given any woman more than passing scrutiny. Ever since Susan's death, he had believed the part of himself that needed a woman had died with her.

"So," he said, trying to think in strictly friendly terms, "are you in Jerusalem for business or pleasure?"

Honey bit her lower lip and watched the fire. "Neither," she said softly.

She seemed to be on the verge of tears.

"Dr. Rothmeyer—" she said, taking a big breath.

"Call me Dave," he interrupted.

"Dave," she complied, "I must seem very peculiar. Actually, I am quite harmless. But I am not here as a tourist, and I have no real business. Actually—"

She paused, and her shoulders shook. "Actually, my cousin sent me to Israel to get me out of a scrape."

David studied her, a bemused expression on his face. What could Ken mean, sending a troubled woman to him? Whatever Honey's problem, Ken must have realized David would have no time to serve as rescuer.

He sat forward and poured her a cup of tea, then handed it to her as he pondered how to respond. "I don't understand," he said. "Did Ken think I could help you?"

Honey smiled wanly. "I believe he thought Israel could help me—you know—in some grand sense of destiny. . . . " She shook her head. "Oh, I don't know! Ken didn't know either. But he said my problem put him in mind of what had brought you here. And he said I'd be safe here."

David was more bewildered than ever, and Honey could see she had only confused him.

"Truly, Dr. Rothmeyer—Dave," she went on, "I am as puzzled by all of this as you must be. I never dreamed I would come to Israel. But then I never dreamed half the things that have happened to me in the last few months!"

Now this sounded familiar. It echoed feelings the professor had had many times since receiving the Consortium letter. His life had taken turns he did not even know were possible, and he still did not know what they were all about.

"Let me get this straight," he said, rubbing his chin. "Something happened to you in the States that Ken believed warranted your coming to Israel? Ken actually sent you here and gave you my address?"

"That's right," she replied. "He made the flight arrangements. Even put it on his own credit card!"

David shook his head. "You *must* have been in trouble!" he joked, knowing that his friend was tight with money.

"It's a long story," Honey said with a sigh. "He wanted to call you, but thought it best if I just showed up unannounced. He thought it would be safer."

David noticed the woman seemed to shiver, though the room was warm enough, and she cradled her teacup in her hands as though thankful for its heat. Suddenly he read more than exhaustion or bewilderment in her eyes. He read fear, an emotion he had experienced in connection with this assignment only once, the day he sat in the airport in New York, awaiting his hosts. It had shot through him when he observed the Arab with the raspy, hate-filled voice telling his little boy that Jews were "the enemy."

For the first time in his life, in that moment, he had experienced ethnic fear. Whatever Honey was afraid of, her look of intimidation reflected similar feelings.

Reaching out and patting her hand, he said, "I can tell that what you need right now is rest. Whatever has brought you here, you are a friend of my best friend. We can talk about all of this in the morning."

Honey blinked back tears and nodded with relief.

As she finished her tea, the professor went to fetch the housekeeper again. "Anya," he called, "please make up a room for Ms. Aronstam. She will be staying the night."

Late the next morning, David was sitting on the veranda, making entries in his laptop computer for yet another disk that he would take to the institute, when Honey appeared. He was pleased that she looked somewhat refreshed. Though it was always a tough transition to change time zones, it appeared she had slept quite well, possibly assured of her safety for the time being.

"Good morning!" he greeted her, pulling up a seat at the table. "I was just about to have some breakfast. Won't you join me?"

"Yes, thank you," Honey said as she sat down.

David could not help but notice how radiant she was in a bright yellow dress, her face aglow in the sunlight.

He quickly shuffled his papers into a file folder and, knowing he should not be too trusting, turned the computer screen so that only he could see its contents. After all, he did not know this woman, and he was under obligation to the committee to consider the security of his work.

In fact, he had given a lot of thought to just how generous he should be with this stranger in opening the house to her. He would learn what he could about her that morning and then decide if he should bring her business to the attention of Rabbi Benjamin. No matter what her problems were, he could not let her stay more than a day or two without the committee's approval.

Anya served them the traditional Israeli breakfast of fresh fruit, vegetables, eggs, cheese, and bread. As they ate, they chatted about inconsequential things—the weather and her plane flight.

David found himself enjoying her company and realized anew how devoid of warmth his life as a widower was. Grief had supplanted memories of human companionship, and he was surprised at how the mere presence of a young woman in his home enlivened his spirits.

Honey looked at his laptop with curiosity. "I've never had a computer," she said. "We didn't even have a TV where I came from."

David gave her a quizzical look, and she suddenly realized that he assumed she lived in Columbus.

With a laugh, she filled him in. "Oh, I didn't tell you . . . I don't live in Ohio anymore. I actually come from Montana." Then, with another laugh, she added, "Not that Montanans don't have TV. My S.O. and I don't have it where we live, but only because we choose not to."

"S.O.?" David said, again baffled.

"Significant Other," she replied. "I guess that's better than calling him 'my man,' like some of his friends would."

David processed this information quickly and was again surprised at his own reaction. Deflated, he thought, *So, she's spoken for. She has a relationship, and she's letting me know up front.*

"I guess so," he replied, trying not to sound disappointed. "So, you must live in the wilderness?"

"It would seem like wilderness to most people," she said. "Actually, there are a lot more remote places in the world, and even in Montana. But we like it there. It's quiet . . . peaceful . . . " Then, looking wistful, she added, "At least, it used to be."

David figured she was alluding to the troubles that had caused her to flee.

He felt quite awkward. He was not used to dealing with people's feelings or problems. He had had enough of his own in recent years and had found it comforting to lose himself in academics, avoiding any interaction that involved the problems of others.

After an uneasy silence, he asked, "Is that why you left? Things got bad for you in Montana?"

It took no more than this to bring tears to Honey's eyes. Fighting them, she tried to look composed. At last, she sighed, as though resigned to unburden herself. "Listen . . . ," she began, "Ken sent me to you because I told him some things that made him think my safety was at risk. He told me you are a bright guy and that, with your connections here, I might find some answers."

"Go on," the professor said.

Taking a deep breath, Honey began to pour forth her entire story—telling David about Pete, about her history with him, about the strange things he was involved with, and at last, about the old star and the crisis that had convinced Pete to send her away. By the time she reached this point, she was alternately sighing with relief, wiping away tears, and shuddering for fear of her situation.

David, overwhelmed, could only listen in amazement, questioning her when she skipped something he needed to know to help him understand. By the time she got to the part about the music box, he was leaning with both elbows on the table, chin in hands, in rapt attention.

As she dabbed at her eyes, yet one more time, he tried to make sense of the whole story. "Okay," he said, "let me see if I have this straight. Pete, and now Ken, as well, think that this little star you have may be something risky for you to own. Neither of them knows what it's about, but Pete thought it was dangerous enough to warrant your leaving home, and Ken thought it merited your coming all the way to Israel?"

Honey sighed. "Sounds crazy, I know. But it was also important enough to my great-grandfather that he went out of his way to get it out of Dachau and into my family's safekeeping for all these years. And it was his expressed wish that we would show it to no one until we could show it to a 'wise man' in Jerusalem."

David leaned back, his eyes sparking with interest. Although it appeared, from Honey's longing references to Pete, that she was not available, her story was intriguing enough to keep his interest.

"Well," he said, "I don't know that I fit requirements of the 'wise man' type your great-grandfather referred to. But I do know a lot of astute, scholarly Jews. Perhaps we could get one of them to look at it." Of course, he hoped he himself could see the little scrap of cloth that had precipitated this mystery. But he did not presume to ask for the honor.

"It's in my travel bag," Honey said. "I'd be happy to show it to you. I'm not sure what my great-grandfather meant by 'wise man,' but you have fine credentials. Ken told me so. Won't you see what you can make of it?"

David brightened. "Well, sure, if you think it's all right. Maybe I can at least help you with the language."

Honey was up and to the door of the veranda before he quit speaking. In a flash, she returned with a large manila envelope. She sat down, shuffled through the manila envelope, then drew out an old letter and placed it on the table.

"Before I left Columbus, I went by my aunt's house. She still lives next door to where I grew up and has some of my family things in storage. I dug through my dad's old papers and found this letter from the Red Cross."

She pushed it toward him. "The star was wrapped inside when the family got it."

David opened the letter and quickly perused the note. It was written on letterhead with the logo of the British Red Cross. It related the same story Honey had given, of the old rabbi and his wish that the star reach his family. "Rabbi Yitzak Aronstam wishes you to keep this private," the note said, "until you can show it to a 'wise man' in Jerusalem.

"At your service," the note ended, and was signed, "Emily McCurdy, R.N."

David glanced up at his guest, handing her the letter. "Did your family ever meet this Nurse McCurdy?" he asked.

"No," Honey said. "As far as I know, we've just done as she said, and left it at that. I have no idea if she's even still living."

At last, Honey brought forth the scrap of cloth and tenderly spread it out.

David's eyes widened. It was, indeed, a "Jew badge" like countless others to be seen in old photos of the period and in museums of the Holocaust.

"May I touch it?" he asked. He felt the same sort of thrill he used to get on an archaeological dig when finding a rare artifact.

"Of course," she said. "The writing is on the back."

David lifted the scrap, tingling with the knowledge that this cloth had witnessed horrors and events he had only read about. Ever so carefully, he turned the piece over, laying it again on the table, and studied the scrawls on the back.

He pushed his computer to one side, lowered the screen so that she could not see his work, then excused himself. "Let me get my magnifier," he said, and quickly ran to his apartment.

Coming back, he leaned over the table, just as the rabbis had leaned together over his long genealogy, and he peered at the cloth through the reading glass.

"The words have faded," he said, "and the substance they are written in has smudged badly. It appears to be charcoal."

Honey nodded. "I am sure he had to use a piece of charred rock or wood, don't you think?"

"They certainly wouldn't have allowed a prisoner to have a writing implement," David agreed.

Continuing to study the piece, he easily lost himself, as he always had, in the joy of such a find. "It's amazing," he said, "how well preserved this is. Considering the primitive nature of the writing tool and considering the natural degeneration of cloth, no matter how well stored. Even in only half a century, it should have blotted and absorbed the charcoal more than it has."

"The family cherished this," Honey said proudly. "Until just recently, I kept it in the safest place I could think of."

"You did well," David said.

Continuing his analysis, "The writing is indeed Hebrew—actually sort of a Yiddish version. You see, even Hebrew script varies from place to place in the Diaspora. A good paleographer, or ethnographer, could tell us exactly where your grandfather came from, by the style in which he wrote his Hebrew characters."

Honey was not sure what a paleographer or ethnographer was, but she got the general idea. "He came from Frankfurt," she said. "I always wanted to go to Germany."

By now, David was not paying much attention to Honey. He had already retreated into the comfort of his calling, having registered deep inside himself that Honey was not for him. Still, he felt a kinship with her, a mutuality based on their interest in Jewish history.

"Interesting!" he exclaimed, his breath fogging up the magnifier. Standing up, he looked at her quizzically. "This cloth seems to refer to some location, perhaps at the death camp."

"What?" Honey asked. "What are the words?"

David leaned over the cloth again and said, "Here, write this down." He shoved a notepad and pencil her way.

The note consisted of five crimped lines. Although the writing was tiny, it was legible enough to interpret. "'Third row from the bottom,'" he read, "'back left corner, fourth brick from the end.'"

Honey wrote quickly. "What in the world?" she said. "Sounds like a treasure hunt."

David had thought the same thing but was too reserved to say so. "I doubt they had any treasures at Dachau," he said.

Honey lowered her eyes. "So, is that all?" she asked.

"No, there are two more lines. Hebrew is a kind of ancient shorthand, and it's possible to cram a lot in a small space." As he mulled over the translation, suddenly his scalp tingled and the hair on his arms stood up.

"What is it?" Honey asked, seeing his look of genuine amazement.

"I don't know what we have here!" he replied. "But I read similar words only yesterday. 'Build your house, O Lord. Return priests to their service and Israel to its House of Prayer.'"

CHAPTER 22

Pete Wester leaned back in the passenger seat of his brother's rental car, trying to sleep. He and Mel were somewhere south of Billings, Montana, in the thick of a rainstorm, driving down Interstate 90.

Little conversation had passed between them since they had turned south toward Wyoming. Once they had reached the Y in the roads at Billings, which offered the choice of traveling directly east, toward North Dakota, or turning off this way, they had relaxed a little. If anyone had been following them, unless the tracker saw their quick exit south, the chances were fairly good that the Westers had lost them at the junction.

Until that point, however, the two men had done a lot of talking, and a lot of looking over their shoulders and in the rearview mirrors.

Taking turns with the driving, they rehashed what had gone on at the meeting to which Fogarty had invited them, the one held after the campers and the dancers had gone to their campsites and bedrolls. That meeting had revealed things to them, secrets that Fogarty would only have shared with men whom he believed to be True Aryans, things too fearsome to speak in public or within earshot of anyone who was of doubtful allegiance.

Even as the two brothers spoke of it in private, within the cocoon of the car, they sometimes hesitated, as though ears beneath the car or in the bushes that rushed past the windows, might hear them.

Pete and Mel were on the run.

The meeting of Fogarty, Monte Altmeyer, and their stooges had lasted until the wee hours. The Westers, captives of Freemen hospitality within Pete's own domain, could do nothing but play along.

For Pete, the situation had been quite troublesome. The fact was that, until only hours before, he would have been proud to be included in Fogarty's inner circle. Things had changed for him when Fogarty called him into the limelight, praising him for something he abhorred, for supposedly breaking up with Honey because she was a Jew.

As he caught Mel's look of shock and disgust in the firelight, he had suddenly seen himself for the confused, fragmented person he really was. He had known, then, that no matter what he thought to gain by joining forces with the Freemen, he would lose his soul in the process, just as surely as he had already lost the love of his life.

He would have run away with Mel that evening, on a quest for Honey, if Fogarty had not intercepted them. Instead, he and his brother had been forced to endure hours more of White Supremacist diatribe as Fogarty and his men took over the living room and held their clandestine gathering.

Unable to communicate freely with each other, the brothers had decided independently that, as soon as that group broke up, they would flee. What they had not anticipated was what they would become privy to during those hours with the brotherhood.

Monte Altmeyer, they learned, had been involved with Freemen, the KKK, and several other White Supremacist groups within the U.S. for years. As a former officer in the German army, he was a skilled military trainer, specializing in guerrilla tactics and terrorist techniques.

Something of a mercenary, he had hired himself out to terrorist groups in the Middle East and in Ireland, and now worked a circuit of militia compounds throughout the United States.

He was well known in Idaho, where he had served as a trainer at Aryan Nations survival camps. His firelight talk in Pete's front yard, the one that Mel had missed as he paced and fumed behind the house, was intended to enlist trainees for a new camp Fogarty was establishing in the hills near Montana's Canadian border.

None of this information was particularly shocking or disconcerting for Mel and Pete. It was not until Fogarty and the German began alluding to certain activities instigated or orchestrated by Altmeyer, activities that had been spin-offs of the camps, that the brothers realized just what they were dealing with.

Pete had brought Fogarty and his friends their second pitcher of beer when the more sensitive information began to emerge. The warm fire and the liberating effect of alcohol led them from speaking in general terms about the greatness of their cause to recounting memories of their favorite feats. They went from horror stories of abuses by the Internal Revenue Service to reminiscences of their own clever tax evasions; from stories of playground skirmishes to tales of skinhead rumbles they had participated in; and finally, from tales belittling "subhuman" races, to accounts of beatings, lynchings, cross-burnings, and church burnings.

At last, as the night wore on and they felt embraced by camaraderie, they filled Mel and Pete in on some of their more daring escapades.

In the gloom of the rain-streaked highway, as he pretended to sleep, Pete shivered, recalling the first mention of Oklahoma City and the Murrah Building. Even now, after he and his brother had gone over and over what they heard, it was hard to believe they had hosted murderers in their midst.

Yes, Altmeyer had been involved in the Oklahoma City bombing! Not directly, not hands on, but he had been one of the masterminds of the coup. It was an awful, chilling fact that Monte Altmeyer had helped plan the disaster from its inception. In fact, he claimed to have conceived of the idea, though there were others who challenged him for that credit.

Woven between these proud confessions was the fact that the ones whom juries had convicted of direct responsibility for the "most horrible crime ever perpetrated on American soil" were actually only naive pawns of greater minds. Certainly not innocent of all involvement, the two who had been pinned by the courts as the primary criminals had only been shoved to the forefront by Altmeyer and other comrades, left to take the rap for actions beyond their own scope or ability.

However, even these revelations had not come close to the horror of the next disclosure. Pete's stomach knotted each time he thought about it. The federal government and state agencies close to the crime had actually managed to strong-arm the courts into denying the defense that would have brought forth evidence of higher responsibility. The two convicted saps who believed they were serving some grand cause, however misled, had been betrayed, not only by their own patrons, but by the governments who were supposed to protect the public.

In fact, for reasons that Pete still didn't understand, it appeared that the government and the Militia, as well as the government and the terrorists, were actually unlikely accomplices.

Pete had never loved the government. From his hippie days until now, he had held the Feds and the state suspect of all sorts of complicity with evil. What he had not realized, until just hours ago, was that the ones he admired, the ones who were supposed to be undermining that establishment, were in league with that very establishment!

And in that one sweeping encounter in the living room of his own home, Pete had also begun to see that the Militia honchos visiting the property were only one tiny link in a network that spanned the globe!

Pete, eyes still closed, could see himself now, sitting on the porch of his handcrafted home, behaving just as naively as the two convicted dupes must have behaved, as he took radio messages and faithfully passed them on to Fogarty. He cringed, now, to think what those messages might have contained, couched in code and transcribed by his ignorant hand to bring about who-knew-what.

As the boasting Fogarty and Altmeyer let their tongues wag on, they had actually revealed that the direct, hands-on perpetrators of the Oklahoma City bombing had been foreign. The public had been kept oblivious to the fact that witnesses at the Murrah Building that fateful day had observed men of Middle-Eastern appearance drive that bomb-laden van into the parking lot. Furthermore, government agents had apparently been aware that some atrocity was being plotted, for they had shown up hours beforehand, making a cursory "inspection" of the grounds and the building with bomb-sniffing dogs.

Fogarty and Altmeyer had chuckled together over the blindness of "the people," citizens whom the Militia were supposedly trying to help with their antigovernment activity, citizens who dumbly took whatever came forth from government memos and from the press as "truth," citizens represented by the 168 who had died that horrific day!

It was the middle of the night before the men grew weary of boasting. Before they crept off to bedrolls strewn about the floor of Pete's living room, they had made oblique references to "other victories," but they had not gone into the details.

Pete and Mel, disappearing upstairs to their beds in the loft, were left to surmise what other ghastly secrets, what other plots, had been set into motion by the network.

Unlike the men downstairs, Pete and Mel had not gone to

sleep. Pete, creeping into Mel's room, had waited with him until they heard the sounds of snoring. Together, they had crammed a few clothes and necessities into one backpack, then climbed out the loft window to the back porch roof, jumped to the ground, and skirted the yard to Mel's car.

They were not much surprised when Willard and Crossley, again playing the role of sentinels, stopped them in the shadows.

"Fogarty and the crew need more beer," Pete explained. "We're going into Thompson Falls. There's an all-night market there. Is there a problem?"

Giving an unspoken dare, he rolled his eyes toward the house as though to say, *If you doubt us, go interrupt Fogarty's meeting.*

"Why both of you?" Crossley asked, eyeing them suspiciously.

"Well, Mel's car is near the edge of the yard," Pete replied. "I guess we could wake up all the campers to move their rigs, so I could get my pickup."

"Can't you take the car without the cop?"

Pete shrugged, pretending to think this over, while Mel jumped in, "Can't do that, boys. It's my rental."

Crossley sneered. "'Course! Wouldn't wanna strain the rules, eh, Top Cop?"

"I suppose Mel could go by himself," Pete suggested coyly. "I'm sure you can trust one of the LAPD to return if he says he will."

Willard looked very perplexed, but Crossley gave a warning pose and shook his finger at them.

"Okay, boys," he said. "But just see that you *do* come back. Hear?"

Pete gave a flippant salute, and Mel headed for the car.

Just as Pete turned to follow, Crossley growled. "Hold it!" He nodded toward the backpack. "Watcha need that for, if yer comin' back?"

Pete looked bemused. "This?" he said, pulling his pack off his shoulder. "Just returning some empties. Need all the cash I can get."

Willard stood behind a scowling Crossley with his arms crossed, but neither of the toughs made a move to stop the brothers as they piled into the car.

Once Pete and Mel were away from the property, they had breathed a little easier.

Mel's first words, after they reached the main road were, "Well, where do you suppose Honey is?"

Pete had already given this much thought. "I have a hunch she would have gone to stay with friends in Cheyenne. She kept in close touch with a couple who moved there from the valley. She's never contacted me, but I think that's a likely bet."

"Maybe you could call and see if she's there," Mel suggested.

Pete thought that was not such a good idea. "I'm probably the last person she wants to hear from," he said sadly. "Besides, if we give notice that we're coming, she might just hightail it. Once we get there, maybe someone can tell us if she's moved on."

"What about Ohio?" Mel asked. "Wasn't she from there originally?"

"Yeah," Pete said, "but there's not much family there anymore. Her folks are both dead, and she didn't have any brothers or sisters."

"Okay," Mel agreed, putting his foot to the gas, "Wyoming it is!"

After speeding down the highway, through the hamlets of Noxon, Trout Creek, and Belknap, the two brothers stopped only in Thompson Falls to get gas and then had taken off again, cutting over to I-90 on a back road, and heading for Missoula.

They knew that when they did not show up at the house within a reasonable span of time, the bikers would get suspicious. Undoubtedly, Fogarty had been roused and told of their escape. In fact, several trackers would probably have been sent after them, heading in various directions: west toward Spokane, south toward Missoula, east toward Great Falls, maybe even north toward Calgary.

But by the time all this was set in motion, the brothers would have been well on their way to their destination.

Now that Mel's snappy rental car had left Montana and entered Wyoming, Pete tried to put his mind at ease. He had time now, in the dark loneliness of his own thoughts, to think again of Honey.

Sorry, Girl, he thought, his eyes moist with feeling. *You gotta know I love you. Please know I love you. . . . I'm coming Honey Girl, coming to find you. . . .*

The image of the little yellow star flashed before him, peeking out of the music box like a premonition. Pete drew his jacket close, trying not to shiver.

All at once, it seemed pieces of the puzzle began to form themselves into a believable theory. All the anti-Jewish rhetoric of the Freemen to which he had been exposed for months took on ever-widening dimension.

"Good gosh!" he suddenly cried out, lurching upright in the seat.

Mel jerked the steering wheel, causing the car to skid on the wet pavement and nearly sending them into a ditch.

"What the . . . " Mel spat, grappling the car back onto the road. "What's the matter with you, brother? You want to kill us?" Glancing over at Pete, he saw that his face was as pale as death.

"That's it!" Pete cried again. "That's the connection!"

Mel, wondering if his brother was in the thick of a nightmare, reached over to shake him. But Pete lurched aside. "I'm awake," he said. "I may be more awake than I've ever been!"

"What do you mean?" Mel was flabbergasted.

"It's suddenly come to me," Pete said. "Something I've been missing all along!"

"Have you totally lost it?" Mel barked.

"No, listen," Pete went on, gesturing wildly. "Remember, Fogarty said that the Oklahoma City thing was actually pulled off by Middle-Eastern types?"

"Yeah," Mel replied.

"Well, think about it! What is the one thing the Militia, the Arabs, and most terrorist groups have in common?"

"Hatred of the Jews? Hatred of Israel?" Mel guessed.

"Exactly! Now carry this a step further. If it's true that the government is in cahoots with these people, or at least isn't pulling the plug on them, it has to be benefiting somehow from their activities."

"I don't follow," Mel said frowning. "How would the government benefit? Why wouldn't they want to squash anti-Semitism, once and for all?"

"Oil, man! Arab oil!" Pete was really wound up. "It all makes sense now! You don't bite the hand that feeds you, that keeps your industries running, that keeps the wheels of commerce humming. You don't fight the oil merchants!"

Mel tried to sort through the logic. "So, if the Arabs blow up a federal building, they get away with it because the Feds are afraid to stop them?"

"Exactly!"

"But"—Mel paused—"how does that relate to Israel? Why would the oil merchants blow up a minor fed building? How does that have anything to do with Jews?"

"Terrorism, man!" Pete declared. "That's the nature of the game! Confuse the world, scare us so we are afraid to move. Keep us wondering when the next 'random act' will take place."

Mel shook his head and watched the road silently for a while. "I don't know," he said sighing. "Sounds awful far-fetched. I don't get how it all ties together. If what you say is true, I don't see how random terrorism is going to accomplish anything for anyone."

Pete sat back and scratched his forehead. "Think like a terrorist," he said. "If you want to accomplish something but do it somewhat secretly, what's the best way to keep people off your heels?"

"Distract them!" Mel exclaimed. "Yeah, I remember the gangs

in L.A. using that tactic! They'd lead the cops on a wild-goose chase down some alley, while the baddest of the bad pulled off some dirt."

"Except this time," Pete said, "the cops are helping them out."

The two digested that for a while. Then Mel added, "But bad dudes always want it known that they are bad—powerful, you know. The gangs never denied everything. They'd leave clear trails often enough that the neighborhood lived in fear of them."

"Okay," Pete said, "so terrorists will sometimes claim responsibility. Like the IRA in Ireland or the PLO in the Mideast."

"Right . . . "

"And we always know who their target really is, no matter who they aim at?"

"Yeah," Mel said. "Like, the Cryps hate the Bluds, or the IRA hates the Protestants, or—"

The men looked at each other with mutual insight.

"Or the Arabs hate the Jews!" they said together.

The car passed over the wet road in swift silence, only the hypnotizing slap-slap of the windshield wipers and the whirr of the rain-spattered tires accompanying their thoughts. Suddenly an awful possibility dawned on them.

"Pete," Mel said, "do you suppose this is the case with other crimes, like the TWA disaster? Or the World Trade Center?"

Pete's hands grew cold. "You mean, like some are unaccountable, no good reason behind them—to throw the world off the trail?"

"And some are directly related to the big hatred!"

"Geez!" Pete gasped. "The World Trade Center was traced to Arabs! I never thought about it. If you wanted to get at the wealthiest, most powerful Jews in the world, the Trade Center is a natural!"

Mel nodded. "Makes sense to me!"

Pete clenched his fists. "Well," he said, "I don't know about

Israel, but I am afraid for one little Jewess. These guys are tenacious and vindictive. They probably suspect Honey's hung around their agenda long enough to be a threat. We've got to find her, bro, before Fogarty and Altmeyer track her down!"

CHAPTER 23

The state of Ohio, perhaps more than any other, was a microcosm of American history and traditional values. Probably no town in the United States typified the heartland more than Columbus, the state capital. Eight Ohioans, two of them from Columbus, had served as U.S. president, and one native son had been the first man to set foot on the moon.

Pete remembered Honey's fond accounts of her state's achievements. As he and Mel drove I-70 into the heart of the Scioto Valley, with its agrarian ambiance, its middle-American feel, he wondered if Honey had ever had to battle anti-Semitism while growing up.

He doubted it. As far as he knew, having lived with her for nine years, religion played little part in her life, and certainly no ethnic cords bound her to Judaism. Most likely she had never given her heritage any more thought as a child than she did as an adult, and most people, like Pete, would not have recognized her name as particularly Jewish.

In fact, now that he thought of it, she had always decorated the house at Christmas with a tree selected from the back portion of their property and had often talked of how wonderful it would be to have children creeping down the stairs on Christmas morning. Though, for both of them, Christmas had related more to Santa and his chimney crawling than to Jesus of Bethlehem, Honey had never made an issue of Hanukkah.

Pete reached into the backseat and pulled his pack into his lap. Fumbling through it, he found a tattered address book, hastily snatched from the guest-room desk as he and Mel had left the loft. It contained current and scratched out addresses and phone numbers of Honey's friends and relatives, going back to her college days, as well as entries which the couple had made over the years.

"I remember Honey saying she grew up in a posh district of Columbus," Pete said. "When we first met, she talked a lot about how materialistic her family was and how she had escaped all that by joining the back-to-the-earthers."

Glancing through the windshield, he saw a highway marker reading, "Capitol Building, High Street Exit, 3 miles."

Above that sign was another that jogged his memory. "Pull over here," he said to Mel. "I think we're close."

Leafing through the book, he found her parents' crossed out address, as well as that of Honey's aunt, Jessie Aronstam, who had lived next door.

After the deaths of Honey's parents, years ago, her childhood home had been sold, and when she moved to Seattle many of Honey's family possessions had been stored at her aunt's house.

"Yeah, here it is!" he said. "She lived on Scioto River Drive in Arlington Heights. That was the fancy suburb she left behind."

"Okay," Mel replied. "That sign says Arlington Heights Exit. I guess we'd better turn off here."

As the car veered down the off-ramp, leaving a view of the "Hat Box Capitol," the headquarters of the state legislature with its famous flattened dome, Pete ran his hands down his blue-jeaned legs, then snapped a look at himself in the visor mirror.

"Calm down," Mel said. "If she's at her aunt's, she'll probably fall into your lovin' arms without a second look."

"Sure," Pete sighed. "She'd just as soon point a shotgun at me." Mel laughed.

At this point, the brothers had been on their quest for four days, driving and catching sleep in turns, fighting bad weather that made travel slower than they liked. They had been hung up in Cheyenne, looking for Honey's friends. At last, they had learned that she had been there more than once in the last few months, but had been too nervous to stay.

"The last time she was here, she said she was going back east," the Wyoming friends had reported. "Something was eating at her real bad."

"Look," Mel went on, "if Honey wanted to hide from you, she never would have told her friends where she was going. She hopes you'll find her, bro, can't you tell?"

The section of Columbus known as Arlington Heights was a grand departure from the city's "Cowtown" nickname. Street after street of lovely brick and clapboard houses recalled the colonial tradition, with its Greek Revival and Saltbox styles. Tree-lined avenues fronted gorgeous parks and playgrounds and world-famous golf courses.

Pete wondered which schools Honey had attended, and smiled to think of an adolescent girl in long skirts and beads, flaunting tradition in this conservative environment.

He saw a lot of churches, but no synagogue. There had to be at least one, he thought, in a city of this size. He wondered if, as a girl, Honey had ever attended one.

In no time, Mel had found the river and the broad avenue that wound along it. Looking over at Pete's address book, he compared the number of the house with addresses on the street.

"We're close," Mel said. He slowed the car to a crawl, and the two men peered out the windows, reading the golden numbers on the porches.

"There!" Pete said. "That must be it!"

Mel pulled the car to a stop in front of a tall white Colonial, complete with pillars capped by a Federalist porch roof.

"Wow!" Pete sighed. "She preferred our log house to this?"

Mel clapped his brother on the thigh. "What did I tell you?" he said. "Hang in there."

Pete looked at the houses on either side of the Colonial. "That must be Honey's aunt's," he said, pointing to the one that matched her address in the book.

Suddenly aware of just how disheveled he looked and how worn out, with dark circles under his eyes, Pete ran a quick hand through his long blond hair, retied his ponytail, and reached for the car door. "Well, here goes nothing," he said, stepping out onto the sidewalk.

As the two men approached the porch, a woman's voice halted them. "Hello! May I help you?"

Walking toward the corner of the house, sprinkler hose in hand, a gray-haired woman in a prim gardening smock, her face shielded by a wide-brimmed straw hat, hailed them from the side yard.

"This must be Aunt Jessie," Pete told Mel.

"Hi!" he called to her. "I'm Peter Wester, from Montana. I'm looking for Honey Aronstam. Has she been around?"

The woman turned the hose spigot off, then looked the men up and down, lifting her chin defiantly. "Clarissa isn't here. And from what she tells me, she's better off without you!"

Pete winced. "Well, ma'am, I sure wouldn't do Honey any harm. You must be Aunt Jessie, right?"

The woman put down her hose but did not remove her gardening gloves or reach out to return Pete's offer of a handshake.

"I'm Jessica Aronstam," she said.

"Well, Honey has always spoken highly of you," Pete said diplomatically.

Aunt Jessie's face softened a little. "She's a fine child," she said. Then stiffening, she added, "What is it you want, anyway?"

Pete glanced at Mel, as if for support, then answered, "Honey and I had words—maybe she told you. I just want to patch things up."

Mrs. Aronstam hrumphed and turned the water on again. "Not likely," she said. "You wouldn't go sending your thugs after her, if that's all you wanted! Why don't you people just leave her alone?"

"Thugs?" Pete said. "What thugs?"

Mel stepped forward, his cop instincts suddenly clicking in. "Ma'am, Mel Wester," he said, putting out his hand. The woman ignored him, but he spoke firmly. "Look, ma'am, whatever you think of Pete, he would never hurt Honey. He's come a long way to find her, just because he cares. Now you're telling us someone else has been here? Looking for her?"

Aunt Jessie turned the water off again and studied Pete. Perhaps his evident sadness and concern convinced her to be less suspicious.

"Look, young man," she said, "you know the family never approved of you."

Pete frowned. "I suppose not," he muttered. "But none of you ever went out of your way to know me, either."

Jessica sniffed. "Well, it's too late for all that now. And I'm afraid you're too late to find Clarissa. She was in a hurry when she left here. Wouldn't even sit down to have coffee with me, and sure didn't tell me where she was going."

Mel tried to focus. "Ma'am, back to the 'thugs.' You say some guys came here before us?"

The woman sighed. "I shooed them away, you can be sure. We don't want that sort hanging out in Arlington Heights! My bridge club was due anytime, and I would have died a thousand—"

"Ma'am!" Mel interrupted. "What did they look like? The men who came by here?"

Jessica shuddered. "Pretty horrid, I'd say. Driving their big motorcycles right up on the lawn! Look!" She gestured at some tire tracks left in the smooth green turf of the Aronstam yard.

"Bikers?" Pete gasped. "How many?"

"Two. They were ghastly fellows," Jessica went on. "One of them was a giant! Seven feet tall if he was an inch! And he looked like something out of a freak show!"

"How long ago?" Mel asked, absently rubbing the side of his hip where, in his cop days, he had kept his gun.

"Yesterday afternoon," she replied. Then looking suspiciously at them again, she added, "Come to think of it, they also asked if anyone else had come looking for Clarissa. Are you saying you know them or you don't know them?"

"We know them all right," Mel said. "They were looking for us, as well as for your niece. But their reasons weren't friendly!"

Pete, frustrated with dead ends, stepped closer to the woman and looked down at her demandingly. "Mrs. Aronstam, Honey could be in really big trouble. These guys you saw are no good, and they mean no good for her! Do you have any idea where she took off to?"

Now the woman grew grave. "I-I don't," she said. "Clarissa's in trouble? She's not just running from a broken heart?"

Pete's mind registered this as a ray of personal hope. He couldn't think about that now, though. "Yes, ma'am. Big trouble," he reiterated.

Mrs. Aronstam shook her head, her eyes suddenly brimming with tears. "I wish I knew where she went!" she exclaimed. "Oh, Lord, what shall we do?"

Pete stepped up and touched her arm. When she did not recoil, he slipped his own arm about her shaking shoulders.

Sobbing, she declared, "I never told those hoodlums anything.

They were scary, but I played dumb, you can be sure! As far as I knew, I told them, Clarissa was still in Montana!"

Pete spoke comfortingly. "That's good, Aunt Jessie," he said. "You did real good!"

The woman heaved a huge sigh and gestured to her home. "They looked at my house," she recalled, "as though they were about to ransack it! But then, the big one refused, telling the smaller one I reminded him of his grandma."

She gave a wan smile, and the two brothers smiled with her.

"Is there anything you can tell *us* about where Honey might have gone?" Mel implored.

"All I know is she came straight here from visiting my son at the university three days ago. She rushed into the house, and I followed her around, trying to chat, while she shuffled through a bunch of my brother's old papers."

Pete translated. "Your son would be the professor, the head of the anthropology department at Midwest?"

"Yes, that's right," she answered, reaching into her smock for a handkerchief and rubbing her red eyes.

"And your brother was Honey's dad?"

"Yes," she said again, seeming to appreciate Pete's informed status. "I couldn't get her to relax or visit awhile. She was bent on finding something. And as soon as she found it—" She gestured with a whisk down the street. "Off she went!"

"Maybe your son knows something. Do you think?" Mel asked.

"Maybe," she said, hesitating. "I asked him about their visit, but he didn't say much."

"Thanks, ma'am," Mel said, catching Pete's eye and moving toward the car. "You've been a great help."

Pete followed Mel to the car and jumped inside.

"Let's go do some digging in the anthro department!" Mel said, starting the engine and flooring it.

"Exactly!" Pete replied. "Spoken like a true cop."

CHAPTER 24

The Wester brothers hurried across the broad-lawned campus of Midwest University feeling out of their element.

"So, these are the college students of today?" Pete laughed as he looked around at the young people who spilled across the quad, rushing for classes. "They look like babies!"

"They could be *our* babies!" Mel replied. "We like to think of ourselves as eternally young. Guess what! We're getting old!"

Pete smirked. "I'll tell you this," he said. "I sure used to handle a few nights without sleep a lot better than I do now!"

Finding a map of the campus in a glass-fronted sign, they located the anthropology department and headed that way.

"Arenstam will never tell us anything, you know," Pete said. "Honey probably gave him an earful, and he'll keep her as far away from me as possible!"

"I thought of that," Mel returned. "What I want to do is find out when the good professor has classes so that we can go by his office when he's not there."

"And what do you hope to accomplish by doing that?"

Mel shrugged. "I don't know. But I never got to play detective on the force. Might as well take a crack at it."

Pete followed obligingly as Mel led the way to the fine old building that housed the social sciences. Greek Revival in style, it was the typical grand university edifice, complete with ivy-covered walls.

Finding the anthropology wing, the two men tried to appear casual as they entered the front office.

Mel was almost disappointed at the ease with which they made their way past the secretary's desk and down the narrow hall that led to the staff offices. Apparently they had arrived at coffee-break time, and no one was overseeing the reception area.

"Even if we do find the right office, what will you do then?" Pete whispered, following Mel like a shadow, darting sideways glances at closed doors.

"Are you asking if I'm flying by the seat of my pants?" Mel inquired. "What would *you* do?"

In no time, they stood where Honey Aronstam had stood only recently, but this time the office was closed and no light shone through the door's opaque, rippled glass.

"'Dr. Kenneth Aronstam,'" Mel read. "So here we are."

The two stood nervously together, ears pricked for the sound of anyone entering the hall. It seemed that anyone not on coffee break must be in classes just now. They were quite alone in the office quadrant.

"What if he comes back? What will we say?"

"He'd recognize you," Mel said. "So that can't happen!"

Pete sighed and shook his head.

"What are you doing now?" he asked, incredulous that Mel had actually placed a hand on the doorknob. "It's locked."

"Oh yeah?" Mel said.

To Pete's amazement, the door was opening, creaking back ever so gently under Mel's guidance.

"Gads! You're crazy!" Pete croaked.

"Like a fox!" Mel replied, shooting another look down the hall and sliding inside the office. He pulled Pete in, then slipped the door shut again, letting the latch click.

Pete stood in the dimly lit office, wondering how they would explain themselves if caught, as Mel did a once-over on the cluttered desk.

"What do you think you'll find?" Pete muttered, teeth clenched.

"Maybe nothing—maybe something," Mel replied. "If this guy's like the typical harried professor, he probably doesn't put stuff away real often."

Pete fidgeted nervously with his belt loops.

"Come on!" Mel snarled. "Get with it! See what you can find!"

Pete, keeping his ears tuned to the hall, sidled up next to Mel and scanned the desk. Suddenly he jolted as if he would jump out of his skin. A red light was flashing on Aronstam's phone.

"Cool down!" Mel spat.

Pete, trying to ignore the light, turned and fumbled through papers on a nearby table. Suddenly he started. "Mel!" he gasped. "Look at this!"

The cop peered over his brother's shoulder and let out a soft whistle.

"Okay, Pete! Okay. You've got it!"

In the Montanan's sweaty hand was a rumpled note, something the professor must have hastily scratched out when he met with Honey. It regarded airline departure flights for New York and Israel, the flights for New York having left three days ago. At the bottom was a credit card number, along with a reservation control number and Clarissa's name, with an arrow connecting it to one of the flights.

As the men scanned the note, the light on Aronstam's desk suddenly stopped blinking. From down the hall, they could hear a woman, probably the secretary, saying, "Dr. Aronstam, here's your mail. And there's a call for you, about the faculty meeting. Do you want to take it here, or in your office?"

"I'll take it in the office," the professor answered.

Pete quickly shoved the note in his pocket, as he and Mel slipped out of the room. Aronstam could just be seen coming down the hall, absorbed in reading his mail, as Mel jerked Pete sideways.

Everything went black, as Mel pulled him into a tidy broom closet.

"So far, so good," Mel whispered.

As Pete stood quaking in the dark, he wondered why he had always been considered the crazy one in the family, and not his younger brother.

CHAPTER 25

Clement, James, and Shofar, the genealogy researchers of the Consortium's computer lab, huddled around a central monitor in their work station. David Rothmeyer stood with them, waiting eagerly as his disks were integrated into the massive bank of data stored in the computer's memory, data regarding family lines of Cohen Jews, compiled from around the world.

"It will be interesting to see how your findings collate with ours around the time of the early Middle Ages," Clement said, his dark eyes looking small but bright behind thick glasses.

"Why that period?" David asked, watching the screen and listening to the soft shifting of the hard drive.

"We have found prominent strands that seem to repeat themselves, being updated or added to in thirteenth-century Germany. They wane during times of persecution, as during the massacres of our people that accompanied plagues and the like . . . "

"Like the Black Plague," James filled in. "Lots of Jews were killed or had to flee, as scapegoats, blamed for the coming of the epidemic."

"Right," Clement said, "and of course they lost

track of their roots. Family history sinks to a low priority at such times."

David nodded. "So, what about these strands you found?"

"Well," Clement went on, "in several of the genealogies that incorporate these lines, there is reference to earlier generations having come out of England. Some even trace the line back into Britain at the time of the Crusades."

"Specifically, following the First Crusade," James added.

David tried to interpret. "You are saying that there is a strong indication that the priestly line can be traced through England and then on into Germany?"

"Quite possibly," Clement replied. "Most Cohen genealogies are pretty sketchy, marvelous as they are compared to other family records. The records of this particular Cohen family, however, are quite insistent on a priestly link, and it crops up more frequently in their records than in those of other families, indicating that they retained the idea, longer than other Cohens tended to, that they had a special, priestly calling."

David was amazed. "You mean, you actually received information like this from people around the world, regarding their ancestry? What form did it take? Letters, manuscripts, what?"

James responded enthusiastically to the question, his nasal voice higher than usual. "It's like a treasure hunt. You never know what people will find when they start digging in their attics, their old trunks, or in the basement stacks of old libraries."

Shofar jumped in. "Family Bibles, even Christian ones, are a great help."

James watched the screen flicker, as it continued to collate information.

"What these records are lacking is a straight line to a present-day heir," Clement said. "They all fade away into dead ends or claim only distant kinship to the *zadokim*. What we need is a definitive connection to the priestly line of Zadok."

David knew this. One of the first things he had learned in this quest was that not every Cohen male had the potential of being in the priestly line. Candidates must be narrowed down to descendants of David's and Solomon's priests, whose names were Zadok. No Cohen of certain earlier branches, such as those descended from Eli or Abiathar, could be considered, because those particular priests had been guilty of actions that disgraced their office, or were not descendants of Aaron's eldest son, a necessary qualification.

As the computer whirred and clicked away, David hoped all was well at his house. He had seen to it that Honey Aronstam had something to do that day, away from the residence, away from his notes and files. He had made a reservation for her with a little tour company and had sent her off to see the sights of the Holy City, then had asked Anya to keep an eye on her if she returned before he got back.

He had not yet told Rabbi Benjamin about his peculiar visitor, as the old fellow was at the yeshiva when she arrived. But he knew he must do so before the rabbi learned of it independently.

For now, he tried to keep his mind on the business at hand.

"It will take quite awhile for all of this to dovetail," Shofar said, pulling up a chair. "Here, have a seat. I'll get you some coffee."

David sat down, and Shofar returned a few moments later with a steaming cup of coffee. David took a sip, then said, "According to my research, there have been so many contending parties throughout our history, I don't see how any particular genealogy will prove to be definitive."

James nodded. "Possibly, Professor. But we must begin somewhere."

"Of course," Clement agreed, "every group that cared at all about such matters has had its favorites through the years. The Cabalists and the Hasidics, for instance, have always contended that some mystic from their ranks must be the chosen one. The Talmudists have the superior scholarship behind them and are convinced that only a great scholar can be priest. Between the Sephardics of Spain and the Ashkenazaics of Eastern Europe, the chasm has always been so great, they could not agree on anything, much less who should be called righteous."

Shofar snorted, that strange little nerdish laugh that David had found typical of computer pros. "Then there are the Reform Jews who think this is all immaterial and deny the literalness of it all," he said. "So far as they are concerned, it is sufficient that Israel as a whole has a priestly function in the world. They spiritualize everything down to broad maxims and vague generalities."

"For our purposes," James added, "Reformism is irrelevant. If we did not believe in a literal priesthood and a literal high priest, we would not be doing any of this." He blew a good-bye kiss toward the computers, and the others laughed.

David was still ambivalent. "All that aside," he said, "if there is no link going back to the last known priest, an actual priest who served in the actual temple, how can we prove anything?"

The young men kept their eyes to the screen and did not answer. So David went on: "Besides, who *was* the last legitimate heir to the priesthood? One of the last priests of record was Caiaphas, in the time of Jesus, and even his credentials are suspect."

"Oh, more than suspect!" Clement declared. "We know for sure that he was not a legitimate heir!"

David was stunned. He had not expected such a firm response.

"What do you mean?" he asked. "I found nothing in my work that discounted him completely."

The three jockeys looked at one another nervously and then back at David.

"Didn't Shalom Diamant show you the lab?" Clement asked.

"Lab?" David repeated. "You mean the one where they have been researching the dyes for the garments and such?"

The young scholars drew aside, whispering together and glancing over their shoulders at the professor, until he felt uneasy.

Finally, seeming to have reached a consensus, they came back to him.

"Surely Shalom means to show you this," Clement said. "He must have overlooked it."

"Show me what?" David asked.

"Go on, Shofar," Clement directed. "Take him in there."

Shofar jerked his head toward a door at the back of the computer room, indicating that David should follow him. Bemused, the professor complied, leaving James and Clement to watch the monitors.

The low door opened on a dark chamber, and David was obliged to duck his head as he entered. Shofar flicked on a bank of fluorescent lights that spanned the close ceiling, and the professor blinked his eyes.

Amazed, David looked around at a room that stretched quite a distance beneath the old city street above, its floor superimposed on the pavement of yet another street that was centuries older. The temperature of the room was surprisingly moderate and even, not cavelike or dank. David noticed dehumidifiers and an elaborate temperature-control system. He stared, mystified at long, polished chrome counters, beakers, bunsen burners, centrifuge machines, high-powered microscopes, and other high-tech lab equipment.

Shofar answered David's wide eyes.

"This is the Consortium's science lab," he said. "The research in here is way out of my league, I assure you. In fact, the geneticists only come here about once a month."

"Geneticists?" David marveled. "What does the Consortium need with geneticists?"

Even as he asked the question, he felt the hair on the back of his neck stand up. He suspected the answer and was not sure he liked it.

"They have been studying the chromosomes of Cohen males for a couple of years now," Shofar replied. He realized such news might be startling, and tried to be casual. "They've made some fascinating finds."

"Chromosomes?" David croaked. "How are they acquiring chromosomes?"

Shofar gave a quick history of the relatively young project. "A scientist in Haifa has collected saliva samples from Cohen volunteers by swabbing the insides of their cheeks. His volunteers were from three separate countries and were not directly related to one another. Running various tests on these samples, he and his colleagues have determined that Cohens across the board share a variation of the Y chromosome, aligning them as descendants of Aaron."

David frowned, skeptical. "Come on!" he grumbled. "Is that really possible? Aaron lived thirty-five hundred years ago!"

Shofar shrugged. "Those are the findings. What can I say? I am no scientist!"

Suddenly David's assignment was more than politically sensitive. It had taken on Orwellian overtones. "Let me guess," he said. "When we come up with our candidate, he will be subjected to this genetic test?"

Shofar shrugged again. "Let's call it a 'confirmation,' not a 'test.'"

Then, leaning back against a counter and crossing his arms, he looked at the professor quizzically. "Have the rabbis ever told you what such candidates were put through in the old days, when Israel cared enough to keep meticulous records?"

David shook his head.

It was evident that Shofar liked telling this story. Clapping his hands brightly, he began, "There used to be a great room in the Temple Cloisters, called the 'Hall of Polished Stones.' It is described in the rabbinical writings as quite a fabulous chamber.

"Anyway, there was a committee in Jerusalem that sat daily in that hall interviewing and looking over hundreds of candidates for the lesser priestly stations in the temple. These candidates had to produce detailed genealogies on themselves, proving their bloodlines, before they would even be considered.

"Then, there were copious doctrinal questions and scholarly questions they must answer. Finally, if they passed those tests, they were submitted to rigid physical examination."

Shofar's eyes flashed with intrigue. "Now get this," he said. "If a candidate's genealogy was flawed, he was publicly shamed by being dressed all in black with a veil over his face and was permanently removed from the court! If his genealogy passed the test, he was examined for physical defects, of which there were 162 that could disqualify him!"

The professor was appalled. "I can't imagine such treatment being tolerated today!" he exclaimed.

Shofar lifted his hands. "If we find a candidate for high priest, he will have to be physically pure, for sure. His line must be proven, and his theology must be straight. So what if he must produce a little spittle? Is that so bad?"

David laughed. "I guess not," he said. Then, looking about the room, he added, "Speaking of the old days, we were talking about the high priest, Caiaphas. Was there something in here you wanted to show me regarding that period?"

Shofar beamed. "There sure is!" he replied. "Step this way!"

Taking him to a large table at the back of the room, he said, "The people who come to this lab to work are some of the most highly respected scientists in the world, and they are of several disciplines: genetics, nephrology, and anthropology. Together, they have made one of the most astounding discoveries of all time!"

David raised his eyebrows. "What you've already told me is astounding enough! There is more?"

"Much more," Shofar replied. "See this?"

He directed David to a glass case, locked with a heavy clasp. The lid was edged with a latex seal that meshed with another along the top of the box itself. Inside the case was a control that kept the temperature and humidity of the contents constant, its little flashing light registering each fraction of variation.

Upon a glass tray in the bottom of the case was a pile of yellow-gray dust and shardlike fragments.

David, with his background in anthropology, recognized the material instantly. "Bone?" he said.

"Exactly," Shofar answered. "But not just any bone."

"Of course not," David agreed. "It appears to be quite ancient. From some tomb?"

"From the casket of Caiaphas," Shofar replied reverentially.

Suddenly it came back to David, information he had read in science journals. He remembered that archaeologists in Jerusalem had claimed to have found a burial box in their digs near Temple Mount and that the box was engraved with Hebrew letters spelling out the name of the ancient high priest before whom Jesus of Nazareth had stood trial.

"Good Lord!" he exclaimed. "Are you telling me that these are the very bones of Caiaphas?"

"The same!" Shofar answered, breaking into a smile.

As David bent close to the case, he was trembling both inside and out, with the feeling he experienced only upon some great, professional find. He had to hold his hands against his chest to keep them calm.

For a long while, he stood before the case, mesmerized. Then he drew back and tried to collect himself.

"Okay! Okay!" he replied. "So, I get it! You mentioned that nephrologists are on the team, right? They've been working with the geneticists, right? And they have run tests on these bones?"

Shofar nodded. He knew the professor deduced the rest.

"So," David went on, "Caiaphas is ruled out as a *zadok*?"

"You have it!" Shofar said.

David was incredulous. "This is the most amazing thing I've

ever heard of!" he said. "So the turmoil of the late Temple period was justified. The rebels who claimed the priesthood was corrupt were absolutely right!"

"They were!" Shofar exclaimed, delighted to be teaching a teacher.

David wanted to linger over the glass case, but Shofar headed back for the door. "We'd probably better get out of here," he said. "If Shalom finds out I broke all of this to you . . . Well, I'm sure he wanted to do it himself."

The professor followed but dragged his feet. "I wish I could meet with the lab team," he said wistfully. "I have a hundred questions."

"Perhaps you shall," Shofar said, clicking off the light and shutting the door behind them.

Again, they stood in the computer room, David's head whirring like the computers themselves.

As they rejoined James and Clement, David rubbed his hands together. "So, going back to the revolutionists in the temple . . . some of them left to live in the wilderness—the Essenes of Qumran, for instance."

"You would know all of that better than we," Clement said. "But we've always suspected that the people at Qumran were revolutionaries."

"Aha!" David shouted. "So, that is the final missing link. We may find everything we need from that point on, but without a record from the revolutionists themselves, we won't have a clue who the last legitimate heir from the Temple period really was!"

Clement shook his head. "Sad, but true. We can only trust that all our work here is not in vain."

As the men stood in silent contemplation of this reality, the computers suddenly went silent, the whirring tapering off to a final click. The central screen flickered, and the windows changed in rapid succession, until a block of intricate information flashed to life.

Clement, Shofar, and James bent close to the monitor, with David right behind them.

"Wow!" James sighed. "Do you believe it?"

"What? What?" David gasped, wedging between them.

"It's practically flawless!" Clement exclaimed. "Your information, your months of research findings mesh almost perfectly with the current genealogies! There is a line, clear as day, running through England! Now, we just need to trace it forward to someone living today."

"Yes," James said, "and then backward, to someone who lived in Caiaphas's time, someone robbed of his priesthood and nameless to history."

The three computer jockeys stood up and stared at David.

"Back in your court!" James said. "Good luck, Professor!"

CHAPTER 26

As David hurried home, his mind buzzing with the information he had received at the lab, he hoped he was making it back before Honey returned.

The moment he entered the house, he intended to contact Rabbi Benjamin at the yeshiva where he had spent the night. He must tell him about his guest from Montana and get some guidance as to how to proceed with her. Rabbi Ben would also be fascinated, he was sure, with the woman's story, and might want to meet her.

As the professor opened the massive old door, however, he knew he was too late. Voices coming from the parlor cued him that the rabbi had already come home and was talking with Honey at that moment.

David cleared his throat nervously as he entered the room, hoping the rabbi would not consider her presence a dreadful security breach. When Horace Benjamin glanced up, greeting him with an effervescent smile, he relaxed a little.

"Dr. Rothmeyer," the rabbi called out, "did you expect to keep this delightful creature all to yourself?"

David sauntered in, trying to look nonchalant.

"I see you have met Ms. Aronstam," he said. "I was just going to call you and ask you to come make her acquaintance."

"Well, that I have!" the rabbi replied. "And she has a fascinating story!"

In front of the rabbi, spread out on the coffee table, were the Jew badge and the Red Cross letter that Honey treasured. It was obvious that the rabbi and the woman had already spent enough time together for her to share her mystery.

Honey spoke up. "I hope you don't mind, Dave. I got back from the tour about two hours ago. It was wonderful! Thank you! What a marvelous city this is! Anyway," she enthused, "the rabbi came home, and well, here we are. . . . "

She gestured to the artifacts excitedly. "Dave," she said, "I do believe I have found my 'wise man.' Rabbi Benjamin seems to believe I was meant to come here!"

David pulled up a footstool and sat down. "I'm relieved, Rabbi," he said. "I was afraid you would think I was out of line letting Honey stay here, considering our work."

He then looked at the woman apologetically. "Sorry, Honey," he said. "But we have certain reasons to keep matters here private."

Rabbi Benjamin leaned back and chuckled. "Don't worry, David. I have already told her."

"What?" the professor marveled. "But I thought—"

"You thought right," the rabbi interrupted. "Our work is sensitive, no doubt about it. But I have lived long enough, and closely enough to spiritual things, that I think I know supernatural intervention when I see it."

David was stunned, and Honey's eyes grew wide.

"S-supernatural intervention?" she stammered.

The rabbi looked at the two of them intently. "Let me give you an example," he said. Then turning to David, "I will be very surprised if you tell me your findings did not mesh with what Clement and his boys have put together."

"That's true!" David exclaimed. "It was almost too perfect!"

Horace nodded matter-of-factly. "That is the way it has been all along with this project, Professor. Not to minimize your scholarship or the work of the computer experts, but it seems quite clear that you are being assisted by powers beyond yourself in all your endeavors."

The professor thought long on this, then conceded, "I would be a fool to claim otherwise."

Honey took this in silently. Such an approach to things was foreign to her. Her spirituality had never gone beyond an appreciation for nature, for mountains, and for human ties. The closest she had ever come to any spiritual quest had been when she and Pete attended an Indian sweat lodge where, they were told, they might see visions. Even that quick dip into otherworldliness had been only a faddish exploit, and they had returned quickly to contentment with mundane things.

Now, here she was—she who had never graced the inside of a church, and who had attended synagogue only as a child—sitting in the Holiest of Cities, at the feet of a great rabbi. That rabbi had just revealed to her a quest much greater than anything she had ever dreamed of—the quest for the one who would serve as leader in the ultimate reestablishment of Judaism.

She glanced down at the little star that had never meant more to her than a cherished responsibility—a responsibility which she did not even understand—and she sensed, for the first time, the hand of destiny.

The rabbi was looking at her now. "And you, young lady, can you say that you have not been led here? Can you say that your coming to Jerusalem is mere happenstance or that the emblem you have protected all these years might not be something very sacred?"

Honey quivered, gripping her elbows tight to her sides. "I-I don't know," she admitted.

The rabbi accepted that and went on. "Now, Professor, I suppose that you are wondering what all of the findings in the lab portend. They can only take any of us so far, but we still have unanswered gaps."

"Truer words were never spoken!" David agreed. "We seem to be fleshing out several centuries quite nicely. There is a strand that leads strongly through England, but the Holocaust period is still sketchy, and then—" He stopped and shook his head. Sighing deeply, he added, "Then, even if we were to find a modern descendent of the firmest line, without proof going back to the Temple period, we cannot prove a thing!"

Rabbi Benjamin nodded. "Shalom meant to show you something related to that issue," he said, "the day he gave you the tour. We ran out of time after we visited the computer room. Perhaps he would not mind if I showed you."

David figured it would do no harm to tell the truth. "I believe I know what it is," he said. "Shofar took me into the science lab."

The rabbi did not take this news as cheerily as he had taken the news of David's having a houseguest. "What?" he barked. "Shofar had no right! That is highly confidential. . . . "

But then, he caught himself. "Listen to me," he said sheepishly. "Have I not just been preaching supernatural guidance? So," he sighed, "you saw the bones?"

Honey jolted. "Bones?" she croaked.

The rabbi laughed softly. "Sounds terrible, eh? Actually, such things are quite common finds in archaeology. Recently, diggers under the auspices of the Jerusalem Antiquities Authority unearthed a very special casket, marked with the name of Caiaphas."

Honey drew a blank. She had heard of the trial of Jesus, of course, but she could not have named Pilate or Herod or Caiaphas, before whom he had been tried.

Quickly the rabbi filled her in. "Caiaphas was one of the last recorded priests before the destruction of the temple in 70 C.E. Actually, he probably did not live that long, as he is referenced as being in office at the time of Jesus, and later discharged by Rome about 38 C.E."

Again, Honey was out of her element. "I never went to Sunday school," she said. "For sure, when I attended synagogue, which wasn't all that often, they never taught about Jesus!" David, seeing Honey's puzzlement, explained, "What is important about Caiaphas is not only his involvement with Jesus, but also the fact that there was a lot of foment at that time, about the legitimacy of the officiating priests. There were sects that had broken away from the temple and then went off on their own to worship away from what they considered to be graft and pollution in the priesthood."

The rabbi explained. "We were able to run DNA tests on the bones of Caiaphas, at least the bones that were in his casket, which we must assume were his. What we found was that he does not fit the chromosomal specifications that would have marked a legitimate heir. Since he was undoubtedly typical of the high priests of the time, appointed by Rome rather than by Jewish law, we can safely deduce that the revolutionists were right. Those filling the office of high priest, until the time of the temple's destruction, were certainly not there legally."

The men were not certain Honey got the gist of what they were pointing out. They were pleasantly surprised when her big brown eyes got even bigger, and she said, "So, this genealogy thing depends on your finding a reference to a legitimate heir way back then?"

The rabbi leaned back and clapped his hands on his thighs. "Exactly, Ms. Aronstam! That is the quandary we face, no matter how brilliantly we piece things together otherwise."

Honey was on a roll, and she began to appreciate the thrill of the chase. "So," she went on, "we have a double mystery, like a candle burning at both ends! We have to find the ancient link, and we have to find the modern one!"

She gazed at her star again. "We have to fill in the blank from the Holocaust. . . . "

Rabbi Benjamin studied her pensive face with compassion. "I could be entirely wrong," he admitted, "but I have a strong hunch that your little star and the message it contains ties in with what we are seeking. Whether or not it relates directly, I cannot imagine that a scribe at Dachau would have risked his life to lead us to anything, unless it was very important to Judaism."

David and Honey looked at each another, sensing the kinship of their mysteries. "Well, Rabbi," she said, "I have come this far on this strange journey. I am willing to go further."

"Of course, Rabbi Ben," David added, "you know that I am committed to the entire venture. What would you like for us to do?"

Nodding gratefully, Horace picked up the letter that accompanied the star and noted the signature at the bottom.

"'Emily McCurdy, R.N.,'" he read. Then glancing up at Honey, he asked, "You say your family has never contacted this woman?"

"Not to my knowledge. I'm sure my dad would have told me."

The rabbi thought a moment, then reached into the pocket of his long black coat. Pulling out a little address book, he said, "It so happens that the International Red Cross has been very helpful in our genealogy work. Some years ago, they began a program of soliciting and gathering information on the families of Holocaust victims. We have been able to incorporate much of their findings into our own research."

Again, David was amazed at the complexity of the Consortium's networking. It seemed he learned something new about it every time he turned around.

The rabbi continued, "If Nurse McCurdy is still living, I am sure the Red Cross can help locate her. We can then hope she will assist you to follow the clues to the treasure buried at Dachau."

David and Honey knew the implication. "Help *us*?" David said. "Are you saying that Ms. Aronstam and I should go to Germany?"

The rabbi gave a wink. "Did you have something better to do?" he asked.

CHAPTER 27

Pete and Mel Wester were not world travelers. Except for one flight to Disneyland with their parents when they were in grade school, and one vacation with Honey to Costa Rica, about seven years ago, they were relative novices. Mel had flown only between cities on the West Coast, and Pete had taken a few turns in crop dusters.

A transoceanic flight was new for both of them, and the one they were on now was not for pleasure. They were running across the world to find Honey and bring her home safely.

After hiding for half an hour in the dark, stuffy broom closet near Ken Aronstam's office, they had at last been able to escape, unseen, from the anthropology department of Midwest University. After a restless night at a dumpy motel on the outskirts of Columbus, they had managed to catch a couple of standby seats on a flight to New York, and then, after several long delays, to Europe. Taking what was available meant they would have to fly into Munich and hope for another set of standbys heading for Israel.

It was not due to any pre-planning that they each had passports. Since Mel never intended to return to L.A., his was among personal documents in the glove box of the rental car. Pete's was in the little binder where he kept his tattered address book and other papers, and which he had hastily stuffed in his backpack before fleeing Bull River.

Flying into darkness for most of nine hours made for an arduous journey, but the brothers felt lucky to have made it this far.

Ever since they learned that Willard and Crossley had gotten off their scent when they turned south toward Wyoming, the bikers apparently having proceeded straight to Ohio, the brothers had breathed a little easier.

It was also comforting to think that the bikers had lost Honey's trail. Mel and Pete were hopeful that the hogsters had accepted defeat and that no tracer was following any of them further. Tenacious as the Militia could be, there seemed no reason to expect that the brother-hood would consider them worthy of an international chase.

Despite in-flight movies, too many trays of food, and the discomfort of too little legroom, Mel managed to catch up on much-needed rest.

For Pete, however, the worst part of the journey was the dead time, for it allowed him to ponder his past. Disquieting scenes tumbled through his erratic sleep, as he relived his fight with Honey and then the agony of sending her away before they could patch things up. On waking, he wondered if she understood, at all, that he was trying to protect her and if she would ever be able to forgive his crazy involvement with the Freemen.

He also pondered the meaning of his work for Fogarty. How many messages had he taken off that despicable ham radio, never knowing what he was relaying or what plot he was aiding? This question had tormented him ever since the all-night meeting in his own home, when Fogarty and Altmeyer snickered over the may-hem they had conceived and carried out over the years. The ugly, unmistakable sense that he was no smarter, no better than the idiots who had aided in the orchestration of the Oklahoma City bombing nagged at Pete's soul.

Gazing out the window at the depressing darkness, he rehashed the messages he could remember, wondering if there was any way to intercept their outcome. But he always came to the same dead end: If he could not even interpret the coded phrases, how could he fight against them?

Somewhere over the mid-Atlantic, as the screen at the head of the cabin gave a computerized depiction of the plane gliding over the English Channel, he found himself dwelling on the last message he had received, the morning before the gathering descended. He remembered that the first words from the strange, grating voice were "Eagle-Eye happening." That phrase, obviously meaning "this is for Fogarty," was the most oft-repeated one in all the messages he received. But what came after was a total mystery to him. Something about "Swastika," "Bailey's Bug," and "Cedars," he recalled. Then, strangest of all, the last word: "She . . . she . . . " what was the word? Yes—"Shekinah!" he remembered now. Try as he might, he could not recall the rest of the message.

Suddenly, however, something did occur to him, and he stiffened reflexively at the thought, bumping his dozing brother as he did so. Mel grumbled and turned over, breathing down Pete's neck.

What came to mind was that the shirt he had worn the morning he took that message was the same one he was wearing now. In their clandestine attempt at packing, he and Mel had not been very selective regarding what they stuffed into the backpack. But Pete had made sure to bring his favorite flannel plaid.

He also remembered that, on the morning when he received the message, he had hastily scratched out the words on note paper and stuffed it into the pocket of this very shirt. Was it possible that the note was still there?

Trying not to disturb his brother further he reached into the pocket. His fingers tingled as he felt the scrap of paper. Gingerly he pulled it out and reached overhead to flick on the dome light directed at his seat. Very carefully, almost afraid to look, he opened the paper and read the words.

A chill of dread moved up his neck. "Relay to Swastika. Bailey's Bug is a go. Cedars ready to drop on Shekinah," the message said.

He had no idea what "Bailey's Bug" or "Cedars" could mean. It occurred to him, however, that "Swastika" was probably the German, Monte Altmeyer. Eagle-Eye Fogarty was not necessarily meant to understand the message, but to serve as intermediary to get the message to Altmeyer.

This made it most likely that the message was of international significance, for Fogarty was only an American White Supremacist, while Altmeyer was a multinational mercenary. It also seemed all too likely that the term "ready to drop on" could mean "ready to bomb."

Pete's throat went dry, and he lifted a shaking hand to turn off the light. Enveloped in gloom, he felt like the loneliest soul in the universe; suspended between earth and heaven, he felt unfit for either.

Yet, what could he do? Not only was the entire message a riddle, but he had never heard the word "shekinah" before and would not even know whom to ask for an interpretation.

He could try to find some government agency that might help. But after everything he and Mel had learned about terrorists and their collusion with the authorities, he did not think that was such a good idea.

All at once, however, it swept over him that he had not relayed the message to Fogarty! In the excitement of the gathering two days later, and all of his duties as the host, he had forgotten to pass the word on to Eagle-Eye!

Perhaps there was some saving grace in that fact. Perhaps, whatever the plot was, he had helped to delay it. Perhaps . . .

Oh God in heaven! he prayed. *Let it not be too late. Help me put a stop to this thing—whatever it is!*

Pete was not used to praying. He had never been a believing man, beyond the nebulous warm fuzziness that came over him when he walked through the woods or thought about how vast the universe was. He had always figured he was a good guy, as good as any, and better than some. If there was a God, he figured that might count for something.

Now, all of a sudden, that kind of assurance seemed awfully tenuous.

The fact was, he was probably no better than Fogarty. In fact, he had, until just the last couple of days, thought Fogarty was great. Now, he thought him demonic. He went numb all over as he realized he had been a member of his camp—politically, spiritually, physically.

Pete's eyes grew hot and teary, and a sense of panic engulfed him. Choking, he took a deep breath to calm himself, then looked out the window. Dawn was coloring the sky gold and pink, and he could see the European mainland in the distance.

Soon, they were flying over the lush green hills of Germany, which were dotted every few miles with glorious castles, a world-class chessboard, reminiscent of the many conquerors and kings who had staked out claims on the Continent.

History never changes, Pete thought. *There have always been mighty men who used pawns to fulfill their ends. I am just a pawn—one little pawn—Help me, God, if you are there, to break one link in the chain of evil.*

CHAPTER 28

The next flight from Munich to Israel would not depart for another four hours. Pete and Mel had been waiting to catch standby seats since eight o'clock in the morning. It was now noon. If the four o'clock flight did not have room, they would have to consider finding a hotel in Munich for the night, then face another round of waiting tomorrow.

On the flight to Germany, Pete had read an article in one of the seat pocket magazines claiming that this airport had now surpassed the extravagant castle of Neuschwanstein as the country's leading sightseeing attraction. Although it had made an impressive scene as they approached it, its glass-sheathed control tower meeting the sky nearly eighty meters above the twin parallel runways and its single terminal spreading out over one full kilometer, Pete and Mel quickly wearied of hours confined to its sleek, luminescent interior.

Views out every window were, except for the continual landings and takeoffs of giant winged carriers, gray and depressing. Built on the Bavarian bogland, the airport landscape was dismal most of the time.

"Looks like we're stuck here at least for the afternoon," Mel said as he read yet another news magazine and watched the waiting area's TV news in German. "Let's take that 'moving sidewalk' down to the shop area."

Antsy with boredom, Pete agreed.

The brothers left the gate where the Israeli jets came and went, and hopped on the human-sized conveyor belt that eased them through a nearly endless, neon-art lined corridor to the main lobby. Here, at least, they might wile away some time in the gaudy little shops that were intended to rob tourists of their dollars, yen, and marks before they even made it downtown.

One huge checkerboard of black-and-white squares, the floor of the main concourse spread out as far as the eye could see, beneath banners and signs luring spendthrifts into temptation. Starting at one end of the lobby, the two men said little as they ambled from one shop to the next.

Mel suggested they should each buy a new shirt, having packed so little in their haste to depart Montana. When they saw the price tags on simple T-shirts, however, they decided against it.

Since their early-morning in-flight breakfast had worn off long ago, the brothers stopped for pizza-by-the-slice and groaned as they had to pay out the equivalent of four American dollars apiece. They sat on shrub-lined benches, making quick work of the "meal," then had white-chocolate yogurt for dessert.

A couple of hours later, one more flight had arrived from Israel, and the big jet was undergoing ground check and refueling, awaiting the takeoff, which, space permitting, would finally take the men to the Holy Land. They would not know, until the last passenger had boarded, whether or not there was room for them. But, they decided to return to the gate. "Maybe we can catch a catnap in the waiting area," Mel suggested.

Shuffling through the x-ray line once again, they picked up Pete's backpack, their keys and wallets from off the belt, and made their way back toward the El Al gate, whose planes, with the blue

Star of David on their tail fins, represented aviation in the modern state of Israel.

The number of the gate was still some distance down the broad corridor when Pete suddenly stopped short, grabbing Mel by the arm, and staring straight ahead. "Am I dreaming?" he asked.

Mel followed his gaze down the long hallway, and his mouth fell open.

It took several seconds for their minds to register that they were not imagining what they saw.

Honey Aronstam and a tall, lanky stranger were standing in the corridor before the El Al waiting area, shaking hands with two women, one a dignified-looking older woman and the other a curly-haired blond.

None of this computed; none of this made sense. "That's Honey—no doubt about that!" Mel exclaimed. "What's *she* doing here?"

Whatever the answer to that question, another blazed louder through Pete's already tormented heart: Who was the fellow she was with, and had he replaced the Montanan?

Pete ducked into a coffee shop close enough to watch the group, and Mel stepped in with him. "What's with you, brother?" Mel grumbled. "Are you going to let her get away?"

Pete's face was red with a tumult of feelings. "She's with some-one!" he muttered. "What would I say?"

Mel sighed, exasperated. "When did you become such a wuss? So what if she's with someone? She belongs with you!"

Pete ran a hand through his long blond hair and smoothed his rumpled flannel shirt. Taking a deep breath, he looked back at Mel as if to say "Wish me luck" and reentered the corridor.

Slowly he walked toward the group, who seemed to be intro-ducing themselves to one another, and then he stood by silently, waiting for Honey to see him out of the corner of her eye.

After what seemed a very long while, but was really only

seconds, during which Pete ran hot and cold, sweaty and chilly, the woman who owned his heart glanced his way.

The look that came over her face was at first disbelief, then bewilderment, then . . . Pete could not be sure what it was.

Surely a thousand questions raced through her mind: How had he found her? How could he have tracked her down? Was he an enemy agent, here at Fogarty's command? And, was that Mel with him? What was Mel doing here?

It was fear that Pete read in her face. But just as quickly, it seemed to be replaced by a softer emotion. Did she see how he felt? Did she see that he was tormented, that he loved her? That, however he had found her, it was love that had brought him looking?

Suddenly she trembled. The man with her reached out to steady her. "What is it?" he asked, darting an anxious look at the two strangers. "Who are these guys?"

"Honey?" Pete cried, stepping toward her.

Rothmeyer started to intercept his advance, but Honey whispered, "It's okay, Dave." Leaning on the professor's arm, she looked at Pete as though the moon lay between them.

"What are you doing here?" she gasped.

Pete's eyes were moist, and he choked as he answered. "I was on my way to Israel to find you, Honey. I would have crossed the world, if I had to. Don't be afraid of me, Honey. I'll never hurt you again!"

Honey Aronstam knew Peter Wester too well to be fooled by a lie. She knew he was telling the truth and could hear by the sound of his voice the agony her loss had caused.

Stepping forward, she let him hold her, and for just a moment, they forgot they were in one of the world's busiest terminals. Oblivious to the churn of engines outside, the murmur of voices inside, they were lost in each other's embrace.

Tenderly, Pete lifted Honey's face to his and kissed her as though his life depended on it.

CHAPTER 29

David Rothmeyer glanced in the rearview mirror of the van he had rented at the Munich airport. Past his own bewildered reflection were faces totally new to him.

Only one of them had he come to know a little in the past few days: Honey Aronstam. He felt he could trust her. As for the others, he had only been scheduled to meet Emily McCurdy, the former Red Cross nurse who now sat in the passenger seat. The rest had been thrust upon him by chance and by wills other than his own.

He did not see that he had any choice but to let the strangers come along, at least as far as the hotel where he had reserved two rooms.

Britta Hayworth had accompanied Nurse McCurdy, the Irishwoman said, as her "companion." David could understand that a woman in her seventies would not want to travel alone and so did not take issue with the young woman's inclusion. He would decide if she should come with them to Dachau the next day, after he got to know her through the evening.

To David's mind, as he glanced at Britta, who sat in the van's second seat, she was pleasant enough company, with her upbeat personality and winsome smile. *Not bad looking, either,* he thought. A little young, barely older than most of his students at the university. But, then, he was not over the hill himself.

As for the men who sat on either side of Honey in the backseat, the long-haired one draping an arm over her shoulders, the professor had no real qualms. Honey had already told David enough about Pete that he was prone to believe the two brothers had literally stumbled into her in a mad dash to save her in Israel.

There was no mistaking the love that sparked through Pete's eyes as he gazed down on the sweet woman. And Mel seemed like an honest sort, as baffled by the events he was caught up in as all of them were.

None of the newcomers needed to know the particulars of David's mission—he and Honey had already agreed to that. As far as Emily and the others knew, this entire venture simply revolved around the mystery of the badge, and the desire of some agency in Israel to know what it meant.

Though it was spring, evening brought a dank chill to the dusk that settled over the Munich bogland. David was glad to find the hotel before darkness descended, and he pulled into the parking lot with relief. He was ready for a good night's sleep and pleased to see that, as usual, the accommodations were first-rate.

The Consortium never spared expense when it came to lodgings, David thought. This was a four-star hotel, its sixteen stories rising up from an elegant boulevard in shining, black marble panels.

"I'll go in and see if they can upgrade us to larger rooms," David said, as the Westers hopped out and began to unload the baggage.

By the time he had reregistered the three women in one suite and himself with the brothers in an adjoining one, bellhops had loaded the suitcases and backpacks on a brass cart and were headed to the sixth floor.

As the group followed the baggage in a separate elevator, David assessed their level of weariness. Nurse McCurdy and Britta had done no more than a major commute across the English Channel, Emily coming from Dublin and Britta from London. He and Honey were not too much worse off for having flown from Tel Aviv to Athens and then into Munich in one day. The Westers, however, looked pretty worn out. David could not have known just how worn out, for he did not know that they had been on the run for days, from Montana to Wyoming, to Ohio, and then overseas.

"You fellows feel up to a good meal before hitting the sack?" he asked.

Even given their state of exhaustion, neither of them was about to turn down such an offer. "Sounds good!" Pete said, and Mel nodded.

As the elevator door opened on the broad, carpeted corridor that led to their rooms, the group agreed to meet back in the main floor dining hall at seven.

"Dr. Rothmeyer," Britta called after the professor, "I've been wanting to ask you some questions. May I sit with you at dinner?"

David turned to her in surprise. "I would be flattered," he replied, a little nonplussed.

At this, she approached and thrust a business card into his hand.

"Thanks so much!" she said, leaving him to gawk at the impressive, embossed card: "Britta Hayworth—Staff Correspondent—*London Times*."

B ritta tried not to behave like a reporter as she sat across from Professor Rothmeyer that evening. The low-keyed dinner was meant for relaxation. But this was a chance she had never dreamed of, to be able to talk with another highly respected archaeologist— Father McCurdy, of course, having been the first.

When Emily had told her about the summons to meet Dr. Rothmeyer in Germany, the young correspondent saw an opportunity for two story possibilities.

She had brought all her charms and powers of persuasion to bear on her elderly friend, convincing her that she would be wise not to travel alone, and that the story of the old scribe at Dachau could be the one that would help put Britta in line for a regular slot with the *Times*.

The young reporter did not let on that the second story, and really the more important one to her mind, related to Emily's brother and the probability of a secret scroll. If David Rothmeyer was working for an Israeli agency, he must know something about the Cave Scrolls and the controversy surrounding them. Perhaps, just perhaps, he could shed some light on the mystery of Father McCurdy's skittish avoidance of the press.

She realized she would have to be coy in her approach to the topic, not wishing to offend Emily with her obvious opportunism. As for Rothmeyer, if he chose to be closemouthed, well, she had run into that before.

Britta had given much thought to how she might broach the topic of the scrolls. It had come to her that a direct involvement of Emily in the conversation would be the best way to avoid the appearance of scheming.

After the hotel waiter had taken orders around the table, Britta, sipping from a goblet of white wine, began, "Dr. Rothmeyer, my friend Emily is the most amazing person. Sometimes I think she should have been the journalist and not me!"

David observed Britta quietly, wondering what it was about himself, lately, that he was so aware of attractive women. He had been caught off guard by the pleasant intrusion of Honey Aronstam into his life, surprised at the magic her presence had worked on him, and disappointed when he learned how unattainable she was. Now, here he was, again, quite conscious of the magnetism of a pretty woman.

Certainly he had associated with many attractive females, both at the university and even in the field—young coworkers, instructors in the anthropology department, even students in his classes. None of them had ever particularly intrigued him.

As for Honey Aronstam, he had concluded that her allure had to do with the setting in which he had met her, the romance of Israel and Jerusalem, and her kindred interest in things Jewish, as much as her evident beauty and sweetness.

How should he reason with himself about Britta Hayworth? He had not spent enough time with her to have any good reason to give her a second thought, especially since, for David, good looks were not "good reason." Yet, in the few hours since he had met her, he had already thought about her more than a second time.

As she reiterated that she was a journalist, he came up with a probable explanation. At the elevator, she had placed a *London Times* business card in his hand, and he had been duly impressed. This was a professional woman, a peer.

Though she was young, her curly blond hair and cherubic face reminding him of a child star, she was adult enough to have made inroads into the staff of one of the world's most prestigious newspapers. He had always respected determination and strength in a woman, and this was evidence of those qualities.

In keeping with Britta's topic of conversation, he asked, "I suppose you are referring to Ms. McCurdy's involvement in this mystery?" He nodded courteously toward the elderly nurse. "If she is like me, she can be close to a wonderful story and not have the slightest idea how to capture it on paper." Then, more pointedly, he added, "I assume that is what you have in mind—turning our little mystery into a feature article?"

Britta blushed. "Guilty as charged," she said.

David glanced down the table toward Honey, who was not deaf to the conversation. He could see that she appeared uneasy at the thought of a possible involvement of the press.

"It remains to be seen," David said, turning back to Britta, "if there is any real story here at all. So far, we have only an old badge with a few scrawls on the back."

Britta took a bite of her salad and lifted her chin. "Dr. Rothmeyer," she said, "your agency would not have sent you to Germany if they believed there was nothing important to be had here." Then, smiling coyly, she added, "I wouldn't mind if I was on hand for some great find."

Emily, appearing to sense Honey's tension, tried to mediate. "The professor is right about journalism. I knew, when I met Rabbi Yitzak years ago that he was a wonderful character and that he had served his people. But I never could have made a news story of those facts."

Britta shrugged. "I suppose it remains to be seen if I can either. First, I should have the good professor's permission to exploit him in this way."

David gave a fleeting glance toward Honey. Trying to be diplomatic, he said, "If I were to be exploited, Britta, I can't think of a more charming exploiter than yourself. You must understand, though, that I am representing a group. This is not 'my' story, to be told to just anyone. This is Ms. Aronstam's story, and it is my agency's story. For now, we have reason to keep the press at arm's length."

Far from putting her off, this kind of statement was just the sort that got Britta Hayworth's investigative nose twitching. "And why is that?" she asked, wishing dearly that she could take notes.

David pulled back and looked at her cautiously. "Aha," he said, "an interview. No, Ms. Hayworth, I will not get into the nature of the agency or why it does anything it does. It is enough that you know Emily's side of things."

The nurse only looked bewildered. "I really have no 'side,' as you say," she replied. "I simply helped an old, dying man at Dachau by sending his family his precious badge."

Britta turned inquisitive eyes toward her friend. "Didn't you wonder about the writing on the back of the cloth?" she asked.

Emily shook her head. "You must realize that we were dealing with hundreds—no, thousands—of prisoners. I have no idea how many I helped in such a way, getting messages to their families, and all. The thing that was noteworthy about Rabbi Aronstam was how we found him that day."

Honey Aronstam had never heard the full story of the rabbi's rescue, and she leaned forward eagerly. "Emily," she said, "please, do tell us how you met my great-grandfather! I have always wished I could have known him."

By now, the waiter was placing meals on the table, the pungent aromas of brautwurst, sauerkraut, hot potato salad, and whitefish in herb sauce competing for attention with the topic of conversation. Digging into the hearty German cuisine, the diners nonetheless hung on to Emily's words, as she gave an account of that distant memory.

"I could never begin to describe the camp or the horrors we came upon. I will try to tell you, though I shiver even now to think of it."

Her eyes were misty as she paused, and David knew she was reliving in a moment the gruesome scenes she had managed to bury beneath years of passing time.

"The American GIs and the British troops who entered with us that day had just loaded the last of the survivors onto the backs of big trucks. They hung like skeletons to the side racks, staring through sunken eyes across the compound where they had endured the worst of hellish nightmares."

Forgetting for the moment about her food, Emily set down her fork and wound her fingers together, nervously weaving them in and out. "I was at the end of the barracks nearest the ovens. . . ."

The young people listened somberly, almost forgetting their own meals.

226

"We had just found a few survivors lying on the ground near the path that led to the deathhouse. They had apparently been scheduled to die that afternoon and were already close to expiring from cold and malnutrition. The troops were lifting their frail, nearly weightless bodies onto their own shoulders, carrying them out, sometimes two at a time, toward the trucks."

Again, she paused. Her voice cracked as she continued, "Suddenly one of the GIs shouted at me to come help him with something. I glanced up toward the oven house, and he was trying to carry an old man—the rabbi—away from the place. It seems he had come upon him, scrambling about at the back corner of the deathhouse. You'll see the place tomorrow, Dr. Rothmeyer. Anyway," she went on, "as he brought him out, the GI told me that he had found the old fellow madly pushing against the back side of the building. It seemed he was fixated upon one row of bricks and sat there, bony and frail, pounding and pressing upon them for all he was worth, as though—" She paused, as if a light had gone on in her head. "I never thought of it before, but it was as though he was trying to close something in!"

Honey quivered, setting her fork aside, and Pete reached for her hand.

"Did the old fellow say anything about what he was doing?" Mel asked.

"There were only two words that I could make out. He kept repeating 'Schuh,' the word which I believe means 'shoe,' just like we would say."

David nodded. "That's right."

"'Schuh!' 'Schuh!' he kept saying. And then something like 'dampen.'" Emily shrugged. "I don't recall anything else. You see, many of the people we rescued that day were talking out of their heads, if they were talking at all. We really gave none of this any mind at the time. The only other thing I remember about that episode was the old fellow thrusting his feeble fist into my hand and releasing his crumpled badge. 'Get this to my family,' he said, in English plain enough that I could understand."

Honey looked sadly at the tabletop and blinked back tears. "My poor great-grandpa," she said with a sigh. "The only things I know about him are what my father and grandfather told me. He was some sort of recordkeeper—"

"A scribe?" David interrupted.

"Yes, I guess so," she said. "What in the world could he have been doing behind that building?" Her voice was husky as she fought back tears.

Emily turned to her, reaching out and patting her arm. "I learned a little about him, once he gave me the name of his son and his whereabouts. Some of his fellow prisoners walked with the GI and me to the truck, where the poor old soul was to be carried out. The folks on the truck greeted him with a bit of energy, something rare in their condition. When we got him into the rig, they cradled him between them, trying to offer him warmth. The people who walked with us said he was an important man, something of a village historian. That is really all I know."

As her voice trailed off, the table was very quiet. Even Britta, for once, was speechless.

Pete took a handkerchief from his hip pocket and handed it to Honey, who dabbed her eyes. At last, David broke the silence.

"Well, I'm no literary critic, but your way with words certainly gives a picture," he said. "If a story does come of this, our journalist would do well to quote you."

Britta agreed, her blue eyes filled with admiration. For a long while, nothing more was said at the table, as each absorbed the sad legacy of inhumanity.

Britta was not so insensitive as to lunge forward with her investigation at this moment, but she would at least prime the pump for later efforts. "As I said earlier," she noted, "Emily should have been the journalist. But then, she is not the only one in her family to be blessed with a fine mind. You might be interested to know, Dr. Rothmeyer, that Emily's brother is a professor like yourself."

"Really?" he said. "Where does he teach?"

Emily brightened. "He is emeritus now, Dr. Rothmeyer. But he still lectures, now and then—at Oxford!"

The last two words were spoken with evident pride, and David could not help but be impressed.

"Oxford!" he exclaimed. "And what is his area?"

At this, Britta looked at Emily as though the thought were new. "Archaeology!" Britta sang out. "Isn't that something, Emily? To think, they are in the same field!"

"Why, that's right." Emily thrilled. "Perhaps you've heard of my brother, Professor. Ian McCurdy?"

David was stunned. The name blazed forth from his academic background like the name of Freud from the annals of psychiatry or Darwin from the field of anthropology. "Ian McCurdy!" he exclaimed. "He is your brother?"

"The same!" Emily replied, sitting up tall and straight.

"*The* Ian McCurdy who was on the Cave Scroll committee?" he marveled.

Britta pretended to be astonished at all these coincidences. "Right!" she said. "Isn't this something? The sister of one of the greatest archaeologists sitting at dinner with yet another great archaeologist!"

"Yes," Emily agreed, "this is amazing, indeed! And to think, Britta is the only reporter who has ever gotten an interview with my brother. He's quite mum, you know, about his work at Qumran." Then, pausing and thinking a moment, the woman seemed to have hit on an incredible irony. "In fact, you two men have a great deal in common, even for your profession! Israeli archaeology . . . tattered writings . . . "

David looked at Emily with a fixed expression. His face did not show the sifting and sorting that was going on in his brain, the amalgamation of facts and seeming coincidences that were surely not happenstance.

Then, not knowing whether to be angered or intrigued by the suspicion that posed itself to him, he turned intuitive eyes on Britta.

"I've read about the controversy regarding the Cave Scrolls," he said, slowly. "I know that the scroll committee hid them from the public for decades, but that's all I know, Ms. Hayworth. Were you hoping that I knew more?"

Guilty as charged! ran through Britta's head again. This time she did not admit her duplicity. Instead, with the deftness that could one day win her a Pulitzer Prize, she rallied, making the best of an awkward moment. "I must confess that the possibility did occur to me," she said. "Perhaps we can help each other in our quests."

Then, in a fit of inspiration, she added, "Wouldn't it be something if our two quests were one and the same?"

CHAPTER 30

More than most places on earth, the backdrop of Upper Bavaria fits its history. Frequently fogged over, the dismal terrain suits the spirit of what transpired there a generation ago. As the traveler passes through boggy stretches, gray and dampish cold, it is possible to believe the ghosts of Dachau and its numerous satellite camps might still linger there.

Indeed, through the headlights of trains and cars along the soggy grasslands, spirits have been seen. Whether sparked by people's imaginations, enlivened by the facts of the area, or whether true phantoms of agony and despair, these spectres are sometimes observed in the striped workclothes of the camp inmates—skeletal, piteous, hands outstretched to the speeding vehicles, as if asking passage away from a horror long past.

Perhaps no odder assortment of travelers ever wended through that bogland than the passengers in David Rothmeyer's rental van. From separate corners of the earth, from places as far distant and unlike as the Montana outback, the cobbled streets of Dublin, the metropolis of London, and a middle-American university in Ohio, they had been thrown together by what seemed more and more to be orchestrated events—events not of their own making.

That morning, they had picked at a hotel breakfast, feeling mixed emotions about the day's venture. David and Britta were, of course, eager to see how the mystery unfolded. Honey was apprehensive about going to the site of misery so closely connected to her family, and Emily had trepidations about returning to the place of nightmarish memories.

As for the Wester brothers, Mel's experience was closer to that of a tourist than any one of the others'. Pete, however, was a jumble of nerves, not ready to see what his Aryan brethren claimed never existed. He knew now that it must have existed, that the story handed down to Honey could not be a lie. He would go along quietly, fists clenched, shame-laden, but ready as he could be to see the truth.

None of the crew had slept well. David had tossed and turned all night, wrestling with an overwhelming sense of destiny. As if sent on a celestial roller-coaster ride for the past several months, he felt more keenly now than ever that something beyond himself was pulling him from one tidbit of information to another.

It was as though some invisible hand had been guiding him when he did not even seek guidance. Along the way it would stop and point a finger at a particular line of type, thrust him into some undreamed of conversation, or even fly him across landscapes he had seen only in books, depositing him here and there as the nameless spirit deemed necessary.

Oh, he knew now what that spirit was. It had to be God. Nothing else could have brought him this far. And he had even learned to pray—tentatively, hesitantly—but truly. Where it was all leading, and why, were the ongoing mysteries.

At times, the information he was now gleaning in his abstract delvings had nothing to do with his own skill as a researcher. It seemed to be planted just where the powers above knew he would dig.

The night before, he had been most confounded by one phrase dropped at dinner. It had jolted him at the time, but he had not digested it until later, as he lay in bed, tossing and turning. Emily McCurdy had related that Rabbi Aronstam's friends at the camp called him their "village historian." This fact, coupled with Honey's recollection of her great-grandfather's being a "scribe," had teased Rothmeyer's imagination all night long.

If this information was true, then whatever the rabbi was hiding at Dachau must relate to Jewish history. *A record of some kind!* David thought. The badge the old fellow had passed on to his family, with its cryptic references to rows and bricks, absolutely had to be a key to the exact bricks he was found working at the day the GI found him.

David tingled every time he considered the possibilities of what the old man had buried there. It could be nothing more than a personal account of his miseries in the camp, but if the man was a scribe he would not have been writing about personal matters.

It had to be some kind of a record.

Again, it could be no more than a list of names of his fellow villagers who had died in the camp. This would be a useful thing for families to have, and for future generations to refer to. But David had been on this assignment, this mission, long enough to have seen the celestial orchestration at work. He felt, to his very core, that he had been brought to Germany as one more step toward the fulfillment of the quest he had been assigned.

Maybe this was faith, he thought. He was beginning to believe that faith was not just an ethereal form of wishful thinking. It was not clairvoyance. He was beginning to see that faith was a certainty.

Faith was the substance of things hoped for, the evidence of things not seen.

Now, where had he heard that line? He would have to ask Rabbi Benjamin when he got back to Israel.

Of course, having worked in the field on countless digs, it had occurred to him that whatever Aronstam had been secreting away that day might have deteriorated beyond recognition. Particularly in this damp climate, it would be miraculous for any form of writing material to survive, walled up in a cold, moisture-riven wall for over half a century.

The old rabbi himself must have been concerned for such things, David thought. As he pounded on the wall, repeating the enigmatic "Schuh," "Schuh," he had also been moaning "daempfen," the German word for "damp." And then, what form of writing material had he been attempting to preserve? If the little badge was an example, with its coalish ink, it would be a wonder if anything legible remained.

Still, as David drove through the foggy morning, heading northwest out of Munich, he did so with a sense of anticipation. He felt certain, based on his experiences all along the way, that he had not come here for nothing.

Gripping the steering wheel resolutely, he peered through the mist and listened to the diesel engine of the German car. There was precious little other sound to cue in on; his passengers were amazingly quiet, each obviously lost in thoughts of his or her own.

The van was nearing the middle-sized burg of Dachau. The low, gray sky seemed even gloomier here. Even though it was late spring, the greenery was less than lush.

No one spoke as the car followed the street signs toward the encampment that lay on the outskirts of town. David wondered if his passengers were struck, as he was, with the fact that life went on here. Houses and yards were typical of homes anywhere else in middle-class Germany. Playsets with swings and seesaws testified to the fact that children grew up here, played, and went to school. Businesses operated, cars streamed down busy streets, people greeted one another on the sidewalks, as they would in any city.

The professor was profoundly disconcerted that the locals could eat, laugh, and sleep here. *Do they think about it?* he wondered. *What do they do with the fact that such a travesty happened on their soil, or that the compound still exists, a perpetual reminder of Aryan guilt?*

As he maneuvered the van onto the main boulevard that led to the memorial, David's stomach tightened. There, beside the road, was evidence that the Germans were not alone in their ability to "move on." A bright red and yellow billboard, an advertisement for a world-famous American burger chain, flashed its commercial message even here.

"I don't believe it!" he exclaimed, pointing to the sign. "Do you see that? Does that strike you as tasteless?"

"Tasteless, indeed," Emily said tersely. The others in the van shook their heads and muttered their disgust, while Pete, his jaw tense, eyed the sign incredulously.

At last they came to a long, high wall that stretched for several blocks along the street. Gray like the sky, it bore no emblems, no words upon its concrete facade. Atop the wall were several rows of barbed wire, and spaced every hundred yards or so were towers, their empty windows staring out upon the world like the eye sockets of dead giants.

"This must be it," Mel called out from the backseat.

All heads were turned, the passengers leaning toward the side of the van that passed closest to the wall. Beyond Mel's simple statement, no one said a word.

David Rothmeyer had visited the Holocaust Museum in Jerusalem. So had Honey, on her one-day tour of the Holy City. Profoundly moving as that had been, the museum was only a reproduction of scenes from the nightmare. This, however, was reality—reality based on memory, to be sure, but as physically present a reality as anything could be.

The impact it would have on them would be beyond definition, past description.

They made their way to the parking lot designated for visitors and piled out of the van. Honey reached for Pete's hot fist. Glancing down at her, he loosened his grip and let her slip her small hand into his sweaty palm. Britta walked quietly beside Emily, who was already choking back tears. David and Mel walked silently together, listening in amazement as Emily began, already, to relive that long ago day.

"This is where the trucks pulled in," she said, pointing to that very parking lot. "It was from here that we got our first glimpse of the emaciated bodies clinging to the iron gate. I can see them now!" she cried.

Stopping in her tracks, she shuddered, her face pale. "Oh, Britta," she gasped, "I don't know if I can go in!"

Britta grasped her close, and Mel reached out his protective hand to steady her. "We're with you," he said. "You can lean on me, if it gets too tough."

CHAPTER 31

The camp at Dachau was laid out simply, constructed for one purpose: the incarceration and extermination of human beings.

Beneath the now-vacant gaze of the first guard tower, the visitors freely entered an open gate, a gate through which prisoners were once ushered against their will.

As they moved along the walkway leading to the interior, they passed between the high gray exterior wall and a barbed-wire fence. Just beyond the fence was a deep trench.

Honey paused, looking at it quizzically. "What was the ditch for?" she asked.

"It was to keep the prisoners from reaching the fence," Emily replied. "They approached it only on penalty of certain death. Guards watched for trespassers from their turrets, submachine guns at the ready."

To the immediate left, upon entering, one long, wooden building sat watch over the huge, rectangular compound. Emily recounted that the Spartan structure once housed the SS, the ruthless officers who oversaw the enforced labor and eventual death of thousands. "Some of the Nazi officers hid in that building when the Allies invaded," she said, "but it was not much of a fortress."

Leading directly perpendicular from the headquarters was a pristine, graveled aisle. Emily walked with the group to the head of the path and with a sweeping gesture, explained, "Along each side of this corridor, the bunkhouses stood, containing wooden beds three levels high, like stalls on a slave galley."

Only two reconstructions remained of thirty-four bunkhouses, which, according to the diagram on a sign, were spaced in dreary, symmetrical balance down that wide path. Just the foundations of the others were visible, the buildings having been so run-down, the sign said, that they had to be demolished.

The Dachau that David and his party observed was a horribly clean place. All remnants of its gruesome past had been raked and shoveled and purged away, much as Lady Macbeth scrubbed at her guilty hands until they wreaked of cleanliness.

In the remaining starkness, the visitors were left to form their own images of the atrocities that had taken place here. It was as if, with the cleansing, a slate had been handed to them, not for the rewriting of history, but for the envisioning of it personally, privately, with whatever memories or imagination each might bring to it.

Nor was there any chance that imagination could overstate what had happened there. Not even Dachau survivors were capable of overstating it.

The starkness of the camp hit Emily McCurdy full force. The horror of that long ago day blazed at her from every open walkway, each exposed foundation. The souls she had seen that day were present in the extreme—the blood, the waste, the disease, and the brutality. She wished there were something to interfere, some professional guide, some taped lecturer whose account would take the edge off her memories. Had there been, she could have said, "Yes, that's good, but not good enough. That's close, but not close enough. I remember it differently."

The blending of her experiences with someone else's could have diffused the emotional impact.

It occurred to her that, in leaving Dachau to the imagination, the German people had displayed wisdom. A degree of absolution had been attained by their stark presentation of their history, their refusal to couch it all in explanation or description.

Only one area of the compound was devoted to images. The headquarters now housed a photo gallery, life-size black-and-white ghosts of the horror that had transpired here.

Though visitors were allowed to come and go freely from the compound, to wander from site to site unhindered, and though there were no guards or custodians scrutinizing their movements, the professor did not want to draw attention to his group by acting differently than most who came here. "We're not just visitors," he said, "but I think we should begin with a tour of the gallery."

Emily took a few hesitant steps into the place and broke into a dewy sweat. It was not so much the hideous depictions spread out through several long rooms that troubled her. By now, there were few people in the civilized world who had not seen such pictures in newsreels of the era and in the endless repetition of war movies and documentaries. Rather, what squeezed her heart and tripped her pulse was the knowledge that Nazi officials, the evilest and cruelest of humanity, had lived and worked within these walls.

Taking Britta aside, she begged off. "I'll wait for you outside," she said, her face pale.

Britta offered to accompany her, but she would not allow it. "I'll be fine," she insisted. "Go see the photos. I saw the real thing."

Quickly she passed back through the entryway and into the dismal yard, leaving Britta to rejoin the others.

As for David, while his mind was centered on the task at hand, he was drawn to the depictions, compelled to take in the horror of the photos. The captions, mostly in German, were obviously directed at the conscience of the offending nation, but the photographs spoke for themselves.

Every horror, from mass shootings at the edge of great pits, to burial mounds of twiglike corpses, was covered in the gallery. Scenes from one of the dormitories showed that the building was devoted to scientific and medical experimentations so grisly in nature as to bring tears to the women's eyes and cause David's stomach to churn.

One chart was of special interest to David and the others, for it outlined the various types of prisoners who had been incarcerated here. The visitors were surprised to learn that Christian Scientists, Jehovah's Witnesses, homosexuals, writers and artists who had offended the regime, and many others were taken captive and held in special bunkhouses. One dormitory was devoted solely to Catholic priests who had spoken out against Hitler. The SS took special pleasure in sending these men off to the experimentation lab.

For each type, there was a special badge, homosexuals designated by pink triangles, for instance, or political prisoners by orange ones.

In each case, however, if a captive fell into any of these categories, and was also a Jew, an extra triangle was added to his badge, to form a Star of David. It was apparent, from the photos, that for such prisoners, existence in the camp was made all the more miserable.

At last, as the little group made its way to the concluding photos in the gallery, the scene shifted. These photos, in full life-size, were of the Allied troops entering the compound, of their carrying the prisoners to the waiting trucks, and of their driving the SS at gunpoint off to prisons and trials of their own.

"This is what Emily described!" Britta gasped as she gazed upon one photo of Red Cross nurses lending assistance to the GIs and other allies. "Do you suppose she's in this picture?"

Mel, Pete, and the others gathered before the photo, scanning it carefully.

"How would we know?" Mel asked. "I'm sure she's changed a lot in fifty years."

David glanced out the window of the gallery and spotted Emily sitting bleakly on the front steps, apparently lost in thought, while other visitors came and went.

"Come on, guys," Honey said. "We should join her. She looks pretty miserable."

David led the group through the door at the far end of the building. Silently they crossed the yard to the nurse's side.

Pete, having said nothing throughout the entire tour, stepped up to Emily and placed a trembling hand on her shoulder. When she glanced his way, her face pale and wan, he found the courage to speak.

"Miss McCurdy," he said, his voice husky and tight, "I feel I don't deserve the honor of being in your company today. For a long time I believed those who say none of this here ever happened." He gestured to the vast compound and the fearsome towers. His eyes welled with tears, but he forced them back.

"I just want to say that I'm sorry," he went on. "It's one thing to deny the history books. It's another to deny your friends, and"—he turned to Honey—"your loved ones." He gave a deep sigh. "I don't know if I'm ready to see the rest, but I know I'm ready to believe. No—I *do* believe! And, well, I just want to ask your forgiveness."

Emily studied Pete's handsome Aryan face. She did not know this young man, but she knew he had been duped by one of the grandest lies of all time.

Reaching up, she patted his hand where it rested on her stooped shoulder. "My forgiveness is not necessary," she said. "Just pray that you can do something, from now on, to dispel the myth."

Then, rising, she smiled sadly at David. "Well, Professor," she said, "shall we move on? We came here to find something, and hopefully whatever we find will bring some healing."

At the back end of the compound, a little bridge led over the deep ditch that ran the circuit of the place. Passing through another gate, the group wended their way through a bower of fir trees and green bushes that, with their inviting look, were strangely out of place here.

This had never been meant to be a showcase. In fact, the Nazi regime had meant to hide their gruesome business from the world. But in designating the site a war memorial, the German people had done what they could to make the place minimally tolerable. Perhaps this pathway necessitated some kind of buffer, something to soften the ghastliness of what the brick buildings ahead represented.

But there was no real way to soften the horror of what that path led to.

Within the bower, three buildings stood, each one bigger than the last, as the ultimate work of the death camp demanded more and more space, more efficiency for its execution. These buildings housed the ovens, the final repository for thousands of unfortunates.

One end of the longest building contained the shower room, where prisoners thought they were entering for a bath. Though legend had it that these showers were never used, not even to gas the prisoners, that was no credit to the Nazis. If it was true that they were never employed, it was only because the SS had decided that such duplicity only wasted time. Better to execute the prisoners at gunpoint and move their bodies quickly into the incinerators.

As Emily made her way up the path and through the trees, she knew what she was about to see. Silently, she turned to Mel. The big, rugged policeman stepped to her side and offered her the strong arm he had promised.

"Thank you," she whispered, leaning on him.

For the first time in her seventy-six years, she felt frail. Emily had always been grateful for her good health and for her robust stature, which defied her age. Today she trembled like an old woman, and her heart beat like that of a bird caught in a net.

Suddenly Honey let out a little cry and buried her face on Pete's chest.

As Pete observed the unthinkable, his face was white as death.

The group stood before the largest of the buildings. Its great doors stood wide open, revealing two immense furnaces, each with its iron doors agape. There was no mistaking the fact that their tunnellike maws were built for corpses, the bottoms of the coffin-shaped oven liners outfitted with sliding iron stretchers for ease of deposit.

Mel placed a quivering hand to his lips. He had seen morgues in Los Angeles. As a cop it had been his distasteful duty to identify murder victims. Many times he had watched as slab doors were opened and bodies were pulled out on gurneys much like the platforms in these ovens.

But, never had a morgue, in L.A. or elsewhere, been outfitted to receive bodies the way Nazi ovens were. In front of the furnaces, on a beam that spanned the room, were suspended hefty iron pulleys, complete with huge hooks. A black-and-white sign attached to the beam explained in cryptic German, English, Russian, and Italian: "Prisoners were hanged from here."

Emily patted Honey's back. "The day I arrived here, GIs were taking bodies off those hooks. The ovens were still smoldering, but those poor folks at least received a proper burial."

Britta's eyes stung, but not from tears alone. "There is a stench to this place!" she moaned. "Is it what I think it is?"

"It must be," Mel replied. "After half a century!"

Emily pulled back and walked again to the pathway. Turning about, she gazed at the scene and stepped back in time. She could see the GI hailing her from the corner of the oven house.

She pointed in that direction. "That is where the soldier called for me," she said. "He had found the old rabbi around back."

David turned his attention her way. Despite the horrors of this place, the quest he was on took over. "Can you show us?" he spurred her.

Emily nodded. Mel offered to take her arm again, but she squared her shoulders and shook her head. "I'm all right," she said.

David glanced around the area and, seeing no other tourists, said, "We're alone now, but we don't want to be caught." Turning to the big ex-cop, he suggested, "Mel, how about standing out front here? If anyone comes along, let us know. We'll try to be quick."

Mel nodded and walked casually over to the first oven house, pretending to read a brief history posted there.

Adrenaline coursing through his body, David followed Emily as she led him and the others around the far end of the largest building, to the back side.

Pointing to the corner, she said, "This is where the rabbi was, sitting on the ground, pushing on the wall."

The spot she designated was overgrown with vines. "Here?" David asked.

"Yes, but the wall was bare back then," she replied.

David knelt on the ground and shuffled through the pocket of his tweed jacket. He pulled out a small notebook, opened it, and found the translation of Honey's badge.

"'Third row from the bottom, fourth brick from the end,'" he read.

He tingled as his eyes fell on the last lines of the directions, but he did not read them aloud: "Return priests to their service and Israel to its House of Prayer."

Like a surgeon, he called for the necessary implement. "Honey, the trowel, please."

Honey reached into her shoulder bag and pulled out a small, pointed tool, which David, in preparing for this assignment, had packed from Israel.

The archaeologist was now in his element. He deftly pulled the tentacles of a vine away from the old wall and ran the trowel down the face, looking for anomalies.

Pete, Emily, Britta, and Honey leaned close, breathing over his shoulder.

"Aha!" he said. "Look at this!"

Along the edges of the very brick designated by the badge, there was no mortar.

'This brick was removed at one time," he said, "and then it was replaced, but not sealed in."

His proficient eyes scanning the adjacent bricks, he noted, "It appears that three others were handled this way. See?" He placed his hand on the face of four contiguous bricks, two on top of each other.

Gently, he eased the point of the trowel between the mortared bricks and the one named on the badge, third row from the bottom, fourth brick from the end.

Suddenly Honey gasped. "Dave," she cried, "do you see that?"

The brick David worked with had some kind of etching on it. He ran his hand over the face and removed loose dirt.

The wide-eyed group leaned closer.

"This is it!" David exclaimed. "Can you believe it?"

There, plain as could be, was a Star of David, scratched into the red clay.

Honey knelt down beside David and ran her fingers over the precious mark. "My great-grandfather must have put this here!" she marveled.

"No doubt about it," David agreed.

Quickly now, he worked the trowel deep into the seams that separated brick from brick. Round and round each edge he worked the tool, pulling ever so gently as he did so, to ease the first brick out. Then, after placing the trowel on the ground, he used his fingers to loosen the brick further, until he had pulled it nearly all the way forward.

As his friends watched, he gave the final tug—and held the brick in his hands. "Here," he said, handing it to Honey. "This is yours."

The woman took it and cradled it to her chest, her eyes welling, while David continued to the other three rectangles, breaking them free and removing them, one at a time.

Now was the moment of truth. All five of the seekers were kneeling, as though in obeisance to the gaping hole in the wall. No light shone through, as the bricks apparently abutted an inner wall, forming only a facade. As the group peered into the opening, they let out a collective sigh.

"Wow!" Pete exclaimed. "Look at that!"

Against the inner wall, where connecting mortar should have been, was a wide green piece of rubber. Flat as a sheet, it was shaped like the silhouette of a foot and was graced with broad straps and rusty buckles.

"It looks like a boot!" Britta gasped.

Emily gripped the edge of the opening and stared at the strange, flat object. "Why, it *is* a boot! The kind the SS wore on rainy days! A lot of them were wearing these over their shoes the day we entered the camp!"

David hurried now, trying not to be clumsy, running his fingers down the edge of the rubber to loosen it from its fifty-year-old burial site. Gradually, he was able to ease it out. As he did so, the top edge separated, revealing that both sides were present. The sole, they saw, had been removed so that the rubber was like an "L" shaped tube.

"This must be the 'Schuh' the old rabbi kept mentioning," Emily said.

"He was worried that it would get damp," David recalled. "So, it must contain what we are looking for!"

Drawing the boot onto his lap, he leaned on his heels and pried it apart, ever so carefully. "Move back a little," he said. "Give me some light."

For a moment, the onlookers complied, but just as quickly pressed in again.

"Yes . . . yes!" the professor marveled. "There is something here!" Spreading the top of the boot wide, he turned the opening toward the group.

"What is it?" Pete urged.

David reached into the boot and pulled forth a dingy piece of fabric. It was rolled in a skin of transparent oilcloth, but through that layer could be seen the dark gray stripes of a prisoner's clothing.

"Where would he have gotten a boot and an oilcloth?" Britta marveled.

Emily was enthralled. "The troops used to keep their paper money in oilcloth. Perhaps the SS did too The rabbi must have come upon a piece of it!"

"Crafty old fellow!" David said with a chuckle. "He must have scavenged for this stuff for a long time. Now it remains to be seen if the rabbi's protective measures preserved his treasure!"

"Take out the fabric!" Britta cried. "Is something written on it?"

David gingerly unwrapped the oilcloth and pulled out the roll of striped cotton. "There's something here, all right!" he replied, loosening one end of the roll to reveal some jagged figures. "Looks like Hebrew!"

But just as he was about to unfold more, Mel appeared at the corner of the building. "Better hurry," he called in a hushed tone. "There's a group of schoolkids coming into the area with their teachers. Must be some kind of field trip."

David quickly rerolled the cloth and stuffed it into the oilskin. "I don't think we need the boot," he said, secreting the little parcel in his jacket.

Honey picked up the trowel and placed it in her shoulder bag. Then, despite David's assessment, she picked up the boot, a souvenir of her great-grandfather's bravery, wrapped the brick in it, and deposited it in the same bag.

David, catching her covert move, gave her a wink, and she smiled shyly.

"We'll have to read the rabbi's message back at the hotel," he said, taking Emily by the arm. "Careful. Don't trip over those vines."

CHAPTER 32

The mood in the van as the six travelers headed back to the hotel was quite different than it had been upon their arrival at Dachau. Though the experience of seeing the concentration camp was unspeakably sobering, the thrill of their find and the anticipation of learning its contents enlivened the spirits of the group.

Heading straight for David's suite, the little entourage fidgeted as the professor fumbled for his keys and unlocked the room door.

After casting their coats on one of the beds, they huddled anxiously around a table under the window and watched as David sat down, brought forth the parcel, and began to open it.

The morning fog had lifted somewhat, and sunlight, the first they had seen since entering Germany, filtered in glorious stripes through the venetian blinds. Emily drew the curtain cord and raised the slats, permitting the light to spill across the table. A distant view of the Alps went unnoticed by the preoccupied guests.

Before unrolling the oilcloth further, David glanced up at Honey, who stood breathlessly gazing at his still hands. "Perhaps you should do this," he offered. "After all, this is *your* property."

Honey smiled gratefully but shook her head. "Go on, Dave," she replied. "This is your quest, as well as mine."

The professor turned his attention to the parcel and pulled back the oilcloth carefully, unrolling it a little at a time until the striped cloth inside lay on top. Although he had handled many precious artifacts in his career, none had merited such respect as this one. Whatever this cloth contained, whether of use to his search or not, it had been created at great risk to the writer.

Gently, he unrolled the striped material as his companions bent close. He was reminded of the day the rabbis huddled with him around the long genealogy scroll in his apartment.

As he began to analyze the writing upon the fabric, he was first of all amazed at the condition of the piece. "The letters are still intact!" he said. "It is Hebrew, perfectly preserved!" Scanning it with the eye of a scientist, he went on, "The ink is of the same composition as that used on the badge. It is a crude, charcoal material, probably made from water mixed with scrapings from burnt wood, and applied with some sort of quill. My guess is that the rabbi made a pen from a piece of stick or a feather. That the writing has held up this well is utterly amazing!"

David's friends glanced at one another.

"Very interesting," Mel sighed. "But what does it say?"

"Yes, yes," Emily spurred David on. "Tell us the words!"

David bent close over the cloth and tried to read it. "Britta," he said, "if you'll look in my briefcase, over by the bed, you will find a magnifying glass. Would you get it for me, please?"

Britta hastened to comply.

"Here," she said, sliding it under his nose.

Holding it over the fabric, he gazed at the first line for so long, the group began to fidget again.

"What does it say?" Britta asked, trying to be patient.

"This starts out as a prophecy and then seems to become a chronicle," David said. "It follows the same pattern of many things the rabbis gave me to read when I began my search. Let's see . . . "

He paused again, and the group shuffled.

"Aren't you reading it backward?" Mel asked.

"Hebrew goes from right to left," Honey said, proud of her new knowledge.

Mel shrugged, looking a little embarrassed, but busied himself pulling up several chairs. They all sat down, except for Pete and Honey, who stood riveted with interest directly across from David.

"It begins something like this," he said. Haltingly, in broken syllables, starting and stopping, he interpreted the tiny figures:

Sons and daughters of Jacob, all you who suffer under the hand of desolation, take heart! The time is coming when Israel will be reclaimed and the land will be yours forever, and your children's forever.

Honey reached for Pete's hand, and he cradled it close to his heart.

"Now, here the chronicle starts," the professor went on.

Let all those who seek to rebuild the Holy Temple pay heed to the story of Israel Ben Kahana.

At this, he stopped and looked up at Honey. "Does the name mean anything to you?" he asked.

She only shrugged, and shook her head.

Going on, he read:

Many are those who say, "Behold, the priest! He is here or he is there. When the Temple is rebuilt, this one or that one shall light the lamps and offer the offerings and enter into the Holy Place to accept atonement for the sins of the people, after centuries of their wanderings. . . . "

David's voice broke. Incredible as it seemed, it appeared that what he was about to read had to do with his exact quest!

Britta, who sat beside him at the table, reached out and touched his arm, squeezing it softly. Moved by her gesture, he glanced her way and, for a fleeting moment, their gazes met.

"I take it this is what you were hoping to find?" she asked.

For once, David sensed that Britta's interest was genuinely personal, her question not part of an interview.

When he turned apprehensively to Honey, the only one present who knew the nature of his assignment, the woman nodded to him, as if to say, "I think it's safe."

"Britta," David replied, focusing on the pretty blond, "the subject matter is related to my work, true enough. I guess we'll see how related as I read on."

Tremulously, he continued his deciphering of the cramped letters:

But I tell you, there is a line, unbroken since the time of Aaron, brother of Moses, and from the time of the House of Zadok, of the reign of David and Solomon, which line is the only true one. . . .

David stopped and breathed out softly. "Wow, the old fellow knew the necessary qualifications! None of the non-Zadokite line were levitically pure."

The five listeners glanced at one another again, having no idea what he was talking about. However, they remained silent, not wanting to break David's concentration.

Holding the glass at an angle to enhance the sunlight upon the fabric, he said, "The letters are hazy here. There's a bit of old mildew."

Then he went on:

Many have claimed to be in that line, to have inherited the priesthood. But only one is worthy to be called High Priest, and his heritage has

been protected from defilement. He will be a descendant of one who
was rescued out of great destruction, who was taken from Jerusalem at
the time of its overwhelming.

"When would that have been?" Britta asked. "'The time of
Jerusalem's overwhelming.'"

David sat back a moment. "My first hunch is that he's referring
to the Roman invasion of 70 C.E. But he could also mean any number of later conquests. Maybe he will tell us."

The writing was laid out in narrow columns, much like the writing on a scroll. The professor bent over the fabric again. "The letters
are so incredibly small!" he noted. "It must have taken the rabbi
weeks to compose all of this, especially in secret. I can guess where
he started and stopped on different sessions, and even how he must
have been feeling on different days."

Honey withdrew her hand from Pete's grasp and leaned on the
table. "Really?" she marveled. "You can do that? How?"

David pointed to one section that had bigger, freer lettering
than the others. "See here," he said. "This is obviously a single ses-
sion. On this day, your great-grandfather either felt pressed for time,
and wrote hastily, or he was in a lighter mood than usual. Or, maybe
it's the subject matter that has him more enthused."

At this, he read:

Now, as to that day of overwhelming, it was a great and terrible day,
and it lasted for eighty-eight years. But it was a time of rescue, for it
was at this time that the soldier who wore a cross spared the young
Kahana and took him across the seas.

The professor sat back again and slapped his thighs. "Yes!" he
cried. "The Crusader period! The rabbi is excited to relate to us that
the subject of this drama was rescued by a Crusader and taken to
Europe. This phrase, 'soldier who wore a cross' has to refer to a

Crusader, and we know that the period of the Crusades lasted for exactly eighty-eight years!"

Britta absorbed David's enthusiasm. "So, you are investigating the Crusades?" she guessed.

At this, Honey laughed softly. "Dave," she said, "do you really think it would do any harm to tell everyone what you're after? Maybe Britta would promise not to make a headline of it just yet."

Mel nodded. "I'll tell you, I'd sure like to know what this is all about. I'm just a guy off the L.A. streets. I promise you, I won't tell anybody!"

All of them chuckled over this, and David lightened up. Looking at Britta, he raised his eyebrows.

"Of course, David," she said. "I won't make anything of it, not without your approval. You can trust me."

The professor was surprised by this unprecedented move on the reporter's part. Pondering her offer for a moment, he at last reached out a hand to shake her outstretched one. "It's a deal, Ms. Hayworth," he said.

Then, with a sigh, he gave a brief explanation of his work, emphasizing the sensitive nature of the quest, but giving no details of the genealogy.

"And so," he summarized, "you can understand that the search for the high priest of Israel is rather like the search for the catalyst to the apocalyptic age! We don't really have any idea where such a quest will take us, or the world around us."

Britta looked back at her friend, Emily, who listened to the professor's tale with an intensity as profound as her admiration of the old rabbi.

"Well, Emily," Britta mused, "it appears we got ourselves into much more than we bargained for."

"I'd say!" the nurse exclaimed.

Pete nodded empathetically. "I don't think any of you could be more surprised by all of this than I am. I sure never dreamed that looking for Honey would take me on the biggest trip of all time!"

The others laughed, and then David bent once more over the writing. "Let's move on, shall we?" he said. "I want to know where the rabbi is taking us next."

Eagerly, the onlookers listened as David read further:

Pay heed, you who have ears . . .

David glanced up at his audience. "The old prophets were great ones for lines like that. I guess the rabbi took after them."

Then, thinking of Honey, he quickly added, "Nothing against your great-grandfather. As the villagers said, he was their historian, and this is the way Hebrew historians write."

Honey hushed him. "Dave, it's okay. I'm just touched to get these glimpses of my ancestor. He must have been quite a guy!"

David nodded, and went on:

Pay heed, you who have ears. Israel ben Kahana was but a boy when the soldier who wore the cross took him to England.

The last word rang strangely through the room.

David raised his eyes for a moment, wondering if any of them could know how awesome such a declaration was.

"England!" he cried. "The computer analysts in Jerusalem told me there was a strong strand of genealogy going through England! The word the rabbi uses here is only a Hebraic approximation. There is no word for England in Hebrew. It is England, though—no doubt about it!"

Britta, particularly, was fascinated by the writer's claim. After all, she was British, and it was amazing to think that this cryptic account related to her homeland. "Are you saying that the blood of the high priest might flow in the veins of some unknown Englishman?" she marveled.

"I'm not saying that," David corrected. "Rabbi Aronstam says that. And he apparently bases his story on an ancient legend." He read on:

Let it be understood that the true priest will be found among the people of Britain.

David stopped and said, "That's another approximation." Then, he continued:

His line is that of Cohen, of the town of Castlemont-on-Wandermere.

At this proclamation, Emily McCurdy suddenly lurched forward in her chair. "Cohen?" she gasped. Then turning to Britta, "Do you suppose . . . "

Britta's heart thrummed. "David," she said, "my family on my mother's side are Cohens. Is it possible—"

David tried to be kind. "Anything is possible," he said. "But you must understand that Cohen in Jewish circles is like Smith in English or American circles. 'There are more Cohens,' my grandmother used to say, 'than there are bagels in New York City!'

"And, while the modern-day Cohens are related ancestrally to the first high priest, Aaron, they are not all high priest material!"

The group laughed, and David added, "It appears likely, though, that, since Kahana is a root-name of Cohen, whoever we find will be called Cohen, or something related to Cohen."

Britta sighed, and Emily sank back into her chair. The young journalist patted Emily teasingly, "Now, now, Emily, just think. If you had married Uncle Reg Cohen, you might be the mother of the high priest. Would you really want that responsibility?"

Emily laughed heartily. "You always see the bright side," she said.

The others did not know the meaning of this private allusion. When it was not offered, Honey suggested, "Read on, Dave."

"Hm," David mused, "the writing here is quite cramped and hurried. Maybe our rabbi was under some pressure to finish this thing."

The hour grows short. Let it be understood, when Israel goes about the business of rebuilding her sanctuary, and when the priest is found, he will be an heir of Israel ben Kahana. And his credentials will be proven thus: The pedigree of Israel ben Kahana extends back to the time of the first overwhelming, when the holy scribes moved to the desert. There they protected the ancestor of Kahana, and this is his name. When you shall find that record, the name shall be written therein, to prove what I write. The name therein shall be "Gabriel ben Zadok," and thus the line shall be complete.

David sat hunched over the fabric for a long while, as the others tried to make sense of what he had read.

The professor shook his head. "Let me see," he said. "'The first overwhelming' would most likely be the Roman invasion of Jerusalem in 70 C.E., and—of course! The holy scribes who went to the desert could be the Essenes! The ones who wrote the famous Cave Scrolls!"

Now it was Britta's turn to jolt. "Really?" she cried. "You mean the scrolls that Emily's brother worked on? What do they have to do with this?"

David sat back and rubbed his chin. "Now don't misunderstand," he warned. "I am not drawing any conclusions here. I could be all wrong about the first overwhelming and the scribes. It's just an educated hunch. You see," he said, his eyes bright, "the people of Qumran believed that the only pure Cohen line, the only Cohen branch worthy of the high priesthood, were the Zadoks."

When the group looked bewildered, he explained, "The Zadokites were the high priests of David's and Solomon's time. Zadok means 'righteous.' After that period, the priesthood was corrupted."

Britta's mind was whirring. "Back up, David," she pleaded. "I don't understand what the rabbi is saying."

Mel, who had no background in any of this, did have a quick, discerning mind. "It's simple," he said. "The old guy is telling us that we will know the right person for the job of high priest because his ancestry goes back to this Kahana kid. And the ultimate proof of everything the rabbi is recording will be in the fact that the Kahana kid is related to the last recorded heir, this—Gabe—what is it, again, Doc?"

David liked Mel's street-savvy analysis. "Gabriel ben Zadok," he repeated with a grin.

"Right," Pete jumped in. "You've got it, brother! Honey's great-grandpa was telling us, or whoever found his note, that the geneal-ogy would be complete with those two links—the Kahanas of England and the Zadoks of—where, Doc?"

"Qumran is a fair guess," David chuckled.

"Okay! Okay!" Pete exclaimed, totally caught up in the treasure hunt. "Then, we just have to find the Cohen of Castlemont, right?"

"No, that's not all," Mel countered. "We also have to find the Gabriel record. Right, Doc?"

"Seems so," David replied, amused that this quest had now become the focus of four new people.

"So . . . " Honey asked, "where do we look for that?"

Britta gave a little gasp, and all eyes were on her.

"What is it?" David asked.

The young reporter had turned to Emily in amazement, and the older woman stammered, "Britta, are—are you thinking what I'm thinking?"

CHAPTER 33

The next day, the little entourage that had visited Dachau departed Munich on two separate planes heading to opposite points of the compass.

The threesome from Montana took an El Al flight to Israel. When Pete and Mel accompanied Honey through airport security, she placed her shoulder bag on the x-ray conveyer belt so reluctantly that she raised the suspicions of the attendants. They had riffled through it thoroughly before they let her pass.

Finding nothing of interest other than an old boot and a red brick, which must have mystified them, they disregarded the precious treasure that lay wrapped in oilcloth with her wallet, her passport, her brush, and her lipstick. Shrugging to one another, the attendants had waved her on.

She sat now in the center row of the 747 as it took off from Munich on the noon flight, safely ensconced between the Wester brothers. In a few hours, they would arrive in Israel, where Honey would release her precious document to Rabbi Benjamin and his Consortium colleagues for analysis.

Meanwhile David, Britta, and Emily were on a plane to England in the hopes that Father McCurdy would receive them.

What inspired this unplanned trip on David's part was a strange story Britta had shared as the group was gathered around the table in his hotel suite.

He had just finished deciphering the words on the striped cotton rag, and they were discussing the missing "Gabriel Ben Zadok" record, when the two Britons lurched as though hit by an electric current. It seemed that a sudden hunch had gripped both of them regarding a possible key to the genealogy. That hunch related to Britta's experiences with Father Ian McCurdy.

The group already knew that she was the only reporter to whom the elusive archaeologist had granted an interview. What not even Emily had suspected, until that moment, was Britta's intuition regarding his elusiveness.

"I felt I had reached a dead end with your brother," Britta told Emily, "until the day you and I had lunch at the Oxford pub. I knew he was hiding something, based on the way he avoided my questions in the interview, but it wasn't until that day that I began to suspect what it might be."

Emily had bitten her lower lip, trying to think back. "What did I say, Britta? I can't imagine—and I wouldn't want to betray Ian."

Britta hastened to assure her she had done no such thing. "No no, dear," she said. "There was no betrayal. Do you recall telling me that your brother and his friend, Cromwell, were going to London the next day?"

"Why, yes, I did. But what—"

"Well, you told me that he was going to visit his study carrel at the British Museum, that Oxford professors are assigned such places for research."

Emily was bewildered. "I don't see—"

"You also told me," Britta continued, "that he visits it only about once a year, just to keep his tenure. It was then that I thought, 'Why would an Oxford don need a study carrel when he is no longer regularly teaching or researching?' From my meeting with you brother, he did not seem the pompous sort who would want to maintain such a privilege out of pride."

Emily laughed. "Ian? Absolutely not! Sometimes I wish he were not so humble."

"Very well, then. Perhaps you can see how my reasoning led me," Britta went on.

David and the others followed her logic closely, caught up in yet another mystery.

"Knowing a bit about the British Museum, I realized that it is a great repository of ancient writings. Though I had not ever heard of it housing any of the Cave Scrolls, I thought it would be a logical place for a linguistic archaeologist to work on such a thing, perhaps even keep such a find safe and secure."

David's intuition clicked in. Recalling how Rabbi Katz and the Consortium leaders had said they believed there was Cave Scroll material yet to be divulged, he jumped in, his eyes wide with possibility. "Are you saying you suspected Father McCurdy was sitting on an unreleased scroll? Are you thinking that the scroll committee never released all of its findings?"

Britta nodded excitedly. "That's exactly what I thought, and still do think, Professor. I knew, as I spoke with him, that there was more to his evasiveness than fear of exposure on the issue of the Cave Scroll Deception Theory."

Pete, Mel, and Honey did not know what this was and looked quizzically at her. But David knew. He had read all about it in various journals.

Quickly he explained. "For a while there, the media was full of the theory that the Cave Scrolls had been kept from the world by the scholars who worked on them because the scrolls might contain something destructive to Christianity. Ongoing scholarship has pretty much debunked that notion," he said, "but McCurdy's avoidance of the press, as the only living member of the original team, keeps the rumor active."

"Exactly!" Britta said. "Thanks to pressure from his sister, I was able to get an interview, and felt quite fortunate. But when Father McCurdy answered my questions about the Deception Theory as adroitly as he did, I began to wonder why he had avoided the press for so long—especially if he could deflect that rumor with a few words."

Diplomatically, she told Emily, "When I asked him that very thing, he seemed to be cornered. I did not mean to make him uncomfortable, Emily. But he was quite nervous, and soon enough, I was ushered to the door by Cromwell and left to ponder it all."

Emily smiled and patted Britta's hand. "It's all right, dear. My brother has been a riddle to me for years. I never did understand why he never returned to Dublin after he retired from Oxford. Now it makes more sense. The faculty there is really quite cloistered, you know. It is quite a chore for the press to climb inside those ivy-covered walls."

David thought a moment. "So, Britta, let me complete the circle of reasoning. It seems that my reference a moment ago to the desert scribes of Qumran may tie in here. Is that what you're thinking? Are you saying that Rabbi Aronstam's reference to the genealogy being composed and protected by the desert scribes could be related to McCurdy's secret?"

Britta held up her hands. "You *are* a fast thinker! That's precisely what I was driving at. But let me tell you more."

Pete and Honey leaned over the table, breathless, while Mel listened with the ears of a cop accustomed to unraveling clues.

"The day after Emily and I had lunch, I went to London. Sorry, Emily," she said, "but I didn't think you needed to know. Anyway, I suspected that your brother was going to pop up at the museum, and so I reserved a slot in the reference room and watched for him. Sure enough, he came in, with Cromwell in tow. Before he got there, I had pumped the reference librarian for information about the research carrels. Just as I had expected, they were used for storage of research materials, as well as for work. In fact, the attendant told me, the ones designated for the Oxford professors are even outfitted with lockable safes!"

Mel nodded eagerly. "So, what happened when McCurdy arrived? Was he shocked to see you?"

"Shocked?" Britta laughed. "Indeed he was! He went white as a sheet, and Cromwell needed to hold him up!" At this, she glanced again at Emily. "Sorry."

The older woman looked a little sad but shrugged her shoulders and sighed. "My poor Ian," she said. "He put himself in this position. I just want to know why."

David spoke reassuringly. "Perhaps we can find out why, Emily. And maybe in so doing, we can help your brother. He apparently carries a very heavy burden, something no one should do alone."

The nurse smiled gratefully. "Are you saying we should go to him?"

The professor nodded. "One call to Jerusalem, and we will be on our way. Honey, if you will take the Dachau parcel to Rabbi Ben, we can try to track down this end of things, okay?"

David, Britta, and Emily agreed not to notify Ian of their coming. It would make him too skittish and give him a chance to cover himself.

Though Emily had pangs of conscience, she put the quest above misplaced loyalty. Whatever Ian had hidden for nearly half a century, it was time, she thought, that he let it go.

CHAPTER 34

Gatwick Airport was fogged over in typical British fashion when David, Britta, and Emily arrived. Deciding that they would wait until morning to catch the bus that ran day and night between London and Oxford, the three got off the airport train at Victoria Station and took the subway to South Kensington, the terminal nearest Britta's apartment.

David considered his good fortune in being thrown, by fate or whatever forces were leading him, into the company of the young English woman. This aspect of his ongoing adventure was, to this point, the most charming surprise.

The more the professor got to know the perky reporter, the more he liked her. He had come to understand that her blunt, businesslike manner, when he had first encountered her in Munich, was pure professionalism. When she allowed herself to be simply sociable, she was delightful.

The three travelers would stay at Britta's walk-up apartment for the night. A short jaunt from the subway station, it lay on a narrow, cobbled street, typical of many London neighborhoods. A renovated townhouse with classical white trim and slender columns, it had been transformed in the 1950s into four flats, one on each floor and one in the basement. The reporter's flat occupied the top level.

When Britta opened the door to her little suite, David was captivated. Nothing gave a better glimpse into a woman's soul than her own residence, he thought. It was there that she revealed, in her furnishings, the colors of her walls, the paintings she had hung, and countless other details, a personality not always observable to an outsider.

While Britta could be brusque and businesslike when going after a story, she revealed a much softer aspect in the way she had decorated her apartment.

Mauve and pale beige were Britta's colors. Her home was casual and modern, in contrast with the classic design of the building. But there was no chrome or black leather in Britta's contemporary abode, a style often found in the apartments of young professionals who put on minimalist airs. Britta's furnishings were of Danish teak and other golden-hued hardwoods, the polished oak floors warmed with large, neutral area rugs. Color was reserved for wall racks full of Franciscan earthenware, its splashes of irises and peonies repeated in full curtains gathered on brass rods across the french doors of the third-story balcony and in throw pillows piled about the floor.

Gilt-framed landscapes of the English countryside were the only other wall decor, except for a large, flowered wreath that encompassed a collection of personal photos depicting family and friends.

The professor was instantly at home, and Emily turned perceptive eyes upon him as Britta took their coats. "She has a lovely way with things, hasn't she?" the elder woman said.

David only nodded, his pleased expression speaking for him.

"Why don't you put your baggage here by the couch?" Britta suggested, guiding David across the room. "I hope you don't mind a sleeper sofa. There are twin beds in my room, which Emily and I can share."

"The sofa will be fine," David said. "I think I'll be able to sleep on a rock by bedtime."

Britta turned to the gas-powered grate in her small hearth. "It will take me only a moment to light a fire, and then I'll fix something to eat!"

She flicked on a switch near the mantel, and instantly a welcoming blaze lit the fake logs in the fireplace. "*Voilà!*" she said, and turned to her guests with a little laugh.

"That's wonderful, Britta," Emily said, taking her own bags to the bedroom. "But we don't expect you to cook, not after traveling all day."

David shook his head emphatically. "There must be wonderful restaurants in this neighborhood," he said. "I saw all sorts of exotic cuisine advertised as we were walking here. Let me treat you both."

But Emily deferred. "I'll tell you what I'd really like," she said. "A nice cup of tea and a little nap. If you'll permit me, Britta, I'll just forage in your cupboards. But I think the two of you should go out for a nice meal."

David liked the sound of that, thinking there could be nothing more desirable than to spend the evening alone with Britta.

But she was not so sure. "I don't like to leave you, Emily. Are you certain . . . "

"Positive!" Emily insisted. "Just show me the way to the teapot!"

The old, lantern-shaped lamps of Kensington Avenue were just coming up as Britta led the way to one of her favorite haunts. She and David had decided they wanted something light, after sitting on a cramped plane all afternoon and downing too many snacks.

"You'll love this place!" Britta said gaily as she pointed to one of the basement windows of a corner townhouse. The window, set deeply into the old stone foundation, was enclosed by a decorative iron fence. Bright geraniums added a splash of color to what could have been a dingy hole.

"The entrance is around the corner on the back side of the building," Britta said.

The block on which the building sat was shaped like a piece of pie, the building itself three-sided and taking up the tip of the triangle. Britta guided David to the narrow, brick stairway that wound down to an open door. Soft, happy music floated up from the cellar, along with the smells of onion soup and pasta sauce.

A bright red sign showing a chubby chef in a tall hat read "Vincent's."

"The after-work crowd has probably left by now," Britta said. "I hope we can get a table."

As David stooped inside the low door, Britta glanced up at him and giggled. "I tend to forget how tall you are!" she said.

The restaurant was really more of a diminutive café. *Any number of people would constitute a "crowd" in this place*, David thought. Fortunately, there was a spot near the door, and the couple slid onto benches, facing each other across a dark wooden trestle table.

The main piece of furniture in the room was a short bar, along which four men and one woman sat, their feet resting on a brass rail. The matron of the place, who also served as the bartender, hastened out to greet Britta the moment she entered.

"Good evening, Miss," she said, her words thick with a Cockney accent. "Back from the Continent so soon?"

"Yes, Martha," Britta answered. "This is my associate, Dr. Rothmeyer." She turned to him. "Do you like onion soup? It's wonderful here." When he nodded, she said to the woman, "We'll each have the soup."

The woman nodded, her plump cheeks bright like an elf's.

After serving each of them a glass of red wine, which she always assumed people wanted when they ordered her onion soup, she bustled into the kitchen, where she also served as cook.

David peered into the cavelike room where the culinary work was done. "And where is Vincent?" he asked, seeing no one else back there.

"I'm not sure there is such a person," Britta answered with a laugh. "I think Martha is the jack-of-all-trades in this place."

David raised his glass and tapped the rim of Britta's drink in a toast. "Nice to be here," he said. "Vincent or no Vincent."

For the first time since he sat with Britta at the table in Germany, where the group had examined the rabbi's scroll, his eyes locked with hers. He thought he read in her warm gaze that the attraction was mutual.

"To tomorrow," Britta said, leaning her glass toward his.

"To tomorrow," he repeated, "and to Father McCurdy."

Britta smiled, and David set his drink down, then cleared his throat. "I have been wanting to share some thoughts with you," he said. "Ideas have been tumbling around in my brain ever since you told me about McCurdy and the possibility that he is in possession of Cave Scroll material."

"Yes?" Britta said, leaning across the table.

"It's been a long time since I paid much attention to the story of the scrolls and their controversy. But I recall that there was one document in particular that sparked a good deal of interest when it was discovered, in the early fifties, I believe. It was called the Copper Scroll. Have you heard of it?"

Britta thought back. "Yes, of course. All of the others were written on leather."

"That's right. In fact, the Bedouins who discovered them originally sold some of them to a shoemaker in Bethlehem, who thought he could use them in his shoemaking business!"

"I read about that!" Britta said. "But there was one that was made of metal, and the scroll team had a great deal of trouble even figuring out how to open it."

"Right," David replied. "It was frozen shut with corrosion. They finally cut it open with a small electric hand saw, mounted on a slide."

Britta nodded thoughtfully, then asked, "So, what does that have to do with Father McCurdy?"

"Well, follow me, now," he said. "Do you remember what the Copper Scroll was all about?"

Britta frowned for a moment, then suddenly brightened. "Yes, I do!" she replied. "It was a list of treasures. The scholars thought it might be a list of things taken from the temple before the Romans arrived, and hidden about the countryside for protection."

"Yes," David agreed. "It's thought that the directions to the various treasures might be in some kind of code. Anyway, so far no one has been able to decipher it. And, according to some estimates, that treasure, if all put together, would constitute enough to pay off my country's national debt!"

"Good Lord!" Britta cried. "That much?"

"That's what they say," David repeated.

Britta shook her head. "I still don't see how that relates to Father McCurdy. What are you thinking, David?"

The professor was about to speak, but stopped short as the waitress-cook-bartender returned to the table, placing two steaming bowls of onion soup before them, with a pewter plate of hard rolls.

Nodding to the woman, David thanked her and waited for her to leave.

Then speaking softly, he went on. "The fact is that the Copper Scroll contained more than a list of treasures and their locations. It also contained an enigmatic reference to yet another Copper Scroll, which, it seems to indicate, would give the key to the code that conceals the treasure locations!"

Gasping, Britta sat back and gawked at the professor. "Do you know what you're implying?" she asked. "You are saying that Father McCurdy may be sitting on the key to the greatest treasure on earth!"

David's heart beat faster, echoing her excitement. "Well, it's as possible as anything else I can come up with," he asserted.

Britta's hands went limp, and she rested them in her lap. "Very well," she managed at last. "Let's assume you're right, that this secret of Father McCurdy's relates to gold and jewels and wealth unimaginable. Lovely as that would be, what does it have to do with your assignment, with what's truly important here?"

When Britta asked this question, David felt himself melt inside. With that one inquiry, she revealed more about her character than many women would do in years. She showed that she had a true sense of values, that what she deemed important was not money or material treasures, but the sort of spiritual quest that David's assignment represented.

For a long moment, he only stared at her, saying nothing.

At last, growing uncomfortable, she squirmed. "What is it?"

"You are amazing!" he said. "Most women would stop at the gold and silver thing! That would be enough for them, and they'd be off on a chase for the golden goose!"

Britta's eyes grew wide. "Perhaps some would," she agreed. "Priests and prophecies and that sort of thing are more to my liking. Besides, I don't think Father McCurdy gives a fig about material treasures, either."

David looked down at his soup, wondering why he was lingering over a bowl of broth when what he wanted was to scoop a far more delicious morsel into his arms.

He swallowed hard and forced his thoughts back to the topic at hand. "I'm glad to hear that," he said, "because that makes what I'm thinking even more plausible. If your Father McCurdy has the scroll I believe he might have, it probably contains another treasure list.

That list would not be of lampstands and golden bowls and trumpets. It would be a list of names—the genealogy that the desert scribes hid, the one Rabbi Aronstam referred to! If I'm right, Britta, Father McCurdy hordes a find that will usher in the millenium!"

Britta was amazed. "Really?" she croaked. "But why would he want to hide such a thing?"

"I hope we'll find out tomorrow," he said.

Quietly the two ate their meal. David's mind was whirling with possibilities—and not only regarding the scroll. He was also thinking about a very different treasure. In Britta he had found something more precious than anything the world could offer him.

He planned how he would manage to hold her hand on the way back to her apartment. The attainment of that sort of treasure did not require a map. It only required courage.

CHAPTER 35

Although Emily McCurdy had never married, never lost her heart to anyone after Reg Cohen, she was good at matchmaking. It was clear, however, that her services in that area were not going to be necessary to get David Rothmeyer and Britta Hayworth together. She had done enough in seeing to it that they had had dinner alone together the evening before. Beyond that, there was nothing she needed to do, because the spark that flickered between the two was growing into a nice enough flame all on its own.

On the bus ride from London to Oxford, the two women suggested that David ride next to the window, since he had "never been privileged," as Britta teased, to see the English countryside before. She sat beside him, pointing out the highlights along the way, and Emily sat across the aisle, enjoying their interchange.

David did not reach for Britta's hand in the presence of so many passengers. But she could still feel the warmth of his touch from the evening before, when, as they walked back to her apartment, he had brushed her fingertips with his and gently slipped his strong hand around hers.

Though surprised by this gesture, Britta had not pulled away. She felt herself eminently comfortable with the professor.

Amazing, she thought now, how much could be said without words! She, who made a living with ink on paper, would have been at a loss to describe the instant bond that that simple move on David's part had created.

Today, as she leaned close to him, naming the hamlets and old churchyards that dotted the knolls, the streams that crisscrossed the rolling green hills, recounting bits of history marked off by hedgerows and ancient roads, she enjoyed the feel of his tweed-jacketed arm against her own and took pleasure in studying his strong profile against the window.

If any part of England could win the undying admiration of a visitor, it was Oxford. As the bus pulled into the modern sector that defined the entrance to the city, it was clear to David that Oxford did not languish on the laurels of its academic reputation. It was a thriving, bustling place.

The university, itself, was actually an amalgamation of thirty-five separate colleges, each one an architectural gem. The bus passed broad greens and expansive rock-walled gardens fronting buildings rich with the ambiance of tradition, and at last parked in front of the quaint pub where Emily and Britta had had lunch not long before. As the passengers disembarked, the two women glanced at each other.

"Hard to believe our last conversation here portended such an escapade!" Emily commented.

Britta agreed. "And it may be only beginning!"

"We will need to take a cab to my brother's house," Emily said. "It is quite a distance out of town."

David crossed the parking lot where the bus sat waiting for its next load of passengers to return to London. Other buses churned in and out of this lot on a schedule of fifteen-minute turnarounds, and eager cab drivers lined up just as regularly to take visitors to whatever part of Oxford they wished to see.

Hailing one of the cabs, David gestured to the women and they all piled in.

"Windham Road," Emily said. "About five miles out, and then a turn to Crossing Creek."

David loved Emily's lilting Irish accent. Coupled with the quaint English place names she called out, it charmed him.

"I wish I could spend some time here," he said. "I know already that I'll want to return."

Britta nodded. "And so you shall," she insisted. "We will see to it, won't we, Emily?"

As the cab wended through the cobbled streets of the ancient village, the two women pointed out the old pub where C. S. Lewis was known to join his colleagues most every day after classes; Blackwell's Bookshop, which was actually housed in several buildings and was said to contain two miles of stacks; and the great bell tower of Christ Church College, where each evening the bell pealed 101 times for each of the first year's enrollees.

"Ah," Emily said, pointing to a cluster of antiquarian stone buildings directly across from Tom Tower, "that is Pembroke College, a rare Catholic institution in this Anglican stronghold. Its specialty is Middle-Eastern studies. My brother is an emeritus member of the faculty and can often be found in the faculty lounge, like a proud member of some British men's club!"

"Do you think he might be there today?" David wondered.

"Usually not on Fridays, Professor," she replied. "He likes to get a start on his weekend gardening on Fridays."

Britta recalled her visit to Father McCurdy's home. "He is a master gardener, David. To see his place, you'd think that gardening was his profession, and not archaeology!"

Emily nodded. "He always says he was born to dig. I guess he just transferred that instinct to the flower beds when he retired."

The cab was now crossing Oxford's River Isis, the upper reach of the Thames, where the university's famous intramural rowing races were held. Britta, whose interests were more literary, pointed to the gentle green slope that led down to the water.

"They say that's where Lewis Carroll told Alice the stories that became *Alice in Wonderland*," she said. "Remember the dream of the rabbit and the rabbit hole? It was against that tree that little Alice supposedly fell asleep and then began her adventure."

David smiled. "Well," he said, "let's hope the chase we're on leads to more than a Mad Hatter's Tea Party. I'd hate to go back to Jerusalem hearing Rabbi Ben shout, 'Off with his head!'"

Britta and Emily laughed with him. But, as the cab passed beneath a tunnel-like covering of ancient oak branches and turned down a winding lane toward a distant cottage, the professor felt a little like Alice must have felt. He only hoped he was on the trail of something real, and not a bizarre fantasy.

I an McCurdy leaned on the handle of his garden hoe, peering down at his rose bed. This time of year, the weeds seemed to leap from the black, turned soil even as he looked on.

"I am getting too old for this," he called over his shoulder. "The chickweed moves faster than I do."

John Cromwell set a tea tray on the glass-topped patio table. "Come, Ian. Take a break," he said. "The weeds will still be there when you return."

Father McCurdy removed his gardening gloves, the fingers of which were worn through, and he wiped a light sweat from his brow, leaving a smudge of dirt above his eyebrows. Just at that moment, the cab from Oxford could be heard pulling into the front drive.

"Oh, heavens!" the old priest fumed. "Not another salesman! How do they find us way back here? Send him away, won't you, John? I'm in no mood for chitchat."

"Shall do," Cromwell replied, and hurried off.

When instead of giving a rebuke at the front door, John was heard to greet someone cheerily, Ian drew out his handkerchief and wiped the soil from his face. Who could be coming to visit, he could not imagine.

In no time, Emily bustled into the garden, greeting her brother robustly.

"Emily!" Ian exclaimed. "You are back from Europe already? Why didn't you let me know you were coming . . . "

Then his voice suddenly dropped as he saw that Emily had brought company with her—not just any company, but the bold young reporter from the *Times*.

Seeing her, the old priest went clammy. The last time he had laid eyes on this girl, she had been at the British Museum. That day he had been convinced that her appearance there was not happenstance, and the reference librarian had revealed that she was on some nameless mission regarding an obscure manuscript. Ever since then, Ian had believed that she might have deduced something about his secret, and he never wanted to be confronted with her again.

When Emily had phoned from Dublin, telling him that she had been summoned to Germany on a Red Cross matter, he had not questioned her. She was an independent woman, who had maintained ties with the service organization. His only concern had been for her traveling alone, and when she assured him that her friend, Ms. Hayworth, would accompany her, his fear for her safety was assuaged. Since his sister knew nothing of his precious scroll, there was no danger that she would reveal anything to the reporter.

"Ms. Hayworth," Ian muttered. He bowed slightly to her and pulled up two chairs for the ladies.

John was flustered, however. Standing in the doorway, he gestured to his friend. "We have yet one more coming," he called. "He is just now paying the driver." He disappeared into the house and returned a minute later with David Rothmeyer.

Emily jumped to introduce her guest. "Ian, this is Professor Rothmeyer. He was in charge of the investigation in Germany," she said. "David, this is my brother, Father Ian McCurdy."

David crossed the patio, his lanky arm outstretched in greeting. Ian quickly wiped his dirt-smudged fingers on his handkerchief and the two men shook hands.

"Father McCurdy, this is an honor!" the professor exclaimed. "I never expected to meet such an eminent member of the Cave Scroll team!"

Ian looked at him curiously. "Glad to meet you, I'm sure," he said, offering him a seat. Confused by this unexplained visit, he asked, "And just how is it that you happen to be here? Did my sister so charm you that you had to follow her home?"

The little gathering laughed together, and as Ian and John offered tea all around, Emily filled her brother in.

"The two of you have much in common, Ian," she said. "Dr. Rothmeyer is an archaeologist, like yourself. And a linguist! Not only that, but his present interest is in Israeli archaeology."

"Is that so?" Ian marveled. "And how do you happen to be working on a Red Cross matter?"

When Britta suddenly spoke up, McCurdy looked at her coolly. "Father," the young woman said, "David has been dealing with old Israeli records, attempting to piece together a puzzle that spans centuries—not unlike the work you did at Qumran."

Such a pronouncement, especially coming from the nosy reporter who had been a source of untold anguish, put the old priest on guard. "I doubt it is anything like the work we did at Qumran," he answered tensely. "That was a localized phenomenon, and our findings related to a specialized sect."

Then looking at David, Ian added, "I'm sure you have read all about it in the journals, Dr. Rothmeyer."

"I have read some," David said, his thin face tightening. He wished Britta might be a little less spontaneous. Better to lead into this thing more subtly. The matter had been introduced, however, and David knew it was up to him to smooth the way.

"Father McCurdy," he said, "Ms. Hayworth's analogy may be an overstatement. My work may be nothing at all like yours, but when Britta spoke to me of her talk with you, I got to thinking that you might at least have some leads for me to follow."

Ian sat back and considered the two intruders carefully. So, the reporter had told the professor of her attempt to interview him. Feeling slightly cornered, he grew agitated. "Dr. Rothmeyer," he began, his voice dry, "as you know, I have kept away from questions for years. Unless your interest relates specifically to the Cave Scrolls, I have little to offer you. And even if I did have, I doubt that I would."

Ian's manner, as contrasted with David's, was anything but diplomatic. The professor was not surprised. He had read enough about Ian McCurdy and his way with inquisitors to expect no spontaneous fellowship.

But David could fire back rapidly, when a situation demanded. Facing the priest squarely, he replied, "What if I were to tell you that I think my assignment is linked directly with what the Essene scribes were all about? What if I were to suggest that I suspect there are things yet to be found in those ancient caves, if they have not been found already, that bear directly on my quest? Would you speak with me then?"

The priest sat back and studied David long and hard. At last, after clearing his throat, he tried to keep steady.

"I don't believe you've told me who you are working for," he said.

David's answer sank into Ian's heart like a harpoon. "I have been hired by an international agency called the Temple Consortium. Have you heard of it?"

Father McCurdy jerked a sideways glance at his secret-sharer, his sole confidant, John Cromwell. John's face was suddenly pale, a mirror of his own.

He was sure that John was thinking of the same thing he was: the little advertisement they had read months before in the *Biblical Archaeology* magazine, the one announcing that a committee of Orthodox rabbis was seeking a Jewish archaeologist with a background in linguistics for sensitive study.

Noting that Ian's hand was shaking as he put down his teacup, John did just as he had the day they ran into Britta Hayworth at the British Museum. Stepping up behind him, he reached out a comforting hand, to support him. And just as he had done when Britta Hayworth came to the house for her interview, he tried to usher the visitors out.

"This is all quite intriguing, I'm sure," Cromwell said stiffly. "But the good Father is not feeling his best today. Perhaps it would be better if you all came another time."

Ian gazed across his garden, his mind wandering along the flowered hedge. His jaw tensed, and David thought he saw the glimmer of tears along his lashes. Reaching up, the priest patted his old friend's hand, where it rested on his shoulder.

"It's all right, John," he said with a sigh. "One cannot evade the world forever, can one? Let me hear what the professor has to say, while you fetch us another pot of Earl Grey."

CHAPTER 36

Ian McCurdy had carried a burden, the intensity and weight of which defied description, for nearly half a century. Like anyone with a grave secret, he had lived in relentless fear of exposure.

For the last decade, ever since the outcry demanding the release of the Cave Scrolls to the public and permission for other scholars to analyze them, he had endured a growing sense that it was only a matter of time before his secret was dragged out of him.

Fleeing Israel upon the death of his beloved mentor, Father Ducharme, ten years ago, he had hoped to deflect the scrutiny of probing questions. But his lot had been so solitary, so foreboding, that he had at last drawn one other soul into his dilemma: John Cromwell, a strong man, who was able to help carry the weight.

He was forever indebted to John, not only for commiserating in his horror, but also for shielding him from the public, a task that Cromwell had performed admirably.

When Emily finagled an interview for her friend Britta, a crack developed in Ian's defense, which, with the subsequent encounter, spread out in fissures, like the crazing on a priceless piece of pottery. Ian knew that Britta Hayworth had seen through him, when the rest of the world's media had only shrugged in helpless frustration and given up trying to break him.

Afternoon was drawing on, the sun settling in a hush over Ian's garden, as David Rothmeyer finished telling of his quest for the priestly heir. It was a tale worthy of the interest of the world's most auspicious archaeologist, and Father McCurdy listened in rapt attention.

At last, when the adventure had been told, when the story had taken them from Ohio to Jerusalem, from the computer and genetics labs of the Temple Consortium to Honey Aronstam's star, and from Israel to Dachau, Ian felt the hands of fate clutching in an ever-tightening grip about his heart. The exposure he had feared for so long now faced him, in the hopeful gazes of the visitors. They believed he could provide the crucial link in the chain of the genealogy, and they were about to ask for it.

Cromwell was in the kitchen, preparing to serve the guests dinner, for they had stayed well past the time that they should be sent away without the offer.

Ian drew a long cigar from his pocket, bit off the tip and lit it, puffing circles into the dewy air of the Thames Valley evening.

"So," he asked the pregnant question, "what is it you want of me, Dr. Rothmeyer? You have not come to Oxfordshire and you are not sitting in my garden only to tell me this tale."

David glanced at Britta, and Emily nodded encouragement.

"I think you already know what we are after, Father McCurdy," David replied. "You must realize by now that we believe you are in possession of the very material that will answer our needs. We believe that not all of the scrolls have been released and that you might very well hold the key to the greatest find in archaeological history!"

Father McCurdy blew smoke out softly, more circles that vanished slowly into the mist. "Go on, Dr. Rothmeyer," he said, feeling somewhat like the mouse *and* somewhat like the cat in a game of cat and mouse. "Surely you surmise something more specific."

David ground his teeth behind closed lips and wondered whether to despise this old fellow or admire him to the hilt.

"Very well," he replied. He took a deep breath, then finally said, "I believe you possess the Second Copper Scroll, the one referred to in the first, the one that gives the key to the treasure list. I believe, based on Rabbi Aronstam's reference to the desert scribes, that the Second Copper Scroll must also contain the name of the extant high priest, the one whom the Essenes held to be genuine. That, indeed, would be the greatest of the treasures they possessed!"

Ian stared into his garden for a long while. His face looked older than it had in years. Emily reached out to him with tender concern, but he shook his head. "It's all right," he said, patting her hand. Then, standing up stiffly, he gestured to his visitors to follow him into the house.

"The nights are always cool in Oxfordshire," he said as he led them inside, "especially in this old stone building. John and I make it a practice to sit by the fire in the evening."

Calling to Cromwell, he asked, "John, while I talk with our guests, would you be so good as to bring us our meal by the hearth?"

John poked his head out of the kitchen, giving his friend a worried look. When Ian nodded to him, he shrugged in compliance.

David was astonished as they passed by the office that sat adjacent to the parlor. Beyond the old French doors, reams of newspapers and magazines were kept in perfect order. Stopping long enough to peer through the beveled glass, he saw thick binders that he assumed were filled with clippings. Every handwritten title he could make out related to the field of archaeology and Middle-Eastern affairs. And it appeared that the ceiling-high bookshelves lining the room contained book after book on the subject. It was the most amazing private resource collection that David had ever seen.

The professor's scholarly heart thrummed at the sight. How he wished he might spend the next few years learning at the feet of Ian McCurdy!

Britta, seeing David's entrancement, pulled gently on his sleeve. "They want us by the fire," she said, smiling sympathetically.

As Cromwell seated the three travelers by the crackling grate, placing standing tea trays before them, he drew near his old friend and peered over his spectacles at him. He sensed that he was about to divulge what the two of them had spent their life's blood to protect. *Do you think this is wise?* his eyes seemed to ask.

Ian glanced up at him and nodded toward a little plaque on the mantel. The others did not notice this gesture, but John fleetingly read the inscription, a verse from Ecclesiastes that some parishioner had given Ian years ago: "To everything there is a season, and a time to every purpose under heaven."

"'A time to keep and a time to cast away,'" Ian added in a whisper, as John bent near.

Cromwell finished laying out the china, then shuffled hesitantly back into the kitchen. Behind him, he could hear Ian begin to talk, and he stopped a moment, looking up at the sunset sky from the kitchen window. As his ears were tuned to the sound of his dear friend's voice, he also hoped for a word from that heaven.

"Give him wisdom," he prayed. "And bless his tired old heart."

Ian glanced about the room at this guests. A tremor passed through his body, which no one present could miss.

"I have never told a soul what I am about to tell you," he said, his voice resigned. "No one, except Cromwell." Then, looking pointedly at David and Britta, he said, "Dr. Rothmeyer and Ms. Hayworth, you are quite aware of the controversy that has boiled around the Cave Scroll team. Well, let me tell you something about that."

He sat back in his armchair and chose his words delicately. "In keeping the scrolls to themselves for nearly half a century, the team members were accused of everything from egotistic possessiveness and exclusivity to defrauding of a public trust. In the past few years, they were accused of conspiring against the secular world to keep some horrid and damning revelation about Christianity under wraps."

David and Britta nodded, knowing the recent media circus the scrolls had inspired.

"I will say that, on the part of some of the international team members, some of those accusations are valid. There was academic pride involved. When a scholar is given a work to do and when he spends years of his life doing it, he begins to feel that the work and the findings are his own. He can easily forget that he is supposed to be serving the realm of knowledge. I will not deny that, on the part of some of my colleagues, an unfortunate possessiveness set in. Of this, they are guilty as charged."

David appreciated his honesty, and Britta listened respectfully.

"Concerning the accusation that they withheld something devastating to the Church, I think that has been sufficiently laughed away by serious thinkers. Not one shred of reliable evidence supports that theory, as I told Ms. Hayworth months ago." He studied her for a reaction, but she gave none.

"As for myself," he went on, his voice stronger with the unburdening, "I bore with the accusations quietly, not because I was egotistical or exclusive or possessive, and certainly not because the scrolls contained something that would destroy my faith!"

Ian gazed sadly past David, past Britta and Emily, as though his mind wandered through a distant time and place. "Where shall I begin?" he asked with a sigh. "I must begin by telling you about my mentor, Father Ducharme, the original custodian of the scroll team."

David had read about Ducharme. Much mystery shrouded the enigmatic scholar, who had descended into a pit of alcoholism and seeming insanity before his death a decade ago.

"I was next in command, under Ducharme," Ian said, "and I was his closest disciple. All along the way, he invested the most important aspects of the scroll studies to me, and he trusted me with the most sensitive tasks."

The listeners could see, from Ian's wistful expression, that he had loved the man dearly.

"I want to put to rest, here and now, the notion that Ducharme was a maniac. Ms. Hayworth," he demanded, "if you insist on making a news story of all this, please do the justice of righting that unfair accusation."

Britta's face grew warm. Out of respect, she again said nothing.

"If any lesser man had borne the burden Ducharme bore, he would have cracked much sooner," Ian went on. "I swear, I have come close to the edge many a time myself."

By now, John had returned, bringing steaming bowls of soup and placing them on the tea trays. In the firelight, his face showed the lines earned by years of stress.

Ian continued, "I will never forget the day—it seems a lifetime ago—that Ducharme called me into his room at the Institut Biblique, the scroll repository. Father Ducharme lived with the scrolls day and night, his private quarters being right next to the scriptorium where they were laid out."

Ian fidgeted with his soup spoon, too engrossed in his story to eat. "He told me that one of the students who helped with the dig at Qumran, a college intern from the States, had brought him a container the day before. It was a clay jar, like the others in which so many of the scrolls were buried. We had a policy that student interns were not to open the jars but were to bring them to the archaeologists directly."

Ian's tone picked up momentum. It was evident that the excitement of that find still came over him whenever he thought of it. "Well," he went on, "Father Ducharme had opened the container and instantly recognized the contents as a second metallic scroll, much like the first, which had raised such interest. It was fortunate, he told me, that the jar had been brought to him and not to one of the other team members, for, as he came to discover, the scroll was of a highly sensitive nature."

Father McCurdy's face twitched as he recounted this. "Ironic," he said. "Ducharme at first felt it was a godsend that the scroll had fallen to him. Later, I am sure, he cursed the day he first laid eyes on it. In truth, it became the death of him."

David felt for old Ducharme. It was evident that the possession of this document had posed no end of testing for him and his disciple. Still, eager to push on, he asked, "So, Father McCurdy, are you admitting that Father Ducharme bequeathed this very scroll to you, that it is in your possession?"

Ian gave David a bleak look. "Do not be so eager, young man, to get hold of the devil's tail. I tell you, it will whip you about without mercy!"

David was stunned.

"Now," Ian said, "let me back up a moment. Regarding my colleagues, upon whom so much censure has fallen: You must understand that some of them always felt they were dealing with classified material. These scholars kept quiet, never rising up in defense or otherwise answering critics, doling out their translations, publishing their books and papers, keeping the wolves at bay because they believed that part of what they had come to know was so potentially dangerous that, if it were wormed out of them, it could usher in . . . Armageddon."

This last phrase shocked the listeners. Britta's eyes went wide with amazement, and David reached for her hand as if by reflex.

"Armageddon?" Emily croaked.

Ian disregarded their horrified expressions. "There were literally hundreds of scrolls, you know. But it was the Copper Scroll that the team felt had the most awesome implications," he explained. "Due to its fragility, it was not cut open and unrolled for four years, but the archaeologists could tell from the reverse impressions of words readable on the outside that it contained a treasure list. Its discovery tainted their view of all the documents, and they held some of them back until such time as their studies led them to feel they were not so volatile.

"Gradually, they published their findings and ultimately the scrolls themselves were released. Even the Copper Scroll, itself, was laid bare to the world. But the furor would not calm down."

Britta needed clarification. "Was the Copper Scroll considered dangerous merely because it contained a treasure list?" she asked.

"Mainly," Ian said. "But not just any treasure! It appeared to contain a list of the treasures of Herod's temple, stored away throughout Israel for safekeeping as Rome's threat of invasion became imminent. The team feared its publication would lead to a scramble by treasure seekers that could devastate the fragile terrain of their ongoing dig."

Then, sighing softly, he added, "More important, they feared that, with the jealousy that continually raged between the Arab world and Israel, delivering up such sensitive material might spark another spate of terrorism, or even war. As it turned out, the Palestinians of Jordan, directly across the river from Qumran, now claim that they should have equal rights, or even predominant rights, to the dig sites and all that derives from them, particularly since it was a Bedouin boy who made the initial find."

He referred, they knew, to the widely celebrated story of the young Arab shepherd who threw a rock into a desert cave, and the resounding "clunk heard round the world," as it hit the side of a scroll jar.

Father McCurdy scratched his head, his brow furrowed with concern. "I must add, also, that the possibility of hidden riches was not all that made this a touchy issue. As you have indicated, Dr. Rothmeyer, the Jews hope to find the key to the treasure list because it is related to their future temple, the one they wish to build on Mount Moriah. Most likely, if the treasure itself is ever found, it will contain artifacts from Herod's magnificent complex, as well as revenue for the temple's operation!"

The old priest looked at David squarely. "Do you understand," he asked, "that the Jews wish to rebuild the temple on the very site now occupied by the Arab Dome of the Rock?"

David grimaced, remembering how horrified he had been when, on his first day at the Consortium gallery, he had realized the international fallout that could come from such a move.

"I do understand, Father McCurdy," he said. "And I also know that the Arabs will never sit still for such a thing!"

Ian leaned forward and studied the professor's pensive face. "Yet you continue to do what is required to bring about the new temple!"

David shrugged. "I am not a religious man," he said. "But, I seem to be"—he hesitated—"appointed."

Ian sat back in amazement. Considering their mutual dilemma, he suddenly wondered if he had more in common with this young man than academics: a mutual sense of fearsome responsibility.

For a long moment, there was silence, until Britta broke in. "Concerning Father Ducharme and some of your scroll committee, she said, "it seems to me that they should be applauded, not criticized! They held out for decades against—"

"Unending pressure," Ian filled in. "Yes, Ms. Hayworth, pressure from all quarters, academic and political. What finally convinced the committee that they could let go without ushering in World War Three was the fact that they believed there was no key to the Copper Scroll. It was, they decided, indecipherable. Any attempt to locate the treasure would only end in frustration."

David sat back and crossed his arms. "Yet, you and Ducharme knew differently!" he concluded. "The metallic scroll which Ducharme possessed was, indeed, the Second Copper Scroll, the one that could unlock the treasure hunt of the ages!"

"And the inevitability of another Holocaust," Ian muttered.

John Cromwell stood in the kitchen doorway, listening in on the conversation. When Ian made this statement, his face grew deathly white. Suddenly he rushed to his friend's side. "Can't you leave him alone now?" he barked, glaring at the visitors. "This is enough for tonight!"

Ian grasped John's flailing hand and held it close. "It is all right, my friend," he rasped. "It was inevitable that this time should come. Since my will is being forced, I must accept it as God's doing."

"B-but Ian," Cromwell stammered. "What of the dangers, what of the horrors?"

As Ian shook his head, his shoulders slumping for lack of an answer, John confronted the guests again. "Should you have any doubts about it, it was not self-interest that made Ian keep his secret. It was altruism, of the purest and holiest sort. Make a note of that, Ms. Hayworth! For years, Ian McCurdy has literally laid down his life for the good of humanity. I hope and pray that whoever is next in line to deal with his despicable treasure will have as good a heart!"

"I will keep all of that in mind, Mr. Cromwell," Britta replied quietly.

Now, Ian turned to David again, scholar to scholar. "Dr. Rothmeyer," he said, "you came here in hopes of finding clues to the priestly line. Perhaps the scroll contains such information, but I have never read it."

David was perplexed. "You mean, you have not read the scroll?"

Father McCurdy smiled wanly. "Not all of it. Strange, eh? Well, let me explain. When Ducharme discovered that the scroll was indeed a key to the treasure list, he asked me to help him translate. Many a night, he and I sat up in the scriptorium, when the others had left for their apartments and hotel rooms. We employed a little circular saw like the one that was used on the first scroll, and bit by precious bit opened the second. But as we got to the end, the metal was so crimped and our work was so arduous, that, without the help of the rest of the team, we felt we could not go further.

"For months at a time, we would ignore the project, involved in other things. Then, as outside pressures worked on Ducharme, as the dread of what he knew increased, his drinking and his demoralization grew as well. I feared to let him near the document. At last, we ceased work on the scroll altogether. After a lifetime of toil in Israel, Ducharme died, poor soul, and I returned to Oxford. Taking the scroll with me, I managed to get the metallic cylinder through customs by showing the officials my card from the Department of Israeli Antiquities. I never returned to Ireland," he said, looking at his sister, "because I was too public a figure. I wished to spare you, Emily, the onslaught of the Press."

Emily's eyes welled with tears. Drawing nearer to Ian, she embraced him sadly.

David shook his head in wonder. Even though he had come this far, actually gaining a confession from the notorious priest, there was no certainty that he had found anything firm to help him in his mission.

Ian must have read his disappointment, for in the next breath, he was giving him hope. "I do not understand why I am being forced, no—led, to help you, Dr. Rothmeyer. The goals of the Temple Consortium are not in keeping with what I believe. The Consortium is not Christian! And they wish to rebuild the temple, with all its antiquated rituals, its offerings and its laws, and its blood sacrifices, for heaven's sake! Not only do I fear the international fallout from the Consortium's plans, but none of their sacrificial system fits with my understanding of the New Testament, which says that Jesus was the ultimate and final sacrifice!"

David knew little of Christian doctrine. He knew precious little, in fact, of his own heritage. "I do not know what to say, Father," he said with a shrug. "That is not my realm. My duty is to get a piece of Israel's past back to its homeland."

The old priest was haggard, defeated. Slump shouldered, he bit his lower lip and choked back a mist of tears.

"I don't know," he said, heaving a huge sigh. "I can only say that I am cornered by a severe but gentle force. Stay the night, my friends," he offered, managing a resigned smile. "We have plenty of room in this lonely house. Tomorrow we will go to the British Museum. I will exhume the battered piece of metal, and we will hop a plane. All of us, yes, John? Yes, Emily? If I am to return the document to its rightful owners, I want to meet them."

CHAPTER 37

Monte Altmeyer paced the glossy hardwood floor of the Wester house in Bull River Valley, Montana. Jim Fogarty sat slumped before a meager fire on the mammoth stone hearth, avoiding Altmeyer's furious face.

"I don't know! I just don't know!" Altmeyer repeated over and over, in his harsh German accent. "I trusted you with some extremely sensitive information, Jim. What made you think you could trust Pete Wester?"

Fogarty's henchmen sat outside on the porch, taking in the cool morning sunlight and listening to Altmeyer rave on. Ever since the Wester brothers had disappeared, the leadership of the White Supremacists had been in tumult.

As soon as it became clear that the brothers were not returning, Fogarty had awakened the camp and announced that there was a security breach. The campers had been interrogated, first as a group and then individually, as the leaders tried to determine if anyone present knew anything about the vanished Westers. What were they up to? Where had they gone? Had they said or done anything to indicate their plans? As this questioning went on, Fogarty's boys ransacked the house, searching for clues of any kind.

By noon, the only hint as to their possible destination was an envelope with Honey's Aunt Jessie's return address, and a vague recollection on the part of Lucy, Hank's wife, that Honey had once spoken of Columbus. On the strength of that, Fogarty and Altmeyer had sent Crossley and Willard off on the wild goose chase that dead-ended in Ohio.

When the second day of the gathering failed to offer any of the lectures or training that had been promised, most of the campers had folded up their tents and packed their rigs in disappointment, if not disgust. Though they did not blame the leadership for this turn of events, they left downhearted, wondering how far their grand cause had been set back.

Only a handful stayed behind, including the "old ladies" of the biker contingent, willing to help with the ongoing search. The leaders had done all they could think of, from this remote spot, to track down the escaped Westers. In addition to sending out Crossley and Willard, other bikers had been deployed, who had headed for major points west, north, and south. Ham radio communications were relayed to and from contacts across the country.

One such communication from Wyoming said word had it that the two had visited friends of Honey in Cheyenne. But where the brothers had gone from there, no one seemed to know.

As for Honey, there was less information about her. If she had gone to Wyoming, she had long since fled. And when she left Bull River, she had taken almost every shred of material that might give a clue as to her destination. Aside from that one envelope, found in a trash basket, no personal address book, no passport, no diary, nothing of any kind was found in the house that would leave a hint of her background or where she might have gone.

One by one, all the tracker groups had returned, empty-handed.

Even Willard and Crossley had returned. Short of roughing up Mrs. Aronstam in Columbus, or vandalizing her house for clues—neither of which the two bikers were willing to do—they had no leads.

They sat, now, on the sunlit porch with the henchmen, bone-weary and defeated.

Despite their tough exteriors, they winced as they listened to Altmeyer's diatribe.

"What made you think you could trust this Wester?" Altmeyer demanded, pounding his fists against his thighs and tromping across the floor. "Were you so blinded by his Aryan looks that you could not doubt him?"

Fogarty slumped further into the wing chair that faced the hearth. "He seemed a simple sort," Fogarty grumbled. "He was easily led. He never questioned any of the communiqués he received. He always followed through on anything I asked of him. Why should I suspect him?"

Then, self-defensively, Fogarty sat up and spat, "It was that brother of his! Everything was going fine, until he came along. He must have planted ideas in Pete's head."

With this, Fogarty's eyes flashed, and he continued, "Yeah, that's it! I'll bet Mel Wester was a plant! He comes from California, right? A cop, right? Put it together, Monte! He was sent here by the ATF!"

Altmeyer stopped his pacing and glared down on Fogarty. "Another government conspiracy, Jim? Come on! Do you really believe all that hogwash?" His foreign accent wrapped strangely around the colloquialism.

Fogarty was caught off guard. His brow crinkled, and he squinted confused eyes at Altmeyer. "Believe it?" he cried. "I teach it every day! What? You *don't* believe?"

Altmeyer looked at the floor and shook his head. "That's right, Jim," he said with a sneer. "I forgot! An FBI agent behind every bush, the CIA beneath every bed!" Then stepping up to Fogarty, he grasped his jaw in his hands and squeezed, forcing the big Aryan to face him squarely.

"Do you not get it? Do you not see, after all these years?" he growled. "*We* are the conspiracy! *We* control the ATF, the FBI, and the CIA! Or had you forgotten!"

With this, he released Fogarty's head and sent a stream of spittle hissing into the fire. Then, his voice low and rolling like thunder, he added in Hitlerian phrases, "We have only one true enemy, Fogarty! Have you lost sight of that? We need to concern ourselves with only one grand task: the extermination of the Jew-devils! This is not just a political war, Jim! If it were, we would not have the allies we have, in every corner of the globe! I would not have been sent to Libya, to the Philippines, to Tokyo, to Belfast! I would not have trained thousands, of every political persuasion, in the guerrilla arts, if this were just a political war!"

He took a deep breath. As if Fogarty needed to hear more, he reminded him, "And it is not just a race war! This is something greater than the sum of both. This is, to borrow a phrase from our Arab friends, 'Jihad! Jihad! Holy war!'" Then, throwing his arms wide, he added, "Why, even the Bible says, 'Israel is a stumbling block to all nations!'"

For a long while, the room was quiet. The men on the porch, ears tingling, strained to hear more.

But Altmeyer had said enough. Too much, perhaps. One could not be too careful, he realized. One never knew who one's friends were, or one's enemies.

Not for the first time, Fogarty felt small. Though he was an imposing figure, with his gleaming silver hair and his six-foot-four physique, he always felt like a peon when Altmeyer was around.

In their circles, Fogarty *was* a peon. His little realm of Aryan Nations, White Supremacy, Militia, and Freemen was but one small cog in a gigantic machine, a machine whose tentacled network spanned the globe. Sometimes, he thought he had a notion of how great that machine was. But when Altmeyer was around, he was easily reminded of just how vague his understanding really was.

When Altmeyer talked this way, Fogarty tried to comprehend. But for Jim and his like, this *was* a political war and a race war. He was lost when Altmeyer talked *Jihad*. He had never had the courage to ask him to explain how anything could be bigger than races and politics; he had not wanted to reveal his ignorance. And, actually, he did not want to know the answer.

For Fogarty, political war and race war were enough. If there was, in truth, some greater struggle going on, it was on a plane he did not need to enter. Besides, Altmeyer was right about one thing: The focus of all these wars was the extermination of the Jews. If that could ever be accomplished, the race war, the political war, *and* the Holy War, whatever it was, would be won.

"Okay, okay," Fogarty said, submitting like a dog on its back. "I hear you, Monte. Holy War, for sure."

Altmeyer tried to calm himself. Sitting down across from Fogarty, he spoke in measured tones. "About this Wester," he said, "are you sure he gave you all the messages that came through?"

Fogarty thought back. "As sure as I can be of anything," he replied. "Why?"

Altmeyer looked out to the porch and lowered his voice. "I was expecting a message from Belfast," he said. "Anything come through?"

Fogarty shrugged. "Not that I know of. Since Wester left, different fellas out there have been monitoring the radio."

Standing up, Fogarty went to the screen door and called out to the porch, "Any of you guys get a communiqué from Ireland?"

Collectively, they shook their heads, and he returned to the hearth. "Nothin', Monte," he said.

Just as Fogarty was about to throw another log on the dwindling fire, Willard pulled open the door and entered the room.

"Uh, I'm not sure if the voice was Irish," he said. "Sounded like a Ay-rab to me. And it was awful raspy-like." He held out a scribbled note. "I wrote this down earlier. 'Scuse the spellin'."

Altmeyer rose from his chair and, with a furious glare, tore the paper from Willard's motor-oil-stained fingers.

"When did you think you might give it to me?" he growled.

As Altmeyer silently interpreted the scrawls, his hand shaking so that the paper fluttered, his face turned red with rage: *Eagle Eye happening. Relay to Swastika. Bailey's Bug must be used. Potency waning. Called you a over a week ago. Cedars heading for Shekinah. Why didn't we hear from you?*

By now, the men from the porch had entered the room, wondering what was going on. As Altmeyer digested the note, the veins stood out on his forehead.

Eyes darting around the room, he surveyed the gathering. "How did I ever fall in with such a bunch of fools?" he cried. "If you represent the Great Aryan Race, Whitey doesn't stand a chance!"

Fogarty's face reddened. Turning on Altmeyer, he shot back, "Now, hold on there, Monte! Wester may have betrayed us, but these fellas here are freedom fighters from the word go!"

Altmeyer fumed, "Get off the soapbox, Jim! We are not dealing with farm takeovers and mill shutdowns now! This message goes way beyond that!"

He waved the note under Fogarty's nose without letting him read it.

Fogarty scowled. "What's going on, Monte?" he snapped.

Altmeyer read the paper again, his face clouding even more. He crossed the big room to the front windows and glared off into the distance, as though his mind traveled the highway beyond the trees and farther.

"How long ago did the Jew woman leave Bull River?" he asked the roomful of onlookers.

There was some subdued discussion. No one seemed sure of the answer.

"She never came to the meetings except a couple of times with Wester," Crossley recalled.

Fogarty scratched his head. "I remember coming by here late last fall," he said. "She was here then. But the next time I came through, on the way to the holiday gathering in Idaho, she was gone. Yeah," he remembered, "I came through to pick up messages on the way to Hayden Lake. Wester was pretty bummed out and asked to hitch a ride with us. That's when I figured out he'd sent her packing!"

Altmeyer considered this. "So," he said, "she left at least four or five months ago."

Fogarty and the others agreed.

Altmeyer started pacing again, looking at the note over and over. "And now we learn that Wester received a communiqué that he never gave to us."

Fogarty answered weakly, "Looks like it." Then holding up his hands, he shrugged. "I swear, I never thought he let anything fall through the cracks. He was always real quick to mention any messages he'd gotten."

The German flashed dubious eyes at his underling. "Qualify that statement, Jim," he barked. "You have no way of knowing what he might have failed to tell you. Meanwhile, he could have been collecting and keeping all sorts of information meant only for the brotherhood!"

Fogarty looked at the floor. "I see your point," he said. "I guess I assumed he was *part* of the brotherhood."

The German glowered. "Once again, you assume too much! Did it occur to you to even ask him if there were any messages when we arrived here?"

Fogarty avoided the leader's furious gaze. "A lot was happening," he argued. "The crowd . . . the visiting . . . "

"The applause! The attention!" Altmeyer shouted. "It is hard to focus, Jim, when you *are* the focus!"

Jim hung his head. Turning to the fireplace again, he slumped into a chair and stared at his feet. He had been thoroughly put in his place, reminded, once again, that he was a small cog in a machine whose size he did not comprehend.

"Let us, as you Americans say, cut to the chase, shall we?" Altmeyer continued. "You may be right about the idea of a 'plant,' an 'infiltrator.' But I think we are dealing with a trio of them. And they are not from the U.S. government."

Fogarty glanced up. To his relief, Altmeyer's angry eyes were no longer on him. The German was pacing in front of the windows again, the note clenched tightly in his fist. The bikers, their girl-friends, and the assorted holdouts from the gathering watched him silently—fascinated, admiring, or just plain mystified.

"What we are dealing with here is an *Israeli* agent and her henchmen!" Altmeyer announced.

Fogarty was stunned. "Israeli?" he croaked. "How does Israel fit with any of this?"

Altmeyer's patience had been strained to the limit. "You ask ignorant questions because you are shortsighted!" he growled. "Must I remind you why the Arabs help your people? Or why the government does so little to stop them?"

Altmeyer shook his head in disgust and wheeled on all of them. "There is a much more important agenda than your anti-American Separatist dogma. In the big pond, you people are mere amoebas!"

The bikers shuffled, looking at one another in confusion.

Crossley, at last, spoke up. "Tell us, Monte. What's all this about Arabs and Israel and Belfast—and what's shakin' down, anyway?"

Altmeyer liked Crossley. He was uneducated, but not dumb.

"That is the burning question," the German replied. "There is something very big about to happen, and I'm afraid Wester knows enough to intercept it."

Grabbing a pad of paper and a pencil off an end table, he scrutinized the biker. "You know how to operate the ham radio?" he asked.

"Sure!" Crossley brightened.

"Good. I need you to make some contacts," the leader commanded.

As Altmeyer jotted down some call letters, one set for his contacts in Belfast and another for a computer expert who could hack into airlines reservation lists, he turned to the demoralized Fogarty. Fishing for something to commend him for, he said, "Jim, I know you picked this place because it is remote. Excellent. But where can I find a fax machine?"

Jim shrugged. "Thompson Falls, I guess."

Fogarty was dumbfounded when Altmeyer snapped his fingers at Willard and ordered, "Warm up the Suburban. I will need a ride to town as soon as I get through to Ireland!"

CHAPTER 38

It was the middle of the night in a hotel room near Heathrow Airport, London. The occupant had not slept since arriving there on a commuter plane out of Belfast earlier in the evening.

The man who occupied the room had spent his entire stay, to this point, in prayer, much of it on his knees, facedown on the little prayer rug that he carried in his suitcase everywhere he traveled.

Bowing over and over, he touched his forehead to the carpet, sometimes staying in that facedown posture for protracted moments, his head pointing due east, toward Mecca, most sacred of all Muslim cities.

Mammed Kahlil was a religious Arab, particularly when he knew his next few hours might be his last.

He had never become used to risking his life in the cause of Islam. He knew that those he worked for thought he was immune to fear, so close had he come to death in his many international escapades. But the possibility of his own demise never rested well on his shoulders.

Mammed was a professional "terrorist." He did not use that term, preferring to think of himself as a "munitions and counter-intelligence expert." Unlike some others, he was not a freelance mercenary, working for whomever would pay him the most. He was a devoted Muslim, believing thoroughly in the cause of the fundamentalist Arab agenda, which included the right of the Palestinians to a formal homeland, the elimination of the State of Israel, and the extermination of all Jews.

Though Mammed lived in New York City, he was Lebanese by birth and went by the code name "Cedars," for the famed forests of his country. He liked the irony of his code name, for, while the famous king of the Jews, Solomon, had used cedarwood from Lebanon in the construction of his Jerusalem temple, three thousand years ago, it was one of the purposes of Mammed's people to forestall all possibility of such a temple ever being built again.

It had been a victory of supernatural proportions, they believed, when almost fourteen centuries ago the Arab world had claimed Mount Moriah, the site of Solomon's vanquished temple, for themselves.

Their prophet, Mohammed, had symbolically laid claim to the place, they were taught, by ascending to heaven from Mount Moriah's flat top. For centuries, a mosque had stood there, the Dome of the Rock, commemorating Mohammed's "night ride" to heaven.

Yet now the Jews, hereditary enemies of the Arabs for four thousand years, wished to reinstitute their ancient system of worship on that site.

Mammed had a long and impressive record of international terrorism to his credit. He had helped to mastermind many a plot directly or indirectly aimed at Israel or her supporters. The world at large saw the increasing frequency of such atrocities, not knowing that most of them were not random at all, but part of a networked scheme.

Not even Mammed, himself, knew all the players or the plans. But he believed in what he was doing, enough to lay down his life in the grand cause.

A few years ago he had fumbled one assignment badly, setting off a container of toxic gas prematurely in a Jerusalem bus station and not fleeing before the fumes attacked his throat. Though he survived, his voice had never been the same.

There had been talk among his superiors of retiring him from his work. Their fear was that his speaking voice could draw attention to him, and the one thing no hired terrorist could afford was unwanted attention. To blend into crowds, to go about his business anonymously like a slippery shadow, was the ideal.

However, Mammed was so good at what he did, his employers were willing to risk using him, and so he had learned to speak as little as possible when on assignment.

At prayer, however, he did use his voice. This night, he invoked the protection and guidance of Allah, gesticulating and beating his chest until the sweat ran off his dark forehead.

The next day he was flying to Israel, where he was due to pull off a direct hit on the very soul of the temple movement. Never before had a violent act been so directly and publicly aimed at this Jewish endeavor.

Eight years ago, one of the heads of the Zionist movement, a figure prominent in the temple agenda, had been assassinated in New York City, by the very same Islamic group that ultimately bombed the World Trade Center and whose plot to bomb the Holland Tunnel was intercepted. But even those acts of terrorism had not been seen as attacks on the temple movement, for the world as a whole was still blissfully unaware that the Jews even had such an itinerary.

Tomorrow, the world *would* know, Mammed thought. Tomorrow, everyone would know that an agency of that movement had been attacked. Tomorrow, the world would question not only why the attack, but they would also begin to question why the Jews had such an inflammatory agenda.

Mammed knew he might not be alive to see the publicity. He

might never be privileged to see the outcome of his own sacrifice, or the pressure it would bring from all quarters against the Jews; Mammed might not live to see his heroism rewarded.

As he bowed again to Allah, he prayed for his wife and little boy. He had not seen them for almost seven months, and the last time he had left them, for this "one more trip away from home," he had spoken roughly to his child.

The memory of that last interaction, a moment that should have been a loving farewell, still haunted him. He and his little family had been waiting in the JFK airport terminal for his flight to Belfast. His child had wandered too close to a group of Jewish men at prayer and had innocently spoken to one. When Mammed found him, he had rudely jerked the child aside and growled at him in Lebanese, forgetting to keep his coarse voice low. "No, no, Faisal! Bad! These are wicked men! Enemies, Faisal! Jews! Not to touch! Not to speak!"

The boy had burst into tears, drawing even more unwanted attention to Mammed than he had already drawn to himself, and so he had snapped his fingers at his wife, commanding her to follow him as they departed down the concourse.

Mammed had never forgiven himself for treating his son that way. He only prayed he would have an opportunity to make it up to him. And he also prayed Faisal would grow up to despise the enemy as he did. "Let me redeem myself," he prayed. "Let my actions tomorrow bring glory to Allah in my son's eyes."

On Mammed's bed, the suitcase from which he had taken his prayer rug lay next to a smaller bag, a toiletry clutch. Although it contained shaving lotion and other necessities, it also contained a small glass vial, wrapped in washcloths, holding one of the most lethal substances ever concocted.

"Bailey's Bug," it was called. Irish scientists, agents of the IRA, had created it. A form of anthrax, it was specially formulated for use in close quarters, for decimation or destruction of narrowly targeted populations. It had been successfully tested on barnyard animals in the farming area outside Belfast. Tomorrow, it would be directed against a very specific human group: the handpicked arm of the Jewish Temple movement.

For nearly seven months, Mammed had been in Belfast, training IRA subversives in the finer points of terrorism, one of his roles as an international "munitions and counter-intelligence expert." The contract between Mammed's superiors in Beirut and the IRA in Belfast designated that the formula for the new "bug" and a sample thereof would be given to Mammed in exchange for his services.

He would have gone to Jerusalem a week ago, but the go-ahead had not been received by a German contact in the United States, Monte Altmeyer, the master terrorist who had trained Mammed and many of his compatriots.

When the Irish formulists warned that the "bug" had a half-life that would be quickly waning, and that it must be used before its potency failed, Mammed's superiors decided to wait no longer.

What had befallen Altmeyer, they did not know. He had last been heard from before departing for some "survivalist" camp in the American outback. As was typical of such outposts, there was no way to reach him except by ham radio, and there had been no reply from him in response to Mammed's last two messages.

Dawn was just creeping through the hotel room window when Mammed finally gave up his prayer vigil. Petitional tears were still wet on his olive-complected cheeks, and he was rolling up his little carpet, when he was suddenly electrified by the ringing of the room's telephone.

As always, Mammed had requested a room with a fax/phone, a rare luxury for which he paid a premium. Before answering the ring, he set down his prayer rug and watched the lights on the machine. It was not a call coming through, but a fax communication.

To his knowledge, the only people who knew his location were his superiors in Beirut and the IRA agents in Belfast. The read-out for the incoming number, however, had a United States country code and an area code unfamiliar to him: 406.

Quickly, the fax printout scrolled up from the paper guide. Mammed bent over the machine, reading the heading on the paper, as the printing continued. "Thompson Falls Midnite Mini-Mart," he read. Brow knit, he grumbled, "Where on earth?"

In his business, it was a fact that communications rarely came from private phones, cellular phones, or private fax machines. Even e-mail was avoided. Messages were often funneled over pay phones or pay faxes in train stations, airports, or hotel rooms. But he could not imagine why he would be getting something from an all-night market in a town he had never heard of.

Until he saw more of the cover sheet.

"Aha!" he exclaimed. "Thompson Falls, Montana! It must be near the militia camp!"

Quickly, he ripped the completed fax from the machine. If this was from Altmeyer, it had taken some doing on his part to track Mammed down. It must be important. Holding the paper as steadily as he could in trembling hands, he read the memo:

Hello, Cedars. This is Swastika. Got your whereabouts from
Ireland. We know about bug. You must move quickly. Hope this
reaches you before you head for Skekinah. There has been a
leak here. Your message of last week fell into wrong hands.
Computer tap at JFK confirms spies headed for Israel. Beware of
two American men—twinlike, tall, big, blond, blue-eyed, one
short-haired, one long-haired; and one petite American woman,
long dark hair, dark eyes; possibly traveling together. Appear to
be Israeli agents. Jihad, Cedars. Be safe.

Mammed's mouth was dry as sand as he finished reading the fax. Tremulously, he folded it and put it in his day-planner.

He picked up his watch from the nightstand and realized his non-stop flight for Tel Aviv would depart in two hours.

Then he finished rolling up his prayer rug, drew it to his lips, and kissed it.

Unlike some of his fellow Muslims, he did not think of the seventy virgins he would receive in Paradise, if he died as a martyr. Instead, he stroked a photo of his wife and son that he carried in his suitcase and prayed that he would see them again.

CHAPTER 39

As the El Al plane bound for Israel taxied down the airport runway, its gigantic engines blasting beneath its wings, its proportionately tiny rubber tires spinning toward liftoff, Father Ian McCurdy watched the passing landscape as if in a dream.

The old priest had spent most of the past decade in some form of prayer, either consciously or subconsciously invoking the protection and the will of God in his attempt to save the world. Today, he felt as though those prayers were at last leading him on a tangible path. For some reason beyond his comprehension and against his better human judgment, against everything he held to be consistent with his beliefs, he was being guided to turn his scroll over to its original owners.

As he sat on the crowded 747, his dear supporter, John Cromwell, beside him, he cradled the scroll on his lap.

When he left Israel ten years ago, he had packaged the fragile document in a soft roll of linen and created a formfitting liner for a large valise, hollowed out to the exact dimensions of the wrapped scroll.

Despite the fact that he had kept it all these years in a study carrel at the British Museum, he had never taken it out of the container for research, had never done more than open the little safe that protected it, peering in once or twice a year to be sure the valise and its contents were still there.

This morning when he and his traveling companions had checked through the x-ray machine at the airport, he had been detained. The image of the metallic scroll caused no end of concern for the check-in attendants, who, due to the increased potential for terrorism, were much more cautious these days than a decade ago. Against Ian's protests, they were ready to open the briefcase then and there, in front of the world, and rifle through its delicate contents.

Fortunately, with the help of David's credentials from the Midwest University anthropology department, and Ian's own faculty card from the Oxford archaeology department, they were able to forestall the search.

Ian had not let go of the valise since retrieving it from the x-ray conveyor belt and refused even now to "place it in the overhead bin or beneath the seat" as the stewardess gave her loudspeaker instructions. Instead he hid it beneath a flannel lap robe provided by the airline for sleeping passengers and hoped the stewardess would not notice.

Emily, Britta, and David shared the center row of three seats, across the aisle from Ian and John. As the plane at last rose into the air, Ian watched from his window seat as the pavement retreated, grew tiny, and was finally lost beneath a wisp of clouds.

Soon the British Isles were no larger than a hand, and the greenness of his native Ireland could barely be made out across the Irish Sea.

For the first time in a long while, Ian had dressed in his priestly garb, a long black cassock and pants, black buttonless shirt, and white, backwards collar. Emily had commented on how dashing he looked, but he had only dressed this way in honor of the duty he was about to perform.

Leaning back against the headrest, he closed his eyes. For years, he had followed the development of the Temple Consortium. Though he never visited its gallery, he had read many articles and seen many pictures of the implements, the garments, and harps being made there.

As a student of the Old as well as the New Testaments, he was very familiar with the nature of the worship and service that had taken place for centuries in the temple of ancient Israel.

Based on the layout of Moses's wilderness tabernacle, which had traveled everywhere with the Israelites in their wanderings before they entered the Promised Land, the temple's focal point was the Holy of Holies, which housed the Ark of the Covenant. Outside the Holy Place, where the priest entered once a year to make atonement for the sins of the people, daily sacrifices were made in the courtyard. Thousands upon thousands of animals were killed there every week, he knew. The calculations made by some scholars concerning the amount of blood that must have flowed from Mount Zion into Jerusalem's underground sewers was staggering.

As much as it troubled Ian to be turning over a list of treasures that could bring the jealousy and hatred of the world against Israel and could possibly usher in the greatest battle of all time, it troubled him even more to think that he could be helping to take religion backward, to the pre-Christian era. *I don't understand, I don't understand,* he thought as he sat with his eyes closed. Yet, he also knew that the prophets, Jeremiah, Ezekiel, Isaiah, and others, had declared thousands of years before that one day Israel would build a "house of prayer for all nations." The prophecies were quite specific regarding its structure and functions. Anyone in touch with world events could see the buildup of the Arab nations against this eventuality.

Why, the Scriptures indicated that Jesus himself would one day reign from Mt. Zion, and his people would recognize him for who he was.

Ian cringed at a horrid notion. Could it be that Jesus, establishing himself as ruler over Israel, would consent to reign over a place where the blood of goats and rams ran through the stones, and the smoke of sacrifices filled the air?

He thought not!

But, about this incongruity, Ian had thought too much and too long. For years, he had wondered about these enigmas in the Scriptures. He could not figure it out, and he knew of no one who had.

All he knew, here and now, was that he was being carried along on a wave of inescapable fate. He was taking the scroll back to Israel, and he was about to turn it over to hands responsible for Israel's future. He could do nothing, now, but trust that the prayers he had delivered up for a decade had not led him astray.

As his four companions were carried, with him, on the wings of destiny, they were all silent, each deep in thoughts of his or her own.

Apart from John Cromwell, who knew Ian's struggles and shared them, David Rothmeyer had the most vested interest in the scroll. If it did, indeed, contain a vital link in the genealogy, the goal of his assignment would be all the closer to fulfillment.

As the plane flew over the English Channel, Britta studied David's pensive face, reading his nervous anticipation. Reaching over, she clasped his hand in hers, and smiled up at him.

She was about to lean his way with a whisper of reassurance, when the rattle of a food cart drew their attention to the aisle. Stewardesses were making their way slowly up the walkway, handing out little trays of kosher breakfasts.

It seemed there was enough time for David to make a quick trip to the lavatory before the cart reached their seats. "I'll be right back," he said, giving Britta's hand a squeeze.

Quickly he made his way back to the rear of the plane, and finding that the lavatory door read "occupied," he waited beside it, stooping under the curved ceiling, which was too low for his tall frame.

The cart was almost to his row of seats when he at last heard the toilet flush in the little cubicle and the sliding lock sign slapped to "vacant."

As the door opened, he pulled back farther and waited for the occupant to exit. The instant this happened, David did a double-take: He had seen this character before.

He might not have remembered just where he had encountered the dusky fellow, or why the sight of him was troubling, had the man not given a cursory, "Pardon me," as he slipped past. The sound of those two words, rasping and strangely coarse, recalled to David the scene in the JFK terminal. This was the Lebanese man who had chastened his little son for speaking to a Jew!

That day, for the first time since childhood altercations, David had felt ethnic fear. Though the man had not looked his way, the professor had been stunned by his expressions of hate.

Today, once again, David was alarmed by his presence. Though he had no reason to be suspicious of the man, he struck an anxious chord in David's spirit. As the professor slipped into the lavatory and washed his hands at the little sink, he relived the scene in the New York airport with a shudder. Never before had he seen such hatred in a man's face, as this stranger directed at the praying Jews. Jews were the "enemy," he had told his son. "Not to touch! Not to speak!"

Feeling clammy, David ran a damp paper towel over his face, closing his eyes. *Why*, he wondered, *would a man who loathed Jews to that degree, be traveling to Israel?*

CHAPTER 40

Later that evening, Honey Aronstam stood at the rooftop balustrade of the house where she had first met David Rothmeyer. It was from this vantage point that the professor had first set eyes on her as she emerged from the taxi upon arriving in Jerusalem.

Now she was the one watching for a cab, this one due to arrive any moment, bearing the professor and Britta Hayworth, Emily McCurdy, and two men whom she had not met. Behind her, seated at the table where David often worked with his laptop computer, sat Pete and Mel. Downstairs, in the parlor of the big house, other men had also gathered.

The rabbis of the Temple Consortium were all there, waiting together in the medieval chamber for the arrival of Ian McCurdy and his priceless scroll. Anya, the housekeeper, bustled about, serving them sandwiches and pouring pot after pot of coffee.

The mood all through the house was one of tense anticipation, of the long-dreamed-of climax to an arduous search.

When David had called from Germany with news of the successful procurement of the Dachau document, Uriel Katz, Carl Jacobs, and Menachem Levine were already headed to Jerusalem from New York.

Rabbi Benjamin had reported to them on the findings of the computer lab, and they were eager to look in on that work. They had not known about the German material until they arrived, and felt it was divine timing that they should have come just now.

Amazed at such a windfall, they anxiously awaited the integration of the Aronstam document into the genealogical chain.

It had not taken long for the new information to be collated into the data files. Since the lab had already determined that there was a strong British strand in the line, the document made the evidence even stronger. It remained for the sorting through and discarding of millions of names to narrow the field.

Several strands within the British records stood out as possibilities, but one by one they were eliminated as dead ends, as the computer programmers manually entered information that continued to pour into the institute.

Honey breathed in deeply of the sage-scented air wafting up from the Hinnom Valley. During her brief time in Israel, she had learned the pleasure of such evenings, when soft, warm breezes blew across the rooftop.

Pete watched her from behind as she stood at the rail, admiring the willowy form that never failed to please him and the thick, wavy hair, which flew free in the air's gentle currents. He believed that the best thing he had ever done was to take Mel's lead and go in search of this woman. Never again, he was determined, would he let her go.

His fondest desire now, was to get her back to Montana, to the beloved home he had built for her with his own hands. How he hoped that wonderful house was still standing, that the Militia had not revenged themselves against him by destroying it! But even if he must build a new place, deeper in the outback, far from the reach of ruthless men, he would see to it that she was never put in danger again.

And once this escapade was resolved, he planned to give her her heart's desire, a beautiful wedding.

For now, he felt as she did, that they must see this venture through. He and his brother had become as caught up in the mystery of the quest as anyone else.

Below, in the parlor, the four colleagues of the Consortium chatted together, their conversation sinking, as was too often the case into a sparring match. Rabbi Benjamin listened helplessly as, once again, Uriel Katz fumed over the ongoing quest.

"I cannot think that the true line leads through Britain!" Katz declared. "Oh, I can see the possibility that it paused there for a while, but for the data to say that it stopped there is just very hard for me to accept!"

Dr. Jacobs sat back in his armchair, rubbing his protruding stomach after feasting on too many of Anya's treats. "And what will you do if the record proves you wrong, Uriel?" he asked.

"You all know that I believe, along with thousands of like thinkers throughout our history, that the first mark of a true priest is scholarship. Of course, not all the great priests were great students. But, surely, the highest of the priests must first be devoted to the Torah, the Talmud, the Mishnah . . . "

Menachem Levine sniffed and turned perceptive eyes on his disgruntled colleague. "Come, now, Uriel! What we all know is that you have set out to prove that the line devolves through Eastern Europe, through Northeastern Europe, to be exact. You and your fellow Talmudists will never be happy unless one of your cold, literalist scholars is put in charge of things!"

Dr. Jacobs, who was usually quite jovial and accommodating, was less generous that evening. "Let's face it, Katz!" he spat. "You are determined that anything less than the declaration of a Katz as the successor is unacceptable! Your fondest desire is to see yourself, yes, *yourself*, installed as priest! You have even created an Internet web page, of all things, setting out your credentials before the world!"

Katz stiffened. "I did not create that page, Carl! You know that very well. It was my students at the Brooklyn synagogue who did that. It has been quite the embarrassment, actually!"

Rabbi Benjamin intervened. "Now, gentlemen, let's be gracious to one another. As for myself, I would be pleased to see Uriel gain the post, if God wills it. He is a great mind."

"If not a great heart!" Menachem muttered.

Jacobs chuckled at this, but Uriel was chagrined. "Horace!" he growled. "How did you come by these two?"

Rabbi Benjamin shook his head. "You could do with some sweetening, Uriel. Your poor wife will vouch for that!"

At this, the other two laughed aloud.

"Now, now, Uriel. I mean no harm," Horace said. "But I do agree that there is more than scholarship and orthodoxy that qualifies a man for this position. We will probably be quite surprised when God presents us with the chosen one!"

"Aha!" Uriel fumed. "There we go with the orthodoxy thing again. Are we not all orthodox here? But, then, I forget . . . you tend toward the Cabalist teachings, don't you, Horace?"

Rabbi Benjamin, coming from a long line of Southeastern Europeans, had been reared in the tradition of the mystics who followed Eliezer Ben Tov. As a result, he did respect certain aspects of the Cabala, believed to be a code for deciphering untenable portions of Scripture.

"I will not debate with you, Uriel," he asserted. "Let us just remember how God surprised Israel with the choice of King David. He was nothing more than an unschooled shepherd. Probably dirty and puny, at that!"

"Amen!" Carl chuckled.

"Well spoken," Levine cheered.

For the moment, Katz had been put in his place, though not the place he thought he should fill.

Meanwhile, Honey, looking down from the roof, spied a taxi cab pulling up to the curb.

"I think they're here!" she cried, turning to Pete and Mel. Then, watching the passengers emerge, she declared, "Yes, I see David, Britta, and now Emily. With them are the men from England! Go tell the rabbis!"

Mel jumped to do her bidding, and Pete joined her at the rail, slipping his arm about her slim waist. "I can't believe we're here, waiting for the greatest find of the century!" he said. "How do we rate?"

Honey smiled up at him. "I've stopped asking that question," she said. "Somehow we got plopped into the middle of all this. I have to believe there's a good reason for it!"

"Well," he said, "I can see why you'd be here. Your star was a key in the whole search. As for me . . . well, I just hope I can help."

Honey perceived the regret in his tone, sorrow for past involvements and causes. She slipped her hand in his, where it rested on the rail.

"I don't know much about God," she said. "I used to think about him some, when I walked through the woods on our property or sat by the stream. But now I think he's a lot bigger than all that. I don't think anything happens without his say-so. If you want to help, I'm sure he'll find a way to let you." Then she smiled lovingly. "Besides, just your being here has already helped *me* a great deal!"

The sound of the front door intercom drew the two lovers from the rooftop, and hurrying down the hall, they joined the rabbis in greeting their friends.

"Gentlemen," David began, "this is Father Ian McCurdy, his sister, Emily, and his friend, John Cromwell, from Great Britain. And this is Emily's friend—and mine," he said wistfully, "Britta Hayworth."

Pete and Mel took their jackets and luggage as Anya ushered them into the parlor.

"Come, come," Rabbi Benjamin offered. "Rest by the fire! Father McCurdy," he said, stretching out his hand, "I am honored to meet one of the world's great scholars." This last phrase was for Uriel's benefit, who needed a reminder to accept the man.

At this, Uriel, too, shook Ian's hand, and Carl and Menachem offered their warmed-up chairs.

"Gentlemen," Ian said, bobbing his head in a bow, "the pleasure is mine, I am sure! I have followed your work for years. I hope I can be of some assistance."

In his arms was the precious valise from the British Museum. He had not let it go, even once, since leaving London.

Rabbi Ben deduced the contents and did not immediately offer to relieve him of it. "You have brought the scroll?" he asked gently.

"I have," Ian replied. "Perhaps you can understand my insistence on transporting it personally. It has long been a part of my soul."

John Cromwell swallowed hard as Ian said this. No one else could possibly know how true that statement was.

"Father," Horace said, "you may rest assured that we will not take it from you against your will. Although we believe it belongs in Israel, you must let God tell you what to do. After all, he apparently entrusted it to your keeping for all these years."

Ian was stunned by this sympathetic observation.

For a long, silent moment, the two clerics stood face to face on a small, oriental carpet before a Jerusalem fire. Etched before the golden blaze in long black frocks, both with snowy hair and guileless faces, they looked more alike, than unlike.

CHAPTER 41

The next morning, the house was bustling with joyous activity, as all the company from across the world anticipated the outcome of the day's findings.

Honey was helping Anya clear the breakfast dishes from the dining room, where the four rabbis, the Catholic priest, John Cromwell, Emily, Britta, the professor, and the three Montanans had devoured a large meal.

In a few moments, all the men but Pete and Mel would be going off to the Consortium's computer lab, where, in the security of the underground workroom, the scroll would be unveiled.

Since women were not allowed in the Consortium lab, Honey, Emily, and Britta were discussing with Pete and Mel a day-long tour of the city, under the escort of the Wester brothers, when Rabbi Benjamin ducked his head in the room.

"Come join us," he said. "We're going to say a prayer over the day, before we depart."

Honey wiped her hands on a napkin and left the chores to Anya. Together, the five guests followed Rabbi Benjamin to the parlor, where David and the other rabbis waited.

"Let's join hands, shall we?" Horace said, gathering his friends and colleagues in a circle. Silence descended on the group.

Rabbi Benjamin looked around at his fellow clerics. The rabbis, all except Katz, had their eyes closed, their heads bowed. Horace noted that Uriel's face was a bit clouded and thought perhaps he was uneasy with the ecumenical spirit. Thinking it best to ease his comrade's mind, Ben said, "Uriel, would you do us the honor of invoking God's blessing on our day?"

Katz glanced at Horace in pleased surprise, then closed his eyes and cleared his throat.

"Hear, O Israel," he began, "the Lord our God is one God. There are no others. God of our Fathers, bless our endeavors. Bring to light the ways of righteousness and guide us to fulfill your will on earth. Help us to establish your sanctuary, once more, among men of all nations. And may your Shekinah glory dwell again among us!"

To this, everyone said "Amen," and the men clapped one another on the backs, like soldiers ready to enter the fray.

But one of the guests had been stunned by the prayer, wondering if he had heard the words correctly.

The scholars and the rabbis were gathering up their briefcases, heading for the front door, when Pete rushed up to David and drew him aside. "Excuse me, Professor," he said in a low voice, "may I see you for a moment?"

David glanced at his exiting coworkers. "Now?" he asked. "What is it?"

"Maybe nothing," Pete said, feeling foolish.

David read deep concern in the Montanan's eyes. Calling to Horace, he said, "I'll be right there, Rabbi. Go on. I'll catch up with you."

Then, turning to Pete, "I'm all ears."

Britta and Emily had left for their room, to get ready for the day's tour. Only Mel and Honey lingered behind.

"What's going on?" Mel asked, joining his brother.

Honey, seeing that Pete's face had gone white, slipped up beside him, too.

Pete's voice was dry. "Like I say," he repeated, "it may be nothing. But . . . "

"Go on, Pete," Honey spurred him.

"Well," he said, "when the rabbi prayed, he used a word I've been wondering about. I know this will seem crazy, but, Professor, can you tell me what 'Shekinah' means?"

David was bewildered, and not a little annoyed at what seemed an unnecessary interruption to a crucial schedule.

"'Shekinah?'" he repeated. "Well, Pete, I don't know why you're asking, but shekinah is the Hebrew word for the glory of God, which the Bible says used to fill the Holy of Holies, the inner sanctum of the temple, when the Lord would descend. 'Shekinah,' 'Glory of God.' Why?"

Pete understood David's impatience. "Bear with me, Professor," he said. "Maybe Honey told you—I used to take messages for the brotherhood, off the ham radio." Quickly he related the incident of the Arab voice coming over the receiver, and he pulled the crumpled note from his wallet, where he had transferred it from his shirt pocket days ago.

David scanned the note, and as he did, his eyes grew round with fear. "'Ready to drop on Shekinah'!" he read.

He looked in dismay at Honey, who grabbed the note and gawked at it. "Oh, no!" she cried. "This sounds like a threat to the Consortium. 'Shekinah' is also the name of the yeshiva where the rabbis are training young men for priestly duties in the future temple!"

"Yeshiva?" Mel asked.

"Seminary!" David explained. "Yeshiva Shekinah, 'School for God's Glory,' houses and trains the very finest young Jewish scholars—Levites and Cohens—for roles in the future sanctuary! Rabbi Ben is an instructor there."

Honey clutched Pete's arm. "Did you say the transmission was from an Arab voice?" she asked.

"I'm no language expert," Pete replied. "But it sounded Middle Eastern." Then, feeling helpless, he added, "The only other thing noteworthy was the voice itself—extremely coarse and raspy."

Now it was David's turn to lurch. "What did you say?" he gasped.

"The voice, it was—"

"Okay! Okay!" the professor said. "I hear you."

"What's wrong?" Honey cried.

"Like Pete said," the professor muttered, "it may be nothing, but I've run into a guy with that sort of voice more than once now. He's definitely Arab, Lebanese by his language; he's an international traveler; he hates Jews, that's for sure! And—"

He paused, making the others edgy.

"Go on, Professor!" Mel exclaimed.

"He's probably in Israel, even as we speak," David replied. "I saw him on the plane heading here!"

Dread filled the American foursome as they all drew the obvious conclusion.

"What shall we do?" Honey groaned.

David pondered this, his palms sweaty. "We don't have enough to go on to alert the authorities," he said.

Pete and Mel glanced at one another, each knowing what the other thought about such "authorities."

"What about the rabbis?" Honey asked, her face full of fear.

David shook his head. "Again, since it could be nothing, I don't think we should disrupt them and their guests. Not today, of all days!"

Honey nodded. "What then?" she implored.

David thought a moment. "Since nothing happened during the night, maybe our fears are unfounded. But we can't be too careful."

Looking the Westers up and down, he said, "Maybe it's

providential that you guys are here. You lock like you could handle most anything. Mel, you've got street smarts, and Pete, you'd recognize the guy's voice if you heard it. Why don't you two hang out near the school for the day? Watch for a burly guy, dark hair, dark beard, dark complexion."

The Westers did not hesitate. "You've got it," Mel said, and Pete gave a thumbs up.

"Honey," David went on, "you can lead them there. I'll go join the rabbis, like they expect me to. Once you get Pete and Mel oriented, which shouldn't take long, come back and get Britta and Emily out of the Old City. Tell them you're taking them to Ben Yehuda Street for a day of shopping. Tell them you'll do the sightseeing thing tomorrow, because Pete and Mel decided to help at the lab. Okay?"

"Okay!" Honey agreed.

David grabbed his briefcase off the parlor sofa and headed for the door.

"Glad you came along, fellas," he called back to the Westers. Then, surprising even himself, he stopped and added, "Maybe God knew we needed you!"

Yeshiva Shekinah sat on one of the typically winding, narrow streets of Old Jerusalem, several blocks away from the Temple Jewels Exhibit. Pete walked so fast, he appeared to be leading the way, as Honey gave directions and Mel followed.

"I never overlooked giving Fogarty a message—never until this time," Pete said. "Now I'm glad I did!"

Honey hurried to keep up with the long-legged Pete, pointing this way and that as they turned corners and descended the crooked, terraced streets of the town. As Pete unburdened himself, she listened respectfully, seeing in him the crusader spirit that had attracted her to him years ago.

"I can't explain," he went on. "I've just had a spooky feeling about this note ever since I remembered it being in my pocket—like, like . . . well, like it was meant to be that I didn't deliver it. Like, maybe, it was a—"

"A warning?" Honey guessed.

Pete shrugged. Seeing that Honey was out of breath, he stopped a moment. "I don't talk to God much, not since I was a little kid. But on the plane, when you were asleep, Mel"—he turned to his brother—"well, it just kind of settled over me that I should shoot a prayer up about this thing. Dang, guys, I'll just say it! I told God I'd like to help if I could, you know, do something to make up for—"

His face turned red, and Honey touched his arm.

"I understand, Pete," she said.

Mel, feeling out of his element, cleared his throat and said, "Bro, you know I'm with you. Where is this place, anyway?"

Honey pointed to one more corner, and once they had rounded it, they saw that it dead-ended at a plain little house, two stories high, probably dating back to the same era as David's place.

"That's it," Honey said. "Rabbi Ben showed it to me once, when we went out for an evening stroll. He didn't take me inside, of course. Women aren't permitted."

A small sign, not in the least ostentatious, was the only adornment on the heavily carved door. *Yeshiva Shekinah* was all it said, in unimposing letters.

Decoration was sparse; a couple of large flowerpots, filled with red nasturtiums, one on each side of the door, provided the only splash of color. A wrought-iron bench sat to one side of the tiled porch, which was little more than a step.

"Check it out," Pete said to Mel. "If anyone wanted to do damage here, there's only one way to enter, and the high windows on the top story are covered with grille work. It would take a fairly powerful bomb to blast through those rock walls!"

Mel surveyed the scene, much as he would have done at a crime scene in a Los Angeles alley. "No, look," he said, pointing to a small flight of stairs barely noticeable behind an iron gate to the side of the building. "A lot of these old places probably have only one door, but I'll bet they use the rooftops for patios, like in the older apartment houses in big American cities—and like where David is staying. There's probably a way in through the roof."

Honey was amazed. "You're right, Mel. Pretty clever. Actually, you can walk from house to house on the roofs. It's like a thorough-fare up there."

"You mean, people aren't freaked by strangers crossing their roofs?" Pete asked.

"Well, all I know is, David and I took a walk with the rabbi one evening to see the city lights come up. We went along the rooftops like we were on a sidewalk. No one asked any questions. They just nodded and said hello as we passed by. You could see entrances to the floors below."

"Wow, strange!" Pete said. "The closest we get to that idea is Santa Claus on Christmas Eve!"

The three laughed, but Mel was still speculating, analyzing the building and the street that dead-ended at the front door.

"One of us could go up on the stairs, and one of us could stay out front," he said to his brother. "But how would we explain our-selves, if the students see us? Tell you what," he suggested. "We passed some little shops not too far back. How about if we hang out there and keep checking the street? Chances are probably about fifty-fifty that anyone wanting to 'drop' something, like the note says, will approach from the street anyway."

Pete shrugged. "Sounds like a plan," he agreed. Then, turning to Honey, he gave an anxious nod. "Okay, kid," he said, "you get out of here!"

Honey shot a worried look at the school and then rushed toward Pete, embracing him and burying her head on his shoulder. "You be careful!" she said, then sighed, "I need you, Pete!"

CHAPTER 42

David arrived at the institute just in time to enter with his associates. Smoothing his hair, he tried to look calm, to focus his attention on the task at hand.

The computer lab was a whirl of activity when the men arrived. Clement, James, and Shofar were madly collating reams of names that continued to pour in from respondents to the Consortium's request for Cohen family histories.

"Good morning, fellows," Rabbi Benjamin greeted them. "I have brought some very important guests."

Clement stood up from his work station, where he had just clicked the enter key to deposit about a thousand names into the main computer's spinning brain. When he saw his four bosses, he snapped to attention. "Good morning, Rabbis," he said, nudging James, who nudged Shofar, so that they, too, snapped alert.

"This is Father Ian McCurdy, from Oxford, and his coworker, John Cromwell," Horace announced.

Having anticipated this visit, the programmers' expressions were full of admiration.

Clement thrust out his hand, at the same instant

as his companions, so that three eager hands waited for Ian's attention. Shaking each in turn, the good Father smiled.

"Quite the greeting committee!" he said to Rabbi Benjamin.

Stepping up to the computer bank, the Oxfordian studied it
with amazement. Reams of paper flowed steadily from printers, each
sheet laden with charts and columns of names, dates, and places.

"So this is the result of your work?" he asked. "All of these are
Jewish histories?"

"That's right!" Clement said proudly. "We are very close to
drawing some important conclusions!" As the computer master
spoke, his eyes were locked on the valise in Ian's arms. He was hesitant to ask the obvious question, but turned eagerly to Rabbi
Benjamin.

"Yes, Clement," the rabbi answered. "This is the scroll, the one
we always hoped to find."

Clement rubbed his hands together, like a hungry man over a
feast, and his two companions pressed close to his back, peering
around him at the marvelous find.

"The back room is ready," Clement said, looking longingly at the
door to the adjacent laboratory. "Rabbi Diamant opened it last
evening for the geneticists. They put all their work away so that you
could have free reign. I—I certainly would like to see the scroll. . . . "

Rabbi Benjamin glanced at his colleagues. Uriel Katz looked
askance at such a notion, but Levine and Jacobs welcomed the par-
ticipation.

"You'll be working with the results," Horace said. "You might as
well see the unveiling."

Elated, Clement turned to his envious companions. "You have
plenty to do," he said. "I won't stay long."

At this, he took a key from his pocket and opened the back
room, then flicked on the bank of lights that ran the length of the
subterranean chamber.

The last time David had seen this place, it had been the

repository of the bones of Caiaphas, ensconced in a hermetically controlled case. Now that case was nowhere to be seen, probably secreted away for further study, and all of the lab equipment used for that work had been lined up neatly on a side counter.

The long, stainless steel table in the center of the room was open for use, the geneticists having thought to set out a little circular saw, a surgical tool the men might need for their task. This lay beside a roll of white butcher paper, which they thought the linguists might want to spread on the work area.

"How surgical!" Ian said. "I feel as though I am about to submit my child's body for autopsy!"

The rabbis did not know whether to laugh or console him.

"Sorry, lads," the old priest said. "Just a bit of the dry Irish wit!"

Surveying the room, he sighed. "Goodness! If we had had such facilities at Institut Biblique we could have worked on those scrolls much faster."

Rabbi Benjamin hated to press him, but he reached out his hands, silently asking for the parcel. "May I?" he asked.

"Oh—of course," Ian replied. "Here, let me set it down."

The priest walked to the lab table, ready to deposit the scroll. But before he did, David, who was now centered on the work at hand, grabbed the roll of butcher paper and handed Clement one end. "Here," he said, "help me spread this out."

Clement, honored to be part of the procedure, quickly pulled the end free and, while David held the roll, draped a large sheet across the table. Quickly, David cut it with his pocket knife, and Clement, finding a roll of tape, secured the piece to the metallic surface.

"Now?" Ian asked.

"Now," David said.

Ian glanced at John Cromwell, as if for reassurance.

John nodded, and the priest set the valise on the table. "David," he said, "would you do the honors?"

The professor had thought that he could never be more nervous, more awestruck by a professional assignment than he had been when he had looked at Honey Aronstam's star. Then, the day he exhumed the document from the brick wall at Dachau, he had believed there could be no greater privilege.

Now, he was about to open the most sought after of all the Cave Scrolls, the one whose portent could reach from across the centuries to shape the destiny of the world!

As he pressed the lock buttons on the valise, the metal tabs flicked up with a snap. Gently, he lifted the lid with its form-fitting liner.

There, snuggled in its linen wrap, was the scroll.

He turned again to Ian, who nodded the go-ahead.

David rubbed the fingers of both hands against his thumbs, like a safecracker about to work a dial. Gingerly, he lifted the linen swaddle from the case and set the parcel on the table.

Next, he turned the bundle over and over, unrolling the linen wrap, until an ancient metal cylinder was exposed.

Ian stepped up to the artifact reverently and gazed upon it with a sigh. "Hello, old friend," he said, "old enemy. We meet again."

Cromwell stood by silently, wondering how Ian would bear up. When the priest stepped away, stalwart and unflinching, John breathed easier.

David gestured to Ian to begin taking apart the pieces that had been fit together after the original cutting.

"No, no, Dr. Rothmeyer," he said. "I am much too old and shaky for such close work. Be my guest."

David swallowed hard. If his colleagues only knew what anxiety he was feeling after learning about the possible terrorist threat, they might not trust him to be less shaky.

Piece by piece, the professor began to lay out the shards of corroded copper, side by side so that they formed a recognizable document, reading from right to left.

The rabbis leaned close, trying to make out the antiquated Hebrew characters.

"See how the language has changed!" Ian said. "It will take some getting used to, as the forms of the letters alter with time. What you are looking at is stylized in the writing form popular in the first century C.E."

It had been years since Ian had worked with such material, but he had given many a lecture at Oxford, explaining how paleographers and linguists determine the era in which a piece is written.

His voice showed the enthusiasm of a true scholar as he proceeded. "It is apparent, also, that this was written by somebody other than one of the Qumran scribes. Their handwriting and their use of language were quite precise and educated. Whoever wrote this is probably the same fellow who wrote the first Copper Scroll, likely a coppersmith, hired to do the work, and possibly borderline illiterate. He would have been copying a script written out on some other parchment and would not have understood much of what he wrote. We can see this from his misspellings, jumbling of characters and, sometimes, outright skipping of words."

The rabbis were amazed at Ian's analysis, but David was familiar with the analytical process and only admired his astuteness.

"It is marvelous that you can deduce so much from what, to the layman, is merely a bunch of graffiti," Dr. Jacobs observed.

"Rather like the pharmacist reading the doctor's prescription?" Levine teased.

Jacobs grinned, but Uriel Katz was more somber. "So, Father McCurdy," he asked, "is this, in truth, a key to the treasure scroll?"

Ian nodded. "It appears to be. We never implemented it. As I told David, Father Ducharme and I worked on this privately. We were under much duress as we did so, and we could only do so much. We never analyzed it in detail with reference to the first scroll. Because we were familiar with that document, though, it became obvious to us that this one was directly related."

Horace Benjamin shook his head in amazement. "Is it possible, Father, that there would be references here to the lost treasures of the Holy of Holies? The Ark of the Covenant, for instance?"

The priest looked at the floor. He had always feared such speculations, for he knew the international skirmish they could create. He answered carefully. "Anything is possible, Rabbi. As I say, we were not after any treasure. We were simply trying to interpret what we had found, though we did not complete that task."

At last, after David had spread out the copper shards in the puzzlelike arrangement, what was left of the scroll was the crimped core Ian had spoken of, the remnant that he and Ducharme had feared to tamper with.

"There, Dr. Rothmeyer," Ian said, "if your genealogical reference is in this scroll, it will be in that section. We saw nothing of the sort in the first part."

David's hands were sweaty as he reached for the diminutive, battery-powered circular saw. "Clement," he asked, "could you please bring me a paper towel from the sink?"

As Clement obeyed, Uriel Katz scrutinized the scroll and rubbed his forehead. "Now let me be sure I understand our thinking here. We are hoping to bring together the references in the Dachau document with scribal notations in this scroll? If we find a reference here to the first-century priest mentioned by Rabbi Aronstam, that should verify his contention that the line goes through a Jew who was taken to England during the Crusades. Am I right?"

"That is right," David replied. "The Dachau document says that the line of Israel Kahana, who was raised in England, descended from a certain Gabriel Ben Zadok, one of the 'righteous' Cohen priests. It says that the legend will be verified if a reference to Gabriel can ever be found and that this reference was recorded by desert scribes, presumably of Qumran fame."

"So," Katz went on, "bear with me. We are also saying that if such and such can be proven, it only remains for some modern line to be linked with this Englishman, and, *voila*, we will have our candidate!"

No one present could miss the sarcasm in Katz's tone.

Neither David nor Ian knew how to respond, but Rabbi Benjamin was used to dealing with his obstreperous colleague. "'*Voila*' indeed," he said pleasantly. "Can you imagine a more definitive trail of evidence?"

Katz had never grown accustomed to Horace's way with him: always able to squelch him, yet remain kind in the process.

Levine, however, was more blunt. "Step back now, Uriel. Let Dr. Rothmeyer work," he said, pulling Katz away from the table.

David cleared his throat tensely and held the saw in crimped fingers. Pushing the little button on the side, which would disengage the motor the moment he let up on it, he set the saw to humming.

With a high-pitched squeal like that of a dentist's drill, it bit into the first thin layer of the tightly wound core. Bit by Bit, David worked through the coiled layers, removing a strip at a time and placing them beside each other, like pieces of onion skin.

"Beautiful!" Ian whispered. "You are a craftsman!"

David worked through the last layer, and when he had unraveled the final characters, placing the last thin section next to the others, the men gathered around the table. All of them knew Hebrew, whether in this archaic script or in the words of a freshly printed Torah. Scanning the frail shards, they looked anxiously for the necessary reference.

"Clement," David called, drawing an overhead lamp close to the table, "do you have a magnifier?"

Clement rummaged through a drawer in a nearby cabinet and quickly produced a reading glass.

Looking somewhat like Sherlock Holmes, with his tweed jacket and serious, thin face, David Rothmeyer read as quickly as possible through a long list of explications on hiding places and the meanings of words in the first scroll.

At last, with a thrill coursing through his entire body, he thought he had fallen on something. "Father McCurdy," he said, handing the priest the glass, "look at these lines, just before the benediction! Do they say what I think they say?"

The rabbis moved collectively closer, trying to get a view while not disturbing the paleographers. "Have you found it?" Rabbi Benjamin asked in a whisper.

Ian began to read the vague, corroded letters of the section David pointed out. "Much of it is missing," he said, "but I can make out certain familiar phrases."

Slowly he pieced together a few words for the listeners. "'*Asher ba'u habrit hahadashah. . . .*'" Then he interpreted, "'The people of the community of the renewed covenant.'"

David nodded agreement. "Go on," he said.

"There is a rusted place here," Ian said, "but I see the next phrase as '*halakah bene sadoq*.'"

David nodded again. "I agree, 'the law of the sons of Zadok'!"

The rabbis were astonished. "The priestly line!" Dr. Jacobs exclaimed. "It is talking about the priestly line!"

"It seems so!" Ian affirmed. "Now here, what is this?" he asked, squinting through the magnifier. "Again, there is something missing. But the next recognizable phrase is '*rebi saddiq*'!"

He glanced up at the onlookers, and as one voice they shouted, "Righteous Teacher!"

Dr. Jacobs and Rabbi Levine grasped each other in a hug.

"They are speaking of the Teacher of Righteousness! The one so often heralded throughout the Cave Scrolls! He was the leader of the commune!" Levine recalled.

"So it would appear!" Ian said, trying not to overanticipate. "But, let us go on. . . ."

Again, he squinted through the glass and read the adjoining

words. Suddenly his old eyes grew wide, and the magnifying glass wavered in his hand. David grasped it from him, fearing he would drop it on the scroll.

"You *do* see it!" David cried. "I am not imagining this?"

The old priest rose up stiffly, straightening his back and gazing speechlessly at the American.

"What? What?" the rabbis cried. Even Uriel Katz was unable to resist the drama of the moment. "Tell us what it says!" he exclaimed.

Ian ran through the phrases in his mind, filling in the missing parts to make a likely composition.

"I do not feel we are out of line at all, gentlemen," he finally said, "in making the following interpretation. This is the culmination of the document, the place where the drafters give their credentials. They are put just before the closing benediction and would read something like this:

"'The law of the sons of Zadok, the people of the community of the renewed covenant, and their Righteous Teacher or Rabbi . . . '"

Here he paused, his entire body atingle. John Cromwell patted his back and whispered, "Go on, Ian."

"' . . . their Rabbi, Gabriel Ben Zadok'!"

At the sound of these words, the ultimate proof of the monumental quest, the rabbis were ecstatic. Jacobs and Levine hugged one another rapturously, and began to dance around, singing, lifting their old knees and stomping their feet, clapping their hands and twirling like boys at a bar mitzvah.

Reaching for Rabbi Benjamin, they drew him into their jig and then held out their hands to draw the others in. Suddenly the entire group, even a previously reticent Uriel Katz, was caught up in celebration, singing and dancing around the metal table.

David, John, Ian, Clement—all of them—laughed and clapped, spinning around the priceless scroll in unleashed joy.

Perhaps, centuries before, the drafters of that document had prayed for this day, when the scroll, prepared under great duress and hidden at great risk, would serve the purpose for which it was created. Perhaps they even dreamed it would be celebrated in this way, received with great joy, for the door it would open on the future and the new day it would usher in.

CHAPTER 43

Mammed Kahlil was used to pulling off his violent acts under cover of darkness, or at least, in the confusion of crowds.

However, this assignment was different. It called for daylight, for the Islamic forces behind it wanted it to receive immediate media focus. And because of the layout of the dead-end street and the yeshiva building, chances were that he would not be able to sneak away unnoticed.

But he was prepared for that eventuality. He was prepared either to die and go to Paradise, where he would be received in honor by the Prophet Mohammed, or to become a bull's-eye of media attention for the Islamic cause.

So long as he was successful in destroying the Jewish school, where youngsters were trained as functionaries in the planned temple, he would please Allah.

Mammed had spent the night in Tel Aviv, and took a cab to Jerusalem in the morning. Dressed in casual attire, he could have been a tourist, a Lebanese businessman, or even a secular Jew. Though his skin was darker than that of most Jews, if he did not speak, he knew he should go unnoticed in the Orthodox neighborhood where the school was located.

Apart from the directions to the yeshiva, which he had received from his employers and committed to memory, he also bore in mind Altmeyer's description of the blond American men and their dark-haired female accomplice. If anything was going to interfere with Mammed's duties, it would be a threat from Israeli counterintelligence.

Bright noon sun flooded the narrow lanes and twisting streets of the Old City as Mammed wended through the marketplace nearest the school. In a small leather case, the strap of which was over his shoulder, was the precious vial full of Bailey's Bug. Mammed held the bag beneath his arm, close against his body, like a tourist might hold an expensive camera case.

He walked through the bazaar as nonchalantly as possible, at the same time considering the volatility of the vial's contents. Though the lid was securely tightened, he could not be too careful in avoiding jarring the bottle. Too harsh a bump from a passing pedestrian or a clumsy stumble over a crack in the lane could spell disaster.

As he skirted clusters of tourists and shoppers along the way, he also skirted his enemies. This was an Orthodox Jewish neighborhood. He was reminded of this every time men in black suits and broad-rimmed hats passed him, chatting together in Hebrew, keeping their eyes to the ground.

How he hated them! How his pulse pounded as he moved ever closer to vengeance.

Ahead he could see the sign for the street that led to his target.

He could feel each beat of his heart now, thrumming, pushing adrenaline through his body. He wondered how many more times it would beat, before it was silenced for eternity.

It had been two hours since Honey had left Pete and Mel in the marketplace near the yeshiva. The Westers felt awkward as they lingered near the corner of the little side street leading to the school. Trying to look like tourists in the small shops lining the adjacent block, they feared their extended "visit" there was beginning to attract notice.

Pete had tried on five pairs of sandals, declining to buy anything, while the anxious shop owner jabbered away about the fine quality of the cheap leather, and Mel had downed his second cup of thick black coffee and a prune pastry at the neighborhood café, when they joined one another at the intersection for the umpteenth time.

"Maybe we should come back this evening," Pete finally said, as they stood at the corner. "If anything's going to happen, maybe it'll be after dark."

Mel was prone to agree. "The professor and the rabbis will be done at the lab soon enough. Dave will probably think it's okay to tell them about this situation, once their research is finished. Maybe they'll want to contact the authorities."

"Yeah," Pete agreed. "Maybe we're in over our heads. Or, like we keep saying, maybe there's nothing to any of it."

Just as he admitted this, however, he noticed a peculiar look come over his brother's face. Seeing that Mel was focused on something behind him, Pete turned around and followed his gaze. "What is it?" he asked.

Mel had observed the behavior of countless drug dealers on the streets of L.A., countless ganglords trying to look harmless as they ambled through the hood, nodding innocently to the patrol car as it passed by. Something in the demeanor of an oncoming stranger was similar.

"What do you suppose he's all about?" Mel whispered, nodding in the stranger's direction.

His words were more of a statement than a question. As Pete

observed the enigmatic fellow, whose description matched that which David had given, the hair stood up on the back of his neck.

The Arab, who had stopped at a fruit stand, pretending to survey the wares, had not yet noticed the Americans.

"Look at how he babies that bag of his!" Pete muttered.

Mel ducked into a small trinket shop and pulled Pete with him. Hiding behind a rack of posters, he spoke softly. "Bro, how about you head on down toward the school? I'll stay at this end of the block, and let's see where he goes."

Pete did not need to think about it. Moving out just before the Arab began sauntering down the street again, he walked calmly but quickly toward the yeshiva. Mel, shielded by the posters, pretended to read a guidebook as Mammed drew near the corner.

As Pete arrived at the school, he was horrified to find that the door to the building was ajar. Two young students sat on the bench by the step, sunning themselves in their cotton vests and debating something they studied. Oblivious to what transpired, they sparrred jovially, their dark side-curls bobbing as their animated heads shook.

Casting a quick look over his shoulder, Pete saw that the Arab had not yet rounded the corner. Quickly, he approached the yeshivites, trying not to startle them.

"Hey, fellas," he hailed them. "You don't know me, but I think you'd better get inside!"

The students looked up at the American with wide eyes then, glancing behind him, suddenly darted into the building and pulled the door shut with a slam.

Pete, wheeling about, saw the Arab approaching.

It was a stunned Mammed who, upon rounding the corner, laid eyes on the big, blond informant. Stopping dead in his tracks, his olive face paled, and he nervously drew his bag from under his arm.

Pete stuck his thumbs in his belt loops and rocked back on the heels of his boots. "Howdy, stranger!" he said, in his best John Wayne. "New to these parts?"

Fumbling with the mouth of the bag, Mammed began to reach inside. At that instant, however, another American voice called out, "Don't even think about it!"

Shocked, Mammed wheeled about, ready to flee, but the instant his eyes landed on Mel, approaching from the head of the lane, he did a double-take.

Though he had been given the Westers' descriptions, they were an awesome duo in the flesh. With their unusual white-blond hair, their husky builds, and their Nordic height, they appeared like warrior angels, ready to smite him.

In a fit of rage and fear, Mammed grabbed the bag from his arm and began to swing it over his head, like an ancient sling. "Stand back!" he cried in a Lebanese accent. "This is Allah's will! You interfere with the will of Allah!"

The two brothers, seeing that he was not going to go down easily, began to circle him, darting the purse as it whizzed overhead.

Meanwhile, the young men of the yeshiva were gathering on the roof, going out through the top-story hatch and lining up along the balustrade. Thirty or forty of them had gathered before Pete looked up and saw them bunched precariously along the parapet.

"Back, fellas!" he shouted up at them. "This guy's dead serious!"

Mammed was working himself into a frenzy, the purse continuing to cut the air above his head. With a crazed expression, he lunged repeatedly at the Americans.

"Jihad!" he cried. "Jihad! Holy War against all Jews, and all lovers of Jews! Allah is the only true Glory! Death to the Shekinah!"

Hearing his ranting, people were drawn to the little street from all corners of the neighborhood. Soon a large group gathered at the intersection, many of them hurling Jewish epithets at the Muslim.

Distracted by their catcalls, Mammed glanced their way for a split second—just long enough that Pete was able to catch the handle of his whirling purse, like the rope of a whizzing tetherball as it spins around a schoolyard pole. Tearing it from the Arab, he took him off balance, and Mel was able to tackle him to the ground.

Instantly, the mob rushed forward, spitting and hissing at the terrorist.

Mel grappled with the would-be assassin until he had him face-down on the cobblestones, then locked the man's arms behind him, just as he had done to many a culprit on the Los Angeles streets.

"Back, back!" Pete warned the mob. "This is a very dangerous bag!" He held it carefully before him, and the crowd fell over one another in their rush to get away.

As Mel took off his belt, using it to tie up the Arab's wrists for lack of handcuffs, the Muslim continued to spew forth his venom.

Pete, meanwhile, had taken the bag to the bench outside the school and proceeded to open it gingerly.

Bringing out a little bundle that lay in the bottom, he saw the glass vial, and broke into a sweat. He was astonished that it had not been damaged in the fracas, but did not think he should handle it further, and placed it on his lap, afraid to make another move.

Meanwhile, more people were arriving on the scene, pushing through the crowd, amazed at what they had come upon. But these were not strangers. These were friends, and when Pete glanced up, he heaved a grateful sigh.

"Honey!" he cried. "You were supposed to stay away from here!"

Britta, who had come with her, hung near David as he stooped to help Mel.

Clustered about the ex-cop and the Lebanese were the rabbis. As the professor helped Mel bring the Muslim to his feet, the rabbis rushed into the school. Seeing that no harm had been done, they called to the rooftop gathering, telling the students it was safe to come down.

Honey, flying to Pete's side, slumped down beside him on the bench. "I couldn't stay away any longer!" she cried. "Oh, Pete, if anything had happened to you . . . "

Suddenly she noticed the vial he cradled and deduced immediately the nature of the attempted assault.

"Don't touch it!" Pete warned. Then, ever so tenderly rewrapping the container in its cloth, he slipped the bundle back into its purse. "Now, I think we have something to show the authorities," he said.

Honey looked up at her handsome man, tears welling in her eyes. "Do you know what you have done?" she sighed. "You have saved the choicest sons of Israel! You have saved Israel's future!"

CHAPTER 44

Ian, Emily, and their dear friend John Cromwell sat in the back of a silver-gray Mercedes limousine, as it sped out of Jerusalem and up the highway toward Tel Aviv. With them, in the side seat, was Rabbi Horace Benjamin, who was accompanying them to the airport.

For the second time in his life, Ian was fleeing Israel under a spate of media harassment.

Within a few hours of Pete and Mel's dramatic intervention at Yeshiva Shekinah, newspeople had descended on David Rothmeyer's house. Word had quickly reached the news hounds that the two heroes were staying there, having been seen entering the place after their bold escapade in the Old City. The Jerusalem bureau of CNN was at the site almost as quickly as local TV news crews, ready to flash the story across the globe.

After the scholars at the Consortium gallery had completed the analysis of the copper scroll, David had broken the news of Pete's message and the possible implications. The rabbis, anxious to go to the yeshiva, had sent Father McCurdy and John Cromwell back to the house under Clement's escort, asking the Britishers to wait there.

Unfortunately, when the CNN staff arrived at the house, demanding an interview with the American heroes, someone had caught a glimpse of Ian inside and recognized him as the notorious press dodger, the famed head of the Cave Scroll team.

Instantly the reporters were on him, clambering over him in the lobby, thrusting microphones in his face, demanding to know what connection he had to the Wester brothers.

Rabbi Benjamin, with the help of David and John, had managed to move the reporters out, then had tried to calm the shaken priest.

"I'll be all right," he said, catching his breath. "I'm just having a bad case of déjà vu."

Emily, left waiting at the old house, when Britta accompanied a distracted Honey back to the yeshiva, had heard the account of the rescue as one wily reporter managed to get to the Westers. She, also, was shaken.

"Ian!" she cried. "What's going on around here? I'm not sure I like any of this!"

Ian sympathized. "I know, I know! I think we've served our purpose in Israel. It's time to go home!"

After an unsuccessful attempt to persuade Ian to stay, at least until the computer collation was done and a more definitive conclusion could be gained from the information in Ian's scroll, Rabbi Benjamin had phoned the airport, making plane reservations on a night flight to London.

After saying farewells to David, whom he hoped to meet again, and to the rest of the American contingent, whom he had only just gotten to know, the old Oxfordian, his sister, and John Cromwell made a hasty departure.

Britta, with her love of a good story, had contacted the *London Times* about a potential feature series and had been assigned to stay on. So she hugged Emily fondly and promised to meet up with her at the Oxford pub when she returned.

Now, as the limousine cruised up the main highway that connected the length of Israel, Ian took what he believed would be his last glimpses of the Holy Land.

Leaning back in the leather seat, he let out a sigh. "I hope you know, Rabbi," he said, "I have a great love for your country. My desire to leave is not a reflection of my feelings for this land and its people."

Horace smiled at him with understanding. "Why do you think we keep such a low profile, ourselves, when we are here?" he said. "The entire political and spiritual climate is so sensitive that, given our agenda, our lives are in jeopardy all the time!"

"I suppose you speak mainly of Arab-Israeli tensions," Ian said. "But I am sure there are many Jews who would not welcome the idea of a return to the old ways—of the restoration of ancient rituals, for instance."

The priest had picked his words carefully, but the rabbi knew what he was referring to. "You speak of the return to animal sacrifices," Benjamin surmised.

The Oxford scholar nodded vehemently and Emily winced squeamishly. "I tried to tell David, and I am sure you must realize, that I consider this aspect of your plans to be utterly antithetical to my beliefs," Ian declared. "Not only do I spurn the notion on the grounds that I consider it a reversion to a more primitive role of religion, but it also flies in the face of New Testament teachings, the teachings, my friend, upon which I base my life!"

Rabbi Benjamin replied with energy, "Father McCurdy, not only am I not surprised by your statement, I would be surprised if you said otherwise. I realize that much of what the Consortium has undertaken, in its efforts to duplicate the ancient covenental forms of worship, is not only unChristian, but antithetical to much of modern Judaism."

Ian leaned toward the rabbi with a puzzled scowl. "Why then do you proceed?" he asked bluntly.

Before the rabbi could answer, however, Father McCurdy anticipated the response.

"I know," Ian said, "you are going to quote Jeremiah and Ezekiel, and you are going to refer to the vast body of prophecy that seems to indicate that such a temple and such worship must be reinstated at the coming of Messiah."

Horace smiled. "You are right," he said. "But I was also going to ask you why you have participated to the degree you have, if you are so opposed to what we are doing."

The luxury sedan hummed its way up the road, carrying Ian away from a venture that had been the biggest conundrum of his life. Sighing again, he glanced out the window at the passing terrain upon which the most fabulous dramas of human history had been enacted.

"You have me there," he confessed. "I have asked God that question a hundred times. Perhaps I will never know the answer."

Horace closed his eyes, as if he had something to say, but did not know how wise it was to say it. He remained in that attitude for so long that the others began to wonder if he had fallen asleep.

At last, smoothing his fluffy white beard with his wizened hands, he cleared his throat and said, "Ian, I am going to tell you something I have never had the nerve to tell anyone else. It is certain I would not share this if my colleagues were within earshot."

The three passengers glanced at one another, mystified.

"Let me begin by saying that, as much as I admire my colleagues, we do not always agree on everything. You know what they say about us Jews." He laughed. "'Where there are two of us there are three opinions!'"

Ian echoed his laugh, and Emily felt less tense.

"Well," Horace went on, "if any of them knew, especially Uriel Katz, just how many friends I have among the Messianic contingent, they would probably disbar me from my position!"

"By 'Messianic' you mean 'Christian' Jews?" Ian asked.

"That is one way of saying it. They call themselves 'Messianic' for two good reasons. One: They believe in Jesus as the Jewish Messiah; and two: The term 'Christian' has too many evil connotations among Jews who have been persecuted. After all," he reminded them, "the mass of Germans during the Holocaust and the greatest of the persecutors throughout modern Jewish history have called themselves 'Christian.'"

Ian was aware of this and nodded sadly. "That is an irony, and a shame," he said. "Jesus was a Jew, and so were all of his followers. Certainly, he never would have endorsed such horror!"

"I believe you are right," Benjamin agreed. "Part of what I want to tell you, and what I have rarely admitted to anyone, is that I have a great deal of respect for Jesus of Nazareth. You might be surprised to know how many of my fellow scholars and thinkers feel the same."

Ian was surprised and showed it.

"But let me continue," Benjamin went on, "before I lose my nerve." At this, he took a deep breath and shot a glance back at the retreating highlands that cradled the Holy City.

"You might also be surprised to learn how many of my fellow rabbis are now participating in Messianic congregations. The Messianic movement is, to be frank, enormous in Israel and among Jews of many lands. It has the potential of the great evangelistic movements that took place in Europe and America in the nineteenth century!"

Ian studied Horace's expression curiously. "Rabbi," he said, "it sounds to me as though you, yourself, have been giving a lot of thought to the claims of Jesus. Is this what you are leading up to?"

Benjamin shrugged. "I may as well confess, I have even attended meetings once or twice. There is a Messianic congregation that meets every Wednesday evening at the YMCA in Jerusalem."

Ian was astonished. "Across from the King David Hotel?" he cried. "Why, Horace, the Y has been a bastion of Christian presence in Israel since the British Mandate!"

"So it has," the rabbi agreed. "Well, I got real brave and went to the meeting there. I tried not to draw attention to myself, but . . . " Again, he stroked his patriarchal beard, and the passengers chuckled.

"You would look like a rabbi even if you showed up in blue jeans!" Emily observed.

Horace agreed. "Then you see how much courage it took on my part to set foot in the place!"

Growing very sober, he went on. "The fact is that my own background is not so rigid as that of Katz and his ilk. He is a Talmudist of Eastern European descent, though he was born in Israel, and lives in Brooklyn. He, like his ancestors, prides himself on a very strict and literal view of Scripture."

Cheerfully, he added, "As for my background, my people are Hasidic, also from Eastern Europe. We take a deeper view of Scripture, one that allows for a lot of things the Talmudists cannot abide. Add to that the fact that I have also been trained in the Cabala. Do you know what that is, Father?"

Ian was familiar with the term. "Cabalism looks for hidden and mystic meanings in the Scriptures, am I right?"

"Exactly!" the rabbi said. "And we find them!"

Ian considered this. "So, how does that relate to the Messianics?"

Benjamin's face took on a look of awe as he related his experience with the strange congregation.

"The first night I attended one of the meetings," Horace explained, "the speaker was a Cabalist! He believed in Jesus as Messiah, and spoke at length of the years he had spent using the Cabalistic approach to his scripture studies. He claimed to have discovered that the name of Jesus, or *Yeshua*, is encoded throughout the Scriptures and is intertwined with references to Messiah, especially in those portions we call Messianic prophecy!"

"The name of Jesus?" Emily marveled. "How so?"

Benjamin spoke in a hush, obviously moved by the profound

topic. "It is literally woven into the fabric of the ancient verses, each letter spaced perfectly in patterns and predictable arrangements in the orginal Hebrew text! I have looked at the material myself, and he is right! It is all there, just as he said!"

Ian was astounded. "Is it also to be found in the sections dealing with the future of Israel, for instance in Jeremiah?"

"That was the most astonishing part of the matter!" Benjamin exclaimed. "The very books that speak of the reinstating of Israel as a nation and of the worship on Mount Zion are interwoven with the name of *Yeshua!* Jeremiah, Ezekiel, Zechariah, Isaiah, Daniel— all of them!" The rabbi's eyes were full of zeal, his hands clasped ecstatically before him.

"So," Ian reasoned, "if this is true, are you thinking that your colleagues may be misconstruing their duties? Are you saying that the blood sacrifices may not be necessary?"

Benjamin stared at the floor of the limousine. "I have never voiced this to anyone," he confessed, "but I do wonder that very thing. Perhaps the encoding is a riddle, meant to direct us to Yeshua, as the ultimate sacrifice! If so"— he shrugged and lifted his hands— "many of the preparations that have already been made may ultimately be unnecessary—the vessels for blood, the training of the young priests in the execution of sacrifices, and so on." At last, with a sigh, the rabbi concluded, "In any case, the great majority of our preparations are perfectly useful. And so, I go on with my work."

Ian agreed. "Particularly the work of locating a high priest!"

"That is correct," Horace said. "The prophets are quite clear that there must be an officiating administrator in the temple, even though Messiah will be the King."

Ian sighed and leaned back in his seat. Suddenly it seemed there might be light at the end of the tunnel he had entered on blind faith. "Well," he marveled, "then perhaps you have answered another question that has been nagging at me."

"What is that?" Horace asked.

"I had no idea what a movement this Messianic thing was," he admitted. "However, I knew that, through the centuries, many Jews have been absorbed into the Church. Many Jews do not even think much of their ethnic heritage and consider themselves to be Christian by creed. My question, Horace, is this: What will you do, if, when you find the rightful heir, you discover that he is a Christian?"

Horace closed his eyes again. Then opening them, he pleaded with Ian, "Pray for us, my friend. The possibility you have posed is not at all remote. There are those among my colleagues who would disqualify such a person without a second thought. Pray that we will have ears to listen and hearts to discern the will of God."

CHAPTER 45

O ver the next few days, the media bombardment of the old house where David lived waxed and waned, but never completely abated.

Though Pete and Mel Wester had offered no information that would keep the press coming back, any new bit of evidence regarding the incident or those involved sparked a fresh flurry of reporters smothering the street outside the house, sitting on the ancient gate, thrusting mikes at anyone who came or went.

The story the Westers gave was simply that they were American tourists who happened to be in the right place at the right time. The Arab had looked suspicious, Mel was trained in spotting suspicious characters, and *voilà*, they were able to nab him.

In the interim since the would-be assassin was wrestled to the ground and turned over to Israeli authorities, however, the international intelligence community had come up with personal profiles on the Westers, and even on Honey, which cast them in a very different, much more complex light. Bits and pieces of this information leaked to the press, just enough to keep them salivating and lunging at any-one who came near the house.

It was quickly learned, for instance, that Pete and Honey were from Montana, one of the U.S. hotbeds of Separatism. This tidbit immediately launched a full-scale investigation into their political backgrounds. When it was learned that they were somehow linked with White Supremacist groups in their area, there was no way that the press was going to leave them alone.

Yet, the Westers had rescued a Jewish community. They had intercepted an Arab terrorist on a mission to seek and destroy. And Ms. Aronstam had a Jewish name! This did not fit with the doctrines it was assumed they would espouse.

Coupled with this was the fact that they were staying in Jerusalem with members of the most right-wing movement in Israel. Then, to top it off, the head of the notorious Cave Scroll team, which had been accused of anti-Semitism, was guesting with them.

The facts, as they emerged, made for a banquet of contradiction and confusion that fed the talk shows, the evening news, and the tabloids for days.

One theory that emerged was that they were U. S. counter-intelligence agents, posing as Militia members or Freemen, yet actually spying on Arab activists! But even that notion did not tie in with Ian McCurdy's presence.

And what about this American professor, David Rothmeyer? Both he and McCurdy were linguistic archaeologists. Were they working on something together?

Of course, all of this attention and speculation caused no end of concern and fear on the part of the Consortium rabbis. They who had attempted for years to keep a low profile were suddenly under international inquiry.

It had not taken long for the media to piece together the fact that the seminary the Westers had rescued was under the auspices of the Temple Consortium. This had never been a hidden fact, any more than other activities of the temple movement had been hidden.

Indeed the Consortium had created a public gallery to display all the artifacts and explain the hoped-for construction of a new temple.

What was covert was the search for the high priest.

That must be kept from the eyes of the world until such time as the man could be ushered safely into his place as Israel's religious representative. Until that time, there were too many enemy forces who would attempt to intercept that find, to circumvent the resurrection of Israel's sacred system.

At last, something happened that alleviated the tensions in the house, at least temporarily.

One evening, as David, Britta, Honey, and the Westers sat with the rabbis enjoying one of Anya's fabulous dinners, the front gate intercom buzzed.

"More reporters," Horace grumbled. "When will they ever quit?"

David stood up and went to the door. "Go away!" he shouted over the speaker. "We have nothing for you!"

This time, however, the reply was a surprise.

"Dr. Rothmeyer?" a dignified voice called out. "We are not members of the press. We have, in fact, just sent the press away. We are agents of your country, Dr. Rothmeyer. We have been sent by your government to ask some questions."

Just enough of this response could be heard from the dining room that the company stopped eating and listened.

"Agents?" Rothmeyer repeated. "One moment."

David hurried back to the dining room and stood in the doorway, looking to Rabbi Benjamin for guidance. "Did you hear?" he asked.

"We heard," the rabbi said. Then, glancing at his colleagues, who looked mystified, he rose up and went with David to the lobby.

After introducing himself over the intercom, the rabbi objected, "You have no right to place demands on us. Although we are American citizens, we are here on international business, living in an Israeli house. You have no right—"

Cutting into his defense, the agent's voice called out again, "Reverend—uh, Rabbi—you are correct. We have no papers from the Israeli government giving us entrance to your house. However, if you will only let us in, we think you will find that we mean no harm. In fact, we only mean to help."

Putting his hand over the intercom, Rabbi Benjamin whispered to David, "Go outside and look at their credentials. Ask them if they are armed. If they are not, let them in."

Moments later, two tall, middle-aged men in dark suits, bearing briefcases and badges identifying them as members of the Central Intelligence Agency, entered the house.

Rabbi Benjamin, not offering to shake their outstretched hands, simply asked, "What is it you want? Whom do you wish to see?"

"We want to see the Wester brothers and Ms. Aronstam," they replied.

"Who doesn't?" the rabbi said, in his best Yiddish twang.

Then, leading the men into the parlor, he sent David to fetch the three.

The moment the three Montanans entered the room, Honey looking intimidated and the brothers angry, the agents tried to reassure them.

"Agents Morris and Dalton," one of them said. "Please, be assured that we are here for your benefit."

Pete, who had never trusted authority, smirked and Mel nudged him. Honey pressed close to Pete and grabbed his hand.

"Mr. Wester," Morris said, confronting the long-haired Montanan, "you are quite the international hero."

Pete returned the agent's gaze suspiciously but said nothing.

"We have been sent to take you home, Mr. Wester, you and"—he nodded to the others—"your brother and Ms. Aronstam."

At this, Pete bristled. "Why should I go home?" he spat. "I've done nothing wrong, and I have not made the personal decision to go home just yet."

ELLEN GUNDERSON TRAYLOR

Dalton, the other agent, stepped in. "Mr. Wester," he said, "you must surely know that we are aware of your past involvement with the Aryan Nations and similar organizations."

Pete's face went red. "It's all over the news! How could you miss it? What no one seems to realize is that I'm done with that bunch!"

Mel placed a brotherly hand on Pete's shoulder, and Pete clamped his mouth shut.

"In that you are mistaken," the agent went on. "We think you have proven a new loyalty. You risked your life, and so did your brother, to save an Israeli school. Rather than doubt your intentions, the world seems to be siding with you. And so are we."

Pete breathed out through pursed lips. "So," he muttered, "what do you want? Why do we have to go home?"

"We believe that with your background, you would be a great asset to your government in tracking down and curtailing the activities of American terrorists."

"Possibly even *international* terrorists," Morris added.

Pete did not need an explanation of that last statement. Having taken radio messages from many foreigners, and having been present the night Fogarty and Altmeyer talked about their international connections, neither he nor Mel were surprised by the agent's assumption. Besides, the CIA network undoubtedly knew about their recent trip to Germany and probably had speculated wildly about it.

As for Dalton's allusion to the U.S. government, Pete gave a sardonic chuckle. "My government?" he growled. "My government is in league with the Militia and their sort up to its eyeballs! I don't trust you guys any more than I trust Fogarty or Altmeyer!"

The agents, to Pete's surprise, were not rattled. "We thought you might feel that way," Dalton said. "So we've brought you something that might help convince you we mean well."

He reached into his valise and pulled out a large, white envelope, emblazoned with the seal of CNN.

As Pete opened it, the agent explained. "We've already told the talk shows they can have you for as many interviews as you care to do. If you have dirt on the U.S. government, now's your chance to tell the world!"

Pete's hands trembled as he unfolded an invitation to appear on *Larry King Live.*

Honey and Mel read the note in amazement, as the agents added, "Rest assured, if what you have to say sounds at all plausible, there will be a full-scale investigation, the likes of which our country has never seen!"

Pete looked into the faces of the two emissaries. Maybe he did read sincerity there, he thought. "What about Fogarty and the others? How do we know we'll be safe?" he asked, drawing Honey closer.

The agent clamped his briefcase shut like the door of a prison cell. "We intend to see them behind bars!" he said. "As to any danger their followers might pose, we will grant you full protection, until you tell us otherwise."

Pete sighed. "I sure would like to see that scum locked away!" he said.

"Very well, then," Morris granted. "We are here to offer you safe passage home, at the expense of the American government."

"And full immunity for any improper involvements lurking in your background," Dalton added.

Pete turned to Honey and Mel. "What do you think?" he asked.

Mel nodded. "We're with you, bro, whatever you decide."

Honey squeezed his hand. "It looks like God has more work for you to do," she said with a smile.

"All right," Pete said. "When do we go?"

As soon as it was heralded that the Montana Contingent, as they were now being called, had returned to the U.S., the talk shows were abuzz with more speculations. Even in Israel, people could not turn on their televisions without encountering some new report related to the Westers.

Shortly after they left, information regarding the substance that the terrorist had intended to drop at Shekinah came pealing across the airwaves.

"A New and Even More Lethal Strain of Anthrax!" it was touted. "Developed for Use in Confined Areas, for the Decimation of Specific Populaces, Schools, Churches, Synagogues!"

The formulation had been traced to Ireland and was called "Bailey's Bug."

Scientists, analyzing the formula under highly controlled conditions, had found that it was viable outside its container for only moments and then was harmless. It seemed to be designed for use in concentrated areas, such as bus stations and other gathering places, making its detection and interception more difficult than the weapons of mass destruction intended for larger populations.

"No One Is Safe!" the press blared to the world. "Beware of all Suspicious Activity!"

One evening, David and Britta sat alone in the parlor of the old house, watching the international news on television. The rabbis were on the rooftop, enjoying the warm evening air.

David was about to turn off the TV, having had his fill of speculations about the terrorist attack when suddenly, flashing on the screen was a scene of a beautifully wooded property somewhere in northwestern America. Scruffy-looking characters in handcuffs were being dragged from a large log house, past a row of Harley motorcycles strewn across the yard.

"American agents of the Bureau of Alcohol, Tobacco and Firearms arrested several members of the White Aryan Nations in Montana today," the news anchor announced. "Led to their hideout by the owners of the property, the Americans who intervened in the recent attack on the seminary in Jerusalem, agents stormed the remote house and broke up a standoff of about a dozen Militia members."

David lurched forward. "Look at that!" he cried. "That must be the Wester house!"

Britta's eyes were wide, her mouth agape. "And those must be the honchos Pete worked for!" she exclaimed, as the screen changed.

"Heads of the group, James Fogarty of the Montana Supremacists, and Monte Altmeyer, German international mercenary, had fled the scene by the time agents arrived," the moderator continued, "but they were caught by roadblock in the small town of Thompson Falls."

The TV showed armed ATF agents handcuffing a tall, silver-haired man and a dark fellow in army camouflage. Spread-legged, they leaned against a black Suburban as the agents frisked them.

Then, switching again to the Wester house, the news coverage returned to the drama of the Bull River arrests.

"I think I see Honey!" Britta exclaimed. "Isn't that she with Pete and Mel . . . look, back behind the bikers!"

Sure enough, as the hogster contingent, the only members of the Fogarty bunch who had remained at the vacated Aryan headquarters, were hauled away, they spat profanities and made obscene gestures with the fingers of their handcuffed hands. These obscenities were directed at a trio of onlookers, who stood on the porch of the log house, watching them go with faces of relief.

"Honey looks happy!" Britta observed. "Wow! She sure has a story to tell!"

David glanced at Britta. "Always the reporter!" he said with a laugh.

"Sure," she replied. "But, just think, if I didn't have a nose for news, I never would have met you."

David's heart raced. Glancing toward the hallway, he made sure that no rabbi or housekeeper was nearby. Then, for the first time since he had held her hand in the London street, David made a closer move. Bending toward the blond-haired darling, he cupped her face in his hands, and kissed her.

CHAPTER 46

June/*Sivan*

It was the time of the Feast of Pentecost in Jerusalem, the ancient and traditional holiday celebrating the first harvest of the year. Pentecost, meaning "fifty days," indicated that the festival was to take place seven weeks after Passover. It was the highlight summer event throughout Israel.

The celebration was like the Sabbath, in that no work was to be done, and families offered their rabbis small loaves of barley bread in commemoration of the harvest and in gratitude for the provisions of God.

All male Jews were supposed to attend services on this day. In Jerusalem, many congregations held special gatherings in the court of the Western Wall.

Though Britta had not been raised as a Jew, she rose with the sun this Pentecost morning, full of excitement for the day. She had plans to meet her relatives from Nazareth, Great-uncle Reg and Great-aunt Deborah, who were coming down to Jerusalem for the festival.

She had contacted her uncle when she first arrived in Israel, but, given the sensitive nature of her involvement there, she had put off a visit until things calmed down.

The *Times* had kept her in Israel, as she followed

up on a feature series that grew out of the Wester saga, and she had been here for several weeks now, staying at the Consortium house.

It seemed to be perfect timing that Uncle Reg should be coming her way now, for the world press had taken its focus off the Consortium for the moment, as it followed the Wester story across the seas.

Meeting David and Rabbi Benjamin for breakfast on the balcony overlooking the Hinnom Valley, Britta was radiant in a simple pink dress, her hair reflecting the golden light of morning and her cheeks flushed with the blush of love. She could scarcely believe how lucky she was, to be in the most amazing city on earth and to be sharing it with a wonderful man like David Rothmeyer.

"Sleep well?" David asked, pouring her a cup of coffee as she sat down.

"Very!" Britta said.

Actually, that was not true. She had tossed and turned all night in her room, savoring thoughts of the professor, as she had done too many nights since they had first shared a kiss.

Rabbi Benjamin glanced up from his Sunday edition of the *Jerusalem Post*. Had the enamored couple looked at him, they would have seen a knowing twinkle in his eye before he ducked, smiling behind his newspaper again.

"Good morning, Rabbi Ben," Britta said. "This is a wonderful day! I'm going to meet my Uncle Reginald at the Western Wall. He's coming down to celebrate with Zachary, his son, who attends a synagogue here."

"How nice," Horace replied, putting down his paper again. "I did not know you had family in Israel."

"My uncle—actually he's my great uncle—was a famous photo-journalist during World War Two. He moved here after doing a photo-documentary on Holocaust immigrants. His work inspired me to become a journalist."

Then, dropping her voice a little, she gave a girlish giggle.

"Would you believe he and Emily McCurdy were sweethearts during the war?"

The rabbi raised his eyebrows. "It is a small world," he said.

Then, as an afterthought, he asked, "Is your family Jewish, Ms. Hayworth?"

"On my mother's side," she replied. "We were raised Anglican. Uncle Reg married a Jewish woman, but even she is one of those . . . how do you say it—"

"Messianics?" the rabbi guessed.

"That's it!" Britta said. Then with a little shrug, "I really don't understand all of that. Somehow, they work it out, mixing the two religions."

"So," the rabbi inquired further, "your uncle's son—Zachary, is it? Is he Messianic, as well?"

Britta nodded. "I believe so. He has been studying Judaism for years, even made his bar mitzvah. But I think he attends meetings in a Christian building."

Horace made no issue of his thoughts regarding the Messianics. He had shared his views with Ian, but David and Britta were not theologians. Besides, he did not wish to get into a discussion of something that, if Uriel or the others were to overhear, could cause dissension on such a bright and glorious day.

"Are the others going to join us?" Britta asked, glancing down the steps that led to the rabbis' bedrooms.

"They were up hours ago," Horace replied. "They should be returning soon. They went to the Wall to do morning prayers before dawn."

Britta was amazed. "Such devotion!" she said. "I don't think I could ever get up that early."

David laughed. "Rabbi Ben and I never went to sleep," he said. "We were at the computer lab! Clement thinks they may have an answer today!"

Benjamin leaned across the table. "Don't tell the others," he said. "They would not approve."

Britta shook her head. "What's to disapprove?" she asked.

"They would accuse me of working on a holy day," he said with a wink. "The way I see it, the computers are doing the work. We only feed them!"

David and Britta stifled grins, not fully understanding his rationale, or the need for it.

"So," Britta asked, "what has the lab been working on since they received Honey's and Ian's material? I thought it all fit together quite nicely."

"It did," David replied. "Since then, it has been a matter of weaving in the mass of e-mails, faxes, and letters that continue to pour in from around the world, from people wishing to offer what they know of family histories. The lab has come quite close several times to a final genealogy. Always, though, there is something not quite perfect. We hope it is only a matter of time before an exact match comes in."

Suddenly their conversation was interrupted by another buzz at the front gate. From down the winding stairs, they could hear Anya answering the intercom. Soon, she was admitting Clement, the computer master, to the lobby and led him to the veranda as she brought the group a tray of breakfast.

When the young scholar explained his visit, however, no one cared about food.

His eyes bleary from a night in front of monitors, he carried a sheaf of paper in one hand, along with an airmail packet. "Rabbi! Professor!" he cried, tossing the papers onto the table. "I believe we have it!"

"The final list?" Benjamin gasped.

David scooped up the computer material and perused it, while Clement explained: "We were just sorting through a pile of mail we received a few days ago. Since the strongest line we had found runs through Britain, we decided to only look at postmarks or e-mails from that area, hoping to narrow the chore. We came upon this airmail package, from some elderly woman in Chesworth, England.

When we collated her information into what we already had . . . *bingo*! It was there!"

Britta and Rabbi Benjamin left their seats and huddled over David's back, reading the letter. Written in the cramped characters typical of old folks' handwriting, it was nonetheless very detailed and well documented.

"Who wrote it?" Britta asked, reaching for the envelope and glancing at the return address.

"Dahlia Knight," David said. "What a name!"

"Dahlia?" Britta repeated. "I have a distant cousin named Dahlia, on my mother's side. Could it be?"

As David and the rabbi scanned the letter's contents, Britta was deep in thought, "In fact . . . I remember mother saying how Dahlia is into genealogy, big time! She has always kept copious records, writing for pictures of all the family weddings, asking for the names of every newborn, every new in-law! Apparently she used to bore the family stiff every time they visited, dragging out photo albums and reciting the family tree!"

David pulled an older letter from the packet, one with a broken wax seal. As he read it, his eyes grew wide. "Listen to this!" he exclaimed. "The old woman says that this letter, handed on by her great-grandparents, refers to a tradition of the '*kohen zadokim*', the righteous Cohen, going way back in her ancestry. She says that the ancient family manor is called Castlemont on Wandermere!"

Benjamin jolted. "That is the name the Dachau document gives as the Kahana home in England!"

David nodded affirmatively.

Then, with a sharp breath, the professor turned to Britta. "Have you ever met this Dahlia?" he asked.

"No . . . why?" Britta replied.

"Well, she's never met your Uncle Reg, but she seems to know about him. Claims that Reginald Cohen, a photographer, is descended from that line!"

Benjamin and David studied Britta's awestruck face. "Uncle R-Reg?" she stammered. "A high priest?" She did not know whether to laugh or cry, and stared at the letter, stunned.

"Now, dear," Horace said, "if your uncle is the one she refers to, he is probably much too old to take up the mantle of such leadership."

David nodded. "Besides," he said, trying to be gentle, "didn't you tell me that your uncle was wounded in the war, that he walks with a limp?"

Britta sighed. "Yes. Does that also disqualify him?"

Horace nodded. "It would, Ms. Hayworth."

Then, suddenly a light flashed through his old eyes. Glancing at Clement and David, then focusing on Britta, he exclaimed, "You said he has a son? A Cohen male?"

Britta gasped. "Zachary! Zachary Cohen! My second cousin!"

David folded up the papers and reached for his ever-ready briefcase. Stuffing them inside, he stood up and looked to the rabbi for the go-ahead.

Horace gestured toward the door. "May we accompany you to the Western Wall, Ms. Hayworth?" he asked. "We'd like to meet this fellow."

CHAPTER 47

Sunlight flooded the gigantic Western Wall plaza as Britta, Rabbi Benjamin, Clement, and David made their way down the stairs leading from the Old City.

Against the wall, in fenced courtyards on either side of a low divider that separated men from women, hundreds of worshipers sang, prayed, and read the Scriptures together, remembering the bounty of the earth and the blessings of heaven.

As always, the men's court was much fuller than the women's, as entire congregations of Jewish males representing many synagogues throughout Israel and around the world met in clusters about the pavement.

This holiday was almost as joyous as Passover, which coincided with the Christian celebration of Easter. It had little of the somber reflectiveness of Yom Kippur, when the nation remembered its collective and individual sins.

For Britta, who had never witnessed this Jewish festival, the sight of dozens of groups dancing and singing as huge, decorated cylinders were carried into the men's court—containers for the Torahs of the many congregations—was awesome indeed.

Old men, in flat black hats or woven yarmulkes,

decked out in striped prayer shawls, leaned against the wall, praying in hope-filled tones for the coming of Messiah and the peace of Jerusalem.

Younger men sat on chairs, hunched together over portions of scripture, reading to one another and praying, their heads uniformly covered with skull caps and their ringlets bobbing with the rhythmic movements of their heads.

On the women's side of the divider, young ladies helped older ones to find places where they could fit small folded pieces of paper into the cracks of the wall's ancient stonework. Each slip contained a prayer, personal or universal. Every crevice of the retaining wall—the only remnant of the ancient temple—was so stuffed with notes that it was a wonder one more could fit in.

The group from the Consortium did not immediately enter the plaza, but stood on the stairs while Britta tried to locate her uncle.

Rabbi Benjamin handed David a prayer shawl which he had grabbed when they left the house. "Here," he said, "you'll need this."

As David spread the shawl over his shoulders, Britta suddenly brightened.

"I think I see him!" she said. "Over against the other wall!"

Rabbi Benjamin and David followed her pointing finger to a sizable group of people gathered away from the fenced-off areas. This was a mix of men and women, some dressed in traditional Jewish garb, and others not. They stood near the tunnel used as a priestly storehouse in ancient times, listening to an animated speaker as he addressed the flock.

"Shall we join them?" Rabbi Benjamin suggested.

The four crossed the plaza, then stood on the edge of the crowd, not wishing to interrupt the meeting, though some of the people recognized Horace and greeted him warmly.

"For the Messianic Jew, Pentecost is a double blessing!" the congregation's rabbi declared, his arms spread wide and his face radiant.

"This is not only the festival of the firstfruits of the ground, but we remember that the Church was born on Pentecost Sunday! On that day," he cried, "the Holy Spirit descended on a gathering of those early Jewish Christians, in a house not far from here, and empowered them to preach the gospel to all nations!" Then gesturing toward Temple Mount, he proclaimed, "On that day, the apostle Peter preached in the court of the Gentiles, and his followers echoed his proclamations about *Yeshua*—Jesus, the Messiah—each speaking in a new and foreign tongue, so that people of the many nations gathered there could receive the story in their own languages! On that day," he cried again, "three thousand of our fellow Jews were ushered into the kingdom, receiving the word of truth and affirming that Jesus was the Anointed One, the one sent for the redemption of Israel!"

For the moment, David wasn't concentrating on the rabbi's message. He was scanning the gathering, looking for someone special.

He did not know what the man would look like, but he knew that, somehow, he would recognize him. As he walked around the perimeter of the meeting, his eyes fell on a dark, handsome man of about thirty, who sat casually on a ledge at the foot of the wall, his prayer shawl thrown loosely over one shoulder and his head bowed in contemplation of the message.

What struck David about this fellow was not only the sincerity of his countenance, but also his peaceful appearance. It occurred to the professor that he looked a little like artists' conceptions of Jesus that he had seen in Christian homes. David was also impressed that the young man seemed to sit apart, as though he enjoyed worshiping God one on one.

As the professor stood watching this stranger, Britta tugged on his sleeve. Wheeling about, David found that she had been joined by an older man and woman, who embraced her on either side.

The elderly gentleman was perfectly British, David could see.

Tall and dignified, he leaned on a cane. His beautiful wife was clearly Jewish, her olive complexion framed by a fall of wavy, silver hair.

"David," Britta said, "meet Uncle Reginald and Aunt Deborah."

David thrust out his hand and shook theirs eagerly. "I am very happy to meet you, sir!" he said, focusing on the tall Cohen.

Reg greeted him with curiosity. "Britta tells me you wish to meet my son?"

"I do!" David replied. "Is he here?"

It was no surprise to the professor when the tall Briton pointed out the very fellow whom he had been observing.

"Thank you!" David said.

Shaking Reg's hand again, he nodded respectfully to Britta's aunt, then excused himself, and crossed the court to the place where the young man was seated.

For a long moment, he stood waiting for him to glance his way.

When the meditator did at last lift his eyes from his prayers and found a stranger gazing on him, he was bewildered. "Hello," he said shyly.

David's heart raced as he drew closer to the man.

"Zachary Cohen?" he said. "My name is David Rothmeyer. You don't know me, but I have been looking for you for a long time!"